M_{THE} C_{HURCH} _{OF THE} H
OUNTAIN _{OF} FLES

The Church of the Mountain of Flesh

Kyle Wakefield

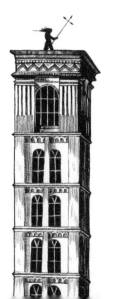

For Zachary,
Who keeps pulling me out of the sea.

CONTENT WARNINGS

Surprises are only fun if you consent to them. If this page
wasn't here for you to skip, that wouldn't be consent.

If you're still here, please be advised that this horror contains
the following sensitive content:

Graphic body horror including decay and infestation of live bodies
Graphic gore
Graphic sickness and injury detail including vomiting
Graphic bloody violence including cannibalism
Slow death
Imagery reminiscent of self-harm
Imagery reminiscent of a miscarriage
Healing a lifelong disability against the disabled person's will
Corrupting and codependent romance
Explicit sexual content including unsafe sadomasochism
Descent of a Catholicism-based religion into cultism
Physical abuse of a child by a parent
Injury of a baby
Death of a parent
Grief
Alcohol abuse
Suicidal ideation
Gender dysphoria
Misgendering and deadnaming
Internalised misogyny from a trans man
Consumption of rocks, clay, dirt and other non-food items
Natural disaster including imagery of people trapped under rubble
Mercy killing of an animal
Mentioned death of a child
Mentioned suicide attempt by a child
Mentioned traumatic childbirth
Mentioned eating disorder

THE OCEAN
AND
THE CLAY

CHAPTER 1

THE DEAD WHALE

I AM NOW DRUNK ENOUGH to feel the sea flowing backwards. Somewhere beyond the cove, a cyclonic core has grown in the water to pull the inbound waves back out. I feel it reaching down my throat to pull my stomach up.

I've been wondering tonight how much of my body is in the sea. Whether it's enough to strain out and build a second one. Flesh from the burns I cleaned with the saltwater, tadpole clouds of blood lost to the sharp edges of rocks, crescents of fingernail and toenail scattered off the cliffs on morning walks. For the last three years, I've been wheedling the sand with my wine bottles, letting the waves wash the tears and red vomit from my face before they stain it. My skin and hair will pull away like lichen soon enough. My skeleton will erode slow like the cliffs, but I will lie here as long as they do.

Yesterday, I found myself moaning, *"I want my mamma, I want my mamma,"* between bouts of vomiting. My mother might have heard me from the valley, if she was awake and the windows were open. She didn't come. There's a monster on my back, a spined thing which towers even when it crouches.

2

If they dragged me home, it would gash the new thatch on the roofs, poison the wet daub in the walls. It's dread.

We buried Nene in the sea. It was the only grave big enough to hold him. We dragged him out beyond the cove, like he was a whale which had washed up rotten on the shore. I'm waiting now to drown myself, let my skirts drag me down to the seabed where he lies, his verdigris skull with marrow pikes between its plates my first and ultimate glimpse of Heaven, but I lay down three years ago to wait for him to come to me. He would walk out of the surf, wringing water from his shorts. He would be cold in my arms, so cold his skin stuck to my nails. He would say he was sorry he'd taken so long. All that water, all those knots, all that weight upon his back, all nothing when he heard me screaming for him.

The moon is high and dazzling, making a night like a day with a clash of opaque shadows painted in. The gabbro cliffs are light-eating black against a blue sky, but sandy brown against this grey one. The half-built houses and streets of Magmate crowd the valley behind the cliff. The sounds of dogs barking, mothers calling children, and clip-clopping hammers and hooves swirl up in its bowl and streak free in distorted howls. There's a group of men, miners, on the prong of cliff to my right, dancing between the slate sky and the red thumbprint of their fire. I hope the dark rocks camouflage me from them.

Lying on my front, I spread my arms and scoop up two handfuls of wet sand. Half gabbro, the sand is solid grey, like the clay we mine in the quarry. I spread it onto my bodice beneath my breasts, let it drip off, and then collapse again, face-first. I miss the passion with which I used to detest myself. It's half-hearted nudging now. Poking a dead fish with a stick and cringing when it lifts its tail.

I crawl down the beach on my belly until the first wave hits me in the face. It's warm, like being struck playfully with a dishcloth. A stronger one bursts down the collar of my dress. *I will drown in this one,* I think. The next few come weaker but

3

recede stronger, sucking my hair up off my neck. *I will fall asleep before the next one comes and drown in that one.* The last wave slings my hair in a wide, shallow arc, sparing my face completely, and then jerks away, as if ripped by a current.

I will vomit into this cavity of sand and suffocate on it.

Wondering why the waves have stopped touching me, I struggle up onto my elbows and part my wet hair from my face. The waves are lapping at the bottom of the sand bank, twenty paces away. All along the cove, a band of beach lies newly exposed, smooth silver studded with stranded mussels and razors.

I give a slow, bovine blink, letting my chin thud against my chest, and when my eyes refocus, the silver band has tripled in size. The sand which foams as it absorbs the last wave is never submerged again. Perhaps I am drunk, and the hours I have been watching the tide retreat only feel like minutes. Perhaps I am drunk, and have forgotten that the tide always retreats in minutes. There won't be a flood. There wasn't an earthquake I was too drunk to hear. The sea is not flowing backwards, dragged into a cyclone over the grave beyond the cove. There is no glow in the water at the epicentre.

I stagger to my feet, shield my eyes with my arms. Between the two prongs of cliff which form the cove, something is glowing blue: The deep, gauzy blue which bruises the tips of yellow flames. It looks like a reflection, but it lies beneath a dun stretch of slate and bronze sky, not beneath the moon.

And it pulls. As I gaze at it, drooling from my open mouth, it needles a hole through my navel and ties a taut string to my bladder.

I run down the sand bank until I'm ankle-deep in the ocean and start throwing up. Thin, dark vomit and lots of it. The retches weld my eyes shut and lash my face to the water. When I look back up with my fist ground against my stomach and see the glow still there, blue-purple bobbing in rings like mug stains on a tablecloth, I howl. The howl hurts, dragged up by wire

4

hook through my vomit-sored throat.

I turn and sprint along the beach. The jetty lies along the cove's leftmost wall. Ersilio, who doesn't tether his fishing nets lest they capsize him nor himself when he works on roofs, moors his coracle by wedging its prow underneath the jetty. Whereas the other boats beached by the fleeing tide are craning their heads up in their moorings, the coracle sits loose in the sand. I drag it into the sea and plunge after it without lifting my skirts.

As I settle in the coracle, I'm sure that the current is aiding me. The cyclone will pull the boat out without a single stroke rowed—but not quickly enough. I seize the oars. I used to be strong, but I have leached fat and muscle like sweat into this beach, and three strokes make my arms ache like I've been rowing all night.

The cliffs move past me at a creeping pace. When I stop rowing to look over my shoulder and search for the glow, my stomach burning with the effort of holding me upright, I can't find it, and the waves seem small and aimless again, jouncing the coracle from all sides. Silence redoubles and compounds my drunkenness, makes thoughts pull down my neck and back like they have weight.

I lie down in the boat. Lower myself carefully on both arms and slam my head down with a bang. If I fall asleep, I might roll and capsize it, and the cold might not be enough to shock me awake.

For the first time in three years, I pray that I live. I pray that I live long enough to apologise to Ersilio.

Opening my eyes supine, I expect to find that morning has come. Instead, I see the moon still high, soaking a hole through a fast-moving black cloud. The two prongs of the headland, bent together in the sky, creep downward in my aspect and out of sight.

Something thin and white moves downward at speed. Much closer to the boat.

I sit up, lurching the boat enough to pull my stomach back into my mouth.

The ocean all around me is full of pale heaps of *something*. They stretch a valley's length in every direction, depressed into wells of seawater in places and stacked into nodulous pillars in others. The white pillar I saw first is twice as tall as me, and wears a purplish balloon as a hat. The valley of flesh is moving with the directionless tide, making glottal mud-bubble sounds as air and water push through its fissures. Its rotting smell is piscine and bovine, treacly blood and stomach gases drenched in salt.

There's a familiar texture to the flesh. The edges of the lumps are soft and thin, and spread and clump on the surface of the water like white hair. Whale blubber. Last year, the corpse of a whale washed up on the jetty after a thunderstorm, and festered there for two weeks. When the fishers rolled it over, the clear skin of the upper flank peeled off the inflated innards in long white fronds like these. This heap of whale flesh is too enormous to be one whale, but too uniform to be a whole whale. No red or grey intestines, no muzzle, no bone.

I gaze for a long time, passionless, panting. There's another yank on my bladder through my navel. Dread bends me over the side of the coracle, stands me up, bends me over further. I stay balanced long enough for my eyes to follow the white masses down into the navy murk of the bottom of the sea, then swerve to follow the fish which swim between them. I stay balanced long enough to notice the silence and stillness of the corpse, to anticipate in vain a great shivering to life, an opening of eyes or mouths, a voice. A voice which asks me why it's so cold and dark down here, where I buried it.

I stay balanced long enough to choose to dive.

When I leap from the prow, the coracle rears up onto its edge and then flips upside-down. As the bubbles clear to reveal the bulk of pale behemoth suspended in the water, the shock of noise and cold doesn't clear with them. My first impression is of a stuffed and swollen head, of lockjaw, of all the world's oceans above me crushing at once. A white star exploding. Tentacles straddling an altar. Legs and wings braided out of tornadoes. My body washing up on the beach at daybreak, tangled in an old fishing net.

The sprawl has no centre. Knots of tentacle, intestine and gibbous-moon saccule are strung between the surface and the distant seabed like a net to strain the ocean clear. Rabbitfish swarm around the myriad limbs like flies around a horse's ears, but the limbs make not a twitch to frighten them away. Just under my feet, two of the little brown fish are worrying their long snouts inside the brain-pleats of a membrane. They are eating it. When I look toward the seabed and see the film and viscera bubbling against it as they bubbled against my boat, I am struck by a thought that there's no such thing as up and down. The bedrock is another surface of another sea, and when I crashed down into the water, I was flying upward into a pressurised, haunted sky. So solid are the walls of flesh around me that the only way I can see into the distance, can fix my drunk, exhausted eyes on unbroken darkness, is by looking up.

Two things happen. Simultaneously or not. Maybe one causes the other.

Blue light rushes into the viscera and I scream a name. A name I think is the monster's. The water seizes the scream and crams it back down my throat.

The blue is scarcely a glow. It's as dark as the water around it, but a hundred times saturated. It draws arteries through the corpseflesh and backlights shadows inside it, the shadows of writhing, dancing things as tall as I am.

As I stare, shocked by the light as though by the swipe of a rag down a dirty window, appendages of noise pour into my head, spread out, stretch my skull away from my brain.

It's a voice.

A voice like whalesong whose high notes wheel in the sky above me and whose low notes vibrate in the base of my neck.

7

Don't be scared.

A rabbitfish darts out of my hair. As it pauses by my arm, I see that it, too, is glowing from the inside. The blue light pulses sore in the hinge of its jaw. It is swimming upside-down, its flat white belly like the blaze on a horse's head.

I open my mouth. Salt water pours in. I let out a bubble of a cough.

Solavita.

"That's not my name!"

Like the one before it, the shout is slurred red by the wine and green by the water. It doesn't carry past my throat.

Then what is your name?

"Not that!"

The enormous voice laughs. In staccato throbs, heat coagulates me, shields me from the deep sea's cold.

You're not scared.

"I've seen you before."

But I haven't seen you.

"No? So you're God, then? You think you're God?"

I do.

I curl up and cackle, like I've been kicked in the stomach. "Oh—for fuck's—sake!"

This isn't the body I buried. This isn't the voice of the body I buried. *This isn't him.* I lay down swearing that nothing could peel me off the beach but him, and something else has.

I have called you because Magmate was once my most loving and most beloved village, and now it lies corrupted. You are my chosen, my prophet. You will restore your people to their faith.

"You—you—*what?*" The water still slurs me. "Do you know why my people renounced their faith? What was done to them?"

Of course.

"What, then?"

An earthquake. Beyond the cliff, you are still rebuilding,

9

eight years later.

"Who MADE the earthquake? Or weren't you God then?"

You know it was me.

"Then you were there when we denounced you too."

You tore down your church. A church built from good white stone in a lowly village is a more precious tribute than a cathedral of gold.

"How about eight houses of good white stone in a half-built village?"

It is a testament to my mercy that I will not ask you to tear them down to rebuild the church. But you will rebuild the church.

Surprise dawns in a shockwave of laughter.

"Who TOLD them to tear down the church?" I shout. "Who led them in denouncement?"

I know it was you.

I am unbearably warm. The blue light could be boiling the sea. The heady thrumming of the voice and the tightness of my lungs wash over me in a cross current.

"And I'll rebuild it, will I?"

If the mob are to repent, the first to repent must be their leader.

"And why would I repent?"

There's a ripple in the water around me. It takes me a moment to notice that the rabbitfish have retreated. It seems like a mannerism of the monster's. A blink.

"Because I've been… ordered, yes?"

God does not barter.

"Nor does He pick His enemies for prophethood."

God does not offer rewards.

"Then why does He suppose His enemy will do it?"

If you refuse, I will choose another, and forever damn you.

"Who will you choose? Someone else in Magmate you stole light and life from eight years ago? Perhaps someone from

10

whom you stole less? Nought but the house from above him?"

What is dead to you can never be brought back.

"There are TWO things dead to me!" I shriek, throwing my arms up in a tremor of desperation. "I'm not asking for Nene back! I know you ATE him! I know the mouth of God destroys what it eats!"

I expect God to ask me what else I want. God knows what else I want.

God says nothing.

"Doesn't matter," I say. "I'm not their leader anymore. They're terrified of me now. Terrified of becoming me. I'm a… ruined thing."

God does pick ruined things for prophethood.

"Only if prophethood will put them back together."

Purpose can put anyone back together.

"I don't want a purpose! I crawled to this beach to gather the strength to drown myself!"

And did you succeed?

With the rabbitfish gone, only the shadows inside the monster are moving.

When the blue light fades to nothing, they vanish as well.

Something has happened to the moon. It is impossibly dark. The monster's shape is a thin phantom in devouring black water.

I open my mouth. *No!* I try to say. *Come back! Bargain with me!* But all that comes out is a whine of terror and a bubble, the last mite of air inside me.

My lungs begin to burn. I've never felt pain like this, the pain not of drowning but of emerging from numbness already half-drowned. When I kick, fresh cold slides up around my calves and slices down. Bewilderment and despair overwhelm me as instead of moving upwards, I turn upside-down and begin to descend.

I surface.

The rabbitfish were never upside-down. I dove in headfirst,

and was upside-down all along.

As gasps rock me back and forth like a coughing fit, I still feel the monster laughing.

CHAPTER 2
THE STRANGERS

I WAS BARELY VERBAL when I started worrying about rockfalls. Looking down at Magmate from the cliffs and seeing how little of the valley the buildings occupied, how tightly pressed into one corner they were, I felt like I'd kicked over a log and found a cowering clutch of brown beetles. The only escapees from the stiff cuboid were the church, a white, black-bordered tower which jutted high above the wattle houses, and the graveyard, which poured backward from the church into the thickets beyond it.

The striped grey bowl of the gabbro quarry, where my father had worked, lay alongside the wooded bowl of the valley, farther from the sea. That was why I was scared of rockfalls: I pictured a miner digging too far into the wall of cliff which separated the two and making it erupt, slide, crumble like the wall of a sandcastle. The Curato told us that the gabbro rock, glassy, spined and as black as rotten teeth, was only found elsewhere on the southern edge of England, and that not even there were the cliffs so black, the sand and clay as grey as thunderclouds. The rabbitfish and herring which thronged beyond the cove were the village's best export, but because it was unique to us, it was the gabbro which was full of God.

I was born bad at sculpting. A month old when my mother pressed my bare feet into a brick of clay at my christening, I'd stamped down with my right foot so aggressively that the remaining membrane had crumbled out when it dried. After every church service, she took me to the side aisle to look at the brick, stroking first the flank which read SOLAVITA DE GASINIS, then the footprint, then the gaping hole. I was born a month premature, earthworm-purple and wretchedly coughing, and that hard kick had been the first sign I'd be strong enough to live.

"Remember," she said, as she walked me to the children's table at my first sculpting ceremony, "being good at it isn't the point."

The footprint bricks were made at christenings, but the sculpting ceremonies happened on a summer's day every ten years. In the village square, under the watchful black eyes of the white church, all two hundred of us sat together to sculpt self-portraits. The tables we used were great geodes of gabbro, with dried grey layers from centuries of the same ritual.

It was Prasede Vpezzinghi, seven years old to my six and therefore my best friend, whom I saw pouring water onto her sculpture straight from the tin jug. She'd laid the head face-up to dig a crevasse of a mouth, and the water turned it into a lake.

"I had a nightmare that Magmate drowned in water like that," I said. "The sea filled up the whole valley like a soup bowl, *shoop*."

"That can't happen," said Prasede. "The wave from the sea would have to be taller than the whole cliff."

"Not if it knocked the cliff down. Like that."

I reached over to poke Prasede's sculpture's cheek. She pushed my hand away and yelled, "Stop it!"

Prasede had a sharp face, with a narrow, long nose and thorny black eyes. Her sculpture of it looked like a cauliflower,

14

handfuls of clay smeared on and drying with peeling edges. I was trying to copy the way she was sculpting her curly hair, crushing sausages of clay into clusters. We both had curly red hair, though Prasede's was copper-gold and mine would only be auburn at the roots for a few more weeks before it turned black. In a vague sort of way, I knew my likeness was a harsher, lumpier thing than hers. Big brow and big hooked nose, thick hair between my eyebrows and down in front of my ears. It, I had decided superiorly, was better suited to talentless sculpting.

Blocked from poking a hole in Prasede's sculpture, I poked holes in mine. I clawed into it and pondered my hands bemired with clay, with my own sticky grey flesh. When I saw that the surface of the ancient table had added to the curly hair a texture like frizz, I ground it down again. Already drying in the sun, the chunks snapped in half.

I looked around the square. All the adults, from fourteen to elderly, were mixed together in groups of families or friends. Most had muddled together rudimentary heads in what felt like a few minutes and were now chatting or helping at our table.

There were two dozen children at the table. The smallest to be trusted with his own piece of clay was a four-year-old named Ario Barostaldo and the oldest was a teenager named Ciecherella. Her face wore all the annoyance of someone who wouldn't have just had a jug of grey slime upended onto her dress if she'd been born a year earlier. The brother sitting next to her was nearly a decade her junior, but he, silent and focused with his knees to his chest, wasn't the one who'd made the mess.

The one who'd made the mess was Ersilio De Aqvancis. He was a dark-skinned, broad-shouldered boy with black hair which cowlicked a constantly sneering mouth. He had formed his own sculpture by piling clods of his clay, Ciecherella's clay, and disintegrated shards of the table into the shared water jug and then upending the jug into both of their laps. He was ten, too old to be acting with the curious clumsiness of a baby. I saw the same destructive glee in his face when he kicked over our sandcastles, slapped our caps off our heads and snuck up to push us in swimming lessons.

Dreamily wiping clay against my mouth and hair, I watched as Ersilio jammed his index fingers into the soggy mountain. "Eyes," he said to little Ario.

I laughed. Ersilio glared across the table at me. He was still glaring as I copied him, planting two fingers firmly into my gritty grey pancake.

"Eyes," I said to him.

He curled his lip and turned away. Stricken, I started piling clay into the new eye sockets, making eyes which protruded from the pancake face like two volcanoes.

My mother arrived at my shoulder. When I turned to look at her, she held up her own sculpture and contorted her mouth to match its lipless grimace. Her black-thatch hair was loose around her shoulders, but she'd sculpted it scraped back in a cap, perhaps because that was how she wore it to church and perhaps because it was easier to sculpt. She'd made her nose too small as well. My mother and I had identical noses, wideset, swollen between our eyebrows and hooked over our mouths.

"Do you like it?" she said. I nodded. "Let me see yours."

"It's not finished yet."

"Oh, Solavita." As she tried to glimpse the peaky-eyed plate-face I was shielding, she noticed my filthy arms, face and hair. "This is very important. It's for the church."

"You said being good at it isn't the point!"

"That doesn't mean you should be silly."

Across the table, Ersilio's mother had also arrived to examine his creation. The creation under examination looked like a pile of horse dung. With one hand petting his hair, she was showing him how to smear the turds together so they'd stay in a pile when they dried.

Once both of our mothers were distracted, Ersilio grinned

and turned the sculpture around. Sticking out of the pile was an enormous hooked nose, so long he was using one wrist to bend it shy of the tabletop.

I gasped. Something began to glow in my chest.

Ersilio frowned. "It's you," he said.

"Yes," I said.

"Because your nose is ugly."

"I know!"

Prasede looked at me with her cheeks puffed out, indignant on my behalf.

"You never cry," Ersilio said crossly.

"Why would I cry when I like it?"

"Shut up! You're no fun!"

When my mother and I walked into the church the following week, the scale of the ceremony struck me for the first time. This ritual, performed once every decade, was the reason our church was so large. Four floors of attic for preparing the clay, a huge crypt with kilns for firing the sculptures, and pews in the nave for two hundred.

The sculptures, which the kiln had turned from grey to silver, were awaiting collection on the chancel. There were tiny heads and gigantic heads, bodies which had balanced upright wet but lay on their sides dry, disembodied fragments on huge bricks of bases. The only likenesses I recognised were those of the other children and the only pregnant woman in the village—she had sculpted her belly and breasts, the stumps of limb and neck peaked as though severed with scissors. My mother found her sculpture at the back, with a small piece broken from its cheek. We couldn't tell whether it had tumbled from a weak seam or been accidentally kicked off by a neighbour. In the time we spent hunting for mine, the crowd of sculptures on the chancel halved in size and most of the village found their seats behind us.

"Oh dear," my mother said at last. "It was next to mine all along. Look."

Where her sculpture had been waiting, there was a large heap of grey shards. When I ran to it and sorted through it, I found one of the eye-peaks I'd made. I couldn't find the other anywhere. It must have been dust.

When I merrily started scooping the heap into my skirt, my mother told me to stop. She went to the Curato and came back with a burlap sack.

The villagers were arranged in the pews by age, with our grandparents at the back and us at the front. The first person I saw when I stood up with my sackful of dust was Prasede. She was cradling her sculpture, a half-body which was mostly hair, on its side like it was a baby.

"I'm sorry it got all broken, Solavita," she said.

"S'okay. It was bad anyway."

"Maybe if you ask the Curato, he'll let you make a new one?"

"He didn't let my mamma make me another baby brick. If it's the wrong day there's no God in it."

"Oh well. You can try again in, um, oh. Ten whole years."

I wrinkled my nose. Sixteen. A grown woman. A far bigger, more intricate body in which to trap treacherous air.

Prasede was sandwiched between two older girls, Ciecherella and Sitha, so I wandered along the pew in search of a space. I had just noticed a space next to Ersilio, whose witch-nosed turd-mountain looked heavy enough to hurt his lap, when the Curato raised his voice and began the ceremony. Shards of clay flew out of my sack and shattered loudly on the floor as I ran to sit down.

Magmate was a village without money. If you worked a trade for your neighbours, they worked to feed and house you in return. The first trade worked by every child in the village was as an assistant to the Curato, tending to the sculptures. The sculptures from ceremonies past stuffed every free space on the chancel and in the side aisles, and with every ceremony, they were jostled backward to make room for more. My favourite

18

clusters to look at were those belonging to the elderly: Single-file lines beginning with footprinted bricks nearly a century old and ending with demure products of either vanity or indifference. The pieces which had fallen from my sack weren't alone on the flagstone floor. I couldn't remember a Sunday service which hadn't been punctuated by the sound of a nose or finger shattering on the floor. After the service, one of the Curato's assistants would dart to rescue the pieces, place them into a burlap sack like this one, and hang the sack from a nail above the cluster. Preserving the pieces of God, no matter how tiny, was of great importance. The frightening appearance of the sculptures themselves, weathered by age or missing appendages, was of none.

At a funeral, a person's coffin was followed from the church by a procession carrying their sculptures, and the graveyard was a tight tangle of sculptures of the dead. When my mother was a little girl, it was a tidy lattice, and a grave with only a footprinted brick was given equal space to one crowded with likenesses. Long before the Curato and his assistants had assented to expanding the graveyard towards the woods, they had resorted to shoving sculptures in wherever there was space. Whenever my mother and grandparents asked me about my father's funeral, which had happened when I was four, I insisted that I didn't remember it at all. It felt less callous, less blasphemous, than telling them I remembered giggling watching the procession bicker about the sculptures. Whether to put them on the windowsill, over by that poplar tree, or on that other, overgrown grave.

Prasede had confessed to me that she had nightmares about walking through a meadow with gaping clay heads instead of primroses. She was especially frightened of the graveyard, and of a sculpture of the Curato's which he kept in the pulpit. He had sculpted a long, thin arm to hold his burlap bag, and when he braced his elbows either side of it during his sermons, it looked like he had a third arm, a shard of his younger self wizened dark and leathery.

It was a strange thing for her to be scared of. Not because the sculptures weren't frightful, but because Prasede's parents were butchers. Bloody aprons haunted the hallways of her house, rusty, hooked things the basins. I didn't understand how a girl could go to bed surrounded by viscid gore and hack-slashing noises and have a nightmare about black, brittle, silent things.

The Curato told us to stand, turn, and place our sculptures down in our seats. My mother had told me the sculptures used to be placed in their piles in the side aisles, but the rush was deemed unceremonious.

"Now, Lord, I commit myself to this earth."

"Now, Lord, I commit myself to this earth," I copied. I picked up the bottom corners of my sack and dumped broken shards all over the pew. Next to me, Ersilio snorted.

"As you committed yourself to the Lord Jesus Christ."

"As you committed yourself to the Lord Jesus Christ."

"Ex magmate exoriebamus, et ad magma revertemur."

The Curato had gathered us children the previous week to practice the Latin phrase. He'd taught us syllable by syllable, and I exclaimed each syllable like I'd dropped something on my foot. "Ex magmate exori, ay, bamus! Et ad magma revert, em, er!"

From the magma we arose, and to the magma we will return. God had made the huge extinct volcano which had made the gabbro which had made the clay which had made our likenesses, and when we died, our bodies would be buried in the gabbro and become one with it. Magmate, the village's name, meant *from magma*. Clay was flesh, and gabbro was God.

It struck me again that none of the adults had put effort into their sculptures. Even those who could sculpt well—the members of the sculpting club who met in the church every week, the bakers, the miners who whittled figurines from pebbles of raw clay—had treated this rare important project as

20

a race to finish first. We could have filled our enormous white slab church with lovely figures, figures which oozed effort if not talent, but instead, we were holding our hands up to God, the inventor of each of our likenesses, and saying, *You're still better at it! Don't worry!*

I didn't see a point in trying either. I scorned Ciecherella, who had stuck out her lip in disappointment when Ersilio had stolen her clay, and Ciecherella's little brother, who had stayed in his chair in the square until dark and thumped the table in protest whenever his mother had suggested he was finished. Every sculpture, whether ramshackle or exquisite, was broken in some way within a year.

"What happened to it?" Ersilio whispered to me.

"I put the clay on the eyes too fast, and left gaps inside, and the hot air got in the gaps and made it explode."

Cackles bent Ersilio double. Drowned out the congregation's "Amen". It was then that I learned my mother was old for a mother. As she glowered at me from three pews away, Ersilio's spun around straight in front of him and clapped her hand over his mouth.

I fixed my eyes forward and beamed. Like his meanness, his laughter was a piece of theatre, not a compulsion, but I was delighted to be the cause of it.

Ersilio and I were not the last, nor the largest, interruption to the ceremony. The Curato had told us that after "Amen," he would proceed out of the pulpit, down the aisle and out into the square, leaving his sculpture in his place, and we were to follow. He was followed first by the elderly and finally by the children.

As soon as Ersilio and I joined the shuffling crowd, its shuffling abruptly stopped. Before Ersilio could shout at me for crashing into him, we felt the end of a cracked whip of murmurs. Then, the Curato shouted, "Signora?"

"Come up!" Ersilio hissed, leaping up onto the pew. He was talking to the other boys, but I climbed up as well. I could now see over the crowd in the aisle to the front of the church, where the huge wooden doors stood open. The Curato was framed in the doorway, talking to a woman I'd never seen before.

If Magmate had been a fortress, with portcullis and drawbridge and real river moat, it would have been no less inviting. The nearest village was high in the mountains thirty miles away, the nearest road fit for horses at the base of that mountain. My mother had told me that the valleys, soft earth and dense forests made it impossible to approach us on land unless on foot. Forty years ago, Ersilio's Indian grandparents, his mother's parents, had come here by boat—not a boat from India, but a rowboat from a merchant ship—and the story was still told like it was folklore, like they had fallen from the sky. At six, the only thing I knew of the wider world was how rarely it came close to mine. A stranger was rarer than gold.

And she was a beautiful stranger. With a mat of curls the colour of cherrywood and a golden face scorched around the eyes by freckles, she shone like a jewel in the sun-soaked doorway. She was besmirched in the black dust of the mountains she'd hiked, from her face down to the trailing corner of the blanket which wrapped the belongings in her arms, but even banded with volcanic stains, her dress was the finest I'd ever seen. Sky-blue linen. The sleeves were slashed to bare slices of the white sleeves underneath and the ladder lacing to which she'd tied gathered heaps of the skirt was bronze.

The Curato was speaking too softly for us to hear him. He was already speaking to soothe. This poor woman had arrived in a village which had seemed to be empty, only for a door to open and reveal her to the entire population and their gabbroic doppelgangers at once.

Her speech was a paradox. Clear projection and long, tremulous pauses.

"My name is... Emerenzia Karafantoni," she said. "I was compelled to seek this village under signs from God. I'd heard... stories about the... sculpting you do... the church of sculptures. I'm sorry to have interrupted your worship."

"Oh, no, you're not interrupting at all," said the Curato. "We are done. We will hang the sculptures tonight."

The woman—Emerenzia—nodded.

"Where are you from?"

"I am from Sansepolcro. From the court of the Marchese di Mantua. But I was compelled to seek you under signs from God… This is Magmate, isn't it?"

"Yes, oh, yes, of course this is Magmate. How far have you walked? Come and sit with me."

The Curato waved to part the crowd and guided Emerenzia into the backmost pew. She sat, jostling her pile of blankets into her lap.

"What can we do for you, Emerenzia? What has the Marchese di Mantua sent you to fetch?"

"Nothing, no, no," Emerenzia said. At that moment, the Curato, and the whole village, realised what was wrapped in the blankets. "We will never see him again. We are staying here!"

The tiny arm, as white as a cockle shell, which protruded from the bundle was the proof Emerenzia's journey was no errand. One of the boys beside me gasped, and a couple in the aisle seized each other and took a step backward.

At first, I simply couldn't comprehend the *irritation* of carrying a baby over the mountain and through the valley on foot. Wouldn't it get dust in its eyes, get hungry and tired, and cry and cry? But the baby wasn't crying. The little arm had dropped out into Emerenzia's lap like a stone.

"What's his name?" asked the Curato unsteadily.

Emerenzia grinned and tucked the blankets down under the baby's chin. "This is my Nene. He is three years old, but he looks one."

Nene's hair was cedarwoody, and his closed eyelids were green in his white face.

"It's dead," Ersilio whispered.

23

I knew I'd ridicule him later for his awe, but I felt it too, a red knot in my throat.

Emerenzia leant down, wound a curl of the baby's hair around her finger, and smothered his face with kisses. When she withdrew, his eyes were open in the blankets, staring up at her.

"Good morning, *angelo mio*," she said indulgently, and kissed him once more on the nose.

The crowd in the church sank in relief as one.

With the Karafantonis settled in Magmate, Emerenzia smothering her son with kisses was a sight as common as the sea. She taught him to walk in the street outside my house, placing him down on one side, rushing to wait on the other, and then rushing back to lift and exalt him for every first step. The baby never giggled or squirmed at her attacks, but his placid stares made her as giddy as any giggle. He had the most enormous eyes, perfectly round and perfectly black, with only a crescent of white visible at a time. He really did look no older than one.

If Emerenzia adored Nene like ten sons, she adored each of us like one. Every child in the village learned to anticipate her ferocious embraces whenever she was nearby, even when Nene was already in her arms. It first happened to me in church, when the Curato asked us to turn to our neighbour and greet, "May the Lord be with you." Instead of replying, "And also with you," she swept me off my feet and squeezed me for so long that I memorised the delicious clean linen smell of her undersleeves. I tottered around for the rest of the day inhaling it out of odourless air. She'd been a washerwoman for the Marchese di Mantua, and was now a washerwoman for us.

When Emerenzia invited me, Prasede, Ciecherella and the farmers' daughter Sitha to a laundry lesson, my excitement surprised my mother. I'd been known to shun anything I perceived as a chore, especially a girls' chore, but Emerenzia made laundry seem as lavish and wild a thing as kicking over sandcastles or covering myself in clay. We arrived at the fountain in our sacks of chemises with our day dresses in our arms and found Emerenzia in the same state of undress, albeit with woollen hose underneath instead of bare legs. Her white linen underdress was floor-length, puff-sleeved and elegantly tailored to her waist, and none of us could decide whether to be scandalised by the fact it was underwear or the fact it looked like a fine lady's wedding dress.

It was nothing compared to the blue dress spread out on the fountain, even while the blue dress was glutted with black stains.

"Oh no, how'd it get so dirty again?" Prasede said.

Emerenzia grinned. "I stomp-stomped to the quarry and rolled around so I'd have something to wash with you."

"What about Nene's clothes?" I said.

"Nene doesn't get dirty either. The big boys carry him all around."

When Nene had turned four, Emerenzia had started sending him to play with the other boys. I knew well the sight of Ersilio carrying him on his shoulders into the woods with Ario Barostaldo capering around them in circles, delighted to no longer be the baby. I thought it was brave of Emerenzia, both because Ersilio was a hooligan and because she seemed incomplete without her son. She'd hiked all the way from Sansepolcro to Magmate with him in her arms, holding him so tightly that when she had first jostled him from her chest into her lap, she had bared a square of blue linen never touched by mountain dust. They were like two pieces of clay dropped on

25

the floor together. Separable along a seam, but pulverised by one another.

Our mothers had bleached our clothes clean, and the stink of ammonia and lye had made our eyes water for days. Emerenzia directed us to spread the chemicals on only the blackest stains, and then handed us each a smooth bar of soap.

"It's called Castille," she said. "It doesn't burn your face off when you breathe it. It's a kindness deserved by all pretty dresses, not just the Marchesa's, no?"

I was so in awe of the perfect bar of soap that I didn't want to ruin it by scrubbing my dress. Instead, I lathered it on my hands, pressed my face down into them, and watched Emerenzia. On the thin sky-blue linen of the skirt, the gabbro stains looked like burns, so she and her Castille were a spirit and spell which could undo fire. When she was finished, the dress's blinding blue unclouded, she spread it out to dry on the wall of the fountain, between herself and Ciecherella.

As she started to help Prasede, Emerenzia noticed the way Ciecherella was looking at the dress. In brief sniffles, like she was looking at the sun to coax herself to sneeze.

Grinning, Emerenzia reached over and pulled the sleeve of Ciecherella's dress out of the water.

"Did you do this?" she said, stroking the embroidery with her thumb.

Ciecherella nodded. She was fourteen and a clumsy embroiderer. She'd made roses on the horizontal seams with a thick black blanket stitch for their foliage. The faded yellow with the lumpy black stitching suited her; Ciecherella Malacheti was a wispy girl with harsh borders. Thin hair worn in knotted plaits, watery eyes above a front tooth gap big enough to whistle through.

"It's so beautiful, and it makes me think of you, *farfallina,*" Emerenzia said. "Would you think about letting me buy it?"

Ciecherella stared at her. Prasede and Sitha stared at each other. I stared at the weird yellow dress.

"I…" said Ciecherella. "I can't use money, and it's my only dress—"

"Of course! You are people of trade, aren't you?"

Ciecherella didn't look down at the blue dress for a few moments. She was far too confused.

The reaction which followed was like that of one meeting God, and that didn't make it overblown. Emerenzia attributed every good thing she did to the goodness of God. In the clamour, as Ciecherella wished the dress was dry enough to put on and Emerenzia told her it would dry faster if she did put it on and we held out her skirts, I was the first to see the boys coming out of the forest.

There were five of them. Three trooped in a line at the back, Nene was running to find his mother as fast as his fat toddler legs could carry him, and Ersilio was chasing Nene in sidestep, determined to save him from tripping and hurtling headfirst down the hill.

They had been at the beach. When they reached the fountain, I saw that whilst the four older boys were wet, with sand dried on their arms in bands, Nene was as dry and fluffed as if he'd just been sent out. And whilst the other boys were barefoot, as we were, Nene was wearing white hose and the only pair of baby shoes I'd ever seen. Next to the dress Emerenzia had just given Ciecherella and a few ceremonial ornaments of the Curato's, those tiny brown leather shoes were the most frivolous garment in Magmate.

"Oh, look at your strong running legs, *angelo mio,* and all for me!" Emerenzia said, scooping her son into her arms. "Look at your lovely eyes all full of sand! Malacresta Malacheti, you give me those trousers right away! I have never seen a thing scream for ammonia so loudly!"

Ersilio, whose long hair was stuck to his neck in diagonal stripes, turned sheepishly to his line of subordinates. *Malacresta,* like *Emerenzia,* was a name which my head still bent out of shape. Ciecherella's parents had a passion for unwieldy names the eight years which separated their children's births had not dulled. The brother was a mute creature with hair cut around the rim of a mixing bowl and a constant scrunch to his nose which pushed his eyes up under his fringe. His trousers were stained green to the waist buttons, and a piece of seaweed long enough to trip him hung out of one pocket.

Ersilio's expectant turn prompted the same from Ciecherella, who had just finished picking her way into the tight sleeves of the blue dress, and the two almost chorused, "Dump them out, Malacresta."

Malacresta harumphed like a horse and tore his trousers off by the hems. As he shook them upside-down, what seemed like the entire beach poured out of his pockets. Pebbles, razor shells and the sand scooped up with them rained down onto the cobblestones for what felt like a minute, making Prasede, Sitha and me flinch away like kittens from a club. Though his face was sullen, the six-year-old, whose tunic was thankfully much too big for him, because he wasn't wearing undershorts, hopped over the lost treasure and handed the trousers to Emerenzia without a hint of tantrum. *"Thank* you," she said.

She turned her attention back to Nene, setting him down on the wall of the fountain.

"Why aren't you the picture of filth?" she cooed. "Didn't you want to go in the rock pools?"

Ersilio, Ario and the last boy, Lalo, exchanged guilty glances.

"Signora Karafantoni, we don't think Nene likes it with us," Lalo said.

"No—" joined Ersilio. "I was going to carry him into the pools and just dip his feet in, but I think he really thought it was too deep and he'd drown. No matter how much I told him I wouldn't let go."

"Oh." Emerenzia frowned. "He cried?"

"No. We really are sure he was scared though."

"Oh, that's just his face! If I thought these big eyes meant he

28

was scared of drowning, I would think all the world was an ocean!"

"It's not that we don't want to play with him, really it isn't," said Ersilio. "Just that we don't want to play with someone who doesn't, uh, like us."

Emerenzia looked down at Nene with tragic eyes.

I thought she, like me, thought that Ersilio was lying. That they found Nene boring. A burden.

As the four boys trooped away together, I gazed upon their filthiness with jealousy. I didn't quite know why. It wasn't that I wanted to be filthy. It wasn't that I felt we'd been made to do chores as the boys played. Perhaps it was that, in their filth, all of them matched. Even Malacresta, who'd been shovelling rocks into his pockets as his friends wrestled in the sea. I was annoyed by the idea that Nene had shirked his place with them. It seemed like a tall order to exclude yourself from a group which didn't care what you did.

"Don't be sad, Signora Karafantoni," Ciecherella said anxiously. "Nobody wants to play with those little swamp rats anyway."

"Yes, I had no particular desire to *raise* a little swamp rat," said Emerenzia. "But I did so want him to be wanted."

Nene didn't seem upset. He stared up at his heartbroken mother the way he stared up at her always. Even though he'd run down the hill to her as if he was desperate for comfort, he hadn't pressed himself into her arms. He'd stood and waited to be picked up.

"Well," said Prasede, "we want him. He can wash with us."

"Yes, and, tomorrow," joined Sitha urgently, "we're going looking for fairy circles in the woods. Perhaps Nene could come and help us pick flowers."

Emerenzia looked forlornly down at Nene.

"You would like that?" she asked his gigantic, staring eyes. "Pick flowers for Mamma?"

Nene said nothing and did nothing.

Emerenzia winked at the three girls. "My favourites are the yellow primroses."

It was obvious that Emerenzia had named the primroses her favourite because she knew the woods were thick with them. Snowdrops, wild roses and the trees themselves were suffocated in their beds by primroses. She wanted Nene to have an easy time finding them without knowing she'd designed it that way, just as she'd avoided embarrassing Ciecherella with her gift by pretending she wanted the old yellow dress in exchange.

The toddler, however, was paralysed by the size of the task he'd been given. Under duress, he nodded when Prasede pointed to the sea of primroses, and stayed rooted to the spot when she suggested picking some.

But Prasede, Sitha and Ciecherella adored him for it. They gave him the role of vase, and piled flowers into his arms as he stood there bewildered. When they ran out of space in his arms, they tucked flowers behind his ears and into his hair. When Ciecherella feigned trying to poke one into his mouth, he cracked a tiny smile.

I told the girls I didn't want to pick flowers. I sat beside Nene on the grass, scheming. Since Emerenzia was from Sansepolcro, and from a Marchese's court, it made sense that she had never thought about letting her son play with girls. In those places, I was told, the softness of a boy was an abomination equal to the dirtiness of a girl. What I couldn't work out was why I hadn't thought about the reverse for myself.

"Solavita," Prasede said, "Can you take some of the primroses from Nene and make a crown with them?"

"For what?" I said.

"For Signora Karafantoni."

"Why are you making a crown for Signora Karafantoni?"

"Because she gave Ciecherella her dress! And the yellow will look pretty with the new one."

"Ugh." I threw myself onto my back in the grass.

"I'll ask Ciecherella then. You're just best at flowers is all."

I was the best at making jewellery out of flowers. I had a knack for knotting the flowers together so they all pointed outward. But in light of my scheming, I had decided to enjoy it no more. Flowers were for *girls*.

When I sat up and saw Prasede walking away, I grew ravenous for an argument. A dissolution.

"Make yourself a crown too!" I shouted at her. "To match your yellow teeth!"

Prasede froze midstride.

Sitha's head appeared behind a tree. "What did she say?"

Prasede turned and stared at me with glossy pink eyes.

When Sitha ran to her and repeated the question, my stomach panged with fear. What if Prasede didn't do what Ersilio had done to Nene? Seize destiny by the neck and cast me out of the group? What if she just cried?

"What the hell is wrong with you, Solavita?" Ciecherella yelled. "With teeth twice as yellow, too?"

"HA!" I yelled.

"Didn't you hear me? I was insulting *you,* you little beast!"

I rolled around on the grass, clutching my sides. "Stuff—flowers in the baby's ears quick!"

"Don't call him the *baby*. He's our friend."

"Well, I'll teach him to call you all ugly then!"

When my mother found out what I'd done, she was more confused than angry. I couldn't understand why everyone was more confused than angry. Did they not see what I saw? Wasn't it obvious, even if the reason evaded us all, that I didn't belong with the girls?

"Do you think I shouldn't play with Prasede and Sitha and Ciecherella anymore?" I asked her eagerly. "They shouldn't have to play with me if they hate me, should they?"

"They don't hate you, Solavita. And you don't hate them."

"I do hate them. They boss me around. I wish you'd let me

play with the boys. Ersilio doesn't boss Malacresta around."

My mother turned to stare at me. Then, she burst into a rant.

"Not *letting* you play with them indeed!" she yelled. "If you want to play with the boys, you go and play with the boys—in fact, you should have gone straight there this morning instead of going with Prasede! I would rather raise a filthy pup than a bully!"

Ersilio, Lalo, Malacresta and Ario were in the quarry the next day, surrounding a huge boulder of gabbro. Exhausted from climbing the cliff, I lay down in their eyeshot to wheeze.

"Do our mammas want us, Solavita?" Ario shouted.

I sprawled out on my back. "No."

"So what are you doing?"

"What are *you* doing?"

"Whoever breaks the rock first wins."

I squinted at them. Each boy had an apple-sized rock in his hand. The boulder was nearly as tall as Ario. If Nene had still been with them, it would have towered over his head.

I scrounged on the ground until I found a rock which fit in my hand. As I carried it up to the group, still panting, I fantasised that I would be the one to break the boulder. I would cleave it in two like a lightning strike, and they would exalt me with their eyes through the smoking fissure.

I struck as hard as I could. The dull tonk of rock against rock sprang up the quarry wall. The four boys glared at me.

"This's what I'm doing," I said. "I'm a trade."

Ersilio raised an eyebrow. "Traded for what?"

"Nene."

The boys glanced at each other.

"Good," said Ersilio. "You're good at breaking rocks."

CHAPTER 3

THE ROCKS

W E NEVER BROKE THE BOULDER. That wasn't the point of the game. The point of the game was for Ersilio to say each of our names in turn, and watch us obey him. "Your turn, Lalo. My turn. Your turn, Malacresta. Your turn, Ario. Your turn, Solavita."

Long after I'd stopped counting my turns and my rock had rubbed a blister on the heel of my palm, Ersilio said,

"Stop making that stupid face, Solavita."

I hadn't realised I'd been making a face. When I concentrated, a huge, aching grin fell out of my cheeks.

I'd thought joining the boys would be a mammoth task. I'd have to impress them, serve them, beg them. I'd climbed up to the quarry sure that I was going to do it alone for a hundred mornings before they finally let me stay. But they were different from the girls in a meagre way: They didn't care about *why,* only *how.* The girls had adopted Nene because they pitied him and wanted to please his mother. The boys had adopted me because I was there with a rock in my hand.

And they were different from the girls in an enormous way.

Once, when Ersilio said, "Your turn, Lalo," Lalo turned away from the boulder, raised his rock to Ersilio, and hit him squarely on the head. The thump was soft but solid. Ario squawked with laughter and fell to his knees. Ersilio brushed his black hair out of his squinting eyes, said, "My turn," and tackled Lalo to the floor. Not one for letting an elbow in his mouth spoil the orderliness of his game, he craned around and said, "Your turn, Malacresta."

All morning, the five-year-old had been echoing, "Your turn, Malacresta," with a jeer about the six-year-old's name. "Malachesta Malacreti!"—"Malacrestacheti!"—"Your mamma gave you a joke name!" Malacresta replied only to the ultimate, wiping his brown fringe out of his eyes, which were bulbous like his sister's and startlingly yellow, and saying the first thing I'd ever heard him say: "Your mamma gave you a joke face."

The boys didn't include me in their fighting for weeks. It seemed they didn't believe I was built to withstand it. Kept at arm's length, I wasn't sure whether moving to fight one of them on my own would make them draw me in or throw me out. Finally, after a month of hungering to be insulted, Ersilio sated me. I told him a story my mother had told me about a fish biting off and swimming away with her hook. "It's okay," he said. "She can just tie you to the line by your ankles and hook fish with your nose."

Instead of laughter, the boys returned a sharp, nervous silence. I grinned madly and said, "I will bite your fat head off for bait."

Since he had a sister, Malacresta was the one to whom I first articulated my preference. That girls were so gentle to one another that disagreements felt apocalyptic. That I would rather be punched in the head than catch a glimpse of sceptical glances being swapped behind my back.

"Cos you're simple in the head," Malacresta said. "You've not got the brains for working out if people don't like you.

34

That's what my mamma said. Fighting with words is for people. It's animal stuff to fight with hitting."

I imagined the causation reversed. That we didn't hit because we were stupid, but rendered each other stupid by hitting. I pictured Ersilio and me sitting face-to-face like jackstraws players, one hit to the head per turn, the loser the first to forget how to lift a rock. Or maybe the winner.

Most of Malacresta's chatter was about his sister Ciecherella, and her fawning fear of Emerenzia's blue dress. She wore it as a day dress for two weeks, picking her way around like there were needles sewn into the seams. At church, she hesitated before she sat down, and at home, she stalked around the dinner table until her brother had headaches from watching her. Their mother, sick of waiting an hour every morning for the application of the laces and pausing on walks for her to catch up, finally procured a hideous beige dress from a neighbour. She had told her son that they were watching the erosion of a practical woman by the vice of frivolity, but Ciecherella's immediate relief proved her wrong. The blue dress now hung above her bed like a tapestry.

The story reminded me of one Ciecherella had told last year about Malacresta's idolisation of a red stone he'd found on the beach. He'd called it his ruby, and kept it in his pocket to play with until, one evening in the garden, he'd tossed it up and not seen it come down. Implacable in his response—half tantrum, half efficient organisation of a solution—he'd ordered his parents and sister onto their hands and knees to help him search for it. By the time Ciecherella found it, stuck between the petals of a lettuce, and knelt before him to coo, "Look, it must be your *magic* ruby!" Malacresta had shouted so much that his face was as red as the stone. After that, his mother had wanted to ask Sitha's father, who made jewellery, to put it on a necklace for him, but he had yelled that drilling a hole through it would decrease its value.

"*Was* a ruby," said Malacresta, when I reminded him of the

story. "Papa said it was a bit of red glass, but you have to melt gold to make glass red. Gold's rarer than ruby."

It seemed like a good point to me.

The boys and I often hunted treasure on the beach. Navy razors shells, stones worn as smooth and round as wooden balls by years under the sea, bones bleached by the sun, bones still black with flesh. The bones of fish were as thin as hairs, the bones of seagulls just as light, despite their girth, because they were hollow in the middle. When I found an intact seagull's skull one day, the air bubbles rendering the arch of the eye socket flakily fragile above the beak, Ersilio warned me not to let any of the boys touch it. They, he said, were sure to break it.

On my way home, I sat on the fountain with the bird skull in my pocket and crushed it. I remembered it was there the moment before my backside hit the wall, and sat anyway. When Ersilio heard the crunch, turned back to me and shouted, "Oh, you *idiot!*" there was a red burn like pride in my chest.

I was eight, Ersilio twelve, for our first seaquake. It happened in the middle of the night, too far out at sea to wake us, but seeing the aftermath in the morning was as thrilling as hearing the tremor. The flood had swelled far enough to level the beach into a lattice of silver ripples and receded quickly enough to leave behind mountains of fish and starfish.

"Papa was so giddy when he woke me up," Ersilio said, as we sat together at the top of the cliff and watched our parents dart around with buckets full of fish. "He said he won't have to go fishing for days and days."

Ersilio's father was a fisher just like my mother. Ersilio talked often about his excursions in his father's sailboat, and how he couldn't wait for it to be his. He assumed that I wanted to follow my mother into the trade too, and I felt no impulse to tell him otherwise. I had no dream for my future more particular than to be like him.

When our parents had finished on the beach, we climbed down into the village to collect the other boys. As we stood on the hillside, bickering about whether to go and help with the fish at my house or Ersilio's, the others raised their heads to watch something over my shoulder.

It was Emerenzia. She was coming from the direction of the square, from church or the fountain, and was holding Nene by the hand. He was five now, and I hadn't seen her carrying him for months, even though he didn't seem to have grown any bigger.

To our surprise, she walked past her own house, the last house on the street, and started up the hill towards us. Her step was unsteady, almost a stagger, and her red-brown hair was down in a tangle. I had never been able to rid myself of the thought that the yellow dress from Ciecherella looked terrible on her. Somehow, it made her skin look yellow too, like it was oozing up inside her.

She stopped in front of us and coaxed Nene forward. "Can he play with you, please?" she said.

Nene grabbed hold of his mother's leg, but didn't grab again after she dislodged him.

Ersilio blinked. "Um, today? We were—"

"From now on."

"Why?" I said.

Emerenzia looked at me sharply. Something ran cold through the part of my chest which burned when I was proud. *How dare you ask why he belongs,* her eyes said, *when you belong less?*

"Those girls," Emerenzia said. "They… spoil him. They

don't worry that he is so... timid."

Emerenzia and Nene went to church every evening, but as I looked at her, I realised I couldn't remember the last time I'd seen her smile in church. She used to beam behind her praying hands and now she squinted, scratched at her lips. She still clasped Nene's little hands between hers, but now that he sat on the pew instead of on her lap, doing so strained them both, made her stoop and him hold his arms out straight.

"That's okay, yes?" she said when none of us spoke.

Ersilio held his hand out to Nene. "Of course."

Emerenzia smiled at him, gave the rest of us a curt nod, and hastened back down the hill. Again, she walked past her own house.

"Back to church," I said.

"Ugh," said Ario.

Ersilio took a break from trying to take Nene's hand to clip Ario across the ear. "He's old enough to understand you now."

"I don't think he understands where he is," I said.

Ario, Lalo and Malacresta laughed.

As he had grown, Nene's strangeness had stretched, solidified. I had never seen brown hair so colourless before, nor a paleness so intense that it seemed less like pale skin and more like fish film laid over bone. His nose was firmer and his mouth was less gormless, but his eyes were still too big for his face. His ears were enormous, and stuck out of his hair like round white flags. Everything was too big for him. His mother was. He stared up at her like she was a mountain no matter what she was saying to him.

"Alright," Ersilio said. "We're happy you're here, okay, Nene? I am sorry that Ario said yuck and Solavita said you don't know where you are. Ario's excited that you're littler than him and Solavita's excited you're even more braindead than her."

"And I'm sorry I called you a pipsqueak!" hollered Malacresta.

38

"Yes, Malacresta's very excited to have competition as the biggest loser weirdo in Magmate. I think you should call him a name to make up for it."

"Yeah," said Malacresta.

"Call him a snaggle-toothed jowly rabbitfish."

"Yeah!"

"We can sound it out together." Ersilio knelt next to Nene. "Do you know what 'snaggle-toothed' means?"

Nene stepped backward, away from Ersilio's hand, and gazed up at me.

"It means his teeth are growing in the wrong place, and when he's a man he's going to look like a walrus."

I stared down at Nene in horror. He was exhibiting, I realised, his first shadow of preference.

Ersilio smirked. "I think he wants your hand, Solavita."

"He thinks you're his mamma!" Ario squawked.

I stuffed both my hands into my skirt like they were filthy. "I'll wear your face if you say that again, you little shit!"

It was too late. All the boys were laughing.

"Go away," I snapped at Nene. "Your mamma wants you to play with *us*. Not us playing her."

Nene spoke then. "Mamma said," he said, "I don't have to do anything scary."

Ersilio, to my shock, looked at me.

It wasn't a day for anything even Nene could call scary. It was early springtime, too cold to swim in the sea and too warm to make a campfire.

"We're going rock jumping," I said.

I had no intention of finding myself in the sea. I'd only said such a thing to frighten Nene away from me.

Nene did not react and did not move.

In stubbornness, I walked forth, leading the boys up the cliff.

"Aw, *yes!*" Ario said. "Sea-tremor rock jumping!"

"Aren't there, like, fish dead in there right now?" said Lalo.

"There are always fish dead in there," said Malacresta.

I stopped at the top of the cliff. Malacresta and Ario had run ahead to play tag and Lalo was lagging behind, but Ersilio and Nene stopped with me.

This part of the cliff overlooked a rocky outcrop of the beach. The highest tides—and this was an unnaturally high tide—churned the water into molten pewter and sucked it back and forth between towering gabbro fangs.

I tried again. I took a step towards the edge of the cliff. Nene followed, and gazed down solemnly.

Ersilio and I looked at him. We looked at each other over his head, then all the way down at the water.

Then, Nene said, "From here?"

Ersilio and I burst out laughing. He stifled himself with his hand, and I threw my head back and guffawed. Ario and Malacresta ran back to us, asking what the matter was.

"Nene thinks we jump from here! You'd be *splattered!*" I said, stooping to shake Nene by the shoulders. "Splattered like a little egg!"

"Oh," Nene said. "Okay."

His eyes were rimmed with red, and brimming with tears, but it was only the wind. If he was frightened or hurt, he would have backed away.

"Come on," Ersilio said unsteadily. "No splattered babies on my watch."

As we climbed down the grey sandy path to the beach, Ersilio tried again to get Nene to hold his hand. When Nene ran harder to keep up with me, stepping on my skirt in his stupid shoes, loathing rose inside me. It was a rag-wringing of my stomach, a tight pressure between my legs. On the hillside, I had only wanted to scare him, but on the overlook, I had wanted to push him off the cliff to his death.

We always jumped from the same rock. It made a windbreak for the sand in its inlet, and the deep pool on its ocean side was wide enough for one of us at a time. Ario reached it first, eagerly tossed his tunics and trousers off, and lunged into the sea. His mouth stretched into an O. "Hoh, ooh, cold, cold!"

"Little baby wuss." Malacresta followed in his undershirt, and contained his howls of discomfort in a closed mouth. I laughed and called curses to the pair, ignoring Nene, who was staring at the rock like it was as tall as the cliff.

"You first," Ersilio said. "It was your stupid idea."

Straight-faced, I tore open the buttons on my dress and threw it down around my ankles. I was wearing long underwear, no hose or shoes, and no undershirt.

And Nene stared. My chest was as flat as the boys', but his eyes were as clouded by premonition as his mother's.

Tears stung my eyes, a hot adversary for the sea spray.

"Come on," Ersilio said. "It's fun, swimming. I'll carry you. We won't jump."

"Take off your shoes," I snapped. "Who the hell wears shoes on the beach?"

"My mamma says I'll cut my feet."

"Of course you'll cut your feet! The skin grows back thicker and they get stronger."

"Mamma wants us to toughen you up," Ersilio tried. "You're big now, like us."

"Take off your bloody shoes!" I yelled. "Or I'll take them off you, you pathetic weasel!"

They both blinked at me.

"Oh, come on, now—you've got one of us offering to carry you and one of us telling you she'll drown you if you touch her and you'd rather give your hand to me? Why? Because I'm a girl?"

"Solavita—" Ersilio said.

"Don't let him follow me!" I shouted, and stormed into the sea.

Letting the salt water scour the tears from my eyes, I swam out to the rock.

"What happened?" Lalo said as I scrambled up.

I ignored his question. "Why aren't you jumping?"

"Water's cold. Malacresta's mamma said he'll have a heart attack."

"Oh, you're all girlier than me!" I said, and jumped off headfirst.

When I hit the water, the water hit me back. Seized me around the neck and flipped me on its axis into a bellyflop. My feet scraped down the sandy wall of the pool and my hair bloomed into my eyes. When I bobbed back up, the three boys and rock above me were swaying back and forth like I was still watching through water.

Then, Malacresta said, "Shit!"

There was blood leaking down my face, washing over my chest in long red hairs as the waves came and went.

My shock was more winded than butchered. In the seconds I tried and failed to speak, a bright-white burn spread out across my forehead. In my haste to dive, I'd almost missed the pool, and a rock had hit me in the face.

"It's not even cold," I managed at last.

After two more stubborn jumps, each shock of cold and burn of salt in the cut more numbing than the last, I walked out of the water washed clean. When my head emerged from my dress, and awe spread across Nene's and Ersilio's faces in unison, delight passed through me in a shockwave. The blood zigzagged like lightning between the water droplets on my skin, which diluted it brighter and pinker the further down it ran. I let it collect on my lip until there was enough to lick up and spit out onto the sand. I'd seen many cuts and had many cuts, but head cuts were special. They gushed and didn't stop. I felt christened.

As we trudged over the cliff in the evening, it began to rain. We arrived in the square with warm sweat and water in our collars. Spectral in the heavy fog of my headache was an image of myself as a renegade warrior in my gore, the group's merciless new ringleader. By stepping back to take the baby's hand, the old ringleader had abdicated.

A shout broke through my delusion.

"Solavita!"

My mother hurried up to me with her apron turned backwards on her waist. Even though she'd shouted for me, her arms went towards Nene.

There was a shriek from behind her. Emerenzia and the Curato stood together in the doorway of the church. The Curato's arms were extended, as if Emerenzia had just run out of his embrace. I thought her fright was for me until she said:

"Did he do it?"

I stared at her. The boys stared at her. My mother stared at her. The Curato stared at her.

We then all looked at Nene, who was beseeching my mother with his black eyes.

"No!" I guffawed.

The Curato took Emerenzia back into his arms and led her inside.

"I don't need a bandage," I said, putting my tongue against my top lip to steady my headache. "I'm fine."

My mother ignored me. She said to Nene, "Your mamma's helping the Curato with some bits and pieces. Would you like to have dinner with us?"

Nene said nothing.

"We have sweet rolls. Do you like sweet rolls? I bet you do."

"See you tomorrow, Solavita!" called Ario as I trudged home behind them. I gave a clumsy wave without turning around. My view of the street was charred at the edges, and every step I took shook another salty drip into my cut.

My mother sat Nene on the kitchen counter to watch her make dinner, and I stormed into my bedroom. When I sat down on my bed, a swoon came over me, the bulk of my headache catching up after three minutes stumbling behind me. The cut had stopped bleeding and the blood on my lips felt and tasted like rust, but I thought there was still blood coming.

With the clot blocking its outlet, it was filling up my head, making it heavier and heavier on my neck.

My mother had ignored me on purpose, frustrating my desire for an argument. I wanted her to throw me onto the kitchen table, to overkill the cleaning and binding of the wound, to tell me a daughter wasn't supposed to do these things to herself, so that I could scream back that I was sick of being a daughter. I wanted her to ask me if it hurt. I deserved a chance at the manly performance of swallowing the pain and lying that it didn't.

Something was wrong with Emerenzia. What was wrong with Emerenzia was that something was wrong with Nene. I should have despised her for the cruelty of uprooting him from the girls' group and placing him back with us, if only because I would have despised my mother for doing the same to me.

But Nene had shown no sign that it had been a cruelty. The look on his face when I'd shown him the edge of the cliff was identical to the look on his face when Prasede had shown him the primroses. His catatonia, that clash of petrified and bored, wide, weeping eyes and no words, was perpetual.

When my mother left to fetch something from the garden, I got up from my bed and went into the kitchen. With my throbbing head tilted, I analysed the look which overtook Nene's face when he realised he was alone with me. It was fear and it was indifference. It was like he was three again, rolled up in his blanket on the pew. All the look betrayed was that he lived.

"What's wrong with your mamma?" I said. "Why isn't she taking you home?"

"Mamma is talking to God," Nene said.

"What is she talking to God about?"

"I don't know."

"Do you know if it's something to worry about?"

Nene shook his head.

"But you're not worried, are you?"

My headache had soaked down my neck and into my chest. I was woozy, lead from the waist up and rubber to the floor.

"Were you worried at the top of the cliff?"

Nene shook his head.

"You should be scared of me. You know that, don't you? That I was scaring you?"

Nene blinked at me.

"You're my friend," he said.

"Friends don't threaten to drown you, Nene. You hate people who threaten to drown you."

"I don't know how."

That was it. It was like I'd told him to pick up a rock. My legs won't bend. It's too heavy for me to carry. I don't know how.

At last, Emerenzia arrived. The Curato was with her. At my mother's encouragement, Nene opened the door.

"Are you the man of the house?" said the Curato. "We're looking for a little boy. Can you fetch him, please?"

Emerenzia picked him up with a theatrical groan. She thanked my mother as the Curato stooped to her shoulder to coo at him. They left, in step like a family.

"Something's wrong with Nene," I said immediately.

"Oh, stop it, Solavita," my mother snapped. "I'm ashamed of you. Don't think that because you're bleeding I'm going to baby you."

"I don't want to be babied."

"Then why didn't you clean up the blood and comb your hair to hide the cut?"

My eyes filled with tears. My mother tutted.

"Such a sweet little boy, Nene."

He's not sweet. He's nothing. He's empty.

"Boys don't cry about their feet getting cut."

"So that's why." With her thumb, she pushed painfully at the skin around the cut, wiping the sand from it. "Because you thought it would make you a boy."

CHAPTER 4

THE BROKEN ANKLE

WITH ONE FINGER, I worried at the quarry floor between my crossed legs. I rubbed away the powdery layer of gabbro dust, then scraped the compacted earth beneath with my nail.

We were sitting on an overlook, black rock above and all around us. The wind was warm and dusty, and we paused between words to cough, spit and rub our eyes. Malacresta was shielding the cut on my forehead with his hand. His sweat was burning it.

"I told Nene he was supposed to hate me," I said, "and he said he didn't know how."

"How to hate?" Malacresta said.

"Why do you want Nene to hate you?" Ersilio said.

"I don't. I just think he should. I terrorised him."

"But if you terrorised him and he still likes you, doesn't that make you feel cool?" Lalo said. "It's like you're a mistress of trickery."

"No, just like I'm a girl," I snarled.

There was a moment of quiet.

"She told us to carry him, you know," said Ersilio.

"Who?" I said. "Signora Karafantoni?"

"Yeah. When we played with him when he was little, she told us to keep hold of his hand and carry him."

"So he didn't get scared?"

"Or so he didn't get dirty. I don't know."

I frowned. For some reason, it made me sad. That Ersilio had only put Nene on his shoulders because he was told to.

And it didn't make sense. Two years ago, Emerenzia had told Ersilio to coddle Nene, and now, she'd told him to harden him.

"But with Signora Karafantoni for a mother, it's so easy to clean you when you get dirty," I said.

"Ah, but with the Marchese di Mantua for a father, you're too *good* to get dirty."

The four boys laughed at my shocked face.

"Oh, you never heard that?" said Ersilio. "She was a servant for the Marchese di Mantua, and then a nomad with a greensick, idiot baby? When you have a baby, you know, even unmarried, you're still looked after. There's no reason she would've left that court unless someone told her to go."

"She said she came here under signs from God," I said.

Ersilio snorted. "Yeah, wouldn't you?"

"But the Marchese's got bags and bags of money. If Nene was his son, he'd keep him."

"And if he did? If he told Signora Karafantoni that she had to leave, but he was keeping her baby?"

I felt an ember of understanding. "She'd run away with him."

"I think she asked him for money too, bags and bags of money," Ario said. "Papa said that dress was too fancy to be a washerwoman's."

"Oh, oh, what if she *blackmailed* him?" Malacresta said. "Like told him if he didn't give her all his money, she'd tell everyone he had a bastard? Maybe Nene isn't even his!"

Ario embellished further: "Or he isn't even *hers*, and she *stole* him out of his cradle!"

I grinned. I liked the idea of Nene being the Marchese's bastard. Far from raising him above us, it gave credence to my dislike of him. It seemed that nobody had asked Emerenzia what the Marchese was like, continuing to speak about him the way they spoke about any unfamiliar noble, about the *concept* of a noble, but that image—sallow-faced, sallow-haired, afraid to walk without carpet, dumb as a rock—sounded a lot like Nene to me. I liked the audacity of this new Emerenzia too, either seducing a Marchese or defying the Marchese who seduced her.

Lalo butted in. "We heard her praying in church the other day, on the front pew. She was talking about Nene, saying, 'Oh, God, why did you choose me for this burden?' My papa said it's rich blaming God or a little baby for something you and some man did without them."

"Well, I say he's not a burden," said Ersilio. "A hundred of him would be easier to raise than any one of you idiots."

"A thousand of him would be easier to raise than your left pinky," said Lalo.

Wedlock wasn't the only reason Nene's birth was scandalous. In one altercation or another about the swapped dresses, Ciecherella had let slip to Malacresta how close the two women were in age. When Nene was born, Emerenzia had been sixteen. I couldn't remember whether she had looked her age when she arrived in Magmate. She certainly didn't now. Something—tiredness, guilt, prayer, lye—had sucked the fat out of her face.

My mother had told me that Nene's father was the villain, especially if he was much older than Emerenzia, but that her being too young was still making Nene suffer. Ciecherella talked sometimes about wanting to be a mother, and her own mother's answer was always the same: *"A baby is not a doll, Ciecherella."*

But wasn't Nene, tiny, button-eyed and catatonic, the closest a baby could get to being a doll?

When I glanced up and saw Nene struggling down the quarry path towards us, I groaned. The boys grinned, amused.

"What's happened to his leg?" Lalo said. At the same moment, Ersilio shot to his feet and bolted up the path.

Nene's gait was laboured. More than struggling to walk downhill, he was lolloping. When I realised that his leg was hurt and that his mother was nowhere to be seen, I raised my eyebrows, impressed.

"Here, do you want help?" Ersilio said. "Can I lift you?"

Nene shook his head and kept limping. Ersilio stuck anxiously to his side anyway, his hands out like paddles.

When they reached us, I saw what the problem was. There was an enormous swelling at the bottom of Nene's leg, a peapod with all the peas squeezed down to one end. The skin around the swelling was shiny and green, an early promise of bruises. His ankle was broken. Lalo widened his eyes in amazement and Ario and Malacresta swore in harmonising pitches.

"Does Mamma know?" Ersilio said, helping him sit down.

Nene nodded.

"Did you walk all the way here by yourself?"

Nene nodded again.

In a moment of vanity, I thought that it was my fault. That he'd seen me climb the cliff careless of my head wound the previous week, and, when an injury befell him, decided to copy.

"You should take your shoes off," I said.

Ersilio shot me a dagger with his eyes. "S—"

"No, I mean it's bad for his foot. Does it hurt, Nene?"

Nene said, "My mamma said—"

"I don't give a rat's ass what your mamma said; if it's pressing it it'll split it."

"She's right," said Ersilio, gently lifting the swollen foot into his lap. "Here."

We all swore when the shoe came off. Nene's foot was blue-purple, round and shiny as a pearl, and the flesh on the sole was maggoty and white. Thankfully, there were no breaks in the skin for rot to settle in. There was a pang in my stomach like jealousy, although I didn't know whether I wanted the injury or the bravery.

"There," Ersilio said, placing Nene's shoes neatly next to each other. "They'll stay safe and sound for Mamma."

When I saw his bare feet together, I nervously said, "Maybe the shoe was keeping it from swelling, actually."

Ersilio sighed and asked Nene, "Do you feel better?"

Nene nodded.

"Good. That's all that matters."

We sat in a circle for a while longer, drawing shapes in the dusty ground. When I finally shook Malacresta's hand off my face, he leapt to his feet, slapped my shoulder, and shouted, "Tag! You're it!"

I struggled to my feet to chase him. Ersilio stood up too. I caught Malacresta easily, seizing the back of his tunic. He dropped dramatically to his knees, pretending to choke.

When I turned to flee, I crashed straight into Ersilio. "Don't play tag! Don't! Don't—" Malacresta slammed into us and tagged me back, and Ersilio grabbed him too. "Nene can't play."

"Why can't I play?" Nene said.

"We'll play a sitting down game."

"No, I'll play tag," said Nene. He got up, only faltering slightly on his broken ankle.

As Ersilio and Malacresta glared at each other, I walked up to Nene. He looked at me placidly as I put my hand to his head.

"You're it," I said.

Then, I turned and walked away with an exaggerated limp.

"Solavita, you rat," said Ersilio. When I turned and saw Nene limping determinedly after me, I guffawed.

"Oh no! He's it! He's it!" shouted Malacresta. Instead of limping, he threw himself onto his belly and started dragging himself with his arms. "Less injured than me, he will get me!"

Lalo and Ario, cackling, copied my limp. Ersilio sighed and dropped to shuffle on his knees.

Nene didn't find the game funny like us, or cruel like Ersilio. He chased us with the doggedness of a runner chasing runners. Malacresta, on his belly, was a surprisingly lethal tagger, lunging to grab our legs, and Ersilio made him get up and shuffle after he headbutted the backs of my knees and folded me face-first into the dirt. When, after ten minutes of the game, with Nene tagged again, I caught sight of tears in his eyes, I felt a rotten squirm of triumph. He saw that I'd frozen to look at him and broke into a run; I had a flash of a vision of sprinting away, making him sprint after me, unspooling the sliver of pain into a fierce, dazzling anguish; and then he caught me.

"Okay, that's enough," Ersilio said. Nene was panting hard with his hand wedged under my ribs and I was staring at him like I'd been grabbed by a ghost. "Sit down. All of you."

"Oh, this baby's made a softhead out of you," I groaned as I collapsed.

"And a hardass out of you."

"And a bone-smashing lunatic out of meee!" Malacresta shuffled up on his knees, threw his arms out, and mock-swooned on top of me. I shrieked in pain as his shoulder hit my chest.

Soon, we were all lying on the floor, pretending to be exhausted, as Nene sat and primly played with his shoes. With his foot lightening, but his leg darkening, the wound was now a uniform blue.

That night, I walked the boys home in the usual order. Ario, then Malacresta, then Lalo, then Ersilio. Only when I turned from Ersilio's front door to mine did I realise that Nene was still there. His house was the first one we'd passed.

"Damn it," I said. "Do you even know where you live?"

"Next to Ario."

"Why didn't you say anything?"

"You were talking."

I sighed, and turned back on myself. The idea of letting him limp home alone was so pathetic it made me angry.

"Did tag hurt?" I asked him, as we walked together in the dark.

Nene looked up at me. After a long silence, he said, "It hurt less with my shoes off."

The reply seemed deduced. Like he didn't want to confess he was in pain, but he wouldn't, or couldn't, lie.

"So do you feel them missing?" I found myself saying. "All those things I talked about?"

"You mean hating?" Nene said.

"And hurting, and being scared."

"I suppose so."

"Why are they missing, do you think?"

"God."

"Did your mamma tell you that?"

"Yes."

I had slowly realised that I was still limping as I walked. It had twisted a knot into my hip, but I couldn't stop.

"What if I told you you had to put your shoes on?" I said. "Would you really feel nothing?"

Nene looked at his shoes and hose, which he was carrying. We'd tried to help him put them back on before we left the quarry, but his foot had been too swollen.

"My mamma told me to keep them on."

"Ugh!" I said. "What if I shoved you over and *forced* them onto your feet?"

Nene said nothing.

"What if... I twisted your ankle in my hands? What if I'd made you run to catch me in tag? What if I put the shoes on the wrong feet and got them stuck there? Would you hate me then?"

53

"My mamma told me…" Nene began. Then, he stopped himself. In the dark, something seemed to shiver in his eyes. "No, she told me not to tell."

"No, tell me."

"Just—try and see!" Nene said.

Fury compressed my stomach and bladder. The sweat on my palms began to crawl, and Nene's blue leg glowed in my aspect like a beacon. When my mouth dropped open, something hot and savage, a possessing demon, poured down my throat and saturated me red.

"Try and see." Because he didn't think I would. *"Friends don't threaten to drown you."* But he didn't think I would. It wasn't me who was tricking him, hypnotising him into missing the signs I would kill him. My first attempt to hurt him had ended with me plunging into freezing water and splitting my head open and my second had ended with me limping on an imaginary wound. He was tricking me. He was clawed into my head, a witchling.

I grabbed Nene by the collar, ratcheted him from his feet, and threw him to the ground. I had seen him smile once before, in the woods with Ciecherella, a tiny crack. The smile which came when I leapt on him and dug my knee into his broken ankle tore a black rent in his face.

And from the smile came a scream like a ribbon pulled through a pinhole. He snagged on every stitch of it.

Electrified, I went downward. I grabbed his ankle in both hands. I twisted, pulled. I used my whole weight to crush it against the cobblestones. His screams compounded into a white peak of dizziness and a pulse of blindness—my illness they were, for mine they were. He made a wet, enormous inhale, pleated the ribbons down their centres, filled his lungs with them.

And then, behind him, a shadow towered, the massive echo of the witchling with straw hair and blazing eyes. When I saw her, I felt at once that she'd flashed out of thin air and that she'd

54

been looming behind him all day. The sight of her tore me from Nene and stood me to attention, but when Nene tried to stand too, she swooped down and enveloped him.

He wasn't screaming now. He was gasping hard in shock. Every note of voice I heard shimmering in his breaths made my stomach roll over. A seaquake was happening inside him.

Emerenzia crushed him in her arms and pressed her cheek against his. "Hush—now—*hush*," she said in a whimper. She was matching her words to his breathing. "Oh, *angelo mio,* it's okay to cry. It's okay to be in Oh, so much pain, isn't it? Pain is God's embrace! How are we to be alive in the kingdom of pain if we do not scream?"

She buried her face in his hair and kissed him, over and over again.

Slowly, the rocking, and the gasping which led it, gentled into nothing.

"Put your shoes on, baby," she said.

Nene did nothing and said nothing as his mother picked up one of his shoes and raised his broken foot. As she jammed the shoe into place, her head juddered downward—as if in anguish at his silence.

She stayed like that, in a crawl, her head down, as she coaxed on the second.

She turned to me. I nearly shrieked. "Why did you wretches take his shoes off? Don't you know what bandages are? *Don't you know why we bind swollen feet? So they don't swell until the skin splits?*"

I dragged my nails across my ribs. "I'm sorry, Signora Karafantoni. I'm so sorry."

"Sei il mio angelo." She buried her face in Nene's pale brown curls again. "Angels are meant to cry, my darling. You mustn't stop. You'll make Mamma go mad if you stop."

But Nene had already stopped crying.

The next day, Ersilio, Malacresta and I met on the beach. We searched for crabs, laughed when Ersilio flinched at a pinch and flung the crab into the sea, then sat on the rocks to skip stones.

Nervous for my answer, Ersilio asked me what I'd done to Nene. He'd heard the screams.

"Signora Karafantoni came," I said dully. "She made him put his shoes back on."

Ersilio jerked about. Buried his face in his hands, punched his thigh, threw his rock into the sea overarm.

"She said it was to protect it from swelling."

"You know that's a lie, right? You know she's just unhinged, right?"

"Sure." My tongue felt swollen in my mouth.

After I'd lost all words and lain down on my back by myself, down the cliff at a gambol came Nene.

Ersilio didn't bother to dampen his delight. "Pipsqueak! Come learn how to skip stones!"

Nene came up to me first. I thought about pretending to be asleep, pretending to be dead. I thought that if I looked at him, he'd possess me again, into kicking him into the sea or dashing his head on the rocks.

"Solavita, I'm here to tell you it's okay," Nene said. "Mamma wanted you to toughen me all along and that's what you did to my ankle, toughened it. I know that's not why you did it. You did it because I don't belong in your friend group and I spoil it. Mamma told me nobody likes me because I came from somewhere a long way away from here, somewhere even further away than Sansepolcro, but I think I'd spoil it there too."

It was the most I'd ever heard him speak. It was more than the sum of every word I'd heard him say before. For the first time, I realised that he wasn't an idiot. And then, I realised that he wouldn't have deserved what I'd done to him if he had been.

"I don't want you to forgive me, you little moron!" I howled, covering my face with my hands. "I want you to hate me!"

"Why?"

"Because it's... *normal!*"

"That's what Mamma said."

I dragged my hands down, looked at him as I pulled on my eyelids. "What?"

"That's what Mamma said when she broke my ankle," said Nene.

Ersilio called again. "Come skip stones, Pipsqueak! Leave Solavita to sulk!"

Nene's face lit up. "Can *you* skip stones?" he called, leaping over me like a hare.

CHAPTER 5
THE CHURCHYARD

W HEN MY FATHER AND GRANDMOTHER had died, my mother had stolen pieces of clay from their sculptures. She kept them mixed together in a vase on the kitchen windowsill.

She didn't see it as stealing from God. Although she didn't fear the sculptures like Prasede did, she scorned the philosophy which kept them hoarded in the churchyard. She said that if pieces of our souls were swimming inside them, sealed by the ceremonial prayer, they should be smashed when we died. My grandfather died when I was eleven, with yellow eyes, purple cheeks and a neck which pooled on his pillow. My mother wanted him trapped in the churchyard no more than she wanted him trapped in his dying body.

And so, at his funeral, she insisted on carrying his sculptures to his grave alone, one at a time. She went about her blasphemy with practiced efficiency and uncanny giddiness, winking at me when I saw her fingers working. She felt each sculpture until she found a crack or a thin spot in the clay, then dug down and tore a fissure open to the air. Handfuls of clay went into the leather pocket on her belt, and, later, the hallowed vase.

The pieces she'd squirrelled from my father and grandmother's sculptures were little shards. Their effigies in the graveyard were still whole. My father had my thundercloud eyebrows but not my nose, unless he had sculpted himself too kindly. My grandmother had made obtuse blobs from infancy to infirmity, and, with tremors rendering her hands unusable, my grandfather had made her final sculpture for her. It wasn't good, but it was loving.

As we left our third funeral hand-in-hand, my mother made a wide-eyed, cringing face and whispered, "I think I nicked too much." There was a sculpture of my grandfather's head with a hand resting on its chin, and she snapped off three of its fingers. There was a section of cheek ribbed along one edge by an eye, a bar of collarbone, a whole nose. Only when I saw the figures in the churchyard, frostbitten of fingers and noses, faces caved in, disembowelled all the way down, did I see my mother for what she was, after the death of her father. A loss that, she thought always, her daughter had had to experience before her. In shock.

When she hurt, she hoarded. After my explosions of cruelty to Prasede and Nene planted the fear that I hated being a girl, she went to Prasede's mother's house and asked for a summer dress of mine she'd given away. I watched from the doorway of my bedroom as she brought it home cradled in her arms like a blue-ribboned baby, smoothed it out in front of the hearth, then tucked it under the pillow on her bed. I told her I still wouldn't wear it. "I know," she said. "It's not for you. It's for me."

She said the same thing when I asked her why, with the scorn she had for tying souls to the earth, she kept the broken pieces of the sculptures instead of throwing them away. Not for Nonno, or Nonna, or Papa. For me.

I never told her what Nene had told me about his ankle. I didn't need to. The same week, the crime featured in one of

Emerenzia's prayers, and the Curato and some neighbours overheard her. The stories about the how and the why were as soft-bodied and colourful as the stories about Nene's father, with only a sliver of backbone: That she had done it on purpose. She gained a pew all to herself at the front of the church, and Nene gained invitations from neighbours to all manner of non-events: To help Sitha and her mother milk the cows, to join Ersilio and his father on fishing trips, to help the Curato light and extinguish the candles. When nobody else had time, the miners took him to the quarry, and sat him on their carts in a helmet which swallowed his head. My mother most often had him at night. I went into her bedroom many a time, wanting water or comfort from nightmares, to find her occupied with telling him bedtime stories or teaching him to embroider. I knew that keeping him away from Emerenzia was necessary, but I wondered sometimes whether my mother did it for herself. Whether she was saving Nene from a certain threat, or saving herself from worrying about a possible one.

So it was that I awoke, one windy midwinter night when I was twelve, to Nene sitting at the foot of my bed.

Awakening was like crawling through brambles. Fragments of noise, flashes of light, and pangs of unease snagged on me in the gloom. It was raining outside, a fine spray which was louder on the window than on the cobblestones, but on the flanks of the houses opposite mine breathed the violet light of a fire.

I sat up, searching the room for my mother. She'd been out on a fishing trip when I'd gone to sleep, and I didn't understand how Nene could be here alone.

He was sitting cross-legged, with his elbows on his ankles. He was nine now, nearly ten, and his limbs had grown before the rest of him. It was like his skeleton had put out vines, with the fat baby calves and forearms still stuck on their ends. His head, with its fine chestnut curls, was too big for his long neck, his eyes and ears too big for that head. He was going to be a

60

gawky, big-handed man, too tall to look down on but thin enough to snap.

"Hi," I said.

"Hi, Solavita. I'm sorry to have woken you."

The way he looked at me was dark and flat. Bloody thumbprints of eyes. There was something laboured and lucid about his voice, ordinarily such an immovable monotone. In a strange way, in being empty of emptiness, it seemed emptier.

"Then why did you get on the bed? Where's my mamma?"

I got up and went to close my bedroom door, which he'd left open. The candles in the hallway and kitchen were lit, which meant my mother had come home. Her bedroom door was wide open as well, and so, I discovered as I ran into the hallway, was the front door. There was a large whitish pool of water on the kitchen floor beneath it.

"She went out," said Nene from my bedroom. He didn't raise his voice.

Not sure what else to do, I pushed the front door to close it. Someone on the other side forced it open again. It was my mother. Her hair was wet, black lines running down into her dark eyes. Her bustle into the house brought with it the smell of smoke.

"Solavita," she said. "You should be in bed."

"Nene woke me *up.*" I looked behind me and saw Nene still staring at the wall. "Why did you put him in my room?"

She smiled. "I didn't. He must have wanted company."

"In the middle of the night?"

"It isn't the middle of the night, darling. You've only been asleep for an hour."

"But you said you wouldn't be back till tomorrow."

My mother went into my bedroom and sat down beside Nene. I was used to seeing her brushing his hair, rocking him to sleep, pulling at the loose threads on his tunic, but she folded her hands in her lap, as if she was frightened to touch him.

As quietly as possible, I sidestepped out of her sight, towards the front door. I had never been annoyed by her fawning over him, had been proud that she didn't consider me in need of the same fawning, but then, as I embarked on a mission which needed her to ignore me, I felt a ripping throb of bitterness.

I opened the front door, stepped over the puddle, and walked into the street in my nightgown. My feet were bare on the wet grit of the cobblestones and the wind came in whipcracks, slinging the rain in a new direction each time. As a gust beat hard against my face, it gave me the smell of smoke, a flash of heat, and a flurry of shouts.

There had been a Mass service that night. The noise could have been the congregation filing home, the fire torches lighting paths through the rain, but it didn't make sense that Nene wasn't there. My mother wouldn't have taken him from church. The Curato's care was the safest of all.

I went back inside. When I appeared, slightly wet and hanging my head, in the doorway of my bedroom, my mother's shoulders sank as though in relief. As though she'd thought someone else had come in.

"Did you go outside?" she asked.

I nodded.

"What did you see?"

"Rain."

"Ah, are you regretting going out in your nightie? Come and sit down." She patted the bed on her other side.

"Is something wrong?" I said. "Did something happen in church?"

"Nene is just going to sit with us for a little bit, okay?"

"Did you go to church to get him?"

"No, darling. There's nobody at church."

I looked at Nene with new unease. I didn't realise until my gaze rolled down off his bony ankles that I was looking for injuries. The broken ankle had been the first and last. If Emerenzia had hurt him again, he would have been taken to Teglia, the physician.

"Why are you staring at me?" said Nene pleasantly.

"Uh," I stammered, "I'm glad you're not hurt."

"Alright..." My mother hauled herself to her feet. "Go back to sleep, please, Solavita. I'll take the guest to the kitchen to—"

The front door opened.

My mother froze. She thrust her arm down between herself and Nene. The door stayed open, letting in a cacophony of new shouts. People were shouting up on the cliffs, their voices wheeling above us like gull-calls.

A man appeared in the bedroom doorway so suddenly my mother jumped. It was Amero De Aqvancis, Ersilio's father: A tall, broad man with a silver-streaked beard and my mother's saltwater-blistered hands. He was wringing water out of his shirt, making new pools on the hallway floor.

My mother was knowing, expectant.

"It's your coracle we need," Amero said at last. "She's down between the rocks. We can't..." He waved his hands in circles. "...reach her."

My mother started to rush at him at *"We can't."* "How could you? In front of the children?"

Amero looked at Nene. He was a stoic man, but he doted on his son. The blunder hadn't been caused by callousness. Just stupor.

"What do you think we can do for him?" he said, rubbing his wet forehead with the back of his hand. "Wipe his memory?"

My mother stared at the floor. She seemed to be looking with misery at the puddles, like they were the last inconvenience she could stomach.

Then, she turned to me and savagely said,

"Do not move. Stay here with him. I'll be home by morning."

"Mamma..." I said. In the corner of my eye, the word sent a tremor through Nene.

"Be quiet. You're twelve. There's nothing you can say to him that is wrong except nothing. Do you want me to send Ciecherella over?"

"No."

When she turned to leave with Amero, I came alight with anguish. I wanted to cling to her leg and scream that she had to take me with her. *Don't leave me here with him, with a wound so raw it isn't bleeding yet, with a spirit so parched it'll drink mine away!* The corner of my room was no longer a bed with a boy sitting on it. It was a black riptide. I couldn't see the shape of him through the clinging, towering ghost of what had happened to him.

I sat. When the door closed, I drew my knees up to my chest.

"Would you like to go back to sleep?" Nene said.

I was silent.

"You must be tired."

"What? How could I be *tired* when… when…" I waved my hands in circles like Amero had. "When there's people shouting all over the place and your mamma is…"

"In the sea." Nene's soulless voice squashed my lungs. "She is in the sea."

I noticed then that he was wet. Shiny cheeks and clinging sleeves. I begged God to let it be from the rain.

"Did you see her fall in?"

Nene took a breath, lowered his shoulders. I felt like he'd inhaled all the air in the room.

"She jumped in."

How stupid, how exquisitely horrid, that on this night, Nene had ended up alone with me. It was so hard to believe that fate could be this cruel that I thought God must have designed it for a reason. This, I thought, was the moment I was supposed to tell Nene I was sorry. If talking about myself was wrong and selfish, I was to say sorry in a quieter way. Shuffle into my mother's place beside him. Fetch a towel and rub his hair dry.

Pull him into my arms still wet. I knew from watching Ersilio hold his hand that although Nene never reached out for affection, he never pushed it away. My mother had told me there was nothing I could say that was wrong except nothing, but I didn't think I even had to speak.

The tugging of fate on my belly was so hard it hurt.

I got up and went to the kitchen, telling myself that I was fetching a towel. And I didn't go back until dawn, when I crept past the door and saw him asleep on the floor.

To the boys, there was no honour, no piety, in pretending we weren't excited. Excitement isn't joy. It's novelty, upheaval in the chest. The first time Nene joined us, three days after the death of his mother, we were in the forest. His house was visible through the trees, still teeming with people.

When I had passed the house on my way up the hill, I had seen blankets and rugs laid on the floor, covering something. The great serpent of them led all the way from somewhere inside to the grass at the edge of the forest.

In Nene's presence, the five of us sat in a listless circle. It was Nene, of all people, who got sick of it first.

What he said was:

"My mamma's death was by design. We shouldn't feel sad about design."

The very wording of it was unbearable. By design, not by *God's* design. We all knew that suicide was an abomination against God. That any other death was the perfect conclusion of His plans for you, but to die by your own hand was to somehow snatch the power from His. In the previous days, the boys and I had agreed that Emerenzia couldn't have killed herself. She'd spent her last days in church, praying as she always had. Her madness had wrested her from God's grace, but not His rule. Ersilio and Lalo thought it was an accident. Malacresta and Ario thought it was murder.

Nene's proclamation made even Ersilio look at him with fright. The other boys had never shared my fear of Nene's disposition, but now, of all times, they understood. Now that he'd watched his mother die, and emptiness seemed the most human.

I asked my mother when Emerenzia's funeral would be, and couldn't believe it when she told me there wouldn't be one.

"What? None at all?" I said. "That's so cruel!"

"I know, Solavita, but certain things cannot be done in good faith. It would be just as cruel to let the entire village gawp at her, feeling about her as they do."

"What about Nene? He's going to live with the Curato now, isn't he?"

"Of course. They'll have a little goodbye service at home, I'm sure. The miners will take care of Emerenzia."

"But nobody will see her get buried?"

My mother was squirming and avoiding my eyes. The event had harrowed her, but I was sure there was more to it. A greater reason nobody could see Emerenzia's body. A greater reason Nene had ended up in our house. A greater horror than a body in the sea.

"She never made a sculpture," was her answer.

"Yes she did."

The week after Emerenzia and Nene had arrived in Magmate, the Curato had brought them clay. She had pressed three-year-old Nene's feet into a brick and then made a quick self-portrait, a pillar with ladder lacing scratched down its front.

"Not at the ceremony."

I lit up bright. I wanted to scream at her, call her a liar.

Emerenzia wouldn't kill herself. She had materials for a grave. A party for a funeral.

Instead, I gathered the boys the day of the burial and told them to sneak out that night.

"Why?" said Ersilio. "You think you'll see her?"

A part of me did. A part of me thought that we'd be able to hide in a bush and watch her descend into the earth. That a sin that made you too evil for a funeral might make you too evil for a coffin, and we'd see the marks of murder on her throat in the moonlight.

As darkness fell, the whole village locked its doors, snuffed out its lights and forced itself to sleep. It was a night for playing dumb, for playing dead as God snuffled at your belly.

With my mother asleep, I snuck out of my bedroom window. Ersilio, Malacresta, Lalo, Ario and I met at the fountain, and crept together to the churchyard. In the dark, the shadows of sculptures were tangled with the shadows of trees. Silhouetted against the low, thick brown clouds were outstretched arms, shocks of hair, bulbous, gaping cameos. We thought we'd find a fresh grave easily, but finding so much as a path through the throng was excruciating. One wrong twitch would knock off a limb, one wrong step knock over a line of statues from us to the edge of the street.

Ario, seemingly bored of treading carefully, ran off into the woods. Just as we'd begun arguing about who ought to fetch him back, he called, "It's here!"

"You found it?" I said, as the four of us turned and ran blindly in the direction of the shout. He met us at the treeline, and led us to a rectangle of freshly dug earth. A grave had been dug and covered again. Tonight.

"That's her?" I said, bewildered. "They didn't even put her in the churchyard?"

"And no marker," said Lalo, leaning over the grave to rest on a tree. "They really did destroy her sculpture."

"Do you think they destroyed Nene's?" I said.

"Maybe," said Ersilio. "He'll get to make another one in, what. Four years."

"Won't he remember making the first one?"

"He was three, Lalo. Do you remember things from when you were three?"

"Yeah, I remember you trying to play quoits with my head."

"You were at least four then." Lalo had been joking, but Ersilio was forlorn. "I don't get it. Funerals are just how we say goodbye. Doesn't matter what kind of a person you were."

"It's not about the kind of person she was; it's about the kind of *death*," said Malacresta. "She slit her throat in front of Nene. Gushed blood all over the road."

"What?" we all said at once.

Malacresta stared at us. "Yeah. Didn't you see the blankets on the floor? Her blood was under them. Big black splashes of it."

"That wasn't blood," said Lalo. "Those were burns. The house was on fire. Blood doesn't dry black like that."

"Burns aren't thick and sticky like that!"

"They melt the fabric and the hay."

"My papa was the one who threw the sickle in the sea! He showed me!"

"Why would he show you that, you little liar?"

Malacresta shrugged. "Dunno, cos he's kind of weird."

Malacresta's father was weird. No stranger to injuring himself at his job in the quarry, he often found his son wherever he was playing to show him cuts, split fingernails and, once, a fluid-filled swelling on his elbow. He had chased him around threatening to pop it on his face.

"I heard banging," said Ario.

We all looked down at him. He lived nearly next door to Emerenzia and Nene.

"Banging?" said Lalo. "Like someone was hitting her?"

"Sure."

I looked at Ersilio. "Your papa told you, right?"

Ersilio shrugged. "Sure, that the body was in the water. That doesn't mean she drowned."

"You think someone put her in the water to make it look like she drowned?" I said eagerly.

He gave me an exasperated look. "No, I think she did one thing after the other to herself."

"Yes, yes!" Ario piped up again. "That's what she was saying, I think, before the banging. She was saying, 'Why won't you die?' over and over again. 'Why won't you die?'"

CHAPTER 6

THE LIKENESS

NENE BEGAN HIS SECOND SCULPTURE without a question as to what had happened to his first. Now living in the cottage next to the church with the Curato, who had cared for him so often when his mother was alive that he might as well have been his father, he had set up the ceremony's ancient tables, water jugs and bricks of clay himself.

Ario was fourteen, I sixteen, Ersilio twenty. At thirteen, Nene should have been at the children's table, but Prasede and Ersilio had conspired to save him a seat between them. With withdrawn, squinting care, he had sculpted a large head and smoothed it until it shone. Still bald, it had his jutting mouth, doleful eyes, fang of nostril. He had yet to grow into his hands, and his slender fingers and flat white wrists wore the grey sludge of gabbroic clay rather prettily.

When he looked up from pawing at the sculpture's neck and saw me watching him, he smiled.

"Do you want me to help you start?" he said.

Because he spoke so little and so quietly, Nene's voice had

seemed to break overnight. My mother had told me and Malacresta, who was with me in my room, that Nene was coming later to lend her a bowl. When the knock on the door had been followed not by Nene's voice but by the tenor of some solemn, gentle stranger, I'd widened my eyes at Malacresta in shock. Malacresta had said, "Wish you were that dazzled when mine dropped."

I had been. The year before, Malacresta's voice had lain down in place after months of rasping and screeching. We had bullied him black and blue for it, the boys because they found it funny, I because I wished I found it funny, but found it miraculous. Unlike Nene, who was more sinuous, and Ersilio, who was denser, Malacresta was the logical elaboration on his childhood self. He'd never wavered in loyalty to the mixing-bowl haircut his mother had resorted to in his infancy out of laziness. Unchanged too were his long hard legs, his swayback posture, his squinting eyes and the canine teeth which grew too high in his gums. He didn't need to have changed into a beautiful man for me to find the changing beautiful.

I rolled my eyes at Nene. "Four years a Curato's son and you think you're a sculptor."

Nene looked anxiously at the head he'd sculpted. Ersilio looked too, and did a double-take when he saw how good it was.

"Yeah, bit sparing on the ears, isn't it?" he said. "Worried they'll overbalance it?"

Ersilio's voice was something different. It was beautiful not only in the way it was born but the way it lived. Dark-skinned like his mother and curly-haired like his father, he was a man in perfect proportion, broad chest in mirror with broad back in mirror with corded arms and enormous hands, the strongest feature above his thick beard the kind eyes which hardened into agate whenever he thought. Deep and thicketed, his voice vibrated in the spine when he was close and thundered in the sky when he was far. When it had first begun to break, I had

71

followed him like a dog, pelted him with questions, just to hear him speak.

I had spent my adolescence horrified by the sickness my friends caused in me. Unmanageable in such a close group, I seemed to have fallen in love with every single one of them.

Nene's manliness was too slender, too painterly, to hold my interest. Malacresta's manliness was merciful and numbing, two fingers in the ears.

Ersilio's manliness was to be eaten. I wanted him as a hunter wants a wolf. To bleach his bones in my stomach and wear his skin.

Using a wooden paddle as a cleaver, Nene cut a fleet of flat strips from his brick of clay and laid them on the table in a line. Occasionally, one of us paused to watch and wonder what he was doing. Quite suddenly, after the others had finished and I had resolved to begin, he said, "I'll be a moment," and leapt to his feet. As he darted across the square towards his house, gold and silver in the sun, the eyes of the whole village followed him. His hair flashed blue as he ran into the shadow of the church.

"Why *aren't* you sculpting?" Prasede said to me.

My clay still sat in a brick, imprinted by eight claw marks.

"What d'you mean?" said Ersilio cheerily. "It's an uncanny likeness."

I smiled weakly.

"Cos your nose—"

"Cos my nose is a big square, yeah, I get it."

I knew Ersilio would sense my temper. To soothe him, I broke off a piece of clay and began to roll it. My listless hour had dried it, and it resisted my moulding like rubber.

"What're you making?" said Prasede. "Head or body?"

"Not body."

I stopped rolling, shocked. It had come out of me like a breath.

Concurrent with my hunger for the boys, another

derangement had spread its roots inside me. I'd begun to resent my body in a calm, natural way, in a way which felt prophesised. I didn't hate the nose Ersilio still mocked, enormous and hooked with ribbed arches of nostril. I didn't hate my tangled black hair, which ripped like cotton when I brushed out the mats. I didn't hate my stern lips, small, watery blue eyes, or the premature creases my temper had wrought between my eyebrows. I didn't hate that I was taller than my mother, feeling large and obnoxious in whichever space I occupied, or the thickness of my neck, or the softness of my belly. Though these were all symptoms of ugliness, lamented by the girls who possessed them in twos or threes and compounded in me into an ugly whole, they were familiar. Mine.

I hated the new things. The things which had dizzied me with pleasure for a month each and then settled to smother and bloat. I was delighted by my minuscule new breasts for as long as they were minuscule and new. Then, my mother noticed them, and told me it was time for my first pair of stays, and my tender thing in the dark became a thing to be wrangled and trussed. The next time I went swimming with the boys, I couldn't decide whether it would be more dreadful to let them see my naked breasts and gawp, or let them see my stays and wonder. I didn't want to be a spectacle, and I didn't want to be a glimpse. I didn't want to be a novelty.

After I had learned from my mother what a period was, I had convinced the boys it was magnificent. For a boy couldn't lose that much blood every month, enough to flood bedsheets and three layers of skirt, and still function. A woman's body was built for it. A woman's body was a fortress which threw off its skin at night and grew it anew in the morning, a soldier impaled on his own sword.

But then, that fabled, powerful body was mine, and I didn't want it anymore. This wound didn't christen me like the cut on my head had. Blood was earned, by bravery, stupidity or enmity. This blood was earned by womanhood, and womanhood wasn't a cause I cared to bleed for.

I couldn't understand why the other girls didn't talk about their pain. If the boys had been subjected to such a hell as this—their bodies mutating from flat neutrality into a shape they neither desired nor understood, their bodies growing shut over their screaming mouths instead of against their backs—they would have talked to each other about it. That was what friends were for. Relief, relief.

I rolled a log as thick as my forearm, and used my little fingers to eke a hollow for a waist. Perhaps I could abide sculpting the shape of myself. Perhaps it was delusional to think that anybody else was paying attention.

"You said you weren't sculpting your body," said Prasede.

I stopped, set the sculpture down, and squashed it into a saucer with my fist.

"Oh, no!" Prasede exclaimed. "Oh, it was so good!"

"It was really good, Solavita," joined Ersilio.

"Yeah, really good big busty lump."

"I love big busty lumps," said Ersilio.

"Don't TALK about me like that! What's wrong with you? You don't even know what it's like!"

Ersilio flinched.

"I'm sorry," he said. "I didn't mean anything bad by it."

He was confused. Insulting me was his way. I had always loved his way.

I sculpted a head, working layer after layer onto the nose. Realising that Ersilio and Prasede were still watching me, I hunkered down over it. The nose, like the pulverised body, was good. Well-blended and crossly faceted.

"D'you ever notice," I said, "people are the only animals who have to have breasts all the time? Pigs and cows only get fat there when they're pregnant."

It was a recurring thought which made me feel dirty, unspiritual. Animals didn't have periods either. Didn't God create humans as the holiest of all creatures? Did that mean periods and breasts were holy?

Of course not. Eve's first period was a punishment. Breasts must have been punishments too.

I glanced up from my sculpture. Prasede and Sitha were staring at me with their mouths open.

"What?" I snapped.

Sitha gave a shaky laugh. "You're calling them pointless?"

"Yeah, the pigs and cows—"

"We're not pigs and cows," said Sitha, who, as a tender to Magmate's livestock, was either offended to be compared to them or offended on their behalf. "We're God's image on earth."

"Then—"

"And since when do you mind what's pointless? You could call anything pointless, couldn't you? Is my hair pointless too? Are Nene's freckles pointless?" She threw a gesture towards Nene, who was returning to the table with a large wooden comb in his hand. "Are the sky and the sea and this clay pointless, Solavita?"

"No," I said petulantly.

"How do they serve you, then? What is the point of them?"

"To be... beautiful."

Nene, having been welcomed back by a shout that his face was pointless, stood by his seat, bewildered.

"But why... why is there *different* beauty depending on sex?" I tried. "Why can't there be no such thing as sex?"

"Because I like looking at boys," Sitha said.

"Well, then, why can't we all look like boys?"

"Because we like looking like GIRLS!" Prasede yelled.

"And I like looking at girls," Ersilio murmured. I glared at him, wounded.

"What's your problem, Solavita?" Sitha said. "How boring to want all people to look the same. It's not like our parents force girls to stay together. You played with the boys as a girl and nobody stopped you."

"And Nene played with us as a boy," said Prasede. "We liked him better than we liked you because he didn't hate us for being girls!"

Nene had put his head down in determined ignorance of the shouting. So had Malacresta, who was often rendered catatonic by conflict, even that which didn't involve him.

"And if it's having babies you can't stand, nobody's going to make you get married to anyone either!" Prasede's anger was insatiable, storied. I had degraded her for being a girl, in the act of degrading myself, for too long. "Being a girl might lead you into dreadful marriages and stupid conversations in the city, but it won't here. Your *mother* is the foreman of the best trade in the village! There's no difference between what girls are good for and what boys are good for, or what we do, or how ugly, or fat, or *pointless* we are! And we don't hate each other either! That's a fantasy you made up in your head!"

Prasede got up, holding the smiley reed of her sculpture.

"I'm going to help the little ones," she said breezily. "Sitha, come with me."

As they walked away, Ersilio slung his arm around me and shook me.

"Had enough of you, they have," he said. "Whining about being a girl."

"It's because their mothers taught them it's blasphemous to complain."

"Oh, yeah? Are you sure about that?"

Together, we watched Prasede and Sitha find places at the children's table. Both had chosen to help little girls. Prasede's charge's hair was as shockingly orange as hers.

Prasede, who would be eighteen soon, was beautiful in clashing halves: Her petal of a bottom lip, noble neck and shining curls were a pedant's beautiful and her orange eyelashes, flinty eyes and coiled portcullis of a jawbone were for those voluptuaries who favoured the savage. She seemed both destined for her father's place in the butcher shop and much too pretty for it, as if her calloused, short-nailed hands against the bloodstained counter would be an anchor dragging something ephemeral down to drown. Sitha, chestnut-haired, rosy-cheeked and staunchly fat, was both plainer and more pleasant to look at. As much as the sight of the best friends standing together gave the impression that one—and it was unclear which one—was leaching beauty from the other, the truth was that each was lovingly cultivating her own. There was a reason that of all the mops of curls at the table, mine was the only matted one.

"Those stupid arms aren't going to stay on her sculpture when it dries," I said crossly.

"Nor Ciecherella's." Ersilio was staring at the adjacent table, where Ciecherella Malacheti was sitting with her parents. "It's a girl thing to make 'em so wispy. I ought to go over and break it."

I rolled my eyes at his invocation of Ciecherella.

Lalo shook Ersilio's shoulder. "You're too old for kicking Ciecherella's sandcastles over," he said.

"I kicked over all their sandcastles," Ersilio said.

"If you say so."

Malacresta, on the other side of the table, shook his head so violently we all turned to look at him. Lalo snorted.

Ersilio narrowed his eyes, fascinated.

"Why the shaking?" he said. "What's the matter?"

Malacresta looked at him. There was a small jolt in his jaw, a jutting of the bottom teeth. Malacresta had moments, even entire days, when panic rendered him unable to speak. The jolt might have been his voice's first denial of the day or its dozenth.

We were so used to it that it didn't impact the way we spoke to him. "Did Ciecherella say something to you?" Ersilio said. Malacresta's look turned into a glare, which meant *yes*. "About me?" There was another change in the eyes, unquantifiable, involuntary. "Something mean? Something nice?" Malacresta reacted only to the latter. He slammed his face down against the table so Ersilio couldn't keep reading it.

I looked at Nene again. He'd been away from the table long enough that the strips of clay he'd cut were drying. He dipped two fingers into the water jug which sat in Prasede's empty place, then carefully rubbed water over a strip to revive it. Then, he stroked it with the wooden teeth of the comb, imprinting it with perfect parallel stripes. Just as I was about to ask him what the hell he was fiddling at, he peeled the strip up and twisted it around his index finger, making a perfect little ringlet.

Ersilio noticed me watching him. He didn't interrupt until the ringlet was safely pasted over the sculpture's ear.

"Oh, you'll be in big trouble with your papa for being too good at it," he said. He looked from Nene's sculpture to mine. "You too."

"Mine's ugly," I said. My sculpture was a pinecone of a thing, with a great spike of nose, slash of mouth and murky trench of merging eye sockets. Unlike Nene, I had hewn hair from the head as I went, and had almost finished hacking the jawline out.

"And gorgeous for it."

"Stop calling me gorgeous, Ersilio."

He frowned. "I thought I was calling you ugly."

As Ersilio returned to his business, harassing Malacresta and gazing across the square at his sister, I looked slyly at the side of his face. I remembered the joke, when we were six and ten, of sculpting each other.

I took the shelf of my sculpture's jaw between the heels of my palms, and squeezed. It was longer and squarer now, like Ersilio's. My fingernails had left stubble-like indents in the hollows of the cheeks.

I stared at it for a moment. A cold stream of dread ran down my spine and into my stomach.

78

I picked the sculpture up, stood up, and dropped it face-first onto the table. The thud reverberated down and out, through generations of dried gabbro.

Ersilio jumped and knocked over a jug, spilling water on his finished sculpture. "Shit, Solavita!" he shouted.

Nene jumped as well. The shock in his eyes was deep and lasting.

"Sorry," I said.

"What happened?"

"Dropped it."

When I peeled the sculpture up from the table and saw its face, squashed flat as though against glass, Ersilio and I burst out laughing.

I shrieked like a seagull when I saw it in the church. It was sitting once more beside my mother's. She'd made a head as well, potato nose and moon eyes, and the two could have been sisters. She watched with good-humoured exhaustion as my laughter bent me double. She'd said it was a sin to be silly, but she thought I'd dropped the sculpture by accident, and that there was fate in it, symbolism in leaving it squashed. I didn't know what it symbolised.

"Nene's is good, isn't it?" she said.

I looked over at the chancel, where Nene stood with his father the Curato. As I watched, he noticed somebody arriving at the door, grabbed their sculpture from the floor beside him, and ran to unite them. The Curato nervously eyed his legs as he skipped through the swamp of sculptures. His own sculpture was waiting for him on the pulpit stairs, where he always sat during services. Whereas my sculpture had been, according to Ersilio, gorgeous in its ugliness, Nene's was ugly in its gorgeousness. When I compared each feature to that of the real boy—the enormous eyes, the neat nose, the ears sticking out of the hair—the likeness was remarkable, but something about the whole was wrong. The curls were the worst, so cleanly cut and pasted, but the same had become of the face. In clay, Nene's features coalesced into something glossy, petulant and overly sweet. There was a gloominess to the real face, a top-heaviness.

"Used a comb to make the curls," I said. "Was clever."

The Curato had obeyed procedure for a bastard with a dead mother: He had sent letters to Sansepolcro, appealing for Nene's father. When I found out, I put to bed my enduring fantasy that Nene was the Marchese di Mantua's son. I didn't realise until later that it was because the Marchese would claim him. The Curato looked at Nene at thirteen the way Emerenzia had looked at him at three, and the idea he could be taken away from him at the whim of a ponce who loved him less irritated me.

For the suicide of the mother Magmate had developed a bitter passion. My mother spoke about Emerenzia with uncharacteristic relish, calling her a monstrous parent, a pseudo-Christian. She'd been made such a monster by her religion, I supposed, that the only death capable of banishing her from Heaven was the death she deserved.

For the son left behind by the suicide Magmate didn't grieve. He didn't seem to have grieved himself, after all. The way my neighbours looked at Nene, with just a ghost of wariness, made me wonder whether they were waiting for him to follow his mother. Become a brute. Die, and seep into the earth. Into *our* earth.

I hadn't tried to terrorise Nene for four years. It wasn't because I'd grown up, learned better. It was because there was no room for him in the part of me that hated. I wondered often whether he and I were meant for one another's bodies, or whether, on the day he arrived in Magmate in his mother's arms, some kind of transfer had happened over the pews. I had enough loathing of ugly, selfish, sexist, brutish Solavita De Gasinis inside me for two.

"Now, Lord, I commit myself to this earth," said the Curato.

I didn't copy. My sculpture was humour, levity. I didn't

80

want to curse it with my soul.

Four years had been one long ache, an ache which should have been slept through. The monomania which presided over all, the chant which rose in cadence whenever a first cramp or snag of a breast against a hand flecked the bruise with red contusions, was suicide.

Emerenzia had taught me what it was. Before then, I had never heard of a person wanting to kill themselves. It had come to me as the most breathtakingly unearthly of horrors, and now, it was soft, familiar and inviting. Cut the throat, slough the skin in all its terrible weight, dance naked in the sky. Like throwing off your clothes to go swimming.

"As you committed yourself to the Lord Jesus Christ."

Every night of the week between the day of sculpting and the day of the church service, my neighbours revelled in the streets. The clay and tools on the ancient tables were replaced with food and wine and bonfires turned the square into a beacon. I had missed the first night of celebrations. The day we'd made our sculptures, I'd waited until nobody was looking and then crammed my leather pockets with leftover clay. I had been proud of my sculpture, the nose, the brow, the cavern of the neck, and planned to make a new one. I had told my mother I wasn't well, taken off my pockets of clay alone in my bedroom, and then gone to bed without touching it.

"Ex magmate exoriebamus, et ad magma revertemur."

I'd lain awake for a long time, listening to the racket of joyous prayer, song and chatter, trying to remember the last time I'd apologised to someone. I'd never apologised to Nene. I'd never apologised to Ersilio. I'd resolved then and there that I'd apologise to Prasede. My hatred of my womanhood was not rational, was not healthy, would not survive to poison the other women's love for theirs. When I attended the following day's celebrations, it would be as a strong, beautiful, clever, outspoken woman.

And I'd come home early for a second time still feeling like a pathetic, ugly, doltish, temper-crippled man.

"Amen."

I pressed my lips against my sculpture. Breathed deep the silver-dust smell of it. "Amen."

I came home from the church service with a tin bucket of water in tow. I rolled up my sleeves, wetted my hands, and scooped from beneath my bed the clay for my new self-portrait. A self-portrait for a bedroom, not a church.

I readied myself by stripping naked in front of the bedroom window. The clay on my hands, overly wet, almost a slip, left pewter stains on my stomach when I unlaced my undershorts.

My breasts were large, veined, and paler than the rest of my body. Let down, they were longer than they were voluminous, and their cleavage made a pointed apex for my stomach. What brought me more agony than the breasts then was the whole body woven to match them. I had fat on my belly and arms, a double hump on each hip, full thighs webbed with the same lilac stretch marks. My shoulders converged at the base of my throat in a V, the perfect pond-reflection of my cleavage. I didn't have the kind of female body prized in the cities, with long neck, sharp chin and high waist, mannish or childish without its breasts, but I had roundness and harmony everywhere. I was beautiful.

All harmonious in disharmony with me.

Listening to my neighbours laughing and singing carols in the glittering square, making the most of the final night of a ceremony that wouldn't come again for ten years, I thrust my hands against my breasts, caked them with wet clay, then clawed down and tore it off again.

CHAPTER 7

THE SIREN

I DECIDED TO BE A SCULPTOR.
 I worked in my bedroom on the last night of the ceremony with a heady conviction I was sinning. Magmate's clay came out of the ground godly, but before the sculpting ceremony, the Curato had lined up the barrows and jugs in the square to be blessed by sacred rites. The clay I had stolen, spread over my naked breasts to sate my tantrum and then used to make a self-portrait to sate my vanity was as sacred as holy water.

I and my idol were damned.

It was a cut gem, a lump from which dry pieces were torn, rather than wet pieces smeared on. The triangle of negative space between ear and jaw, the jagged parting through thick hair, the long dent between thin lips and the slanted sides of neck tendons were steep-sided trenches. The weak chin and ears were wrought carefully and then pushed backward until they caved in. The eyeballs were excavated from the eyelids, the irises scooped from the eyeballs. I made the texture on the eyebrows and lips by mixing a slip and dribbling it on like butter. I knew it would probably crumble off when it dried.

I could have kept sculpting it forever, pushing and pulling, watching each new layer melt into the last, leaving fingerprints as I filled in my fingerprints. I liked the fingerprints in the hollows of the chest below which the bust ended and in the hair, but I wouldn't have them near the nose. The nose swelled forth from the slip-textured brow like a knot, a hive, a spire. I wondered whether I might wake up the next morning and, with fresh eyes, realise it was grossly oversized. I knew that my friends would. They'd coo at me to stop being unkind to myself.

My mother didn't ask me where the clay was from. Desperate to cultivate a hobby which would eclipse my moping, she asked me if I wanted more. I decided I'd make a sculpture of breasts, like the marble goddesses in Rome. I gave them a large belly, spindle thighs and no head.

I had discovered the only thing capable of sating a temper of despair: A temper of monomania. Magmate's sculpting club, a dozen people my mother's age who met in the church in the winter and on the hillside in the summer, fought to give me advice. When I followed their directions to turn my sculptures on my wooden wheel rather than in my hands, the sculptures turned out bulky and listless. Every moment my hands were empty, they panged. If they couldn't have clay, they pined for too much food, knives and sickles and oven-flame, wads of my flesh, Nene's neck. I made portraits of my friends and club-mates, rough, fat naked bodies, and a fleet of bowls for Malacresta's polished stones, Ersilio's fish knives and Prasede's meat hooks. If all the Curatos since the founding of Magmate were right, and our sculptures really did take bites out of our souls, I was soulless. My temper didn't swim in hollow centres, ready to be freed by my mother's poking fingers. It was the material. It seethed deep and even in the skin.

I was eighteen when Ersilio decided he'd had enough of

staring at Ciecherella from a distance. On a windy lilac spring night, he, Malacresta, Lalo, Ario and I made a campfire on the beach. Ciecherella, presumably looking for her brother, came down the cliff path towards us. Lalo and I snickered and shook Ersilio by the shoulders. "No, seriously, stop," he said to his lap. "She's going to see. It's not fair on her."

"No couple like vicious wind and proximate fire," Ciecherella said, putting a spread hand down on Malacresta's head. "Ersilio's idea, yes?"

Lalo couldn't contain his smirk. "What makes you say that?"

"The fact you've made him sit downwind."

"All so his favourites can sit upwind."

These supposed favourites were me, Malacresta and, as she sat down between us, Ciecherella. Her yellow dress was in need of redyeing, and thirstily drank up the sienna firelight. Ciecherella and Malacresta's faces had the same piscine gape. In the same way that scowling had lined my eyebrows and squinting Malacresta's nose, she was so often smiling that her wide mouth and limpid brown eyes were permanently bracketed by dimples. Ersilio had never told us which part of this girl made him stare, but it may as well have been her teeth, with the rabbity gap at the front, for how hard he toiled to make her laugh.

She soon tugged Malacresta down into her lap, which allowed him to glare at Ersilio out of her sight. He wouldn't have been angry if Ersilio hadn't been so pathetic. Patheticness, he clearly thought, stood a good chance of charming her.

The conversation eventually turned to a work story of Ersilio's. On account of his agitation, Ciecherella asked him to reexplain some aspect of tending the sails, and now that he was speaking directly to her, his explanation was even more bewildering. When she said she still didn't understand, he jabbered, "Uh, stupid, yes. Me. You could come out with me some time if you wanted. I'd do a better job of showing you."

Ciecherella smiled and tilted her head. "Surrounded by all your friends, Ersilio, and none of mine?"

Her calm acknowledgement of what he wanted made him nervier and more excited. "Well, yeah," he said with a bright grin. "I mean, they've been bullying me about you since that time I kicked your sandcastle over, when we were kids, so there's no point in waiting till they're not here."

"You kicked over," Ciecherella said, "every sandcastle I ever made. And every dandelion patch I tried to make a wish on. You were like a demon haunting my happiness. Everything I tried to play with you materialised to spoil."

Ersilio laughed. "Yeah. That's how boys say they like you."

"And the fact you think that's an apology proves you're still a boy. A pathetic little boy."

Lalo clapped his hand over his mouth. Malacresta's glower turned into a grin. My heart sank into my stomach, but there was a pang of humour too. Surprise, at least.

"Oh," said Ersilio. "Yeah, that makes sense. That's okay."

Ciecherella got up, linking her arm with Malacresta's. "Don't look so sad, little boy. I don't hate you."

Ersilio put his head into his hands. "I am sad," he said, "because you should."

The moment she left, we rallied around Ersilio to commiserate him. I said that it was ridiculous and unreasonable for her to still care about something he'd done as a child, and he didn't want a ridiculous, unreasonable wife. Lalo said that he thought she'd give him a chance. Ersilio shrugged and said, "Don't want a chance. Chances are for people with debt."

It sounded angry and jilted, and angry and jilted wasn't at all like Ersilio. So when Lalo dragged me to the beach the next day to show me that Ersilio was staggering about in an enormous crowd of sandcastles he'd made, I was nothing but relieved.

"Ah, praise God, the sculptor is here!" Ersilio said, holding his arms out to me. "Come and show me how to make these look cool."

"No," I said with a burgeoning grin. "I think that would defeat the point."

"Not a chance! There's no way she made all those sandcastles as a kid without help!"

"Some people enjoy making things. Some people even prefer it to kicking things down."

Ersilio stretched his mouth out like a crying baby and said, "Wah."

Lalo was looking at something on the ground. "He's lost his mind," he said. "We're leaderless now."

"Solavita, STOP him!" Ersilio yelled. "He's going to kick all the seeds off!"

It was an enormous bunch of dandelion clocks, sheltered from the wind by a rock.

I picked them up, and was admiring how intact their fluffy heads had stayed when Ersilio barrelled into me, tackling me to the floor. "Now I have to start again!" he yelled, white seeds stuck in his hair and beard. "Do you have any idea how hard it is to pick those stupid things?"

"This is *asinine*, Ersilio," I said. "She isn't going to change her mind. She told you no already."

"This is what I said—she told me no, *and* she told me to apologise. Not *but*. I'm not *trying* to get her to go out with me. She just made me feel like a meatheaded thug who'd hurt her, and I *care* that I hurt her, okay?" Ersilio got to his feet. "*Levati dai coglioni*. She wanted me to apologise so I'm apologising. You bunch of clowns."

"There's another dandelion patch near the cliff in the forest," Nene said.

We all glared at him. He'd been standing so quietly on the rocks that I hadn't even noticed he was there.

"What?" he said. "He sent me to search."

"Sweet prince of my heart, perfect angel," Ersilio said,

kissing Nene hard on the cheek as he ran past.

Ciecherella was brought to the beach not by invitation, but by the same incredulity at rumours that had brought me. Prasede and Malacresta were with her, and when they saw what Ersilio had done, both of them turned and stormed away towards the sea. I started to tell Lalo and Nene that we should go too, to give Ersilio space to say his piece, but Ersilio was already saying his piece. He handed Ciecherella the floppy bunch of dandelions and said,

"I didn't know how many sandcastles the average girl makes in her lifetime, so I made as many as I could. And I swear on my mamma, I picked every dandelion in Magmate. These are just the survivors. It's okay, I know they make a sad bouquet and it's not like you can do anything with the sandcastles, but I just thought you probably thought so when I ruined them, too, and maybe all that made it hurt was that someone wanted to ruin them."

I was facing Nene as I listened to this. I turned away so quickly a tendon twanged in my neck.

Ciecherella was grinning. Ersilio was still looking at her with the tragic eyes of a wounded animal, so she'd probably been grinning the whole time.

"Finally," she said. "I can make a wish without you stealing it."

"I'll put my hands over my mouth, look," he said.

"No, don't," she said. "I need it for my wish." And she leaned forward and pecked him on the lips.

"ACK! I'M IN HELL!" yelled Malacresta from the distant corner of the beach. We turned just in time to watch him throw himself into the water with his arms at his sides like a salmon.

Ersilio asked Ciecherella to marry him the following year. It had been a year of easy, quiet togetherness, her watching him tidy the jetty with her feet in his coracle, him watching her dye her yellow dress on his back on the fountain wall, and the proposal was done without a single jeering onlooker. The first we knew of it, Ciecherella was approaching Nene in the street, asking him to talk in private, and leading him away to her house.

"It's the dress," Malacresta said gloomily. "She wants to give it back."

Nene's mother's blue dress had been under Ciecherella's bed for thirteen years. After her death, I supposed, both keeping it and returning it to Nene had seemed equally cruel. It had only reoccurred to her as she'd realised she wanted to wear it at her wedding.

As we all expected, Nene skipped back to us empty-handed. He wouldn't hear of taking the dress away from her. She'd promised that after she'd worn it, she'd make it into a tunic for him to wear at his own wedding.

There was nothing obscene about the gown in the church, the things it should have reminded us of. Magmate washed the silt of bad memory out to sea and kept the jewels. The jewels were a girl who redyed her ochre dress every year in resplendent, indelible blue, still as nervous of the hem and sleeves as she'd been in childhood, and a fisherman in shirtsleeves grinning so enormously his best-man-but-best-woman-but-best-man leant to his ear on the chancel and returned the command which had sealed their friendship: "Stop making that stupid face, Ersilio." Even the mute ringbearer was shocked out of his temper when the groom brought him beer and toasted him as his brother. Even I, when my mother told me it was my turn next-but-two, or next if I wanted to marry Lalo, felt giddy thinking about it. I would have married any one of my friends, married them all one after the other, if this was what a wedding was.

Our Curato had been sick with a cough in the weeks before the wedding, and banished himself to bed to save his strength for it. When he came across the chancel in his white and gold chasuble, with Nene linked to his arm and holding him upright, we realised this would be his last wedding. The next month, he retired. Knowing that we'd wait years to receive a replacement from whichever Vescovo had the authority, and that we might be too inconsequential to said Vescovo to receive one at all, he suggested that his son should replace him. We believed Nene when he told us he was delighted to become Curato, but only because Nene was delighted by everything. As I listened to the first Mass in his voice, that sweet, immovable voice which could not or would not draw a distinction between Love-thy-neighbour and Wrath-soon-kindled, it struck me that we might never know what Nene wanted. Or even if he wanted.

When the Curato died in the autumn, and attendance at church began to dwindle, we all gave each other the same reason. We still loved God, honoured Him as the life in the ocean and clay, but Nene's services oppressed our spirits. We'd now watched this poor lamb lose three parents before he was twenty. His most adoring parent only came close enough to adore him because church was the club with which his mother broke him. And we couldn't bear to sit and watch him, knowing he was trapped there.

That was what we said.

Nene had been installed to assuage the village's fear of the Vescovo sending some young Curato from the city, some *outsider*. It had evaded only his installer that to the village, Nene was an outsider too.

Of course, because he was Nene, the depletion of his congregation didn't pain him. He said that good Curatos are happier the less they are needed.

Distaste for seeing him trapped was my excuse for not attending church. It was also my excuse for falling in love with watching him swim. What a weird, mesmerising swimmer Nene was, floating in jellyfish blossoms, at odds with the push of the tide. He often slung himself onto his back mid-stroke and blew out air until he sank to the ocean floor. During the minutes he lay underwater, whether I was watching a jouncing patch of ocean from the beach or the kelp-haired cadaver of his body from the cliffs, I always thought that any other onlooker would feel sick in their belly and think about leaping in to save him. It was just as well for his pleasure, and too bad for his safety, that he only had me.

He had another habit of ferreting in the rock pools for crabs, sitting them in his hands, and talking to them in coos. Once, after a seaquake, Ersilio and I went to the beach to harvest fish and saw him already there, dancing along the shoreline with starfish clinging to his arms. He was picking them up from the flood-banded sand, laying them backward on his forearm to see if they were alive, and tossing them back into the sea.

My mother now believed he was completely mad. That his newfound fearlessness was newfound apathy. If everyone he ever loved is in Heaven, she said, then death is just a front door with mother and father tapping their feet in wait, asking him what time he calls this. Nene loves everyone, I replied. She scoffed. If you love everyone, you love no-one.

To Magmate, Nene was cold-blooded. I saw it as a sign of my own cold-bloodedness, my superior understanding of it, that I did not agree.

One late autumn evening, my mother and I had a vicious argument. She found me on my bedroom floor with my knees to my chest, crying. Having walked in on the same a hundred times, she made no greeting, no lament. She just asked me how she could make me happy. I didn't know, I said. More clay, perhaps. Clay, my mother said, was the exacerbator if not the root of my madness. My new sculptures were gaping, half-finished, contorted creatures, all with my nose. How did I think that made her feel? That her own daughter wanted to rip herself apart?

I stormed out of the house, through the forest and up the cliff. I curled up on the grass and continued crying, making hacking-sipping-shrieking noises which must have carried like a seagull's squawk to those below me, and didn't notice Nene lying in the sea until the sun began to set. He was on his back with his arms flung out, a white asterisk on pewter sand.

At sixteen, he was still a strange-looking thing. When we were children, smallness, green skin and bony limbs had seemed like nothing more than a sickliness to grow over, and I'd waited with annoyance for stature, noble ivory and big hands to arrive as suddenly as his voice had. Instead, he'd halted upward growth at my shoulder and grown only inward thereafter, developing raw-boned thighs and a waist above which the two corners of his ribcage curved like the fangs of a snake. His hair had taken one struggling step from cedar to gold and lost its footing in a colourless murk which, like his skin, was only saturated by the green of the sea. And in the midst of all which endured, perhaps the most stubborn of all, those massive, doleful eyes. Black gibbous moons. They wilted down at the corners like they had weight.

It was winter-cold and the tide rose in peaks which blurred him from view, but there he lay, as if asleep. I had moved in thirteen years from seeing his peace as something evil to something human which crippled me with envy, but on nights like this, it was purely fantastical, a song in the depths of a forest, a dancing light in the sky.

I got up and went down the cliff, stirred and pushed by the freezing wind.

When I arrived on the beach, Nene was nowhere to be seen on the surface. I looked at the spot of sea where he'd been lying, beyond a black shelf of rock. From a low vantage point, the tide looked even crueller. The waves weren't vicious, but slow, rolling mountains, grey gods breathing deep in their sleep.

I unlaced my dress with freezing fingers, and stepped out of it. I had more vitriol for my petticoat, and cast it to the wind. I took off my shoes and hose. In my white chemise, undershorts and stays, I mounted the shelf of rock and jumped in without looking down.

Nene had had a view of my climb from the seabed. As the cold of the sea burst down my throat and the bubbles cleared, I realised I'd overestimated the water's depth. He threw his head back as I crashed into him, offered his hair as a cushion for my face and his hands as roots for my legs. As he swam out of my way, twisting himself around my ankles like an eel, I thought the shock had starved him of air. When I lay down on my back on the seabed, though, he lay down with me.

The cold sliced me anew with every ripple and the tide was like a man kneeling on my chest, pummelling my head back and forth. I only lay there for a few seconds before hunger for air began to roll me inside out, but in those seconds, I felt lassitude drawing on me through the water. I felt sure that, if I could only train myself to hold my breath for as long as Nene could, I'd be able to lie next to him until he pacified me forever.

I lay there suffocating.

I was suffocating.

Nene turned to look at me.

I contorted and threw myself up for air.

Panting jounced me, like slapping myself in the face. I dragged myself along the rock face, the tide skinning my hips and knees against it in slow, hard presses, until my feet found sand.

As I staggered out of the water, wide-eyed and hyperventilating, a blanket of horror came down on my shoulders. What had he done to me? He was a siren. He had woven a spell through that pocket of sea to make me calm, and it had disintegrated in a crash when I'd surfaced. Had he not turned to look at me, I would have lain there until I drowned.

When I turned and saw him walking out of the sea after me,

my panting gave way to a whimper. I crouched down over my dress and glared at him through my wet hair.

"How are you?" he said.

"I know what you are," I blurted.

Nene tilted his head. Then, a look came over his face and chisel-cracked it in two. One half was terror, the other relief.

As quickly as I'd blurted the question, I blurted the thing which would keep me from learning the answer, the thing I'd say if I wasn't scared:

"You're a girl, aren't you?"

Nene's face coiled shut again. He looked down at his body. His flat chest, concave in the middle, nipples pinched and yellow in the cold. The hair on his legs which was so fair it was like a shimmer.

"Because I look like a girl?" he said.

"No, because you can have the body of a man and the soul of a fucking girl."

He raised one eyebrow. "So, too, can you have the body of a girl and the soul of a man."

Red light tore through the green murk in my head. Rage, a gauze, fluttering against my tongue and sucked down my throat.

I stormed up to Nene and barrelled my full weight through his middle. He went down on his back like he had when I'd broken his ankle—that was his fault—and when I went down on top of him, my tide-battered hips and knees panged. That was his fault too. Hungry not for consequence but for sensation, I put my hands around his neck and shoved his face under the water, and then, remembering how long he could hold his breath and how quickly the ankle had healed, I let him go again.

"This is stupid," I said. "You can't. You won't."

Why won't you die?

Instead of shouting at him or saying sorry, I turned and ran.

"Solavita, wait!"

94

I crushed my fist into my mouth and kept running, snatching up my clothes. One of my hose slithered out of my arms, and I left it behind on the sand.

"Solavita!" Nene ran after me. His wet hair flew over my shoulder as he grabbed my arm. "It's okay! I forg—"

I spun around and threw myself to the floor. "SHUT UP! You cold little broken..." I started crying. "No! I can't! I don't know why!"

Nene held his hand out to me.

"I *forgive* you," he said again, more firmly.

Still hugging myself, I looked up at him. "And doesn't it *eat* you?"

I got up without taking his hand. I told myself that made us even.

What he did next was worse than forgiving me. I turned and left, no longer hurrying but in a drunken, wounded walk, and he followed.

When I realised, I turned away from the cliff path and walked down the beach instead. I needed to see just how far he would follow me. When I reached the jetty at the wall of the cove, with him still beside me, fresh despair filled my throat.

I walked down the jetty, and he followed. At the end of the jetty floated Ersilio's coracle. He often got so comfortable in the boat with Ciecherella next to him that after mooring, he sat down to debone his catches on his knee. On the floor of the boat, trussed in fishing line, was a knife. Raw pine handle serrated by his fingerprints, obsidian blade shimmery with fish guts.

Nene saw me pick it up. He turned and went away from me, hurrying on the jetty, then walking on the beach. It was my turn to follow now, to cling, to step on his feet.

He was gazing at the ocean when I caught up to him, loomed up behind him and dragged him throat-first to the ground.

Fish knives were for fish. *Why won't you die?* Green and jelly-

95

eyed, he was a fish. He would die. His blood would be the same white slime. As I landed on top of him for the third time that evening and made a feint to his neck, Nene's hand reached for the knife, curled around it, and then fell away again, passionless.

"You have to mean it," he said.

The blade travelled down, unchallenged. It traced the hard spike of his Adam's apple, used to popping out gizzards and eyeballs.

"Did your mamma mean it?" I said.

Nene closed his eyes and smiled. "With everything inside her that was godly."

"She meant to slit your throat with the sickle, didn't she?"

"And poison my broth with ammonia and lye, and hold me down in the fireplace, and beat me in the head with a leg of the table. We went off the cliff into the rocks together. She held me so tight as she tried to drown me, but I wouldn't drown. And then she drowned. It was your mother who found me. She sailed inland for the night and there I was, sitting on a rock in the middle of the sea."

"Who's your father?" I said. The knife now dangled above Nene's face.

"God is my father. He got my mamma pregnant by magic."

"*Non dire cazzate!*"

"My mamma used to tell me God chose her for her goodness. I think He really did. You understand what I caused in her. She would have been the perfect mother, but I was the perfect child, and perfect children make monsters of mothers. I was meek and mild, I was cold and dark, I was nothing. She's the proof God makes mistakes... you can crave to serve Him and He can crave to serve you in return and still give you a gift that will *destroy* you—"

"No! No! That can't be!"

But he was Nene. He did not lie or joke.

So I wasn't a woman who hated herself. Without malice,

God had crammed me into a body, a purpose, which was going to kill me. I'd been Emerenzia's echo since we'd twisted Nene's ankle together and I'd die like her, after a decade of trying to crawl out of my skin. My madness would whirl around Nene until his black eyes drank it down and he would feel it not.

It was happening already. He was stretching my skin away from my bones. He could turn my anger into misery, numbness, sleep. He could make me nothing.

"You should be deranged," I said.

Nene opened his eyes. "Deranged are the people who see some great evil in only feeling love."

Passion seethed back into my mouth. The passion which had made me show him the cliff to see fear. Break his ankle to see pain. Pull out whatever there was to be pulled out.

I collapsed into his green aura and kissed him.

He tasted like salt, and his cheek was wet against mine, and a piece of my hair was trapped between our mouths. He threw his head back, knocking me down onto my elbows. Our teeth crashed together with a hard pang and I kissed him again with my top lip smarting. I had done it to be cruel, agitate, call him a liar, but like every other thing I'd done to be cruel, it wasn't working. It wasn't working on either of us.

I staggered upright, pulled back my hair, and wheezed out air like I was underwater. Nene was staring at me, and I knew he was staring at me, which meant I was staring back.

"Well?" I said. "Did you feel that?"

Nene said nothing.

With a snarl, I dragged the knife through the sand and brought it up above my head to plunge down. I must have meant it this time, because the knife disappeared before it came within a foot of him. In the red gloom of sunset, there was an enormous flash of light between our throats, whiter than white-hot and dripping like a wound, and when it crashed down off us, my arm was covered in molten obsidian. It poured down and through me, made a borehole in the ditch of my elbow.

I screamed and collapsed on my side.

Nene screamed too. It was a growl, lockjawed, a burst of power wilting.

"I thought I *said,*" he said through hard, surprised breaths, "that my mamma meant it. You don't get to kill me when you mean it. You just get to see me saved. That's *all.*"

He pulled himself from under my legs. I whimpered when he gently took my arm and shrieked when he pulled it. We crawled down the sand bank, and he plunged my arm into the sea. The salt ate through the lava-cracks, turned blood back into fire. I wailed, drooled and thrashed in agony.

Nene took my face in his hands, tilted it to look at him.

"Please don't cry, Solavita," he said. "There's a horror about you crying I just can't bear."

As black blade had turned to black liquid fire, his eyes had turned to ichor. The power, wherever it had come from and wherever it had gone, had passed through him in a bolt.

"And please don't tell." He drew my face closer. "You and I only work when we're trading. You had to kiss me for me to kiss you back, you had to cut my throat for me to burn you, and you had to tell me you're a man for me to tell you I'm an angel."

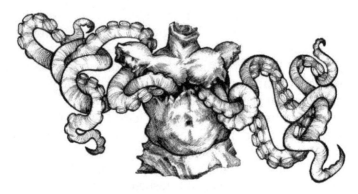

CHAPTER 8

THE CEILING BEAMS

E RSILIO WATCHES ME VOMIT SEAWATER for a long time before he announces his presence.

It's dark. I'm on my hands and knees on the beach. The last thing I remember is drowning. Searching for the coracle and seeing nothing but white and purple whale flesh. Gulping air so thick with rot it burned my mouth. Thinking, as my suicidal brain toiled in vain for the attention of my panicking body, that God was still laughing at me.

Did you succeed? He said, as I hung upside-down. If He didn't leave when the blue light winked out, He saw that I hadn't.

When Ersilio's hand lands on my back, I imagine all possible scenarios. I washed up on the beach and he found me. He saw me rowing out of the cove and swam after me. He saw me rowing out of the cove and took his sailboat after me. He was in the coracle when I stole it, and I was too drunk and hypnotised to notice.

"Were you trying to kill yourself?" Ersilio says.

The question is cold, matter-of-fact.

100

I'm still drunk. I'm falling over and over again from the same precipice. I'm still tangled in the tentacles, the head-swelling voice.

"Nene," I whisper, knuckling my swollen neck. "I saw Nene."

The hand on my back clenches.

"In the sea, right beyond, where we buried him. He had the body of dead whale guts, a whole valley of them, and he didn't have Nene's voice, but he *called* to me!"

"Solavita, Nene—"

"That's not my name!"

"Then what is your name?" Ersilio throws himself down onto his stomach to look up at me. "You don't have another name!"

"God picks ruined things for prophethood if a purpose will put them back together."

"What?"

"Rebuild the church."

"PRASEDE!" Ersilio bellows.

I cry out and sprawl out on my back.

Two bodies and one voice surge up to us: Prasede and Malacresta. The revelation that Ersilio has company isn't the end of my horror. Without saying a word to me, the three of them swarm my bodice's laces, lift my legs, and yank my dress clean off. Something large and soft, a blanket or someone else's dress, is wrapped around me to replace it. It doesn't feel warmer or even drier. "What the *hell* is wrong with you?" I yell at Ersilio as he hefts me to sit up. "You gave up! You promised!"

"On swimming out to save you? Yeah." Ersilio's hair and trousers are soaking wet. "Not on stopping you shivering if the sea spits you out again."

"How did he get so far out there?" Prasede says.

"I think he took my coracle," Ersilio says.

"You think?"

"Washed up without it, didn't he?"

I let their conversation lap and recede over me until some line or another goes up my nose—perhaps one of them saying Nene is dead, or I rowed out to commit suicide—and begins a fresh fit of spluttering.

"Alright, three, two, one." Ersilio, Prasede and Malacresta lift me off my back and onto their shoulders.

"NO! NO!" I scream as they carry me down the beach. I thrash and beat Prasede and Malacresta until I'm hanging upside-down on Ersilio's back. He starts up the cliff, and the sea grows smaller and lower in my aspect. "You *can't* take me away! We didn't finish bargaining! What if he calls me again? What if he cries for me and I'm NOT THERE?"

My wails flatten into moans and then into nothing as my throat rolls shut. As we descend into the valley, Malacresta, thinking my silence means peace, tries to lift me upright again. I bite and scratch at his hands until he jumps back.

Denied scream after scream, I fasten my hands around my neck. Something has congealed there, into peaks which are tacky against the heels of my palms. I bite for air, and feel something flapping in my throat, like the undersides of a luted seam of clay.

The trio plant my feet on the ground at the bottom of the hill. I don't lift my head up until Ersilio shouts for my mother. She opens the front door of our house and gives a whimper of shock when she sees me.

"Went in the sea," Ersilio says. "He's thrown up half the cove."

I'm sorry, Mamma, says the lump in my throat.

My mouth doesn't copy. I stare at her with my tongue bulging behind my lips.

"Why did you go into the sea?" she says.

"He said he saw Nene," says Ersilio.

My mother's eyes widen. Prasede gasps. Under my arm, Malacresta flinches.

"In the cove?" my mother whispers.

"Out beyond, where he was buried."

"Is he still there?"

"I don't know. He won't even tell us what he said." Ersilio braces his elbow against the doorframe and buries his face in it. "*Shit!*"

Prasede puts her hand on my back. Prompted, my mother puts hers against my brow.

"To bed," Prasede says.

I turn to her and sink my hands into her collar, shaking my head. *No, you can't make me stay with my mother,* I try to say. *How cruel to my mother!*

When Ersilio extracts his head from the doorframe and sees me grappling with Prasede, he wraps his arms around me and throws me over his shoulder. Screaming without a voice makes a ghoulish sound, like air oozing out of a stab wound in a lung. As my mother runs to shut the front door, to hide me from the neighbours I hear calling from across the street, I toss my shoulders and strike my head against his back. This adventure is the beginning of more fuss, more pity. They'll keep me from wine and my nose will block and my hands will shake and I'll *feel.* Held down in my new bed, hammers rap-rap-rapping at the new roof above my head.

Prasede, Malacresta and Ersilio wrestle me into bed. Ersilio climbs on top of me to hold me in place. I cough, and the raw walls of my throat stick together and pull into my mouth.

"What's on your neck?" my mother says. "Ersilio?"

Ersilio props himself up to look at me. He reaches for my neck. I thrash my head to throw him off, and he reaches again no less gently.

Behind them both, Malacresta gives a big sniff of panic, staggers in a circle. Prasede runs her hand through his hair and pushes his head against her chest. "It's okay, he didn't really see him," she says. "He's drunk."

I thrash again in rage.

"A swelling at the front," my mother says. "It looks like two dents, but it's a swelling."

"I see it." Ersilio's rough fingers push at the sides of the peak of flesh.

I open my mouth to tell a joke that he'll snap my neck. The joke crawls about beneath the blockage, blooming an itch.

"What?" My mother comes to Ersilio's shoulder. "Is there something in his mouth?"

"Same something." Ersilio presses a bitten fingernail into the skin of my neck and shows her. It is caked in a residue like grey spores. "Is it from the sea?" he asks me, as I gaze at him with drunken eyes. "Did you swallow something?"

I open my mouth wider. The itch in my chest knots into a pain as I try to force it upward.

"You can't speak?" Ersilio whispers.

"Oh, what has he *done?*" my mother says shrilly. "What did he say on the beach?"

"Something about being picked for prophethood. And rebuilding the church."

"It's not true! It can't be! Do you think it's true?"

Ersilio gives a laboured groan. "Don't know."

"But if Nene—"

"We *can't*—waste time worrying—that Nene really was there. What matters is that he *thinks* Nene was there, and he'll drown himself trying to get to him. Meloria, please. That's why we brought him back again. He might already be dead from whatever this shit is in his mouth."

I smile and throw my head back on the pillow.

"Good, that?" Ersilio says. "Being either right or dead?"

When I try to speak again, the tug on my chest brings my stomach with it. I contort, pinning my arm, and am violently sick on the floor.

The stream which comes out of me is red and black, wine and clay or half-digested blood. My mother's wail, a pure sheet of agony hammered into a scale of notes, makes it clear which she thinks it is.

The excited murmuring outside the door compounds into a single knock. Malacresta goes to the door to let his parents inside. When Ersilio hears his daughters' voices, he stares in horror at my pale, red-mouthed face and dashes from the room, slamming the door behind him.

After they go home, my mother wanders into my doorway and says,

"Ersilio told me you told him Solavita's not your name."

I sit up and try to glare at her. She's a black shadow in the hallway and I can't find her eyes.

"I was *hoping,*" she sighs as I hunch down with my back to her, "that meant you'd chosen a new one."

I turn back to face her. For pride's sake, I maintain my glare. *I'm dying and you're upset that I don't like my name?* becomes *What's the point of choosing a new name when I'm dying?*

The look on her face—no, the tilt of the black shape of her head—tells me dying is the point. She doesn't want to bury me next week as Solavita.

I lie awake, waving my arms above my head, trying to savour my last night of drunkenness. The lump in my throat fattens, swelling my gullet to crush my windpipe. I picture it as a ripe plum, tight black skin and blood-pus innards. I'm stupid in the way I'm stupid when I wake up from a blackout, with the gangrene of sunrise in the sky. A wheedling whine in my ears, the taste of wine yellow and rubbery in my mouth, pain smouldering in the fissures below each. The dead whale's voice lacerated my head, hollowed my cheeks and jaw out to their hardest, reddest membranes.

In my bedroom, the shapes of my sculptures seem endlessly unfurling, stretching toward the ceiling. My bed is guarded by my two dead ones. Myself with a flat chest, myself with a hundred eyes, myself with a screaming mouth. Nene's head with solid, trailing hair and the right heaviness in the eyes. Nene's body with the vertical crease from his throat to his sex carved in one thumbstroke. On my desk is a hideous thing which I began after he was dead. I began it as a bust, fiddled doe eyes and swan neck and couldn't remember his mouth. So I made it a mad thing instead, the elbow to a severed forearm digging a raw-edged welt in the belly, gritted teeth and a wrinkled nose to twist away half the likeness and a hand slung across the eyes to shade the rest. Every few months, I drank a bottle of wine and smeared on more curls, bit down on the wrinkles in the nose, deepened the arch of the back. Now, it sprawls off the desk on a caterpillar body of ribs. If they keep me in this room, I'll ruin the other sculptures likewise. The ones I made whilst he was alive. The ones which still have his face.

I know it was you, the dead whale said.

Nene, not God, was the one who watched as we pulled the church down. He was perched on the ruins of the bakehouse, which were so fresh that the beams were smoking and moving underneath him. His eyes were wide and calm. Misery and indifference.

You know it was me.

In the first sober days, I begin dragging objects across my lower belly, trying to simulate the ache I felt on the beach. I wheedle my navel with the windowsill, the corner of the desk, the water cups my mother brings me, the hard wingtips and noses of sculptures. The flesh there grows long red welts like map lines. One night, with the weight of a full bladder pressing down on me, I dig my hands into my belly in my sleep and wake up running to the window, believing I am summoned. As I drag myself back and forth across the windowsill, drawing tentacles in the sky with molten eyes, I perceive for the first time that it isn't Nene I want. I don't want a ghost, a mimic, an animal rutting against a dead man's brain or a fragment of time repeating.

I want for God what God wanted for me. Purpose.

Ersilio can be heard before he can be seen. His voice carries like thunder, and he's always merrily talking to someone: Soothing my mother, shouting advice to the workers on the roofs, or cooing at his daughters, who walk him to our front door and kiss him goodbye. The sight of him cosseting Nedda and Lagia, who are eight and ten years old, reminds me of the sight of him carrying four-year-old Nene on his shoulders. At thirty-three, Ersilio still looks every bit the brute—thick neck and hard pot belly, eyes deepset in crags of sunburnt brown cheek, black hair receding at his temples and curly beard stained grey—but he has a way of greeting, of teasing, of loving with cross, brazen vigour, which makes him the most beautiful creature in the valley.

I always sit up in bed when I hear him coming. He's the only person for whom I feign strength.

Today, he and his youngest daughter Nedda come into my bedroom together, their arms interwoven behind their backs. The moment he lets her go, she presses her cheek against his arm.

"Solavita's over there," he says. "Make a noise." I knock twice on the top of my table, and Nedda directs me a wave and a beaming smile.

Ersilio wouldn't have brought his daughter to miserable Solavita's miserable deathbed unless she begged him. He must have decided that it was impossible for me to traumatise her, given that I am mute and she is blind.

Against the vivid brown of her skin, the scar tissue which shrinks the lids shut over Nedda's missing eyes is as pink as her fingernails, and pleats when she smiles. Her development of a wide, hideous grin identical to her father's, despite the fact that she went blind as a newborn, is the closest thing to a good miracle I've seen. Ersilio takes great pains to plait her hair every day, applying his genius with knots and cluelessness with fashion to bizarre arrangements more for her fidgeting hands than for our eyes. Today, she's wearing two fat pigtails which start in knots at her temples and finish in burlap butterfly bows.

107

"Nice colour in your face," Ersilio says. "My wife married me in blue."

I bare my teeth at him.

He comes up to me, places his hands on my swollen neck.

The crowd which dissipated from the street on the night I was dragged home, bored of drunken tantrums, burgeoned back when word spread of what I looked like. The whole front of my neck is silver-grey and taut, too shiny to be a bruise. My sallow sober face is an island in a mire of greasy dark hair and greasy dark neck. With no mirror in my room, I have to examine myself in the opaque window after dark, marrying my masochistic pleasure to the onlookers' sadistic.

"You're sure you don't remember eating something?" Ersilio says as he presses the sides of the swelling. "A bit of seaweed? A fish?" I glare at him. "My coracle?"

"We will make you a new coracle," consoles my mother.

"I liked my coracle. It had all my cool knives in it."

"Well, you should have kept your cool knives in your sailboat."

"When I go into my coracle to *cut the nets free* from the sailboat? And to debone my catches?"

"You should be doing at least one of those things in your kitchen."

My mother and Ersilio's relationship is one of joking vexation. Amero De Aqvancis retired years ago, relinquishing the tools of his trade to his son, but my mother, with nobody to relinquish hers to, refuses to retire. She teases him for being a reckless child and he teases her for being a stubborn hag.

"Are you drinking?" Ersilio says.

I jounce my lungs for my voice. Then I shake my head.

My mother thought that vomiting blood was a death knell. Neither I nor Ersilio had the heart to tell her that alcohol has been making me vomit blood for months. Thin crimson vomit from the whitest of wine. Shit blood, too. Rends holes through the membranes.

"No wonder you're blue."

I try to smile.

"What about sleeping?"

I glower at him. Every night since I saw God has been a sober night, which means a night of discovering bruises, hearing voices, and fighting down retches. Only last night did I remember that the voice I was trying to retch up was a voice I'd loathed the high, clear sound of for twenty years. Muteness and speaking are drunkenness and sobriety: Feeling nothing, and feeling hellish everything.

Ersilio takes my glower for the misery it is and pulls me into a hug. When the jolt makes me cough, he lies us both down on our sides. My mother tells him to get up, so that she can hug me instead. "Nuh-uh," he says, with his chin against my scalp. She sighs, and takes Nedda into the kitchen.

I need to tell Ersilio that there's nothing to pity. That this sickness is divine. That God will call me back any month now, week now, day now. Muteness is good for my dignity. There's no way I could turn that into a jape.

"Go to sleep," he says when he feels my chest jouncing. "Malacresta can take the girls home."

To make him happy, I close my eyes.

Everything is purple. The sky is in blossom, the sea dark and viscid.

A cliff of a wave looms up beyond the cove. It swallows the two prongs of the headland. Standing on the beach, you wait for it to crest white, but it just keeps getting taller. The tide flees from you, sucked off the lilac sand into the monster's mulberry maw.

You're safe on the cliff now. The mulberry sea is flat, and it laps at the rock face only half a pace below you. Boats float past you, bumping against the grass. The sailboats strike their heads and the coracles roll like wagon wheels. The water crawls slowly upward, submerging your feet, making the grass squelch.

You're watching from your bedroom window when the sea starts pouring over the cliff. The noon sun dyes it from purple to red. You do what you always do when you see wine. You open your mouth.

I wake up, my open mouth drooling on my hard, hot pillow. Only when I roll over, buoyed by the rising red tide, do I remember I'm lying on Ersilio. He has moved onto his back, and laid me on his chest.

"Are you okay?" he grunts, as my head nods into the crook of his arm.

"Mm," I say.

I seize my neck. Ersilio stares at me.

"Shit, Solavita!"

"Hih," I say. The sliver of voice in the breath is so thin we wouldn't have heard it if we hadn't been waiting for it.

Ersilio leaps up and runs into the hallway, shouting for my mother. It's then that I realise Nedda is in my room. She's standing by the desk in a shaft of sunlight, watched from the shadows by the swarm of sculptures. I pray Ersilio runs back for her, because as hope wraps me into a panic attack, I throw myself onto my stomach on the bed and begin a fit of hideous noises. The banging of my head against the wall, chokes and retches, gasps whistling through pinholes in my blocked throat, the stretching of my cheeks and unsticking of my palate by silent screams. I make another "Mm." A "Huh." Then an "Ah," full-voiced and shriller than any noise I've ever made. The note shivers uncontrollably upward and tweaks into silence.

I stop hitting my head, shocked.

Nedda looks at me. I'm sure she's never heard such a noise. The last time I did, I was fourteen or fifteen, with Ersilio shaking Malacresta for voice cracks.

"Ah," I say again. The flat note echoes. "Ah!" I squeak. "Aah-ah! Ah!"

"What are you doing?" Nedda says.

"I thought…" Mucus bubbles into my mouth, and I cough it loose. Then, Ersilio comes in with my mother.

"Can you speak?" my mother cries, as Ersilio picks Nedda up and kisses her hair. "Speak to me, darling!"

I thought my voice was breaking.

"I'm going to kill myself with a rock," I say. My mother shouts for joy and throws her arms around me.

My heart deals in absolutes. I spend days or weeks apathetic, no drop of emotion to make ripples in the water, but every peak of euphoria gives way to a trough of despair. When I wake up the next morning from a dreamless sleep, try another "Ah," and hear my own voice smoothly answering, I hurl my water cup across the room. When Prasede remarks that the swelling on my neck has shrunk, I run to the window to check, then punch the glass until the impacts reach my elbow. Two days, then three. My neck pales to match my face. The callouses grow short and dry and roll away on my fingers. My breaths come easy and wide, and the stuffy nose from wine withdrawal gives me relief in delicious crackles.

Each changing of the guard over my bed ends in an argument. My carers can't understand why my passion for death is inversely proportional to my health. If I wanted to die, wouldn't I have been passionate in sickness instead? Without that moment of hope, that hallucination of hope, I would have slid down into death with dignity. Now, I want to club my brains out before the open curtains, toss myself onto a sharp-winged sculpture and die hanging down like a flag. My life has been an abyssal spiral of neverminds, and the voice cracks were the ultimate.

The dead whale was the penultimate.

When my mother ventures in again, she is carrying a bundle wrapped in burlap. She puts it on the desk, then changes her mind and carries it to the bed.

Carefully, without looking at me, she lays the clay in my lap and unwraps it. It's a small block, two closed fists, maybe a head.

She dithers again. Gets up to leave and then sits back down.

"It doesn't have to be good," she says.

I scowl down at the clay. This was the right thing to do if

111

she wanted me to live. Clay is the only thing about which I will suffer the declaration *This is all there is to life.*

"I'm not a prophet," I say. "There was wine and a dead whale, and I hallucinated."

She doesn't say anything. She just watches me paw at the clay. She knows that I'd rather she left me alone with it. It will never cease to bewilder me that I can love my friends so loudly and bodily but never touch my mother without revulsion.

I stop sculpting when I am holding something construable as a head. Still raw at the front, hacked flat at the sides.

"I could be Sole," I mutter.

She looks at me, her eyes wide.

"Sun?" she repeats.

I start thumbing a pair of eye sockets, too low down on the head.

"Would you like me to tell Malacresta and Prasede when they get here?"

I thumb a second pair of eye sockets without filling in the first.

"Okay," I say.

When my mother leaves, long after dark, I am so unbearably tired I believe I am dying after all. That my recovery was an oasis, and this is the fever coming back to throttle out the last. I fall asleep with dried clay on my hands, rubbing crumbs of it onto the pillow and my lips.

White and placid. You're standing high up again, watching the beach. Nothing is moving, but everything is out of place. It must have moved before you fell asleep, shuffled back and forth by your thumbs.

Look at the mess you've made.

There's a tall white tower between the prongs of the headland. If you walked to it, you could use the roof, the flat black roof with the iron cross on the top, as a stepping stone to hop from one prong to the other. The steps which lead down from the tower's front door are embedded in the sand, which lies bare and smooth as far as you can see.

The old church, beached like a razor shell.

The sea is in the sky, a black sagging sheet over the naked cove, and white dead whale drips from it. Bladdered tentacles hang like a chandelier above the church.

Your throat hurts.

More tentacles come down from the sky. Tornadoes of white rot. More buildings appear around the church. When God multiplies, victims multiply to satisfy Him. There's nowhere you can go, destroyer. The church won't have your filthy feet on its roof. You belong nowhere but below it.

Your belly hurts.

I wake up running. I slam into the windowsill with my arms around my waist. As I wake up fully, I contort my arms palm-outward to grind my elbows into my navel, enjoying the pain for as long as I can.

When I remove my arms, a cramp remains in my stomach. A crumpled feeling which wants stretching out. Then, through my side, there's a tug.

I turn north, toward the forest. When the first tug's echoes converge into a second, it's a visceral stretch and twang, straight from my centre.

Just last year, my bedroom window was glassless, and I could have escaped through it. Not anymore. It'll have to be the door. My mother's bedroom door is closed, but there's light in the kitchen.

Please be Malacresta. Please, God, let him be alone.

It is Malacresta, and he is alone. He's sitting on the kitchen counter with his legs crossed, a little piece of sandpaper splayed on his thigh. When he looks up and sees me standing in the hallway, I imagine the two holy pains blazing from my belly and throat in sheets of silver.

And I know even that wouldn't make Malacresta brave enough to grab me.

"See you in the morning," I say, opening the front door.

"Prasede!" Malacresta yells.

I hurl myself outside and stagger forth, pin-straight. There's no light to follow this time, but my stomach strikes its head against my front over and over again for as long as I run toward the forest. I run through a tunnel of buzzing air which will electrocute me if a foot hits the floor on either side.

Shadows bother the current behind me. There's a shout of "Solav—" and then a chattered interruption.

Eight years have passed since the earthquake, and all the buildings are still unfinished somewhere. As I encroach on the forest, houses scalped without their roofs or eyeless without their window glass turn into animal graveyards of splinted timber and stinking manure. The east side of the square, where the stone church steps lead up into empty sky, is the loneliest of all.

As I stagger up the hillside, a croaking murmuration of sparrows rolls downward past me. I think about the rabbitfish which swarmed around the whale, and turn back on myself to watch them.

Nene and Emerenzia's house was felled by the same earthquake which felled all of ours, but we didn't rebuild it or tear it down. The new Magmate was built one long step away from it, so that it now sits alone at the bottom of the hill instead of at the end of the street. The earthquake caved the roof in, flipping the walls upside-down and propping cruck blade and ceiling beams into a steeple exceeding the height of the old house. As I cling to a tree and gaze at its black silhouette against the candlelit village, I realise that it has new steeples. Three or four. Twinging in the sky like stiff shoulders.

The presence of the monster, or, rather, the presence of the air against my face which is charged by the monster, makes me feel like a pig. It makes me small and hungry. It makes me want to drag my face along the floor until my cheeks scrape off and my molars hit stone. It makes me feel like I'm pissing and shitting myself, like there's liquid pouring out of every pore of me. With a percussion of tock-thuds like the grinding of a gristmill, cruck blades unfurl in the sky, ceiling beams slither upward and splay, the house struggles and rolls to pin its arm beneath its dislocating back. Neither speed nor violence, neither wings shooting into the sky nor wings slamming into the hill and knuckling trenches through the grass, can convince me I watched them grow. That house has always had wings. They beat when Emerenzia was angry. They tore off the roof. They are the reason we were too scared to harvest the wood.

I walk out of the forest. At the bottom of the hill, one of my carers sees me and shrieks. Between us, the house drags its knuckles and thrashes in its bonds, so tightly wrapped in sparrows that the crescents of impossible candlelight which open and close between them are like yellow eyes. Through beating wooden wings, under a cruck blade's blind swipe, over trenches as wide as streams, I walk. The front door slots its handle into my hand and the wall opens wide to swallow me.

This is a sorry place, says the voice leagues above and inside me. **A house of God in ruins because of you.**

"And *my* house in ruins because of you!" I yell.

The hallway of the house, dripping with ivy and moss, hay floors sliding from the hillside beneath, hurtles through phases of light as the roof above it wheels, and the eyes which open in crescents between wings are the night sky's black. I am surrounded on all sides by writhing havoc, once again searching for the centre of God and once again finding He is nothing but limbs bent around each other.

Is that not life, Prophet? Hurting and being hurt in return? The repentance encouraged by sin and the sin encouraged by repentance?

I bare my teeth. "Is that why you chose me? If it's not because you know me?"

There's a commotion behind me, lower and yet louder than the bellowing of the wood. A human voice is a texture which does not belong in this air.

"SOLAVITA!" my mother screams from far away.

Why, Prophet?

"Say my name!" I shout. "And I will say yours!"

"SOLAVITA!" Ersilio screams straight behind me. Multiple bodies slam into the wall where I entered.

Sole.

The name in God's voice is a clearing nostril. Unsticking membranes and a shaft of heady pain.

"Lord?"

Why did I choose you?

"Because I turned them away from you, all of them, every last man, woman and child in Magmate, and it was *right*... and I'm the only one you can turn back with a bargain."

Then let us bargain.

With my eyes fixed on a panel of mossy wall which has not moved yet, I stumble to the floor. To my knees.

Your voice is now God's. Will you speak when I speak?

"Make it a man's voice, and I will speak just to hear myself."

Your body is now God's. Will you treat it as such?

"If it were a man's body, I'd be God on my own!"

The last syllable shrieks, thins in the sky above me until it disappears.

Will you rebuild what you destroyed?

I seize my throat and cackle. Chirruping dolphins, cleats breaking ice.

"In my image!" I squawk. "Amen!"

Amen.

The moment Ersilio and Prasede burst in and see me kneeling there, creaks judder across the roof from wingtip to wingtip. The waning callous on my neck splits. Then, the house collapses on top of us.

An avalanche of birds, wood and sawdust, Prasede's arms around my middle, the concussion of the noise, and the pain, a white sliver of day torn through the night, aren't enough to knock me down. Like the knife Nene melted in my hand, flesh is pouring in molten rivers into my collar and down my gullet,

117

but the hole in my neck is already gone. Luted, in a clean liquid swipe.

I don't speak a word as they drag me from the house. They have no idea that I can. When Prasede perceives that I'm not fighting, she gingerly gives me to Malacresta, so that she might join Ersilio and my mother in staring at the dead monster with her mouth open.

When Malacresta sits me down on the hillside, it's because he needs to sit down. When he speaks to me, it's because he needs to hear someone speak.

"Sole." He gives me a frightened smile. "Gonna feel wrong calling you that for a bit."

I straighten my back and tilt my head. My eyes are red, my hair hangs in viscid stripes and my heart is beating so hard it's tossing my head. The lump in my throat rolls over, arching its belly upward and throwing out its arms. All flesh stretches to accommodate its new volume.

"You didn't need to say so," I say, with a deep, masculine timbre like Ersilio's.

Malacresta scoots back three paces on his backside.

An earthquake in my neck. Fat, heavy vibrations through the roots of my teeth, the marrow of my skull.

An aftershock of laughter. Ecstasy seizes me through the mouth, slams my face down into the ground. Malacresta screams when I sprawl out on my back, screams again when I resume speaking.

"Now *that's* God!" I say. "He summoned me and then keened for me like a dog, Malacresta! He told me to do His bidding and then bent around me like *wind,* Malacresta!"

Malacresta's screaming brings Prasede, Ersilio and my mother running down the hill. He points at me and jabbers, already expecting to have to beg them to believe him. He thinks the voice will disappear now that we have company. He doesn't know that it is *mine.*

"It's—"

118

"What?"

"He just—"

"What? What's happened? Whose voice was that? Where did it come from?"

"Inside him!" Malacresta chokes. "It was inside him!"

"It still is," I say to the grass between my teeth. "And it always will be. And it always was. All God did was drag it into place."

I know what my neighbours are thinking the next morning, when I leave my house sober for the first time in years. I know what they're thinking when daylight falls on my wattle-beige face, my clay slip hair, and the rainbow of bruises on my forehead. I know what they're thinking when I climb, dragging my feet and holding my middle, to the top of the churchless church steps in the square.

I know what they're thinking when I open my mouth and out pours the voice of a man. A sublime voice newborn in a fossilised face.

What a poor mimic of Solavita De Gasinis.

I never saw such life in her eyes.

THE EARTHQUAKE
AND
THE CHURCH

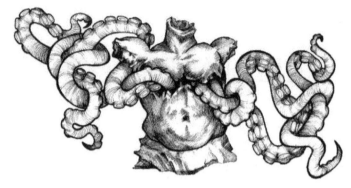

CHAPTER 9

THE SPEECH

NOBODY IN THE SQUARE IS WORKING on their own house. Some builders are distributed by expertise—the strongest pour foundations, the nimblest thatch roofs, parents fetch and carry to include their children—but it's as common to see neighbours exchanging jokes from each other's roofs, or mixing up pairs of cruck blades cut from the same timber. Opposite the grey gash of the church crypt is the bakehouse, a new hearth encircled by a salvaged timber skeleton, swarming with builders. The baker and his son are at the foot of the hill, laying cobblestones.

I don't know what my neighbours know about my illness. I know that they gawped at my neck through the window, they never knocked, they all believe in monsters and there's a wooden spider the size of a black poplar curled up on the hillside where the Karafantonis' house was. When the spell in the beams broke, it sent back to earth ten times the hay and timber it infected. Each plank is a branch, new planks half-formed at odd angles, splintering aside the grain of the old. The enormous weight of the roof flattened the walls and foisted the rigid limbs into the sky.

The people who followed me only spoke to each other. Builders torn from their work asked my mother what was happening, and Ersilio told Malacresta and Prasede to take his hands and form a barrier between them and me. I climbed the church steps alone. My voice crouched, shunted its knees against my throat, unsettled my teeth as it gnawed.

As a child, conscripted to act in nativity plays or sent by my mother to knock on neighbours' doors, I harboured a dread of public speaking. I'd count the actors' lines before mine, the neighbours' footsteps before the door opened. Once I'd agitated my mouth open, I'd speak in a gush, and regret the way I'd spoken once I'd finished. Humiliation didn't fill the act of speaking, but bookended it.

My mother would soothe me by telling me that Jesus was nervous before his speeches too. I thought the idea was absurd. If Jesus was made to give speeches, shouldn't the Lord have made him confident?

As I raise my head to look at the crowd and say, "Good morning," I realise Jesus could have just liked his voice.

Two words are enough to make my teeth and heart sweat. It's a voice like old velvet, black with gashes of blue where the pile splays. A decade of forcing my old voice to sound deeper gives it a laboured, nasal quality I don't wish to train back out, because it lends a blink of delusion that I trained it this deep myself.

And God was right. It is God's voice. As I love my voice, I love my God. Euphoria has split the skin of my blasphemy like a compound fracture.

"My apologies," I say, "for not knowing how much you know about what's happened to me. For, um, blindsiding you, and continuing to blindside you, with the opening of my mouth. The truth is…" I pause to roll my tongue and lick up my own echoes. "Last week, before I took ill, I received an order from God."

Before I left the house, I prepared myself to be laughed at, shouted at. What I didn't prepare myself for was blinking, expectant silence.

"He told me…" I say. "He told me…"

Blue light. Spinning head. Rabbitfish. Not my Nene.

"Eight years ago, I did something terrible, to outline the most terrible night of our lives. With a wrath I'd harboured for many years, I took advantage of your shock, pain and grief, and turned you against your God."

I make the mistake of looking down the steps at Ersilio. He's staring up at me not with anger or shock, but the same look he gave Ciecherella amongst his sandcastles. Round, glassy eyes like a seal's. He's focusing hard on my face, as if he's trying to see the mimic through my mouth. His best friend might speak with this voice, but would not say these words.

"The more I think about what I did," I say, "the more I think I destroyed this church to destroy myself. What breaks my heart is that I forced you all to help me. For that was the only moment, I suppose, that I found myself surrounded by people as broken as me. As you all stand before me, you have healed. I needed ten years, three monsters, and a miracle to heal myself. Now, we must heal our victim. This church must be rebuilt."

And my body rebuilt along with it. The deep echoes of my voice ensconce the secret truth. *Pulverise my ancient foundations and draw a new shape in the pit. Grind and hydrate my shards into new clay. Bubble beneath my own skin.*

Gabbro angel crouched in my neck. Dirty ice split with black blade. Shivering into liquid as the cruck blades came alive.

I am glad I am a passionless public speaker. It keeps my swollen, leaking heart safe in my chest. It keeps God where He belongs: inside me and nobody else.

"It's terrible of me to expect such a favour of you," I say. "I told God as much when He came to me. He said that choosing me was the key to changing your minds, but it was also the key

124

to changing my mind. We must pray it's a sign He's merciful, and wants to redeem me."

And not a sign He was my lover. Wants to crawl inside me.

And not a sign He is vengeful. Wants to crawl inside me and split and slough me in front of you.

Finally, voices murmur in the crowd. The dozen people who followed me here have turned into three dozen. When I catch the murmurers' eyes, they fall silent. I'm being discussed, not addressed.

"How did God speak to you?" a man yells from the back of the crowd.

There's a pang of fear in my chest.

"I saw God beyond the cove," I say. "Then in the Karafantoni home."

The crowd bends like a wheat field towards the hillside. The rippling of their noise compounds into coughs of anger. Cries of "Ugh!" and "How *dare?*"

I claw at my stomach. Making my neighbours believe in God was never the problem. We turned our backs on God in disgust, not unbelief. Nor was making them believe the disease in my throat, and the behemoth on the hill, were His work. The problem was making them believe in my change of heart.

"Please," I say. "I need you to say that you'll help me! I'm just your neighbour. I'm not a tyrant. I know that you don't love God, but don't you love *me?*"

This only makes the crowd angrier. Still, they're not shouting at me, but at each other. Not one of them is trying to get closer to me. Yes, they're angry at my change of heart, but they don't believe it was me who changed my heart. I'm not doubted as a drunk or reviled as a traitor. I'm pitied. I'm God's victim.

My horror seethes into fury. Threats bubble over the pleas on my tongue.

"LOOK at me!" I yell. Ersilio curses, and starts up the steps towards me. "I AM who I say I am! You can believe it without liking it!"

"Solav… come down," says Ersilio. "This isn't the way."

"Then what is the way?"

"I don't know. We can work it out. Just come home, please, before you kill your mother."

When he grabs me, I throw him off, back away and bellow again. "Don't you UNDERSTAND? Do you really think the Lord intends to plead for the pleasure of our love? Do you think the Lord needs our love? Do you think the Lord *pleads?* The Lord shook Magmate to the ground eight years ago for no reason at all, and He will do it again with reason! If we don't rebuild the church, He will tear the village to the ground on the day we lay the last stone. He will reach His tentacles from the sky and make the sea swell over the cliff, red with our blood! Embarrassed and spurned for the last time, He will kill us all!"

I nearly collapse when I close my mouth.

"You didn't tell us that," Ersilio says.

Two hot tears leak down my cheeks.

"Is it true?"

I raise my fists and shout, "I saw it in a DREAM—"

And he covers my mouth with his hand and drags me down the stairs.

I spit and hiss and flail, but only to show that I'm angry. The whole week since I met God I have spent being dragged screaming away from Him, and I know that Ersilio's arms are inescapable. Malacresta takes my legs at the bottom of the stairs, Prasede my middle. My mother tries to stroke my face. Finally, as we reach the edge of the crowd, someone yells it.

"Whose voice is that?"

A roar of agreement behind the shout, a raging river with its dam pierced.

It's mine! It's mine! It's MINE!

"Mm cwthos os aw cod ath ig—" I say with Ersilio's hand muffling me.

"Don't let him," Prasede says. There's a roar of

126

disagreement from the crowd. They want to hear me.

Ersilio removes his hand, and I continue my song: "Lift up your voice and with us sing. Alleluia! Alleluia!"

"Oh, what the fuck?" says Ersilio.

The crowd roils with disgust.

"Thou burning sun with golden beam, Thou silver moon with softer gleam! O praise him! O praise him!" I start laughing. I want to haemorrhage delicious deep noise until my body deflates. "Alleluia! Alleluia! Alleluia! Thou rushing wind that art so strong, Ye clouds that sail in Heaven along, O praise Him! Alleluia!"

"Shut up shut up you're hurting my *head!*" Malacresta wails over my racket as they haul me inside and throw me down on my mother's bed.

"The flowers and fruits that in thee grow, let them His glory also show—"

Prasede steps forward and slaps me across the jaw. I open my mouth for an *O praise Him* and she raises her hand again in warning.

"O—"

She backhands me across the other side of my face.

More people have followed us than I thought. Ario, Lalo and Sitha are standing in the doorway, and more who followed them: Ario's parents, Lalo's father. The man who yelled at me from the back of the crowd is there too. I don't know him well. I know his name is Benghi and his wife was pregnant at my first sculpting ceremony.

"All in all, huh, ten followers," I slur through my slapped mouth. "Or ten gawkers. If you'll work in exchange for your spectacle it's all the same to me."

"We are not your *followers,*" says Ario Barostaldo, elbowing his way through the crowd. "Nor do we care to look at you for longer than it takes to figure out who you are, and how to get Solavita back."

I cackle.

127

"Oh, come on, it's funny," I say. "Look at me. I'm finding it funny. It's fine."

Ersilio puts his head in his hands. My mother turns away, on the verge of tears.

"This's stupid. There's a monster dead on the hill and a new voice in my neck and you won't listen to either."

"That's what you told them eight years ago, you idiot," Ersilio says. "Believe but don't obey."

"Yeah, short life before the afterlife our only chance to rebel," says Ario. "That's what *Solavita* said."

I sit bolt upright and sink my fists into Ario's collar. As people try to lever us apart, I drag him close and snarl into his face, "Yes, she did indeed, but she is dead, and I killed her!"

Ersilio grabs me around the waist and slams me down onto my back. Released, Ario retreats to the foot of my bed, where his parents are turning to leave.

"Did you really see it, Solav…" Malacresta cuts himself off. "God sending another earthquake?"

I lock my jaw, terrified.

You've shouted your lie. Now speak it.

"Not an earthquake."

I know this is the way to get them to obey me. The violent pang which made me shout the threat in the square was something like a revelation. For now, with my shaken body and slapped face, I've forgotten it.

"Then what?"

"Tentacles coming out of the sky."

"And doing what?"

"Crushing the houses."

"The sea swelling over the cliff, you said, too," Prasede says.

"Yes."

There's a long, itching silence. I wait for one of them to call me a liar.

Then, Lalo says, quiet as a breeze, "I don't want to die."

128

At the front door, Ario is pushing his parents away from him. "No, Mamma, Papa, no," he says. "I don't want to die."

And so it is that the parents leave and the children arrive. The first knock at my mother's door comes from a couple in their early twenties who were married at a campfire on the beach last year. Then, a group of teenagers, more curious than ambitious. Sitha's sister comes to fetch her home and ends up running to fetch their mother instead. The rest of the families tell their children, with a patience like they were invited to watch me skip rocks, that they are busy today. Every greeting is the same: "Did she really see it?"

I repeat the lie again and again, my voice darker and fiercer every time.

"I was standing on the cliff. An enormous wave reared up beyond the cove. The sea pressed flat against the top of the cliff. It might not have been a wave at all. And then it poured down the cliff. Red.

"Tentacles coming down out of the sky.

"Crushing the houses.

"Impaling people on their barbed ends.

"The valley became a lake and God hung in it, rolled and splashed in it.

"The sky wasn't the sky at all."

When dusk falls, there are a dozen people in the house. Most are too young to know how to build. Worst of all, in the midst of lying to taste my voice and letting my mother plait my greasy hair, I realise Ersilio is gone. The last time I saw him, he was leaning in the hallway by the open door and shouting into the street, probably to one of his daughters. He never said goodbye or told us where he was going.

Near midnight, I excuse myself to bed. The people in my little crowd shuffle and glance at each other. I add that they may leave too.

"Where should we meet tomorrow?" asks Papena Tegliacci, Sitha's mother.

"Do you think I have instructions?" I say. "Perhaps God floated me blueprints through the water? Don't you think slaving cluelessly is to be the bulk of our punishment?"

The group blink at each other again, frightened.

"Uh, the square, I suppose. We can sit with our neighbours. Examine the... site."

I stumble to my bedroom tired, itching, furious. Without lighting a lamp, I go to the window.

My reflection glares in at me, black and hackled, pale under the eyes with sickness.

The idol looking out with God in its neck isn't God, but maybe the one looking in is.

"Tell me what to do," I say.

I wait a few moments for the last stragglers from my front door to disappear.

"So you convince me to do this with a prize, but leave me to convince them with a threat? A false threat?

"What prize could God offer *them?* People back from the dead? Wondering where their sculptures went? Houses back from the dead? Floating on the cliff like ghosts with nowhere to land?"

The answer comes to me then, cold and seeping.

God isn't meant to offer prizes at all. I told my neighbours that God had threatened to kill them because that's what God would do.

To my delight, in the patch of street rendered visible by my reflection, I see Ersilio. He's sitting in the doorless, wall-less doorway of the new butcher shop, beyond where the cobblestones stop. As he plays with something in the long grass between his knees, there's a stab of fear inside me—*Is it a bottle?*—before I realise it's a flowerpot.

I wonder if he's been there since the dozen people left. Now, he sees me, alone, with my hair in three long wiry plaits, leave the same doorway and stand in the street looking at him. With every step I take towards him, I expect him to get up and run away.

I sit down in the grass next to him. He and I don't speak love. We let it foam in the wakes of our jokes. When he let me play with him when we were seven and eleven, he didn't say, "There's nothing wrong with a girl playing with boys." He said, "You're good at breaking rocks." I think he used to do it to uphold his own callous image, but now, he does it to uphold mine. Maybe he always did.

I lay my head on his shoulder. He lays his head on mine.

"Lot of them," he says eventually. "Sole the seller."

Unlike the new voice, the new name still pierces a nerve of embarrassment. I want to shout that it isn't my name just as much as I did Solavita. If he hadn't made the switch on his own, I might never have corrected him.

"Nothing to do with the fact they're the kids we grew up with."

"Nothing to do with the fact they're kids."

I grin. Kids. Too young to think for themselves, or too young to be apathetic. Those with lives left are the ones afraid to die.

"Listen," Ersilio says. "I'm not going to do it."

Black blight spreads through my lungs and there's a roaring in my ears.

"Why?" I try not to let my voice catch. "Think you're too old?"

"I know God can tell the difference between a true repenter and someone who's repenting in fear, and a God who doesn't care about that difference will never have my allegiance. I'm sorry."

I scowl. "Is that what you think of me? You think I'm repenting in fear?"

"No, Sole."

He's practicing the name. Using it more than he needs to.

"Fear of what? How... badly I wanted to die?"

He says nothing.

131

In desperation, I grab his hand. "You don't think *God* is the one repenting in fear?" I say. "You don't think *He's* the one who's been left lonely and unloved, and is now begging us to take Him back? You don't want to do it for that power? To be *His* God?"

"I'm going home." Ersilio is unmoved. "I've missed putting the girls to bed too many nights. I just need you to promise me something before I go. I don't need you to stop. I don't need you to tell me why you're doing it. I don't even need you to tell me you're sane. I just need you to still be the person I think you are."

I bare my teeth. "Who do you think I am?"

He looks down at his lap in shame.

"Don't you know that it serves God to wipe Himself from the memory of the men He possesses?" I hiss. "Don't you know that if I was possessed, I wouldn't know?"

"Are you the man who gave that *speech* from the church steps eight years ago?" Ersilio says. "Do you remember what we did? You wanted it then, at least, didn't you? I have nothing if you didn't want it then. You know that!"

"You swore after that night that you'd never lose your mind again. That you'd put your children first."

The first note of his reply makes me freeze. He is crying and it shrieks. "It puts my children first," he says, "to keep them from the arms of the God who murdered their mamma."

That night, I drink. Only a little and only to sleep, but I drink, and crash into the square the next morning with the bottle still in my hand. The sun has barely risen and the sky's complexion is white and pinched, but there's already a small crowd on the steps of the church. I climb up behind them and join them in staring down into the crypt.

With the church floor torn up three years ago, the crypt, a gabbro-skinned pit which could fit twenty-seven of our houses inside it, three-by-three-by-three, is open to the sky. The remains of the church still powder the cracks between the stone blocks, a flesh-coloured amalgam of red floor tile, white wall and grey clay. Malacresta and Lalo are standing down there, with their hands on their hips.

"What are you doing?" I shout.

Malacresta looks up. "Nice of you to join us."

"Answer my question."

"We're doing, uh, measuring."

Neither has a string and neither is standing near a wall.

"Brilliant," I say. "Keep that up."

Near noon, I lower my face from a swig of wine and see Ersilio standing by the bakehouse, staring at us. He has a daughter on each arm. Lagia, a skittish ten-year-old who favours loose hair and brown and black wool, is clinging to his left and Nedda is swinging on his right.

When Nedda was learning to walk, the scars over her eyes were still red. It was a daily event to turn a corner in the remains of the street and crash into Ersilio's broad back. He led her walking backwards with slow, finicky steps, frightened to remove himself from the world in front of her in case she tripped into it. Now, she walks as if she can see, faithful in both her father and the world.

I dash wine off my mouth with the back of my hand and stand. Instead of returning my venom, Ersilio lets go of the girls and encourages them to greet me.

Lagia clasps my hands, kisses my cheek, and then bounds up the steps in search of her uncle. When Nedda reaches me, I crouch so she can feel my face. I open my mouth to compliment her plaits, which Ersilio has wrapped with yellow twine to match her dress, then close it again so she doesn't smell the wine.

When Nedda covers my cheeks with her hands, I stumble onto one knee, dropping the bottle. A sharp pain dawns in the centre of my throat, a red pendant hung between her thumbs.

Ersilio sees that something's wrong straight away. He breaks into a jog, calling first my name and then Nedda's.

Nedda is as rigid as me, craning her head back, cloudgazing with her pink shells of scar tissue. Ersilio reaches us, puts his hand on his daughter's shoulder, and goes rigid too.

The pain in my throat breaches, splits the skin and surges out. My possession squashes my scream into a winded moan. It's a more tactile possession than the presence of the monster, as tactile as a larger man sitting up inside me and shrugging me on like a coat. I collapse on my backside, pulling Nedda down with me, her fingers hooked into my mouth and nose like proboscides.

Malacresta's hand makes a fist in my hair from behind. "Sot," he says. "Let her go before I scalp you!"

"I'm not..." I say.

"He's not..." says Ersilio.

I'm not hurting her. She's hurting me. She's eating me.

"Look at her neck!" shrieks someone in the square. It takes a second, a third, a *fourth* spire of pain in my neck to make me realise they're talking about me. There's a shimmering liquid pain and a plucking pain, like the edges of a cut being pulled back and scoured for dirt. Though my eyes are now squeezed shut, I am *seeing,* in swaying red colours, the square, the crowd and Nedda in front of me. When I bring up my hand to seize the wounds on my neck, my hand rears up above my aspect— and clamps over it, snapping it to black.

In the bloody, sticky dark, eyelashes tick against my palm.

I think everything inside me is being drawn up towards Nedda, think my bodyweight sits calcified in her hands, think my head is so full of blood I must claw my neck open wider to release the pressure—and then, it ends. Every piece of me snaps back into its socket. My teeth burn and the soles of my feet itch. When I put my bloody hand back against my neck—flexing my palm against the skin which saw, stung, and blinked like a posy of eyes—I feel only skin.

"Eyes on your neck!" Malacresta falls onto my back. "Bleeding, blinking eyes on your neck!"

Of all the replies I could make, the one which breaches is, "Gone now."

And then I look up and see Nedda De Aqvancis looking back at me, with eyes as pale and splintered as the scars on her face. They were born coated in cataracts, with only the thinnest sketches of iris.

"Can you... see me?" I stammer.

Ersilio answers my question with a wail. The last barrier between his petrified daughter and the crowd, he falls to his knees and buries his face in her bodice like a worshipper.

When the crowd's gaze rolls from my neck to her face, there's a seethe of excitement. Some step forward and some back. Lagia screams, and Malacresta jumps off my back and lands on his backside next to me.

Nedda nods.

I groan in shock, and collapse onto my face to scour her handprints off on the street.

CHAPTER 10

THE EARTHQUAKE

IT'S AT ONCE A RELIEF AND A TRAGEDY, realising that nothing which mattered to you as a child really matters. I spent hours catching bugs which died in my hands, building sandcastles which washed away. I lived under the law that boys and girls were opposite at their cores and couldn't tolerate each other only to learn that I was the only intolerant one, and the only intolerable one too.

Ersilio and Ciecherella's first daughter was born a neat year after their wedding. When the quickening happened, and Ersilio ran to tell me instead of his family, I thought it was because he was scared, but he was so delighted he forgot to be scared until the labour started. As he lay on the floor of his bedroom, the only position which would keep his wife's hand held but hide from her the sweat and tears on his face, I thought about what he used to say when we harassed him for having a crush on her. *"Stop it. She's going to see. It's not fair on her."* The baby's name was Lagia, but Ersilio and Ciecherella called it *Panina* because it was so fat it looked like a pan of bread rolls. For the year that it was their only child, I heard a threat to butter it, dip it in soup, bake it in the oven or sell it to a family in need at least once a day. We learned quickly that when Ersilio passed us in the street and shouted, "Do you want to see the beautiful bread I traded for a trout today?" it was best to pretend we'd never heard the joke before. I once shouted that I knew he was talking about his fat baby, and that carrying his fat baby behind his back with one hand was a sure way to drop it on its head, and he gave me a look of disappointment so wretched it made me feel guilty.

The second baby's birth was longer and bloodier. Ciecherella's face passed beyond white into blue, and I saw her mother sobbing against the wall in the corridor twice instead of once. It reminded me of the stories my mother had told me about my own birth: Feeling like you're being ripped apart by a wolf, by a whole universe, only to give birth to a purple gnat. When, because Ciecherella needed attention more urgently, the physician handed the baby to Ersilio, he experienced, despite his franticness for his wife, a tremor of hesitation. He looked at the tiny creature and then at his enormous thick-fingered hands and said, "I'm... too big."

It was at Ciecherella and Ersilio's wedding that I first noticed Malacresta's attachment to Prasede. With me claiming both titles of bridesmaid and best man at random, Prasede insisted that the maid of honour should walk with the ringbearer, and it was remarkable how well Malacresta suffered their linked arms. Instead of relishing his mute spells as a chance to hear her own voice on the double, Prasede sat with him in complete silence, a state which usually made her squirm as much as Malacresta being touched. We sighingly presumed they were in love, and joked about the wild, miserable places they were going to keep it secret. I couldn't imagine either of them lying down in the dirty woods or on slimy rocks or in a quarry cave full of spiders, but it was clear to none of us what they'd do for each other.

In my most defeated moments, I thought that me and Nene

made sense. If girls and boys were born in destined pairs, if nurturer went to brute and commander to mute, there was a balance about furious me and tranquil Nene. But the thing between us wasn't love. The kiss was a quick fugue just as quickly squashed, and the bond which persisted was blackmail. You tell about the kiss and I'll tell about the knife.

In the two years that followed, I managed to forget what had happened for as long as Nene wasn't near me—and yet Nene was near me. Incessantly. He sloped around after me like we were children again, met me in doorways as I arrived and hung in them as I departed, refused invitations to sit down if standing up gave him a better view of me. He couldn't have failed to notice that my mother didn't want him around anymore, but he came to our house to help her with cooking, gardening and embroidering as if she was still inviting him. That he was known to be quiet and that I was known to detest him were blessings, for they meant nobody remarked on our utter silence and fierce ignorance of each other's eyes. I felt him carving himself into my skin in silence and twitching my sleeves down to hide the brands. One stupid kiss, and I was covered in him everywhere but the face.

And he was fine.

We'd made no transaction not to talk about it to each other, but he smiled and chatted happily in my desperate silence even when we were alone. He wasn't a joker or an actor. He truly wanted nothing from me other than to be near me.

The transaction was bitterly unfair. You tell about the kiss which branded me on the inside and I tell about the knife which branded me on the outside, with a thick purple scar which quarters my palm, veins my forearm and ends in a clot on my ditch. For a fair exchange, my kiss should have ruined Nene. Disgust should have split him like rot every day, made him scour at his mouth until it bled. And *kept him away from me.*

And then, Ersilio noticed. A dozen friends had visited his house for a dinner party, and he had invited me to stay late. He didn't stare at Nene as he loitered in the hallway for half an hour after the others had left, but at me as I stared at my lap with my arms folded, refusing to acknowledge Nene's presence.

"Solavita's staying to help with the babs," he said eventually. "You're welcome too if you'd like."

"Oh!" Nenc exclaimed. "No, I couldn't possibly intrude."

With his spell broken, he skipped out of the door.

Ersilio's head snapped to me with the slamming of the door. "That poor moron's in love with you," he said. "You know that, don't you?"

I slouched lower. "S'not my goddamn fault."

"No, but it's your responsibility. If you care about him, you'll sit him down and tell him it's not healthy to fall in love with someone who bullied you."

"I am perfectly healthy, thank you very much!" Ciecherella said, swanning into the room and dumping Lagia into his lap.

Ersilio, putting his finger out for the baby to grab, didn't join in on Ciecherella's joke. "You're different," he said. "You're a victim of love stupidly expressed. He's a victim of sadism. You're in love despite it."

"And he's in love *because* of it," I finished.

"If you don't do it, I'm going to," Ersilio said.

I scowled at him. I was shocked and insulted that he thought I liked Nene's attention. "Then do it."

The next week, there was a rainstorm which made the whole valley smell like cobblestones. It began at sunset, as a glowing pink fog over the sea, and thickened and darkened with the dusk. Rain in the summer was rare, and my neighbours invented excuses for needing the water—dirty hair, thirsty flowers—and met in the streets. I took a walk. I wove through people who stood as still as pillars, sat for a while on the wet wall of the fountain to watch the mossy surface seethe, and then, through sheets of rain which shone gold between lamplit windows, I saw Nene by himself on the hill.

When he saw me, he stopped walking and clutched at his side.

If I wasn't so used to seeing him swimming, it would have taken me a moment to recognise him. His hair was black with rain, his face white with cold, and his clothes clung glossy and ribbed. His red tunic was plum above the unchanged ivory one and his tan trousers were walnut above his unchanged red hose. Even at my distance, I could see looks colliding on his face, dappling it in portions. I thought he was frightened of me, then delighted to see me, and then, just as I decided he was beseeching me, he turned and ran into the forest.

"What the…" I muttered.

Before I could reason with myself, I ran after him.

In torrential rain, the path through the forest was black and cacophonous, the path up the cliff yellow and slippery. Nene walked up carefully, so I, ploughing at a stagger, muddying my legs to the knees under my dress, caught up with him at the top.

He turned to look at me, seeming confused.

"Did you want me to follow you or what?" I panted. "Stared at me like you did."

"Yes," Nene said.

"Ersilio spoke to you then."

"Yes, he did."

"So what? He thinks you're a doormat who trots around after his bully? You are."

"I know I am."

"You think I should've corrected him? Do you *want* him to know I kissed you first?"

"No."

We stared at each other. I waited for him to tell me what he wanted, and realised, with a pang of rage, that he wouldn't.

"What then? What do you want me to do? You *told* me not to tell anyone. Do you have any idea how lucky you are that nobody knew you were down there with me? They would have asked you what happened, and you would have told them

141

immediately because you can't lie."

"Nobody speaks to me," Nene said.

He turned and sloped away from me.

As he walked in the direction of the sea, the setting sun licked soft the edges of his shoulders and waist. The tornadic pillars of rain over the sea, the freshly turned beach, and the village in the valley all glowed red and bronze. The streets were still full of people, blocking lanterns and reflective windows in shadowy bars. I thought fondly about Ersilio, who hated the rain, and Ciecherella, who loved it. The last time it had rained, she had taken their daughters, Nedda still newborn, into the street and dabbed rainwater into their mouths. Ersilio had shouted from the front door that they were going to catch their deaths, and she had pulled him outside to drape over them like a coat. I hadn't seen any of them out tonight. One for her, one for him.

The sound of the rain on the cobblestones was a high hiss, and below it, hymns rumbled in the belly of the church. With Nene's services scarcely wanted, the only people who still gathered there liked to sculpt, liked to sing, needed the company or cared about keeping the candles lit.

It came over me then, as I prepared to chase Nene down. It made me swoon on a precipice I could have fallen to my death from.

The enormity of what I'd been hiding. Not an angel among us, a pure light which had split my arm. I was thinking about how I'd protected him. Whimpered into his hand and let him scour the wound in the sea. When I'd gone home with my arm gashed raw and my hands full of blood, my mother had watched me bandage it with a haughty chin and heaving chest, like a hostage I'd tied to the stove. I'd told her my lie, that I'd fallen down a rock face and lacerated it, unprompted. She was scared that if she asked, I'd tell her the truth. The truth she still believed.

Not an angel among us but a madness. Not a pure light but

a pair of hands which turned knives only onto people the world would believe had stabbed themselves.

Nene turned to face me again.

"I don't want you to tell anyone," he said. "My mother said nobody was supposed to know what I was. Whether they called us liars or believed us and worshipped us wouldn't have mattered. I wasn't made to affect people. We would have stayed in Sansepolcro if I was."

"So why were you made?" I said.

"I don't know," Nene said.

"You don't *know?*"

"No. God wouldn't have neglected to tell me my purpose if there was one."

"You think you've got no purpose?"

"I think my purpose is to have no purpose. For… people to affect me."

I frowned. Something about it made sense. Arriving so blank and apathetic, showing blips of rage as a child and long blazes of happiness as a man—as if he was learning.

Did that mean that Emerenzia had never rebelled against her purpose? That her purpose had been nothing nobler or more specific than to *affect* him?

"When you melted the knife," I said, "Did you do it?"

"No," Nene said lucidly.

"An instinct, then?"

"No. If I controlled it—even if I was doing it unconsciously, like pulling my hand from fire or scrunching my eyes shut underwater or something—I would have stopped doing it before it killed my mamma."

"And your broken ankle?"

He blinked at me. "What about it?"

"How could your mamma and me break your ankle when you were a baby? Was that before the… defence mechanism… before it started?"

"That was *when* the defence mechanism started. It was

143

healed the next day, and I was never allowed to be injured again."

When he saw how the news affected me, he smiled. He was right, of course. The day he'd come down to the beach to forgive me for attacking him, he'd bounced and run around with Ersilio like he'd never been hurt.

I was barely angry. Anger required surprise. All my other attempts to hurt him had ended up enriching him; why not that one?

"Why do you love me?" Nene said.

I bristled in contempt. "I don't love you."

He could see that I meant it, and he wasn't sad. "Then why did you kiss me?"

"You know why. You told me you could only feel love. I was calling your bluff."

Nene grinned a fiery, gaping grin. "I love you," he said, giving me a reeling attack of vertigo, "because you hate me. You feel something deeply and perpetually that I have never felt. The very core of your being is distant and unknowable to me, like a star. I want to eat it out of your mouth."

I stared at him with my throat inflated. There was a prickle of delight in my scalp.

"That's not love," I said.

"No?" said Nene. "Why not?"

He saw the answer on my face.

Because I hate you, and that's how I feel about you. I want your unary, deficient core. It can't be love making me want to eat the virtue out of you.

There was a change in the air which made me suddenly aware of how wet I was. The rain getting harder or maybe softer, or maybe Nene looking at me too intensely to bear. He rolled his sleeves up and flexed his hands, and then, with raindrops glancing off his eyebrows in explosions, he stormed up to me and pressed his open mouth against mine.

A stillness after our teeth crashed together. Too cold to hurt.

What have we done, again?

And something else and something else. I thought about eating things out of him. When his tongue slithered against my top lip, I fastened my teeth around it, watched the effort of freeing it furrow his brow. His mouth tasted like water again, this time petrichor instead of ocean. The silver-green miasma that, every time it rained, planted in me the hunger to pry up the biggest cobblestone I could find, dripping with soil and weeds, and swallow it whole.

I was suggestable. Every tug I answered with a wrench. He put his hands on my waist, so I raked troughs between his ribs to gather his tunic and drag him. When he moved his hands to my neck, and the sensitive hollow beneath my jaw lit up lilac, I burrowed my mouth down until it found the same hollow on him. Nene was suggestable. My clumsy attack on his neck made him throw his arms around me and squeeze my head between his elbows, and when I clawed into his waist in retaliation, he shoved his face against my scalp as well. I couldn't convince myself that my mission was working, because I couldn't remember whether my mission had been to devour his gentleness or to crush him, nor could I feel, even as I let him pull me to the floor in step with the downpour, whether I was angering or softening. I landed in the mud on my backside, then my back. When Nene put his head on my chest, letting the rain blaze down onto my face, I shouted, "Ugh!" and pulled him back.

He kissed me again. His mouth stretched wide against mine, and a tremor went through his body.

"Don't move," he said. "I need you here. I need to hold you."

I felt it first in the small of my back. A long, reedy groan like a hunger pang and a sliding shift, like a sheath of gut peeling up from my hip. My whole back began to vibrate. The plane of me that was pressed against the ground, not Nene. The ground, not Nene, was vibrating.

145

And then it reared up and roared.

I screamed and grabbed Nene's neck. Yanked off-balance, he fell and headbutted me in the face. Instead of getting up, he splayed out on top of me, used his arms, legs and head to hold me flat against the ground. In moments, my neck and back felt broken, my belly liquid, my head scooped hollow. I had never heard such a loud noise: Not animal and barely natural, the grinding of rock against rock was a monotonous, omnipresent seethe which vitrified valley and sky. And through the steady seethe, crashes. A huge gob of rock unfastened from the headland opposite us, spiralled into pieces and hit the sea in a long whipcrack. With the white scum of rain still on it, the sea was swelling and tossing like tar. Silver fish were crawling up the sheer sides of the cliffs and being licked back down in bands.

Sitting up took an age. The only glimpse I snatched of Magmate before Nene nuzzled and slammed me back down with his neck was of black peaks twisting and buckling, folding the lamplight in their windows inside and inside again—and of one window extinguishing still and quick, in synch with the CRASH of a boulder coming down.

I thought I'd never get up. It wouldn't be long before a rockfall poured us into the sea, before my teeth were shaken from my gums and my bones from their sockets, before the friction in the air boiled off my blood. The seething of the world grew so dense and tight against my head that I felt like I'd been shaken deaf and was hearing nothing at all. It was just an ache. A sinus ache, chewing on my cheekbones and eyes.

After what felt like an hour, the earth ran out of screams and coughed, ran out of coughs and whimpered. The white absence of the black seethe was as loud as the seethe itself. Nene rolled his head inland on my chest, shut his eyes, and sank his mouth into my shoulder.

He didn't kiss. He bit.

I gave a moan, half hunger and half shock, and pressed his

head down with the back of my hand. He bit harder, and dug his hips down between my legs. He needed to lance himself into something which held him to the earth, and I needed to feel pain splitting the numb shell of my skin. We needed.

At last, I stopped shaking and sat up. Magmate swayed into view. Its black peaks were still as tall, but unfamiliar. All was silent.

Then, like the rousing chorus of the hymn the earthquake had paused, dogs began to bark, and people began to groan.

I shot to my feet. Memories of vibrating left my fingertips swollen, my skin pouring upward. Nene sat up beside me, his mouth lolling open.

"Youp…" I couldn't speak. My voice was stretched out of shape. "Youpush… pushed…"

You pushed me down before the earthquake started.

I covered my mouth with my hand and ran.

As I ran down the yellow mud path, I didn't feel where I was landing. I slid on my feet, thrashed a somersault into a pencil roll, and then, with mud in my eyes and my skirts held up around my waist, I was running on flat ground. Through the forest and out of its mouth. The aches soaking down from my head to my legs splintered sharp with every footfall.

The closer I came to the village, the slower I walked, and the slower I walked, the less my footsteps and panting drowned the groans. I couldn't pick out one voice. It was one huge groan made of groans.

The first building I came to was the bakehouse. Its cruck blade had been shot across the square, and the lacy tangle of beams it had dragged with it jutted up from the ruin like a dorsal fin. The square was a thatched tunnel: Tremors had crushed the walls together into a wreckage twice as tall, and beams straddled the street on the floor and in the sky. The church, opposite the bakehouse in the square, was still standing, but wall mesh and beams were tangled around its tower from the steps to the cross on the roof. It was all moving.

147

Timber, wattle and thatch shrugged and rubbed against each other and tiles fell to smash on the street in a stream.

As I stood and stared, buildings contorted and spat people out. Some crawled out wailing or coughing. Others walked out, materialising in the street and on the high peaks of the wreckage like spectres.

One more silent person behind me. Nene, in his wet, spotless red tunic, gazing up at the bakehouse with reverential eyes.

In the fog of groaning, the first word I heard was my name. The shout came from behind the carcass of a house, nearly intact but on its side, which lay across the street.

"SOLAVITA!"

"I'm here. Right here."

Two people black with gabbro dust ran around the house's hanging bowels and slammed into me. The first was my mother. She dug her face into my chest and didn't move. The second, who embraced me quickly and then threw himself away to look around, was Malacresta. His short hair looked burnt, and the yellow of his eyes in the grime was alarming.

"Are you okay?"

"Yeah," said Malacresta. "We both… we were outside."

Outside. I stared around wildly. How many people had been outside, enjoying the rain?

The people in our eyeline were still spectral. They stared with blank eyes at the sky or with irritation at the sources of noise. Focusing on the neighbour choking on the floor relieved the eyes of the everglade of slag which choked him.

How many people had been inside?

"Ersilio," I said.

"Ciecherella," said Malacresta.

We let go of my mother and ran.

I thought my mother would go to check on Nene, but when we slowed down to climb over a beached string of wall beams, I glanced back and saw her climbing after us. The route from

148

the square to Ersilio's house was no longer a straight line. We clambered up and slid down, came to dead ends and ran out of the village into the hills.

In the middle of Ersilio's neighbourhood sat a gabbro boulder the size of a house. Flattened and keeled-over houses lay around it, and enough people to fill those houses, two dozen or so, stood staring at it. I couldn't see Ersilio or Ciecherella among them.

We stood and stared at the boulder too. There was something wrong about it, something wrong beyond the fact it had been part of the cliff and was now down here. Despite the size of the wreckage and the fact it matched the size of the crowd, there weren't enough houses. One was under the boulder.

Ersilio and Ciecherella's house was under the boulder.

The shiver of revelation went through all of us at once. Malacresta screamed and shot forward, and I followed, but by the time we reached the ruin and ploughed up it, a dozen people had beaten us. It was a savage show of people climbing on their knuckles and smashing rocks and flinging them, narrowly missing their neighbours' heads, losing their balance and tumbling down the slope. The boulder had shattered into chunks the size of our heads, and some disintegrated into apples in our hands, but there was too much of it. Ersilio would have been killed by the same weight of sand or straw.

To my right, two men screamed in unison. I looked up just in time to see the one explode out of the rubble and knock the other off his feet. The blood pouring down Ersilio's face was full of gabbro dust, a wet black octopus. He ripped his leg free with a blind sweep which flung a wall of his house down the slope.

"She's down there!" he wailed, staggering upward on a twisted leg. "LAGIA!"

"CIECHERELLA!" Malacresta added.

The crowd swarmed up the slope after Ersilio, trying to look

149

after him. He fought them. With everyone caked in rock and blood and heavy-limbed with shock, their fighting looked animal and ritual, like a bear throwing off hunting dogs. There was a tiny mewl from somewhere beneath him and he threw himself onto his front, launched a boulder over his head, then a toybox, and wrested from the filth a black gob of knitted blanket.

As he splayed out face-down on the slope with the baby against his face, her fat bread-roll arms fisted in his hair, Malacresta wailed for his sister again. The wail went through Ersilio in a fit. A woman approached him and knelt, trying to pull the baby out from underneath him. When he curled up, refusing to relinquish her, she said something which ended with, "—other baby."

It crashed down on me with concussive quiet. Somewhere under the boulder, along with Ciecherella, was a newborn baby.

As I stood there, rain sliding down my back, Lagia's cries of fear coring my ears, waiting to hear Ciecherella and Nedda crying too, Prasede arrived at the ruin. She was carrying a blackened pile of clothes, but when she saw Malacresta digging in the wreckage of his sister's house, she dropped them into a puddle and ran to fetch him down. He stood between us in a tight-fisted shock, nodding and mm-hming as she murmured into his ear. The crowd had dragged Ersilio and Lagia apart, and now swarmed him to attend to his wounds. He was lying flat on his back, shaking. His hands still beat at his face where his daughter had been.

In the sky, whinnying and braying wheeled. The cows in the farmers' fields had fallen down, the horses bolted and mangled their legs on broken fence. Search parties' lanterns blinked on the cliffs, scanning the dark for changes in the ocean. The idea of a flood was just another tremor in an endless barrage of tremors.

Then, it happened. On the north side of the wreckage,

150

exactly where Malacresta had been digging, three men heaved up and flung back a wall. It streamed gabbro in waterfalls and reeled back to expose a pristine white belly. The shout rang through the night, joyous and fierce: "There!"

Two spasms in the crowd. Ersilio got up and started running and so did Malacresta. The same voice yelled again, in sudden panic: "HOLD HIM! HOLD HIM!"

What looked like twenty people jumped on Ersilio and knocked him to the floor. Prasede and I ran for Malacresta and seized a shoulder each. Only when he was firmly on his back, with me on his legs and Prasede on his chest, did he start fighting to get up.

"I'll kill you!" he said to Prasede. "I'll rip your head off!"

"Ah, yes?" She kissed his cheek. "Will you borrow one of my knives, or will you sandpaper it off? Polish it nice and shiny. I can sit on your desk with your stones."

Her voice was shaking, and his whole body was shaking. When I got up off his legs, he drew them up tight around her. In the silence after the discovery, empty of relief and of panic, what had happened to Ciecherella dawned in two long parallel howls. If we had released Malacresta, and the crowd had released Ersilio, they would have crawled straight to each other.

The men who'd lifted the wall were staring down into the pit with their hands on their hips. "That'll do it," one said; another: "That's that." When they tried to lift the wall back into place, it was suddenly much too heavy.

I got up, leaving Malacresta with Prasede, and ploughed up the slope. I had gone to help them lift, but as I shouldered a corner of the wall and turned towards the splayed innards of the living room—and the splayed innards of Ciecherella, who lay with her head beneath the kitchen table and a beam impaling her through the chest—I grew terrified that my friends would think I'd gone to stare.

In the crowd beneath me, there was a flurry of, "Okays,"

and Ersilio got up.

I watched him walk up the slope placidly, failing to draw the connection between his hopeful eyes and his wife's intestines. He'd gotten further than Malacresta before he'd been tackled. It seemed likely to me that he'd seen her intestines then, and also failed to draw the connection.

When terror dawned, it dawned in my groin like anger. I dropped the wall, ran down the slope and flung myself into his arms. "She's dead!" I screamed, as the wall crashed down behind me. "You can't help, Ersilio! She's dead!"

It was as I'd suspected. Malacresta's howls didn't waver, but Ersilio stopped walking, straightened his back, and nodded. "Okay," he said. "Okay, okay." He sounded like he'd had enough of a playfight.

I found Nene in the square, staring up at the church. I didn't know why I'd gone looking for him. I had neither the strength to tell the village what he'd done nor the presence to remember what he'd done.

With ribbed white walls and black grating, the church was Nene's massive reflection. If I thought I'd seen him look at the wrecked bakehouse with pleasure, he looked at the intact church with naked misery.

He wasn't the only one there. Forming a silent, dense core to the array of howling and screaming, a congregation had gathered at the church steps. A few were inside, inspecting, with injured posture, the upright pews, the still-lit candles. More were in the churchyard, shaking their heads up at the statues. The statues which broke during services without being touched.

Not a hundred yards away from the church, the fountain, made of the same limestone blocks, had collapsed like someone had squashed their thumb into it.

My mother was suddenly at my shoulder. "They found her, the baby," she said. "She's alive, but—"

"Look," I said.

My mother looked at the church, and didn't speak again.

My friend Lalo ran out of the church door, weighing neat rows of candles with valley of ruins, and tore at his hair with both hands.

At the bottom of the stairs, an older man grabbed Nene by the arm. "Lucky for you, eh?" he said. "Your house of God intact and ours in heaps?"

"Lucky?" a woman shouted. "You think this is *lucky?*"

"I don't know." The man dragged Nene towards him without resistance. "Do you think it's lucky?"

Nene said nothing.

The man stamped his foot and jostled Nene again. "DO YOU THINK IT'S LUCKY?"

Nene looked over the crowd at me.

"God doesn't deal in luck," he said softly.

"Oh, fuck," said Lalo as the man and woman threw Nene to the ground. He did nothing. I did nothing. Nene did nothing.

"You're *right*—God doesn't deal in *luck*—so what does He deal in? Everything for a reason, right? So what's the reason?"

"It's a *miracle!*" someone shouted. "A beacon! I'm going inside to pray."

"Will praying bring your house back?"

"A punishment, then!"

"Yes—for letting our worship be led by this little moonling child! This bastard child!"

"Or just for not worshipping properly at all."

"Look at him! He's not even fighting back! He doesn't even care! Do you even care?"

"Look—your house is over there in pieces. You haven't looked at it once! Not a speck of dirt on you, so you weren't *in* there."

"Oh—leave him alone. Magmate was wrong before he ever got here. It was built on a belief in bad art."

"If God hated our art why did He preserve it?"

"Because He wants us to have somewhere to crawl when

we pick ourselves up!" I yelled.

A few people turned to look at me, and the shouting paused.

"Solavita!" Lalo prompted, as I stared down at Nene. "Tell us what you mean!"

I'd been thinking about Lalo when I yelled. About something he'd said about Nene when we were children.

"But if you terrorised him and he still likes you, doesn't that make you feel cool?"

"I'm just thinking about how it would feel to be God," I said. "Rolling houses on top of people as they smile up at my rain. Impaling a mother of babies on her own roof. Listening to them screaming and crying... and then watching as they, with no other roof left to shield their heads, limp into my church, throw themselves at my feet, and thank me in raptures for killing their neighbours instead of them."

Nene watched me from the floor. In a crowd blackened by the dust of their houses, there was a wrongness, a pure menace, about his cleanliness.

"And?" Lalo called.

"And what?"

"How would that make you feel?"

How did that make you feel?

I dug my wrist into my eye. "I'd get off on it."

When I left the square and staggered back the way I'd come, they were arguing more ferociously than ever. I was no longer numb. I could smell the cobblestones again. Anger was burning in my fissures. My natural state, the core of my being. I'd show Nene what it meant, what it could do.

I found the wreck of Ersilio's house spread up the hillside like it had exploded. To find Ersilio, I only had to follow the sound of the newborn's screams. It was the worst sound I'd ever heard, raw and red and jagged, so fierce in some notes that it grated.

Ersilio lay slumped against a thorn of beam by himself, holding the black bundle under his chin. Every time the scream grated, his face screwed up in despair.

Finding Malacresta was harder. In the bared chasm of the house, Ciecherella's colours, ochre dress and deep, terrible red, were gone under heaving green. Her brother was lying on top of her.

When Ersilio saw me, his eyes withered. It was such a familiar look. This was the face he pulled whenever the baby in his arms stopped crying or fell asleep. Whenever he spotted someone on their way to relieve him.

I meant to sit next to him and hold him, but I knelt in front of him instead. He was staring deeply and desperately into my eyes, and I didn't want to deprive him.

Or deprive myself. I saw God in those eyes.

"Do you see the church?" I cast an arm in the direction of the square, where the riot hummed. "The only building not razed, and it's immaculate. Not one candle out inside. Not one sculpture cracked—"

Ersilio pawed like a kitten at the blanket, trying to show me the baby. I reached out and helped him uncover her.

She was covered in blood. There was a chasm over her eyes. Something black and viscous, like a slug, glistened in the red. It was a piece of her eye.

"Why are you telling me that? I know the hand of God doesn't discriminate—" The effort of talking hurt Ersilio. Words came out in high coughs. "But she's too little."

"Because I'm pulling it down."

Ersilio stared at me.

I collapsed into his lap and pressed my forehead against his. "Let's pull it down, Ersilio, let's pull the monstrous thing down before God kisses it with another day! Let's show Him what it's supposed to mean for a hand to not discriminate."

With my face so close to his that our eyelashes touched, I watched as, through the dirty scrunch of grief, madness broke. Ersilio grinned. His teeth glowed orange in his black, bloody face.

And so it was that Ersilio tied the blinded newborn's sling to his chest, put the two-year-old likewise on his back after wrestling her from his neighbour, and followed me to the village square. The shouting crowd's shadows reared and jostled on the church's pristine flank. Those who knew what had happened to Ersilio gave themselves away with the way they looked at him. They couldn't believe he was walking. They'd expected him to lie mute and winded under the blanket of his grief for a year.

And tomorrow he would.

But tonight he was mad. We were all mad.

As we climbed the stairs together, the crowd bent around us, pressed behind us, shouted at us. In the savagery of their shock, they were betrothed to what I'd said. They'd found it lucid, workable. They would have eaten each other if I'd told them it would make them feel better.

"We all know," I shouted back, as Ersilio went into the church to examine its construction, "that this disaster, like all things, happened at the will of our God. Through God, all things are tolerable. But like a theatregoer who finds his pleasure in believing the scenery moves by magic rather than by pulley, I have always found my sanity in the invisibility, the distance of that hand. Magmate, do we not adore God for the right reasons? Do we not adore Him for His ruthlessness, His rapture, for destroying as recklessly as He creates—and does a single preserved building not *rip* from us the luxury of imagining our lives undone recklessly? This earthquake was not a wave! Not a gust! Not an upended table, throwing its contents to the ground! That which deprives all is force, and that which deprives with decision, which drives ceiling beams through a mother's heart and purpose-hewn splinters through a baby's eyes in one house and refuses to snuff out a single candle in its own, is being. What God has shown us tonight is that He and His infinite power are a Marchese and his infinite gold and that we, in want of new bodies, new homes, and loved

156

ones brought out of their graves, are the peasants His avarice STARVES!"

The crowd's agreement was not animal and barely natural. A monotonous, omnipresent seethe.

Ersilio came up behind me and whispered in my ear.

"We need to prop it up on supports. Tall enough to reach halfway."

"Gather your beams and cruck blades!" I shouted to the crowd.

"We need to gut it until it's leaning on nothing but them."

"While you're digging through your houses, look for hammers and saws!"

"Then we pull the supports out. Horses or cows."

I searched the square for Sitha and Papena Tegliacci. When I couldn't see them, I dove into the fleeing crowd.

Encroaching on the barn at the end of the southmost field was like encroaching on the bakehouse. Every structure was in ruins, some pieces of fence snapped and others cut, and a spectral group of horses watched me from a corner. As I summited the wreckage of the barn, there was a foam of female chatter, followed by the moan of an injured cow.

"I don't—" I called.

"Hold on!" shouted Sitha. I leapt back as, from behind the flank of a brown cow which was lying on its side, a hand thrust out, purple with blood to the elbow. Between the last three fingers and the heel of the palm it held a long knife like a tent spike.

Sitha was sitting back on her heels, cradling the cow's head on her lap. Her parents were nowhere to be seen. The bloody hand belonged to Prasede, whose heaving shoulders and copper hair were hunched almost out of sight. I shuddered when I noticed the cow's legs, which were so broken they looked like the tangle of roots beneath an onion. The two women were surrounded by the bodies of culled creatures, huge heaps in small stale pools, and pails of shimmering blood.

The cow on the floor moaned again.

"Cucciola, cucciola," Sitha soothed. "One, two, three."

Prasede spasmed and violently slit the cow's throat. The spasm was a mercy, to force the blade through the thick hide as quickly as possible. Through the babbling, ringing sound of blood gushing into the metal pail, Prasede yelled, "What do you *want?*"

We decided to burn the supports instead.

I returned to the square to the sight of a church like an insect, with curved cruck blades wedged against every window. As I searched for Ersilio, I was winged on all sides by people running past with toolboxes, drawing the crowd into bundles. Ersilio had sent groups to the beach to gather tools from the fishing boats, and they had returned enlarged by the flood watch parties. A swarm set to work caving in walls, kicking down pews, smashing up sculptures. A woman lifted her little boy up to watch her pinch the candles out one by one and another woman crashed past them to kick the candelabra up the chancel. A group of teenagers were using a pew as a battering ram on one of the windows, pounding until the lead grate popped out and the glass shattered.

Ersilio greeted me with open arms. "Upstairs," he said. "Quick, before they take the stairs."

With his mouth at my ear, I gazed across the square and saw Nene. He was sitting cross-legged on the wreck of the bakehouse, watching the crowd with vacuous black eyes like Sitha's horses.

When he looked at me, a hot pain zipped from my shoulder to my scalp. I fancied I saw the same happen to him. Throat to tongue. He bared his teeth and tossed his head.

Ersilio and I jostled and chattered as we ran up the stairs. It was light and sublime like his wife wasn't dead, but also light and sublime like the endeavour wasn't real. The church was the boulder we bothered with pebbles, knowing it would never really break. Ersilio threw himself down and started ripping up floorboards, numb to the baby on his back he was jouncing and the baby on his front only a hair's breadth from the backswing of his hammer. He bore down through the floor and took a sledgehammer to the joists. I felt the church tossing in our vice-grip, chewed through to the bone.

"It's going to go," I said. Ersilio didn't hear me.

"Ersilio."

He smashed another joist. Looked up at me with his mouth square.

"Don't let Him take you to Hell with Him."

We ran down laughing. We leapt in unison over someone picking nails from the stairs.

"Everybody out!" I crowed. "Don't let Him take you to Hell with Him!"

We stood on the steps with people pouring past us and looked. The church was leaning hard on the supports on its north side.

"Going to fall towards the forest," Ersilio said.

We looked at each other. We realised what would have happened if it had fallen any other way.

Members of the crowd came forth to give us beams, flint, knives. Prasede and Sitha appeared, with splinters on their arms, and handed us rags soaked in white lard.

At the moment that Ersilio's torch ignited, painting his dirty face crass ochre and red, the trussed white dragon gave a groan and a shudder.

"Speak again," he said as he offered me a light. "They'll need to hear that they won't be damned. Tomorrow."

Of course they'll be damned. Wasn't that the point?

"It's not belief we shirk tonight," I shouted to the crowd. "Just fealty. It's *because* we believe that God is above us, poised to come back for the rest of us tomorrow, that we must vow to live for Him no more! If Heaven and Hell are God's dominion and our toil on Earth is our freedom to choose between them, that makes it our only chance to rebel! We can be... grooms drinking before their weddings, soldiers whoring before their homecomings, prisoners stuffing themselves before their hangings, and if fire is our punishment for doing as we love, then…" I rested my forehead against my best friend's, pressed his full winded weight down upon me. "Fire we must love too."

I always wondered what Malacresta thought of it. He'd run to me before he'd run to his sister, so I was afraid to ask where he'd been when the tremors had come. I can only imagine how strange it must have been when, long after he lay down with his sister's body, in the afterglow of the end of his world, he felt a new tremor begin, looked up at the sky, and saw the church, the only building left to reflect sunlight into the valley, grow two wings of fire, belch black from every pore, and keel onto its back. I should ask him.

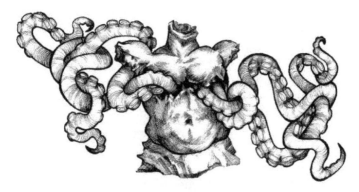

CHAPTER 11

THE CROW

A S I WALK INTO MALACRESTA'S BEDROOM, I have to duck under the garlands of bronze and brown agate hanging from the ceiling beams. He's sitting at his desk in a tight tangle, one leg curled under his backside and the other bent behind his shoulder, throwing rocks from a bucket into two piles. When I see a nub of yellow quartz in the left-hand pile, I surmise they're a 'Keep' pile and a 'Throw back onto the beach' pile. Behind the piles are a quartet of clay dishes holding the 'Keep' piles of weeks past and a purple conch shell rayed with razor shells.

In my first years as a sculptor, I thought Malacresta was as mad as me. He walked home from our adventures on the beach with his pockets so full of rocks he had to hold his trousers up with both hands. When he was little, he polished the rocks by pouring them into a wooden barrel and kicking the barrel down the street with a thunderous noise, and now, he polishes them with sandpaper on his thigh, with the grim mouth and blistered fingers of a leper scratching his sores. Once, he told me that he wished the gaps beneath his high-set canine teeth were wider, so he could twist them out with pliers and replace them with jet or jasper.

It was after the earthquake that I accepted how different we were. Despondent after losing my sculptures, I couldn't bear the sight of the mobiles hanging from his wrecked ceiling as we peeled it off the street. Since his treasures, unlike mine, were salvageable, I offered to pick through the house and rescue them. When he told me that he didn't care about the rocks, that they were just stupid rocks, I thought he was listless in grief for his sister and resolved to do it anyway. Prasede stopped me. She said he'd enjoy the challenge of starting a fresh collection. To Malacresta, there's no such thing as waste. He doesn't polish rocks to make them beautiful. He only keeps them at all in case he decides to polish them more.

"Hi, Malacresta," I say.

He doesn't reply. He's examining a bit of gabbro the size of a shoe, tossing it from hand to hand.

At twenty-eight, a year younger than me, Malacresta wears his grief much better. He's got a face like a catfish, an upper lip pulled tense over the lumps of his errant canines and bulbous eyes the colour of tiger's-eye. His faceted cheeks and nose and the straight line of his bowl cut over his eyebrows make me think about sculpting him every time I look at him. Leaving the edge wide and raw, scraping his forehead up into it.

"Cold outside. First bit of winter. Builders still at it, though."

He jerks his head up in a nod. He picks up the purple conch, and hits the rock with its point a couple of times.

"Hey, um. I should say. Thanks for leading the charge on measuring for the church, you and Lalo. We're going to start drawing plans soon if Ersilio doesn't come. I think he will, though. He just needs a bit of time, between getting over the church coming back and…"

Malacresta stands up, closes the gap between us in two strides, and slams the enormous rock into the wall by my head.

162

The CRASH stakes me from ear to ear. The rock breaks in half. One half falls from his hand, bounces off my shoulder, and shatters at our feet. For the entire succession of noises, Malacresta stands frozen with his arm up, staring over my shoulder.

He crouches and, with the intact half of rock upturned in his hand, collects the broken pieces.

"Thought it might have opal inside," he says. "No. Just more rock."

He goes back to his desk and tumbles the pieces into the right-hand pile.

I don't need to ask why he's angry. I'm aware that I burdened him with my sickness, went back on a vow to my village, made spectacles of power I couldn't control once, twice, three times without a single word to warn, explain or apologise. I'm aware that the greeting he interrupted was yet another of those farces of ignorance.

Besides, now that he's flung a rock at me, he's not angry anymore.

Two weeks have passed since Nedda's healing. The moment after she nodded that she could see is a burnt hole in my memory. The crowd cared as little for the clutch of eyes which had lived for three blinks on my throat as I did, and thronged her to ask if she could see them. Ersilio hung onto her dress and sobbed until he realised that the grabbing and shouting was frightening her, at which point he scooped her up and carried her home. Malacresta was the only one who helped me. His help was dragging me up by my hair, calling me a five-eyed red devil and kicking my wine bottle into the crypt where it shattered.

I go to his shoulder. Alongside the yellow quartz in the 'Keep' pile are a few bone fragments and four eyeballs of obsidian.

"Ersilio would trade you fish for those," I say. "Have you ever made knives for him?"

"Nah. Don't know how to cut. Just polish."

"Don't you ever want to learn?"

"Why? You want a knife?"

"No, I was hoping you'd like to make stained glass windows."

He sits up slightly. Puts the stone he's holding down on his desk, between the two piles.

"What do you mean?"

"You know, stained glass windows, like in the churches in Spain and—"

"I know what they are."

My knowledge of stained glass windows is three people removed. Malacresta's father went to Sansepolcro twenty years ago, admired the churches crammed with painted icons and marble friezes, and was told by a Vescovo about the churches in England and Spain, where the daylight shines in rainbows through pictures made of glass. As tall as houses, and set inside lacy lead nets. Rosy faces, sharp bands of robe and veil, angel wings like chunks of crystal. Though Malacresta doesn't waste time dreaming of the jewels he'll never have, finding in dull white quartz all the beauty of a diamond, I think he makes exceptions for those dreams. His agate mobiles saturated and spread down. His bedroom mosaicked by the sun.

"For Nedda," I say. "I keep thinking about the first thing she ever saw. Half-built village. Bare church crypt. My yellow eyes and sot mouth. I want to fill the world with beautiful things before her cataracts come out."

Malacresta sniffs with laughter.

After the earthquake, we used the stone, lead and iron from the church to build houses. This house, where Malacresta lives with his parents, is one of them. We confiscated God's finery for the families of His victims. I stand no chance of building a church as strong or tall as the old one, but I can build one more colourful.

"Or, well, just because we can."

"Can we?" Malacresta says.

"What do we need? Lead for the outlines, and dye for the glass? We can make the glass here, can't we? They made the window glass for the houses here."

"They made the new windows by melting the pieces of the old ones back together."

"But originally. When the village was founded. They made it from the sand."

"You need plant ashes too," Malacresta says. "To lower the melting point of the sand."

He's still facing away from me, trying to hide the hungry glittering of his eyes. It's too bad I can hear his voice glittering.

"And you get plant ashes how? Burning some leaves? We've got leaves."

An annoyed silence. Then, "Yeah."

"What about colours?"

"Powdered metals. Melt them in with it. The Lord rest you if you're wanting red. You need gold to make red." I smile to myself. "Oh, it's you. Of course you bloody want red."

"Malacresta, if you do this for me, I'll melt you the King's crown."

Malacresta slowly turns around in his chair.

"Good on you for getting something done," he says to his clasped hands. "We were sick to death of measuring for you."

Deep in the forest by the base of the cliff, at a midpoint between sand and plant ash, there's a furnace. The founders of Magmate built it to make window glass, and upon swiping lines through three hundred years of moss and mould, Malacresta and I discover that it is built from the same limestone blocks as the church. As Malacresta walks around it, the spit of the mossy dome in his green *palazzo* trousers and hose, and points out to me the crucibles, the annealing chamber, the blowpipes abandoned in the cracks of the floor, I admire again the aimlessness of his learning. Whereas Ersilio and Prasede are admirable for learning things at the moment they need to, Malacresta's head is stuffed with things he never intends to need. Between definition and application his mind leaves a wide, misty chasm.

"And what's an annealing chamber?"

"For annealing the glass after you make it."

"What's annealing?"

"Makes it stronger."

"How?"

"Don't know."

"What about the blowpipes? Wouldn't they be for making bottles?"

"Yeah, but you make sheet glass that way too, see, by blowing a bubble and then cutting it open." He demonstrates with his hands, cupping them into a sphere and then splaying them flat.

"So you've done that, then?"

"No. I saw Caro do it."

"Didn't you ask if you could try?"

"Didn't want to bother him."

I think about making a joke that I'll hire Caro instead. If he was Ersilio, I would have. But his ego is softer, and I don't want to snuff out the first spark of ambition I've ever seen in him.

By the third week after Nedda's healing, my team of builders is twenty strong. The newcomers, still, are younger than Malacresta and me by enough that we never played with them as children. The last walks into the square as we're sitting on the fountain wall with my sketches on our laps.

"Signora, ignore my family, please—" The young woman screws her face up as her father shouts a plea at her. "I'd like to do something to help you, if you'd have me."

I look over at her parents. The laughing mother's name escapes me, but the miserable father is the very man who heckled me in the square and followed me home after my speech. Benghi. His daughter tells me her name is Abriana Cvradi.

Still staring up at her, I realise she is the first newcomer to introduce herself. The others just walked over, picked something up—a string, a spade—and joined us in pretending to be busy. With no plans drawn yet, and me preoccupied with Malacresta as he alternates between kicking the crucibles to life and licking his wounds at my side, there's nothing to help me with.

I point to Lalo on the steps of the church, and promise Abriana he'll find her a job. Her mother playfully shakes her father, and the two turn around to leave the square.

"Isn't it backwards?" I say to Malacresta.

"What d'you mean?"

"The ages. Shouldn't it be the people closer to their graves who're scared of God?"

He sniffles. "Maybe they don't want to spend the short time they've got left building a stupid church."

I look sadly down at my sketches. I don't want him to think of it as a stupid church. I want him to care about making it beautiful as much as I do. I thought beauty might suffice in place of holiness.

He sees he's hurt my feelings and retracts. "I reckon they don't see it as being about God at all. They see it as being about you. And the only ones who can stand you are the young ones."

"Even though I healed the little girl?"

"If you think a kid's stupid you think everything they do's stupid."

The next morning, as I stare at the blank page I'm meant to be drawing a plan on, Malacresta arrives and throws himself down next to me as usual.

"Any luck?" I say to him.

He thrusts out his hand. Sitting in his palm is something which looks like a dirty hailstone. It's spined along one edge as if it was snapped from something larger—perhaps it was the only white part of an irredeemably ashy crucible—but it's a piece of glass. When I look up at him, he's smiling with dimples in both cheeks, his eyebrows up under his hair. I smile too. He complains often that during his mute spells, I coo and make zany faces at him like he's a child. It's because I'm unconsciously mimicking him.

"Did the rest go bust?"

He thrusts out his other hand. There's a web of white blisters on the heel of his palm.

"You need gloves."

I'm cooing again. I know he doesn't have gloves. It's my job to get him what he needs.

I tap my sketches into a pile. "Come on. No more fire until you've got gloves. Let's think about making pictures."

If he could speak, he'd tell me I was being ridiculous. He made a speck of glass. It'll be weeks before he makes it clear, months before he colours it. But I know him. He'll give up before then unless I give him a vision.

I decide to take him to sketch from my sculptures. When I walk into my bedroom, I think about him sorting his rocks into neat piles, and realise how disgusted he must be by the state of it. The earthquake shattered every single sculpture I'd made, and, in the way of the old church I claimed to detest, I kept every shard. The ones I made later—my hundred Nenes, my better portraits, and my horrors—are outnumbered on my desk by dirty burlaps and socks. As Malacresta sits down, I hand him my sketches, say, "Sorry, been meaning to take these to the beach," and set about piling the junk up by the door.

I sit down with him. We stare together at the empty, dusty tabletop. I feel lighter, like he's torn a rent in me and let in a bubble of air.

I point Malacresta to a sculpture of an angel's wings. Not Nene's wings, but an orderly quartet, sharp edges hooked tight in a spiral. It's a geometric design perfect for glass. Malacresta does a wobbly, stained sketch of a single wing and then shoves the pencil at me.

"After this," I say, "we should go to the graveyard, and sketch the one I did of Ciecherella. I've got sketches I made to make the statue, but we'll start a new one. I've got nothing better to do."

Malacresta glowers, and when I don't understand what he's trying to say, he takes the pencil back and draws something on a blank page. A rectangle with a triangle on top, and a cross perched on the triangle.

He is amused when he sees, days later, that I've drawn my plan for the church underneath his doodle. It's a willowy sketch of a willowy building, a coral-like tower with fish-fin awnings, pitted with windows.

"Like it," he says.

"You do? I'm worried I can only think in clay."

He narrows his eyes. "Why can't you build buildings out of clay?"

"No idea."

I turn the page to show him a far blacker, more detailed sketch. I drew him from memory, frowning down at his furnace. His fringe is a thicket of horizontal slashes and his teeth are gritted. "Make a window of that," I say. "Yellow eyes and sharp green teeth."

He grins, tonguing his teeth. "Like I said I'd do when I was ten? Jasper walrus tusks?"

"To stop you biting your nails."

I point across the square at Nedda, who is dragging Ersilio by the hand. There's a crisp wind, and the flapping of her yellow skirts makes her look like an enormous tulip.

In the first weeks after her healing, it was he who pointed things out to her. That's a mountain. That's a tree. That's your uncle Malacresta. That's a statue of Mamma.

"Make a window of her," I say. "You won't find a prettier medley of colours. Brown skin and yellow dress and big white eyes. No purer picture of God, either."

"What about her in her baby blanket covered in eye jelly?"

There's no contempt in Malacresta's voice, nor his face. He loves his nieces, and spends more time playing with them than he does with his sister's statue in the graveyard. It was a joke, like the green teeth.

Even so, my mind supplies his picture with companions. Red ceiling beam through yellow heart, white church shattered over green hill, blue bones moving under skin, purple blood swelling between teeth. I picture a church like a mudslide in a quarry bejewelled with death and monstrosity, NON VOGLIAMO MORIRE scrawled in the beam above the chancel. An artefact for strange explorers to uncover long after God has killed us for the insult.

"Whatever you like," I say. Malacresta laughs.

When Ersilio starts coming towards us, I hunch over and start furiously drawing, pretending not to see him. He stands at my shoulder and watches me.

Nedda bounces up to us and puts her hands out. Since Malacresta is disquieted by touch, Ersilio taught her to greet him by letting him lay his face into her hands on his own. Then, it's my turn. Even after her healing, she still touches faces to greet.

"Don't worry," Ersilio says. "No soul-sucking today. Cataracts are shrinking all by themselves, aren't they, *pulcino?*"

Nedda grins and nods. The sketch of iris around each of her cataracts has darkened and emboldened.

Ersilio encourages, "Nedda has a question about your voice."

A quick shock rolls down my throat.

"Oh," I say. "Yes?"

"Are, um, um," Nedda says in an anxious monotone. "Are you Solavita, who Papa used to take me to visit? When I couldn't see, you were a man with a woman's voice. And now I can see, you're a woman with a man's voice."

I stare. It never once occurred to me that Nedda didn't know I looked like a woman.

"I'm the same person, yes," I say. "I just… changed out of my woman's name, when my voice stopped sounding like a woman's. I'm a man with a woman's body, sort of."

"A woman's body?" Nedda says.

"Yeah, give it back," says Malacresta. I snort.

"When she was tiny," Ersilio says, "I taught her how to hear the difference between a man's voice and a woman's voice. I remembered you in the middle and said that you didn't count, you sounded like a woman but she was to call you a man. Now, I've got to teach her how to *see* the difference between a man and a woman, and you're jumbling it up for her again."

"So stop teaching her there are rules."

"No! I'm a great teacher and my rules are helpful! It's much easier to add that Sole is an unhelpful bastard who doesn't care about rules and loves to make things difficult—" Ersilio kneels down and hugs his daughter. "But we should call him what he wants, because love is more important than silly old rules."

Malacresta grins. "I thought it was to stop him bashing his head against the wall."

"Isn't letting your best friend dash his brains out a worse sin under God than calling a woman a man?"

When Ersilio called me *he* for the first time, Nene was dying, and I was in a trance. Ersilio and my mother had been arguing about me for nearly an hour, and I had snapped at one *she* or another and started slamming my head against the wall. It wasn't a signal. I didn't think he could have had a clue why I was upset. When he turned to my mother and continued their conversation, supplanting a *he,* I stopped hitting my head and stared at him, horrified. When he didn't look back, I got up and tried to punch him. He caught my hands.

"Is that the scariest thing about seeing?" I ask Nedda. "Who's a man and who's a woman?"

"No," Nedda says. "I also don't know why the sea is the colour of the sky or how the sky and blood can be so bright when everything else in plants and animals is brownish

pinkish, or why things go blurry if I look at them too long or…"
She stops speaking when Ersilio puts his hand on her shoulder.

She looks up at him with something like fear. He kisses her cheek and says, "I know. It's okay."

Malacresta and I exchange glances.

I decide to change the subject. "Would you like to be in a church window?"

Nedda blinks. "What do you mean?"

I hold up two sketch pages. On one is my church, wearing Malacresta's church like a hat, and on the other is a handful of portraits.

Ersilio leans over Nedda to look. "Sole," he says, "Sole, Sole, Sole, *please* do not tell me you're making stained glass windows before you've put the walls up."

I bristle. "We're not *making* them. We're just drawing them."

"Just planning your decorations before you've planned your structure?"

I stab my pointer finger into my sketch. "That's the damn plan of the structure!"

Ersilio sits down. "That's not a plan. That's a concept. It's very pretty." His thick thumb traces the thin door. "It will take you a thousand years and then it will fall over."

Malacresta and I look at one another over the sketch. When Ersilio picks up the pencil and starts to mar our fantasy with pillars and crossbeams, triumphant smiles crawl over our faces.

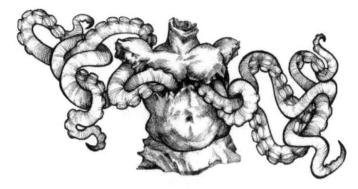

CHAPTER 12

THE HAMMER

E RSILIO'S PARENTS RAISED HIM with a rudimentary knowledge of everything—carpentry, first aid, cooking, mathematics—but it's not the things he knows that make me need him for the church. It's the way he learns. His father started taking him on fishing trips to laze and watch, but he asked to be taught straight away. Our physician, Teglia, believes men don't belong near pregnancy and childbirth, but, horrified by the idea of being useless to his wife if she fell ill, he harassed her until she gave up and taught him. He enlisted Prasede to teach him how to plait his daughters' hair, then slapped her hands away whenever she tried to take over. My neighbours still regard me and my followers with scorn, but Ersilio endears himself to a draftsman at the bakehouse at dawn and throws me a completed plan at dusk. Malacresta and I exchange glances as we lean over it, silently agreeing to feign scepticism to preserve our pride.

It's wattle and thatch and white plaster, with a rectangular, high-ceilinged nave and a stubby tower. Eight thin holes in the two side aisles for the stained glass windows, and larger ones for clear glass in the attic, chancel and transepts. It looks more like Malacresta's drawing than mine.

I'd thought that I'd already pictured the ugliest possible church, a black anthill with curses and horrors gouged in its sides, but this is more noxious to me by far. When one of my sculptures comes out mutant, dismembered, I stare at it for hours, but when one comes out competent and plain, I flatten it and start again. Boring is uglier than ugly.

Malacresta's face has fallen too. I think he's realising for the first time that he won't be making cathedral windows as tall as houses. Instead of making a fruitless complaint about the size, he says, "They're rectangles. Can I have arches?"

"Yeah," says Ersilio. "Probably."

"Everything's a rectangle," I say. "Eight arched windows will clash."

"If what I think's pretty will clash why am I here?"

"Oh, what a shock that the design drawn by me, a boring man, is boring," Ersilio says. "That the design for a building that will stand up, despite having been built by idiots, is boring. Decorating it is up to you. Consider it a more exciting challenge than decorating something which was already pretty."

I sigh out my last speck of petulance. I should have thrown myself at Ersilio's feet the moment he threw the plan at mine. Tearing down the old church was his wife's first funeral. His second wedding. *Our* wedding. And now, he's rebuilding it, for me. He's too good for me. He's the last bright stain on my soul.

"It's great," I say. "Thank you, Ersilio."

His eyes soften. "You're welcome, Sole."

I stand up and throw my arms around him. He stumbles, surprised. Malacresta snorts his contempt.

"I promise," I say into his warm shoulder. "I'm still the same person I was. I won't change."

"Hmph," Ersilio says. "You can't go promising that. I just drove you to the brink of madness by showing you a joist."

Our chain of command for rebuilding is the same as our chain of command for demolishing. Ersilio tells me what he needs, and I command it. Knowing how much more well-liked he is, I tell him he should make the commands, but he knows that without the façade of leadership, I am useless. I don't contribute an idea of my own until there's a freshly dug foundation around the crypt, ready for timber. All the timbers from the old houses, and those cut for the new, are spoken for, and we don't want to fell more trees. I look up at the forest and find my view blocked by the splayed corpse of the monster which gave me my voice.

For a month, this wood went untouched due to an unspoken fear of a curse. Burning it would spread the blight through the air, and building with it would spread it through the streets. But even if my neighbours were right not to want to pitch their houses on the sloughed bones of God, there's no such argument for a church.

When we climb the hill with our hacksaws, the tunnels and tangles of timber seem endless. The new wood God's possession grew on top of the old is of the same blackened, rain-smoothed texture, and wears the same boils of moss and mould. When Malacresta swipes the moss away with his new glassmaking gloves, he exposes circles of lighter, less weathered wood. It was a spell of replication.

The first black beams go up in the square. Our neighbours' scornful glances tinge with horror as they recognise the wood, then gentle again as they grow bored. The people who heckled my speech or tried to pull their children away from joining me still wish me good morning and, knowing that my project is complex and exhausting, ask me how it's going. It reminds me of Ersilio's lesson to Nedda about my maleness. Care that he ruins the rules if you must, but never more than you care about him.

One day, as I stand in the square with the draft plans, my mother comes to hold my hand. She asks me every day if she can help and, knowing she's sixty and I'd go mad with terror if I let her up a ladder, I say no.

Today, instead, she says, "Do you feel powerful, darling?"

I stare down at her. She could be asking if I'm less depressed with something to do, or if I like watching people obey me.

"I'm happy about Malacresta," I say. "I thought it was a stupid idea, the windows, but I've never seen him so focused."

"And do you feel like a leader?"

I frown. As far as the timbers go, I'm barely of any use. I walk over to shoulder any beam being lifted, to hold any ladder without a spotter. The only times I feel like I'm in charge are the times I see people wobbling on ladders, or crawling along beams, or running across the square with tools in their mouths. I refuse to let my mother do dangerous work, but if she's not helping here, she's out fishing alone on the open ocean. I'm not worried she'll be hurt. I'm worried she'll be hurt under my watch.

"Why would they see me as a leader, Mamma? I'm standing here doing nothing."

"Why else would they let you?"

We look at each other.

"I'm only asking," she continues, "because I can't see any of them refusing to call you Sole."

A lump enters my throat. The only people who know my new name are the six who learned it on the first night: Her, my three friends and Ersilio's daughters. I never expressed a desire to impart it on more people. I never told my mother that *she, Signora* and *Solavita* feel in the middle of conversations like mosquito bites, dull for a moment, then a mounting, concentrating ache. For some reason, the bites hurt more in the presence of the people who know better. When my mother and friends hear someone call me *she, Signora* or *Solavita,* they wince at me, or, worse, wince at each other. It's like they're waiting for me to attack the offender, even though the offender doesn't know they're offending.

And why won't I tell them they're offending? Why did my best friend have to start calling me *he* on his own? Why did my mother have to tell me to pick a new name? Why is she the one now encouraging me to tell it to the village? I insist that my agony is with not being accepted as a man, but I didn't care about the village accepting me when I tore the church down with Ersilio, when I sequestered myself with Nene, or when I poured God down on the square. The one who has constantly refused to accept me as a man is me.

I take a deep breath, check there's nobody around us.

"God is going to change me, Mamma," I say.

She stares up at me.

"In return for the church, I asked Him to make me a man. That's why my voice has changed."

"And how long will you take to finish? Ten years?"

I swallow. "Ersilio said it would be less if we got more people."

"So you're going to wait five years? Until you look like a man? When they could call you a man now?"

I bare my teeth. "I can't demand respect I can't give to myself, Mamma."

In my solitude after the conversation, I feel flattened. Such a gentle conversation too. I feel like I argued with her, screamed my throat raw in front of our neighbours. I'm surprised I didn't. I always scream loudest when it's self-loathing I'm smothering.

The builders are laying the skeleton of the floor down over the crypt. As I hop from beam to beam, they glance up, worried I'm coming towards them. I wanted Ersilio, but he's up a ladder with his mouth full of nails. Nedda and Lagia are swinging their legs from the floor beam under him. Malacresta and Prasede are nowhere to be seen. He's started dragging her to the furnace with him, to regale her with his haphazard experiments.

Ersilio's plans include a square hole in the corner of the floor for the crypt stairs. The stairs, cut from the same stone as the cladding, survived the demolition of the church.

There's an obvious reason Ersilio kept the crypt accessible. The village's kilns are in the crypt, two squat white domes huddled in adjacent corners. They were built at the same time as the furnace in the woods, but, since they were used to cure the sculptures used in our rituals, they belonged in the place which housed religious relics.

The idea makes me angry anyway. Nobody has touched the kilns in years. The last to use them was me, and that was long before I started using the crypt to store something else. After we tore down the church but before we tore up the floor, it was the perfect, the only, hiding place for something huge.

I hop over beams to the corner. A group of women, including Abriana, the newest arrival, are collecting nails from a bucket on the crypt stairs.

"Good morning," I say. "What are you looking after today?"

Abriana beams at me. "This little opening, Signora." Mosquito bite. "Measuring the beams is fiddly work."

"Ah, the little frame?"

"Yes, Signora." Mosquito bite.

I gaze into the crypt, through the gap between two beams. The only stain which remains is the dusty wine stain from the bottle Malacresta threw weeks ago. Even so, I put my tongue against my cheek, steadying nausea.

"I can't help feeling the floor would be stronger if we added vertical support beams underneath it."

"And fill in the crypt?" one of Abriana's companions says.

"Yes. It's distasteful to keep it in our sights. We'll build a new kiln. ERSILIO!"

Ersilio doesn't hear me, but builders between us do. I watch in surprise and pleasure as a human chain forms in service of my shout. A woman on a beam calls to a man on his feet, who calls to Lagia, who calls to Ersilio. Ersilio looks up, and takes the nails out of his mouth.

"I don't want to look at the crypt," I say. "Can we cover it over?"

Before Ersilio has time to shrug yes, the components of the human chain put down their work and start hopping over to the staircase.

Ersilio finds me at the fountain an hour later.

"I didn't think about it when I drew the plans," he says. "I'm sorry."

The pain and fear in his voice make me nauseous again. I want to assure him he didn't hurt my feelings, but that would mean telling him why I really made the irrational order. To test which one of us was the leader.

Before we began, I pictured the rebuilding of the church as a frenzy like the demolition. People swarming a skeletal tower like ants and dispersing from a finished one. The reality is wary and self-conscious. In the mumbled conversation of the builders, every shock of a hammer hitting a nail is a punchline. I have to wait until the skeleton of the nave is nearly complete, the supports sledgehammered into the crypt, for my frenzy.

I am eating lunch with Ersilio and Malacresta on the wall of the fountain when, to the south, there's a great roar which reminds a nerve in my stomach of the earthquake.

We look up together. I have just taken a mouthful of bread, and when I see the approaching crowd, I freeze with my cheeks bulging. There are twenty or so. They walk in a ring, a flower squashed down in the middle, because they're carrying someone between them. Someone horizontal, a dead weight. Most of the clamour is chatter, but there's a man crying and a woman making shouts which sound part dismay, part disgust.

As they lay their burden down, one man, the crying man, charges up to me and starts sobbing words I can't understand. I stand up, and Ersilio stands up as if to protect me. Malacresta jumps up onto the wall of the fountain to look at the body. Dumbfounded, I blink into the man's face until a woman, perhaps the woman who was shouting, pushes in front of him to translate.

"Signora De Gasinis, Signora De Gasinis, right hand of God, you have to help him—please, God, please! He fell from the roof while he was working."

When the crowd parts to show me the man on the floor, all I see is blood. He lies on his back with his shirt rolled down around his waist, a wet black border for a torso as red as bare muscle. The hands of the people who carried him to me are red with blood, but his hands aren't. They lie on the street at his sides, short fingers and arthritic knuckles black with dust.

Above me, Malacresta jerks and retches. That's when I see it too. The man didn't just fall onto his front. He fell onto his hammer. Most of the hammers I've seen during Magmate's rebuilding are identical, white pine handles and black cloven heads. All that is visible of this one is a finger's length of handle, saturated scarlet, which sticks out of a layered geode of stomach flesh like a broken bone. Using the angle of it, I draw the rest of the hammer. Seven, eight, nine inches under the ribcage. Claws puncturing a lung or heart.

There's a lot of blood, but not enough. All sinew has caved inwards rather than outwards. I have a quick, giddy thought of grabbing the handle and pulling, releasing a stream with bludgeoning pressure.

After disgust, there's guilt. This is my punishment for worrying about how my builders getting hurt made *me* look. Then, I recognise the man. He isn't one of my builders. His purple lips and one grey eyebrow ripple with memories of sneering and pleading. Sneering at my bedside, and pleading with his daughter not to join me. This is Abriana's father.

"His name is Signore Cvradi," says the woman, who is not Abriana's mother. She's holding the weeping man in her arms. Brother and sister-in-law, I decide. "I know he isn't of the church, but he was working on our house, and when he told Abriana not to join you it was only—"

I hold my hand up to silence her. My face is creased with the shock of such sudden noise. Ersilio and Malacresta look at me, back away from either side of me.

I shout, putting my wrist to my chin when I remember I've got a mouthful of bread,

"You want me to HEAL him?"

"He meant no ill will to you, Signora; just because—"

"No! No! You brought him to me instead of Teglia? Do you have slag for brains?"

The slick on Benghi Cvradi's stomach is rippling with fresh trickles, but he hasn't moved. I haven't seen his chest move.

"You think he's dead, don't you?" I say.

"*Yes,* Signora!"

"And that life and death mean nothing to God! If He grew a voice which never existed in my mouth and eyes which were gouged out eight years ago in the little girl's head, He can cram back a soul which hasn't finished leaving, yes? But *look,* Signora!"

The people in the crowd leap aside as I throw myself onto my knees next to the body. I thrust out my hand.

"This is *my* hand, Signora! It has no power! God takes it up as a tool whenever it can draw someone to His cause! He healed me to hold me, and the little girl to hold my foreman. Look! See how He has no use for an old man who has spurned Him twice!"

The woman's wailing increases. Curious about the texture, and desperate to punctuate my point, I lay my hand flat against Benghi Cvradi's bloody stomach.

Through our joined flesh, the man's broken ribs pull down on my elbow. The contact hums, like struck metal.

Twenty new faces blink at me.

"Oh, eat shit and die!" I yell.

It's funny. It's funny. As God claws up my spine again, I start laughing because it's funny that He has made being the bigger person into a theatrical device. It's an epiphany about unconditional love which makes me stuff my fingers down my throat as if to rip off my bottom jaw, which makes me crawl on top of the body and straddle it, swallowing it with my skirts. "You sick little pest!" I gasp through the lattice of my fist. "Dirty hypocritical animal!"

A scream cores my head as the wound yanks down on my arm again. Not enough power. I apply my other hand. The wound pulls me down by the shoulders, bloats the spaces between my bones, heats up my back until it vibrates and sings.

Another scream cores me whole as the echo of the wound splits my throat, from chin to cleavage. I have two mouths, and my head and neck are gore chunks on a string. I'm screaming twice, and if I sit up, my scalp will hit my heels.

I am conscious at one moment of sunlight bursting down onto me, the crowd backing away in shock. I am conscious at the next of a jolt in the back of my neck as the handle of the hammer touches something hard protruding from the wound in my throat. Blindly, savagely aware that the power guttering into Benghi from my two hands is still not enough, I thrust my face against the geode of flesh and hammer. Clench the handle between my teeth. Drag a pulsating hand up to feel my own wound.

Not eyes this time. Long bones, strung with punctured neck. There's a ribcage on my throat.

In my head, in my bones, through the mouth which is open against the mire of his belly, I taste him. I taste his flesh and the metal of the hammerhead, a hot spring of life and a thorn of cold death.

I push.

I don't pull. I stagger onto my elbows and push, sit up on top of him and push. I swoop upright in a whirl of flying hair and dripping throat and with the palm of an open hand of a shaking arm locked long and straight I push. Blood as thick and black as tar swells through the red rings of the geode. I rock again, forcing my whole bodyweight down onto the hammer, and it hurts so much that it brings Benghi back to life.

He wakes up screaming. It's a greasy yellow scream of pain, pain which eclipses confusion, pain which should be Hell dragging him down rather than Heaven pulling him up. When he sees me crouching on his chest, crushing a weapon down into his heart with both hands, he whimpers and struggles. I lunge down and hiss into his screaming mouth, "Now, now, that's no way to say thank you!"

Then, I rip the hammer out and hold it high above my head. CRUNCH.

Charcoal slash from earth to sky.

Everyone screams except me. I shut my mouth so the blood doesn't come in. The blood comes in anyway. The pressure of the haemorrhage is so dense and omnipresent that it swallows my head, becomes its texture, becomes nothing. This is just God carefully changing the colour of my skin from somewhere underneath it. I'm a red creature now. I press my red hand down through the red haemorrhage to reach Benghi's ribs, now a blown-open ruin of red bone and string, and tell my brother the blood that this is no way to behave in public. When we scream and dance and dirty the floor in the light of day, our neighbours call us mad.

And the blood stops.

To the crowd, it is like I hit the seam once and luted it. Only I existed in the moment for a hundred years. Only I felt the leather hard pencil-shaving crucible-crust resistance of Benghi's wound sucking my life into its mouth to chew. When I stand up, one hand holding him around the waist and the other the liberated hammer, the wound's double-hackled echo long gone from my neck, I still feel it. God, Nene, Mamma, Ersilio, I have never been so hungry, and I am still... being... eaten...

"One second I drop him," I slur. Benghi's brother and sister-in-law run out of the crowd, and I push him into their arms. "Go lie him down out of my sight! He's got a lot of blood to make back!"

The first person I see when my composure sways back is Malacresta. He's standing on the wall of the fountain exactly where he was, with both his hands over his mouth and tears streaming from his eyes. Ersilio and Lalo are all the way over in the church, clinging to wall beams from the tops of ladders. I think that Ersilio ran back to keep Abriana and his daughters from seeing, and Lalo ran back to see over the crowd. The valley of blood I'm standing in looks like it gave birth to me.

When I raise my hands to look at them, the crowd jerks as one. God is a dramatist. He marks my speeches with tense silence and my route across His stage. He directs that the dead man be laid by the fountain at such an angle that his haemorrhage dyes the water and paints the white stone.

"Fuck off," I say to the crowd. "Go back to your houses."

They don't move.

"Don't tell me you want jobs in the church now."

They exchange glances, embarrassed.

"You have *houses* to build!" I shout. "What, you're going to live in the church? Sleep on the pews? Rear your children on wafers and wine?" I shove my hand back into my mouth. It doesn't feed me more blood, just adds finger-blood to lip-blood and tongue-blood. "Always something worse to eat. Alright, someone find them something to hit at! Don't give them hammers. Not me! Leave me alone! I don't know what I'm doing."

I kneel next to Malacresta and slam my head down into the fountain. When I drag my sodden, bloody hair back out again, I don't think I've ever carried anything so heavy.

I don't realise I'm expecting my mother to be home until I open the front door, a black and red spectre, and am surprised by the dark hallway. She was there too. She saw.

Do you feel like a leader?

Signora De Gasinis, Signora De Gasinis, right hand of God. A stranger addressed me as *Right Hand of God* and all I heard

184

was two *Signoras.* Embarrassment doesn't suit me. I'm an attention-hungry lout from top to bottom. Kick Nene to make him fear me, kiss Nene to make him love me. I yelled for the acceptance of Ersilio, for the business of God, for the savage love of the mob, for the terror and awe of the witnesses to my power, and all that I yelled for I hated because I let them call me *Signora.* I'm sick of *Solavita* in the mouths of hecklers. I'm sick of the flapping skirts on my silhouette in fire and gore. Fifty people betrothed to my church. They have already taken me for a sadistic, sottish beast, and I am glad for it.

But I will not be a she-beast.

I storm into the kitchen, the blood in my hose and sleeves leather hard and pulling on my every hair. In my chalky, sticky hands, I seize my mother's scissors from the counter. They're rusty and blunt, used for snipping open fish. As I walk to my room, I work my hair around and around my wrist, making a tightly twisted rope. Hacking through it pulls bruises into my wrist and rubs blisters across my palm. I eke a jagged diagonal line and sever the final piece far too short, to spring up under my eye. The black dead dog of my hair hits the floor by my desk with a thud.

I tousle what's left in front of the window. Nearly dry, shedding trimmings and flakes of blood, it lies flat on my chest when I lean forward, but sprawls on my shoulders in large, circular curls when I stand upright. I part a fringe in front of my face and hack it off severely short, nearly at my hairline. It gives a serrated top jaw to my black eyebrows serrated with frown lines.

I grin and widen my eyes. My mask of dried blood cracks down both cheeks.

What happens next happens in a fugue. I might blame it on shock at what they saw in the square, but I think they've lived this moment in their heads so many times they're bored of it. The front door opens while my hands are in my hair, and all I have time to do before my mother, Malacresta, Ersilio and

Prasede walk into my bedroom is stand up. When they see me at the window still covered in blood and with my hair cut like a man's, they turn to each other with mutters or to me with waiting hands so as to join in, like lions, in my evisceration. I didn't realise my mother had so many pairs of scissors. She cuts the skirt and sleeves off my black wool dress and Prasede cuts the skirt off my white linen underdress. The fluffing out of the white sleeves under the dark ones reveals a syrupy map of bloodstains and the white skirt is so saturated it hits the ground with a splash. From behind me, as he cuts the jagged hair at my shoulders straight, Malacresta yells at Ersilio to get me a pair of his trousers. Both men own two pairs of trousers, but whereas Malacresta wears his green hose and green *palazzo* trousers together every day, Ersilio has kept the black trousers he wore for his wedding under his bed for ten years. Their wool is dyed a finer black than my tunic, gabbro to its blue slate, and they have long braided cords threaded through belt loops. I tell him I won't take them, they're his best. He kisses my blood-grained cheek and tells me I'm his best.

The women's final affront against the dress is to slit the lining at the shoulders and stuff it with wadded offcuts of the skirt. The illusion it creates is less of a masculine feature and more of a masculine choice. The men who are born as men cultivate their sharp edges too: Malacresta stuffs his hose into the wide bottoms of his trousers to make his thin legs match his chest, and Ersilio keeps his beard long and square under his ears. Like the voice and the haircut, the shape makes me feel dark and solid, not because it is dark and solid but because it is right. I am pulled up into my own mouth, saturated through my own eyes. I look like someone who chose.

As dusk gathers, with Benghi Cvradi's blood rolled off but not washed off, still stinking of wet dog in my hair, I return to the square. With my smattering of followers now fifty strong, I pondered the poetry of addressing them from the church steps, but there's a more visceral poetry in standing on the fountain wall. In the still red waters and black scabs of moss. In the fact that, even though I stormed away still retching and Ersilio followed, leaving nobody to give commands, there are people around it on their hands and knees, scouring the blood from the cobblestones.

"Good evening," I say, as the crowd nudge and shuffle. "I am sorry to have left you so soon after we saved Benghi. Can anyone tell me how he is?"

Abriana is standing at the back of the crowd. She doesn't speak until I look at her.

"He's perfect," she says. "Tired and in shock. The wound is no more."

I smile and rub my face. "Tired and in shock we all are. I would even dare to say Signore Cvradi was granted the most pleasant view." Abriana laughs, and the laugh spreads through the crowd in a rumble. "Now, with so many more of you looking at me, I thought it was only fair to tell you a kind of truth about me. A leader must be honest about himself to those who look up to him, or he's not worth looking up to. I'm sure a few of you have heard my closest friends calling me by the name *Sole,* perhaps by *he* instead of *she,* and I wanted to extend you all the same offer. I trust you to understand that that's because I'm a man. I've always been a man. This hasn't come about because of God, or because of the voice He gave me. I was a man when I was born here twenty-nine years ago, as agreed to by the mother who gave me life. I was a man when Nene Karafantoni perished inside and all around me, as agreed to by the God who splayed him out. I was a man when I tore the old church down with you all, and it was a stain upon the bond we forged that night that I did not tell you so."

Ario Barostaldo hollers from the middle of the crowd. I see his face sticking up the moment he speaks.

"You're not a *man,* Solavita," he says. "We can all see you're just dressed like one."

Lalo is standing next to him. "She's got a man's voice now,

bloody hasn't she?"

"I don't care about that!"

"Good!" I say. "You shouldn't care about that! Did I tell you to call me a man because of the voice God gave me? No. I told you to call me a man because I *told* you to."

"Well, what if I threw a massive fit that damned you and your entire village to Hell and then demanded that you do me the favour of calling me the Emperor of Rome?"

The crowd laughs. Ario grins, encouraged.

"What makes you see this as a favour to me?" I say. "This is a favour to you. I've entrusted you with the name and titles to which you may address your curses."

"Well," Ario says, elbowing his way through the crowd, "what if I consider calling you a woman a more effective curse?"

I hold my hand out to him. He pauses, perhaps looking at the blood dried black in the creases.

"Then you come up here, Ario Barostaldo, and try to hurt me with a curse to someone else addressed."

Ario takes my hand and steps up onto the fountain wall with me. He is a hard plank of a man, a hand taller than me, but he glowers at me with a slouch.

"I don't care for a sycophant, Ario. Look at me hard in front of your village and say, 'You're a hypocritical bitch of a woman, Solavita De Gasinis.'"

The resolve in his mouth fails. He realises he's got an opportunity to surprise me, stab me somewhere newborn and soft.

"You're a hypocrite and a worthless drunk, a liver-eating parasite of a man, Sole De Gasinis."

I slap his shoulder. "Brave man, Ario. Brave man."

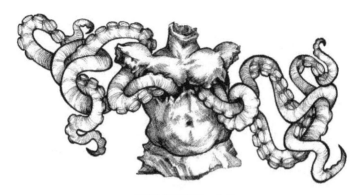

CHAPTER 13

THE BAPTISM

WITH THE FOUNTAIN FULL OF BLOOD, I go to the beach to wash my hair. In the months since God dragged me into the sea, this is the first time I've lain down on the sand. Put my head into the path of a wave and let it sweep my hair down the bank. I imagine the sea sighing in relief, with the weight of my hair quartered.

After half an hour of scrubbing, I get up and walk backward. My hair is still saturated enough to stain the silver sand with a dark trail. With flat pools collecting on the padded shoulders of my tunic and my short fringe scratching my forehead, I walk to lie down on the seaweed-covered rocks. Melody to the tide's rhythm is the sound of necklaces of moisture running from the lichen carpeting the cliffs into the rock pools below.

White sunrise is spread thin by fog. The trees on the nearby cliff look like they're hovering above it and the faraway cliff is a dark rolling cloud with its head down in the sea. When I breathe, I think I feel cold points of condensation running down the inside of my skull.

God swells out of my second hour of tiredness. He is a

headland leaning down through the mist, a droplet dyeing dark the cotton sea. When I feel the change inside me, the foaming dizziness, the defensive inversion of every organ into a petrified knot, I realise that I am not being called. The tug on my belly fastens me hard against the rocks. He is germinating beneath me.

Viscera inside and all around me. The tide a heartbeat chewing on turgid membranes. The streaming lichen capillaries carpeting hard skin. The pimpled seaweed which covers everything from the cliff path to the sea floor the flanks of massive lungs. I, lying at the heart of the seaweed, am a parasite lanced into the lungs, irritating brief twinges in the monster as I drink. There's a swarming itch on the flesh of my arms, a pulling on my body hair. When I look at my hands, I see black ovular particles crawling out of my sleeves. At first, I think they're worms, but when I roll onto my front and my hands crush gobs of red slime against the seaweed, I realise there's a spell on the blood on me. The largest clumps wriggle in places I forgot to wash. In my navel, in the creases behind my knees, in my hair. A clump darts out of my nape and across my face, and I moan as I crush it against my mouth.

All around me, the seaweed turns red. Its yellow pimples fill with blood and burst. A whipcrack of red sparks travels from my shoulder to the base of the cliff. I turn my head to follow a second, a third, a fourth, then look up and see a bubbling scarlet tongue of lichen hanging from the top of the cliff. Something is happening to the sand touched by the red seaweed on my other side. With sounds like cutlery shaking in a drawer and oil spitting in a pan, it is springing up into long, fine teeth of glass. It is happening under the sea as well, and the waves are gaining hard purple facets, receding slow like slime.

An ache swallows me. It's a thick golden ache which pools in my jawbone, my collarbones and my hands. Perhaps it was planted by the blood clot I crushed on my mouth. My flesh has visions of pick axes scoring borders and digging chunks. Of a circle of sky above a crescent of quarry, and a rolling over of the world which replaces it with a circle of floor. Of being poured full of water until it swells and sweats it out, and of a fist coming down to squash it out of shape.

I am clay.

I gasp in delight and seize my face. When my fingers sink into my liquid flesh, a tongue of red lichen and seaweed which stretches from me to the top of the cliff struggles loose. I grind my teeth, moan open-mouthed, gouge a trench from my ear to my chin. My other hand digs at the back of that hand, collects flesh from between my tendons and shoves it up my fingers. I should be yearning for my tools, but I sculpted my finest with only my hands. Three red tentacles of undergrowth hang curled in the sky, anchored on the rocks and sloughing visceral chunks into the rock pools.

I rub my molten fingers against my molten jaw, harvest clay, spread it on the edge in thin layers. Not a mite of air trapped. I work a trough under the edge with my middle fingers, rest my middle fingers together at my chin, put my thumbs under the bulbous ends of my collarbones and push them upward. Use flesh to lute the rent in their wake. The question of whether I control what I'm doing, whether I'm possessed by a design, is as small in my mind as the question of whether it hurts. Pain is everywhere, coating me, and therefore, when I rip holes in myself, I am creating gaps in pain to breathe through.

Limbs burst up. Feelers made of single fronds and tongues as tall as the cliffs. Like the wood in the house and the whale flesh in the sea, there is far more seaweed in the air above me than there ever was carpeting the rocks. A sheet of lichen tossing and pulling against the top of the cliff hurls down into the sea a chunk of gabbro the size of a coracle. As the tentacles fold inward over me like a flower, I see limpet shells studding them and crabs as red as tomatoes running up and down their sheer sides. For the first time, I have watched the whole spell take hold in crisp daylight and sobriety: Not an array of

191

monsters or a monster with different forms but a monster without a form, which splays out all it touches into breathing, appendaged echoes of itself. A version of it lives in my neck, next to my new voice, when I heal. I mimic the wound and heal it on my own flesh, and my patient mimics the remedy. As I lay my half-sculpted hands on my chest, I wonder whether, the next time I heal, they will bear the wound instead of my neck.

I watch, with my hands melting into each other, as the red flower learns how to move. Each tentacle comes in alone, sways backward in tentative synch, and becomes part of a blossom breathing as one. It's like watching a foal try to walk, a puppy try to open its eyes.

I spend as long on my hands as I can, long enough for the surf to fill with glass and the tentacles to dye and drag up every mite of flora on the beach. My fingers sponge clay away from each other and my fingernails slide out of place as they catch on my tendons and knuckles. Hands are harder to sculpt than faces. A hand is five limbs strung together, and both of them must match. When I finally throw them out in surrender, I have convinced myself that the red flower above me is Nene, and I shut my eyes tight, so I don't have to watch him die.

CHAPTER 14
THE CONVULSIONS

THERE HAD NEVER BEEN, nor would there ever be, another ritual like the first bath after the earthquake. As my neighbours ran down the cliff and lunged into the ocean at my sides, their hair belched gabbro dust with every footfall. They blew black snot out of their noses, cried black tears, spat out black licked from their teeth. Their wounds bled black. Oozed it thick and slow. The gabbro might have been eating into their flesh for how violently they tugged and slapped at themselves to get it off.

I was dizzy with relief that I was dirty too. Having stood on the steps as the church crashed down, Ersilio and I were covered in white dust. The dust clung to the bloodstains on Ersilio's face, making white tears like cracks through his dark skin.

As I dragged him and his daughters through the water, holding Lagia on one shoulder and him on the other, his weight didn't feel like his at all. Nedda lay in his arms, still screaming like something barely animal.

Teglia had parted a crowd of the wounded with both hands

to find the baby. Before she so much as touched the creases of blood, she had confirmed that her eyes were destroyed. Gouged out by splinters like the flesh around them. The black slug on her cheek was her left eye and her right eye was nowhere.

All she could do was clean. The baby's face was so small that a bandage would have suffocated her.

Nedda had always looked too small for Ersilio's enormous arms, but only now did I fear that they'd crush her, that he'd either forget how tiny she was or stop caring. He still scrunched up his face when she screamed, bounced her, and cooed, "Papa's here, Papa's got you tight, Papa's going to make it stop," but *make it stop* didn't mean what it had at the ruin. Nedda, who was going to die, had not died yet, and he was desperate for her to die so the noise of her dying would stop. He was desperate for her to die so he could hug her without reserve, crush her flat into his front.

I scooped up seawater with my hand and rubbed it against Ersilio's cheek. My hand came away black and red. All around us, people were groaning at the pain of salt water finding their wounds, but he didn't seem to feel it.

"Mamma, Mamma," said Lagia, twisting backward in my arms and thrusting her head over my shoulder. When she didn't see her mamma, she started crying too.

Magmate haemorrhaged. Children were crying, and parents were crying in frustration as they tried to soothe them. People were throwing their clothes off and scrubbing naked buttocks and breasts with the flats of their hands. To our right, a woman was rubbing a wound on her husband's leg which had bloomed a pool of blood as wide as a bathtub. They were both laughing.

From deep inside the valley, and then cresting the cliff, came the eviscerated, bloodthirsty screams of Malacresta Malacheti. Everyone in the sea turned to watch him come down. His father had tossed him over his shoulder headfirst, and he was beating Prasede and his mother in the face as they tried to catch his arms. He had needed to be dragged off Ciecherella's body, and it had taken all three of them.

They set him on his feet at the edge of the rocks. Out of screams, he stood before us all with his hands on his face and his sister's gore down his front like a red vomit stain.

Prasede said something to him. He tore at the laces of his tunic—seemed to tear them down the middle—and launched his soiled shirts into the sea. Half-naked and half-red, he threw his arms out, pulled his face into a harrowing smile, and pitched himself into a bellyflop.

"Ersilio?"

"Want to do it now," Ersilio said. "It's better than bleeding out."

"*Merda.*" My hand came up in a vice-grip beneath Nedda.

He never tried to drop her. He was asking me to do it.

Nobody slept the following night. We set up beds on the clifftop with salvaged hay and sheets and then wandered, worrying that being the first to fall asleep would look like apathy. Like a spider, my grief scuttled away whenever I grabbed for it. I just felt dirty. With the church's white dust coating my throat and stomach, I felt like I'd eaten a corpse.

The night after that, aching and fluey, I fell asleep before sunset. I woke up again after dark with my mother and neighbours asleep around me, long pink scars of cloud in the sky, and Nene standing over me.

He was only looking at me, and I only looked back. He was a bloody creature in the dark, sharp cracks in his lips and an agitated flush on his throat. He was wearing his red and white tunics over white undershorts. No belt and no trousers. His legs, knock-kneed in red hose, were tentacular.

I hadn't seen him for two days. He hadn't been in the ocean, for he hadn't been dirty. The last time I'd seen him had been when I'd caught his eye through the crowd before the church fell. He was gazing at me the same way now. It was like he didn't realise two days and two hundred feet had passed us by. Like he still thought he could stop me from doing it.

"What do you want?" I said.

He sat down beside me and crossed his legs.

"I don't have a bed," he said.

Of course he didn't. We hadn't made our own beds. To pretend we could protect our loved ones on the cold clifftop, we'd made each other's. Nobody loved Nene.

I peeled back my blanket and sat up. My mother and I had made beds on the edge of the camp. She was fast asleep beside me, with her back to me. Chatter still hummed at the other end of the camp, but I didn't have time to identify the voices before Nene's head pressed against my chest. As I froze, dropping the blanket on top of us, he wriggled to tighten the embrace, curling up with his shins flat against my thighs, like a baby moulded to the womb. When he sank his mouth into the crook of my neck and breathed out, lassitude staked my belly to the floor. I rolled onto my back, pulling him on top of me.

He murmured something. Poured it hot into my collar.

"What?" I said.

"It won't be as big."

Down under the sea, the earth roared.

Terror rolled my lungs shut. Nene covered his mouth with a corner of the blanket and ground his head hard into my neck. The moment the aftershock's growl spiralled up into a tremor, he started shaking. Crying.

Two by two, our neighbours awoke. A child awoke screaming and within a few seconds screamed himself sick. The tremors weren't strong enough to fling us, but people flew to their feet like they were being attacked, threw themselves to the ground and covered their heads, or picked up their children and started running. My mother woke up just in time to see me reach up, seize Nene around the throat, and thrash until I was on top of him. When I wrenched the blanket from his hands, he covered his face with his arms. "HOW DID YOU KNOW?" I screamed into his face. I used my grip on his throat to slam his head back and forth. "HOW DID YOU KNOW? HOW DID YOU KNOW?"

He didn't seem to hear me. He was drooling through bared teeth. His middle was bucking and twisting beneath my weight, his knees beating at my back. If this was crying, it wasn't a performance. It wouldn't be long before he followed the child who'd screamed until he vomited. I pulled back my fist to strike him, and he sat up and drove his head into me so hard I flailed. Bolts of dread shot out of him, punctured and deflated me.

There was nothing I could do but hold him back, feel the fit of anguish toss and shake him.

In a moment, he'd be calm again. I wanted to remember.

The aftershock stopped. The unrest in its wake was a crawling buzz in the small of my back and the sound of children, and Nene, crying. The children's mothers soothed them back to bed, and only Nene was left. He moaned and heaved against my chest, rubbed his face against my neck like a dog. When he started dragging his bared teeth across the palm of his hand, I snatched it away to stop him. My mother had sat up in bed, and was staring at us in shock.

I felt it start to happen. The gentling. He breathed deeper, withdrew his teeth from the lips on my neck.

"What did you say?" said a voice behind us.

I turned, nearly dragged off-balance by Nene's weight.

A ring of neighbours stood around my bed. Amero, Lalo and Prasede at the front, and their families pulled with them. Ersilio was elbowing his way past his father and Malacresta was staring over Prasede's shoulder.

"Solavita, what did you say?" It was Lalo who'd spoken. "Did you say 'how did you know?'"

A rumble of agreement behind him.

Terror hissed in my sternum, green and tight. It was too late. They saw Nene in my bed. They'd heard me shouting. They might have thought we were fighting—

—but they weren't stopping me.

"He fell on me," I said. I let go of Nene's wrist and made a show of shoving him away. "When the tremors started."

Nene lay back on his elbows. He'd stopped crying.

Malacresta said, "No, but what did you *say?*"

"What did I *say?* What do you care? I said no. Get out of my bed, no."

"You don't have to lie for him, Solavita," Lalo said.

I threw the blankets off my legs and stood up. "DO YOU THINK—" I yelled, "I would LIE for that little rakefire? Do you think there's a SINGLE EARTHLY FORCE I would let throw Nene Karafantoni into my lap short of a tremor? *How did you know* indeed. If he'd known, he'd have made his own burrow to caterwaul in. Now fuck off back to yours!"

Lalo mumbled, "I just heard you ask him."

I silenced the second rumble of agreement by punching Lalo in the face. It was a flabby, open-handed punch, one I'd feel as a cramp and he'd feel as a sneeze.

"If you think I'm the one protecting him from you, you've forgotten who I am!" I yelled. "You're the ones protecting him from me, and if you don't feel like doing that, you'd better turn your backs. He's *mine.* Do you understand?"

Lalo sloped away immediately, with an exasperated toss of his hand. Ersilio pressed at my chest until I faced him. I couldn't stand that he'd dragged himself out of bed for me. Malacresta, too.

"Go to bed," I said. "I can hear Nedda crying."

He did.

My mother, still sitting up in her bed, played with one

corner of her blanket and said,

"It's only going to get worse."

"Go to sleep, Mamma," I snapped. "It's over."

"Tell Nene he should go."

"What, you think I'm going to tuck him in?"

"Not from your bed. From Magmate."

She rolled over and went to sleep.

In my eyeline, Malacresta, Lalo and Amero were sitting up in their beds, watching us. They wanted to watch whatever I was about to do to Nene. If I sent him away, they'd believe me, and if I gored him, they'd like me.

I put my elbows on my knees, stoked the coals in my eyes, and glared back. One by one, they murmured curses and lay down to sleep.

It wasn't that I couldn't think what else to do. I thought clearly about telling Nene to get out of my bed, carrying him to the edge of the cliff and dropping him, and telling him to jump. The thing I did was the thing I couldn't think about.

Pulling the blanket over our heads, I leaned down towards Nene, pried his hands from his face, and pressed a kiss between his eyebrows. The kiss was closed-mouthed and completely silent. Then, I kissed the top of his head. He stared up at me with wet, pink-quartz eyes.

More thrilling than his hand curled around the hand which ached from punching Lalo, more thrilling than the warm legs bent between mine, were those eyes. I bit my lips together against the desire to suck the tears out of them. Taste them before they were gone.

"It wasn't to protect you," I mumbled into the hot roots of his hair. "It was to protect me."

Then, I put my feet against his hips and donkey-kicked him out of the bed.

Ciecherella's funeral was softened by the fact it wasn't just Ciecherella's funeral. The families of the four victims of the earthquake agreed to lay them to rest together, as quickly as possible. Two speeches each. Ciecherella's parents shared one and Ersilio took the other. He gave Nedda to me but took Lagia up with him, perhaps because he knew she'd waste time and provoke laughter by babbling to him.

It was hardened by the fact the church lay shattered on top of the graveyard. Four new graves were dug on the outskirts of the woods with the knowledge that, in ten years, enough of us would be dead to join them back.

Marcovaldo Boscholi was an eighty-year-old great-grandfather. He'd been sick in bed before the earthquake, and crushed squarely by the chimney when the roof slid down. Pippo Del Vacca was a four-year-old boy, shaken out of his mother's arms and clawed dead out of the wreckage by the same arms five minutes later. Tanina Totollo had sustained a cut on her neck from a nail so small that she'd kept it out of the sea. She died of lockjaw two days before the funeral. I saw her spasming under her blankets from the other side of the camp.

Only four. In a village of only two hundred, it was a massacre.

Magmate's broken bones loomed over us at the service. Ascending back to the camp and replacing the ruin with open teal sky was a relief.

For a spell, Ersilio and I sat intertwined on the grass, watching the cooking fires on the beach. With so many dead cows and fish, the whole village was absorbed in a frantic effort to use or preserve the mountain of meat before it rotted. Prasede and Sitha had been busy butchering and pickling beef, the fishermen hanging fish on wooden poles and wires to dry them into stockfish. The beach stank of dead flesh during the day and of smoked meat during the night.

Then, Ersilio laid Nedda in my lap and told me he was leaving his daughters with me. I agreed, and watched him walk, with his hands in his pockets, back down into the valley.

Looking at Nedda's wounds made my hands itch. The web of cuts looked like a web of creases, the brown dots of scab like grime trapped in the creases. I felt like all I had to do was brush the grime away for her, and she'd stop scrunching her face and open her eyes in relief.

I thought about the moment Ersilio had nearly drowned her. Knowing it would haunt him for the rest of his life made me sorry, for a terrible second, that she'd lived.

Night had barely fallen when Malacresta's footsteps thudded up behind me. "Get up and come with me," he said. "Now. Now!"

I spun to face him. "What's the matter? Is it Ersilio?"

"Yeah."

And I had a thought like a premonition that Ersilio had killed himself.

"Brute's been digging around in the street for wine. Sitha saw him with his arms stacked with bottles. No idea where he is but he's drunk enough to die."

I turned again as if my mother was there, ready to relieve me of the children. She was busy with the fish, as were all four of the grandparents. I handed Lagia to Malacresta, and we ran back and forth across the camp, searching for someone to give them to. When I saw Nene alone on the outskirts of the camp, fussing with his bed, I stopped. Malacresta stopped beside me.

Suggesting we leave them with Nene was a bad idea. I knew that the earthquake had compounded my neighbours' unease at Nene's apathy into disgust, but I didn't know whether they were disgusted by him as though by a man, or by something more nebulously, baselessly sinister. And if Malacresta didn't think he was dangerous, he'd wonder why I'd suggested him. Why I'd stopped to look at him. Why we always seemed to be together.

As I opened my mouth to say *Never mind,* Malacresta shouted, "Oy! Pipsqueak!"

Nene looked up.

"Since you love sharing your bed so much."

Malacresta dumped Lagia down on the bed. Nene smiled at her. When I offered Nedda, he lifted her out of my arms.

Malacresta turned violently, as if set off by the contact between my arm and Nene's. "Let's *go.*"

We walked down the cliff in silence.

"If he's laid out drunk on her grave," Malacresta repeated as we walked to the graveyard, "I'll gut him, I'll kill him, I'll kill him." When Ersilio wasn't there, though, his vitriol softened into fear. "Oh. Really thought he'd be there."

We found Ersilio deep in the woods. He was leaning against a tree, his splayed legs squashing a patch of dandelions. His shoulders were unsettled forward by a knot in the trunk, and his hands were in his lap. Just as I spotted him, he took a slug from a glass bottle, then ripped his head to the side like he'd spilled it on himself.

"*Coglione!*" Malacresta broke into a run. I could have wrestled him back, but I was charmed by the return of his anger, the way it had waited until he'd found Ersilio alive. When Ersilio peered around the tree and saw us, something bright flashed through his slack-jawed face. Guilt, awoken from a dead sleep. "*Merda! Sei proprio un coglione!* We thought you'd killed yourself! Why the hell do you think she married you? To look pretty? To be her *children's father!* You worthless *dog!*"

When I caught up to them, I saw that there were three wine bottles at Ersilio's leg. Two were empty. One was half-empty.

Ersilio recoiled his head with scorn, the purple stains around his mouth like the blood from being punched.

"This isn't about Ciecherella," he said. "Not her or Lagia or Nedda. Tomorrow, I'm going back at the crack of dawn and never leaving my little girls until my dying day, I swear, never, never, but I needed... to get *me* out of me first."

He flinched as Malacresta shot forward and kicked the tree next to his head.

I felt again the sinking premonition of Ersilio's suicide. Saying you'd only drink once, only drink once more, was a lie by existence. People who really were only going to drink once or once more didn't say so.

Ersilio wasn't a habitual drunk or a desperate drunk. This was something he'd calculated, looked forward to, on nothing but word-of-mouth.

I was hurt that he hadn't told me. I would have helped him hide it from the Malachetis. I would have looked after his daughters, instead of abandoning them to chase him.

Malacresta turned away, rolling his ankle against the floor. I sat down next to Ersilio, removing the half-full bottle from his reach.

"Just tell me you don't think I didn't love her," Ersilio said.

Malacresta didn't move.

"I'm ugly and stupid and a bully. And I stole your sister from you without caring that you needed her. And I'm going to be a *terrible* father, half a blight on those little girls' lives when they were born and a total blight now I'm all they have..." When Ersilio's voice whined upward, I learned exactly which thoughts he'd been trying to drown. "Tell me you think all that. Not that I didn't love her."

Malacresta turned back to us, a wide, cringing mouth under the hands on his eyes. "Fine," he said.

"Just tell me—"

"I just did, you fat dalcop."

I leaned my head on Ersilio's shoulder, and twitched the bottle at Malacresta. As the two of us slugged the rest of the wine, Ersilio never tried to take it. Perhaps a nerve in his head had told him that as long as he left some, he wouldn't be sick.

We announced our departure before Ersilio fell asleep, bargained Lagia and Nedda from Nene, and then wobbled back down the cliff to sit on the hillside. Having both had our first and only drinks at his sister's wedding, we were narrow-eyed and sloppy-voiced from our three mouthfuls of wine. Lagia slept in Malacresta's lap and Nedda slept in mine.

"You know Prasede and me met arguing about which one of us had to marry you," Malacresta said.

I blinked at him. "Where did that train of thought start?"

"Me being cross with Ersilio, obviously. I was thinking about them tousling me on the head at their wedding, making me their little... mascot. Prasede said we ought to get married so we could moan about Ersilio in private. I said, I probably have to marry Solavita. She said, Solavita thinks she's a man. I said, well, maybe you have to marry Solavita, then."

I snorted. "Bonded on the gallows."

"S'not just you. I'd be a lousy husband. Only some people are meant to have wives. Just like only some people are meant to sail boats."

I watched as he realised what he'd said.

"They both thought," he said, "see, that I wanted the other one. I wasn't jealous of him for her attention. Or jealous of her. For his attention. I just couldn't get rid of the part of me that thought they never liked me in the first place. That they just used me to get at each other."

I said nothing.

"That makes me twice as bad, right? That they were both right?"

"No, Malacresta. That's not how that works."

At sunrise, after two hours of sleep, Ersilio wandered out of the forest, carrying the three bottles. Malacresta and I stood up in disbelief.

"Where the hell are you going?" Malacresta yelled.

Ersilio looked up at us with yellow eyes. His headache was

creasing his entire face. The pain seemed so murderous as to
have sobered him.

"Back to my little girls," he said.

When my mother told me that a party was forming to examine
the wreck of the church, I ran to volunteer. It wasn't fair to
make my neighbours clean up my mess without me.

To my relief, when we reached the site, we realised almost
all the materials could be reused. The glass could be scooped
up and melted back, the limestone walls lay in enormous
chunks, and the iron brick fittings and lead window grates had
only warped. When one of my neighbours suggested what we'd
use it for—beautiful houses for the families of the dead—I
decided we'd have found a way to recycle it from powder.
We'd get eight houses out of the church with ease. I couldn't
believe I'd had to see it lying in pieces to realise what a waste
it had been.

I knew Ersilio would try to refuse the gift of the house. A
week clear of his indiscretion on the night of the funeral, he
believed it made him worthy of sleeping on the street forever.
I'd have to introduce it as a gift for his daughters. Stronger than
wattle and daub, it would shield them from the next
earthquake.

As people ran back and forth between the eight piles, I
noticed a woman standing alone on the intact church steps. Her
name was Fotena Del Meda, and she was close friends with
Sitha and Ersilio's mothers. Under her gaze, oozing from
beneath the church's wrecked western wall, were masses of
gabbroic clay dust. Sculptures from the graveyard.

As I watched, a man climbed the steps and wrapped his arms around her. When she laid her head on his shoulder and started to tremble, realisation sent a tremor of nausea through me.

When we cleared the churchyard, we would find the bodies of our ancestors still in their graves, but their sculptures were destroyed. In my rampage to kill God, I had killed centuries of our history, the entire output of our culture, and the memories of the loved ones of those who still lived.

"All my papa's sculptures are under there." Fotena pointed to one corner of the pulverised churchyard. "He's dead!" She laughed, almost incredulous. "He can't make new ones!"

My stomach wrung itself. In my mind's eye, her grief shot up the cliff, rebounded from the head of every neighbour. Everyone I knew had a dead relative. I'd destroyed my father's sculptures too. I deserved the hell I'd suffered the week before, when I'd peeled the roof of my bedroom away from the powdered remains of my own sculptures.

I climbed the church steps, and joined the couple in looking down. The clay dust was ankle-deep on the church floor and shin-deep in the grass. I felt a shudder of revulsion of the macabre. It had been frightening to others as hordes of figures, but it was frightening to me as powdered flesh, as mulch. I was seeing for the first time how much earth had gone into the practice.

"I'm really sorry for your pain," I said. "I hope we can collect the clay along with the other materials and find your father again in new statues.

"The ritual... was an inhumane thing. It glorified God by degrading us. It was my hope when we tore the church down that we'd rebuild the village to glorify us. If you'd let me, I'd like to glorify your father. I'd like... to make you a new likeness of him."

My proposal beat the proposal about the houses to the top of the cliff. When I ascended to the camp in the evening, I was accosted by Malacresta and his parents, who were thrilled by the thought of a statue of Ciecherella.

The following day, I declared that my job would be searching the rubble for pieces of clay from the dead's sculptures, to reuse in their new ones. I didn't find one of Della Del Meda's, but I found what I was really looking for. It was the enormous witch's nose from Ersilio's first ever sculpture, which he'd made with stolen clumps of Ciecherella's clay. When I presented it to him, he puffed his chest out and said, "Oh, yes, I remember that piece distinctly. Plucked it right off her face for my purpose. Look, *Panina,* it's Mamma's face. Give kiss."

On my first venture into the tedium of clearing rubble, I had found myself a job which would exonerate me from it. A job which would keep me housed, fed and honoured forever. A Godless, churchless Magmate would still need a graveyard, and I would make the gravestones. Every day, a new family came to my bed to talk about a person they'd lost. I had never had such easy, fond conversations with strangers as those about the dead.

As the fugue of raw grief cleared, and trudging down the cliff at dawn to work on rebuilding the village became routine, my sculpting tent on the hillside became the place for parents to leave their children. Only used to caring for the sweetly behaved De Aqvancis girls, I was worried that any strange children might be determined to call me names, knock things over, or antagonise one another with the aid of my chisels and knives, but they were far too mesmerised by Ciecherella.

I sculpted a memory of her standing in the rain, with a fringed shawl over her shoulders, her face turned skyward, and her cupped hands outstretched to catch droplets to drink. To gain a reference for her wet hair, I stripped off my dress on the hillside and ordered Ersilio and Malacresta to dump a bucketful of water over my head. To gain a reference for her likeness, I bribed Malacresta to sit still on a stool. He kept whining, "But I don't even *look* like her," no matter how many times I explained that he looked enough like her to show me what she was not. The siblings' faces were not the female and male versions of the same face but the tranquil and agitated. I looked at the way his upper lip tightened over his teeth and knew that hers had hung slack, looked at the pits of scars from chewing his lips and crushing his pimples and knew that her skin was smoother, looked at him squinting at the tent canvas over my shoulder instead of into my eyes and knew that whatever revulsion he had of looking at people had not prevailed upon her.

She was life-sized, and mounted on a base which her blowing petticoats swallowed. Having grown up to the noise of sculptures breaking all around me, I vowed that mine would withstand gale and downpour. I still feared that she'd fall on any child who glanced at her.

"My mamma said," said a little boy one day, "I'm not supposed to ask you for some clay because you said clay's not for bad sculptors."

"*Cazzate,*" I said. "What'd she tell you that for? Doesn't she think I was ever a bad sculptor?"

The child's eyes filled with awe. I thought he was delighted to have heard a curse word, but then he said, "So can I sculpt?"

I gave him a lump of clay and sat down on the floor to show him how to start. I was guiding him by the wrist to carve a seam with the most childproof tool I could find—a wooden spoon—when the door of the tent fluttered open and Nene came in.

All of the children turned to look at him. Nene was something of a ghost to the children. He slept alone in a bed he'd made for himself, had stood alone on the hillside at the quadruple funeral, had sat alone on the bakehouse to watch the mob, and, before that, had lived alone in the house beside the church. That their village had chased God out and burned down its church, and this greensick young man with hay-coloured hair had once been the Curato, was all they needed to

208

know to be intrigued by him. But he was kind, and they were children, so it was not the same insidious intrigue as their parents'.

"Hello." Nene smiled down at me. "Are you teaching lessons?"

"I am teaching *one* lesson, to *one* boy—" I said, rolling my eyes when the crowd of children moaned that they wanted lessons too.

"Oh, you can teach one lesson to two boys, I'm sure," Nene said, coming in and leaning against the table next to me. When I continued to stare at him, he added in a lower voice, "I'm not allowed to build anymore."

Nene and I found out that the little boy's mother had told him that amateur sculpting was honouring God, and he wasn't a child of God anymore. I explained to him that we could take the clay away from God, just as we'd taken the earth, and sculpt badly for our own pleasure.

"So when God was here," said the child, "how *did* you know if you were sculpting too good? Did God come down and tell you to stop it?"

Nene laughed brightly. "I am sure he did not," he said. "God's the biggest mess-maker of us all, really."

After Nene had spent a week with me, Ersilio and Malacresta told me that he had indeed been banned from building. It wasn't for the reason I'd thought. Every day, Nene had lifted something, either alone or in a group, convulsed, and dropped it. He had apologised and insisted that he just had poor grip, soft hands, but Ersilio and Malacresta thought he was hiding an illness. I didn't disagree. Just as his pale skin never tanned and his wiry legs never grew muscle, his poor grip would never strengthen and his soft hands would never grow callouses. He was wonderful with my charges, speaking to them in soft, musical tones which placated the older ones and mesmerised the little ones, so I liked him with me.

Finally, I saw it for myself. He was carrying a plank for a

little girl to rest her sculpture on, and a tremor passed through one of his shoulders which caused him to cross his arms and send the plank to the ground spinning. The children laughed, and he recovered quickly, singing, "Sorry, sweetheart, looks like I got possessed by the ghost of a circus juggler," as he swooped to pick it up.

When he stood up again, I saw something move down his back. It looked more like a gust of wind bothering his tunic than a spasm bothering his muscles. Only when he caught my eye on standing up did I know I hadn't imagined it.

I was relieved to find myself alone with him that day. With the children's questions gonging in my ears and the curls of Ciecherella's hair bending my eyes out of focus, I nearly groaned in joy when he said,

"I thought I'd go to the rock pools. Come with me?"

It was a black and platinum night. The clouds swirled like curds in a bowl, and cold wind flew up our clothes as we descended the cliff path. Nene walked beside me with a pronounced stoop, his shoulders rolled forward as to suck the hollows above his collarbones into ravines. On instinct, as we started wobbling our way over the slimy rocks, I held my hand out to him.

He gave me a confused smile.

"You're having pain," I said. "Convulsions. Aren't you?"

I gave up and dropped my hand. Only then did he take it.

A thrill of fear shot down my back at the contact between the cold insides of our wrists. I had offered it to comfort him, and now he'd accepted, I was imagining his veins rearing up like cobras to lance the blood from mine.

We were still holding hands when we sat down on the seaweed. Steel waves crashed against the short sheer face beneath our hanging legs.

What happened next I wanted to pretend not to see, like I was watching an actor forget his lines. Nene put my hand in his lap and enveloped it with both of his, then let it go. He drove his golden head into my shoulder, then withdrew it before I could kiss it. Then, he started to brush my hair back behind my shoulder with his knuckles.

Finally, he remembered his line. "I am having convulsions."

"Oh, sweet relief," I said. "We're overdue for a trade."

"A trade?"

"You drag me somewhere cold and wet and tell me something about being an angel I should have asked you, and then I kiss you."

Nene laughed. "I absolve you from kissing me for this one."

"Maybe I want to."

His thumb was still hooked into my hair, resting at the base of my throat. It was a cruel choice of membrane. Afraid to unseat him with a twitch, I couldn't even breathe.

"I am having convulsions." It was another carefully curated speech, one I'd interrupted. "Tremors through my shoulders, tremors through my belly. The big ones make me feel like my bones are moving. I feel them coming, the big ones. They squeeze my bowels, like food poisoning. Not so much the small ones. I dropped a beam on Signora Tegliacci's foot last week."

"Oh, dreadful choice of victim," I said. "I bet she reacted like you'd run her through."

Nene laughed, but didn't reply. "I never used to have them. Something's changed inside me. God is moving."

I decided not to interject again. I knew that, in some roundabout way, he was answering the question I'd screamed on the cliff. *"How did you know?"*

"On the day of the earthquake," Nene said, "I didn't feel anything until the moment I saw you from the hillside. I got a feeling in my stomach, that squeezing feeling... the dread that something terrible was about to happen. Not to Magmate."

"To me," I said.

Nene looked at me with tragic eyes. "To me, Solavita."

Fear pierced my throat.

"On top of the cliff with you," he said, "it kept getting stronger. It turned into rolling inside my shoulders, and while I was kissing you, it made me lie down. Solavita, it's the same pain I feel when people try to kill me, the lightning, the power. Every night, Solavita, I think I hear God speaking to me from somewhere in the sky and then I wake up and realise it was a dream. God doesn't give me premonitions. I didn't convulse because Magmate was going to convulse. I convulsed…"

He clenched his fist in his lap.

"And so Magmate convulsed.

"My mamma used to tell me about her prayers. How, ever since I was born, God hadn't been answering them. I'm not an angel. God has no job for me. He doesn't speak to me in a way I understand, or in a way that might make sense somewhere beyond my understanding. He speaks to me in fits and aches and *thoughts*. God has been nowhere for as long as I've been here. Solavita, I think I'm God."

And with our hands enfolded in his lap he stared at me.

And with the fondness washed out of my face I stared at him.

"Ridiculous," I said. "If you were God you'd drag me to Hell for what I did to the church."

Nene said nothing.

"The audacity you'd have to cry on me in the aftershock if you were the one causing it."

Then, madness threw up a spiralling wave, blinded and gagged me, slung me at him.

"YOU WERE THE ONE WHO CAUSED THE EARTHQUAKE?" I shrieked. "STAND UP! Is that what you're saying?" Nene stood up. I stood up with him, my hands around his neck. "Are you saying *your convulsions* caused the earthquake? Your convulsions blinded Nedda and killed Ciecherella? SAVE ME FROM DROWNING MYSELF TRYING TO DROWN YOU!"

"I think so," Nene said.

I collapsed onto my knees again. My hands slunk down his front and found his wrists. "You're the—slaughterer, the Marchese, you, you," I sobbed.

"I think so," Nene said again.

"Why wouldn't you warn everyone when you warned me?"

"You were the only one I could make follow me."

"THEN WHY SAVE ME?" I howled.

As I knelt on the ground, Nene sank to his hands and knees on the seaweed and shoved his face against my middle. He mumbled something I only felt, in a rumble.

"What?" I snapped.

"Because I wanted somewhere to crawl when I picked myself up."

He put his hands on my waist and forced me to my feet before him.

The shock made me step back and clutch his head for balance. When his mouth stretched open against my stomach, a terrible pleasure ran down my legs. I wanted him to do it again, pour confession after confession into my belly, glut me on it.

"I beg, beg," he said. I nearly moaned. I put my hands hard against his head, and he reached up to hold them there. "Godless, furious creature that loathes me, you're the only one who can forgive me. You're the only one who understands that I'm just an animal, just a sick, stupid animal! It's not my fault people catch fire when they touch me! It's not my fault the earth shakes when I do!"

I knew he was right. To be born of God but with no duty, to be placid but blossom such madness, to have a body which spasmed as though rutting against a core too gnarled and yet too beautiful for it: Nene contained God.

My speech to the mob was a farce. God was a sickness, an animal. God was a tremor.

I'd made love to the earthquake. I'd kissed the earthquake with my mouth open as it dragged its gabbro fangs down my back. I'd let it bite my shoulder as it murdered my best friend's family. I'd punched my friend to guard it. I'd kissed its forehead to comfort it.

And the earthquake had made love to…

"Nene," I said, with retches inflating my throat. "Nene. Nene. Nene."

It was all I could say. He gazed up at me, unsmiling but pleased. He knew what I'd realised.

"Nene, if God is a tremor, if you didn't mean it, then why did the church survive?"

A meaningless convulsion through a meaningless body.

Only stilled in one place.

The earthquake had made love to the church.

Nene kissed my stomach. I whimpered. He kissed again, harder, to be felt through the ocean-soaked wool of my bodice.

"It's silly," he said. "Isn't it?"

I nodded. It was silly. Not that there was a power which had connected his body to the earth and the body he clung to to a building, but that the building it had chosen was the *church.* The club with which he was broken, and later, his home. Perhaps it was his home because it broke him.

I dragged him out of my skirt by the scruff of his neck and looked at him. As I stared at his red mouth and eyes, not in knowing what he'd done but in unhinging as I pondered it, from manic horror to manic delight, I was complicit.

"They want to kill you already," I said, "just for sitting on the bakehouse! If they find out what you really did, they'll tear you limb from limb. They'll eat you alive in the square."

"I don't fear that," Nene said. "You're the one who fears that."

"Why would I fear that?"

"That someone else might eat me alive before you can," he said.

Madness seeped across my face from my mouth. Lockjaw grin and wide eyes. Earthquake on its knees. God on His knees.

Every failure to destroy him made me love him more. Every attempt to destroy him made him love me more. To be struck was to be touched.

"Put your head back where it was," I said. "You're not done repenting yet."

Nene rocked down onto his hands and knees and shoved his face back into my stomach. With my bodice sealing his mouth, his moan went into my bones, made me vibrate from tailbone to nape. I threw back my head and cackled. Thought I felt my jaw unhinge. I wanted him down my throat, in my stomach, in the viscera which coiled around my bowels. I wanted him rolled tight to fit inside my bones, sheeted thin and stretched over my face. I wanted him everywhere.

When his arms went around me, they went under my dress, swiped a scale on the folds in my hose and found the cold, wet skin of my thighs. Still grinning, I tore my skirt up and fed him the flesh I most wanted to see him devour: Not my thigh or my sex but his own hand.

He looked up at me with his hair wet in his eyes and his mouth smeared open by the knuckle of his thumb.

"Yes!" I said.

Stop holding me. Shake me to the ground.

He opened his jaws around my sex. His teeth chisel-cracked the nerve which broke me in half down the middle. I tightened my fists in his hair and pulled up, and he dragged his nails up my thighs and pulled down. I crumpled into his lap in a white crash. He writhed his hips beneath mine, sharp and impermanent and hungry. We had gone down to the church on a new day and found whole pieces of wall intact, but on that night, in the dark, and the madness, it had seemed to disintegrate into seafoam, and float for a moment, before the green mouth of a wave sucked it under.

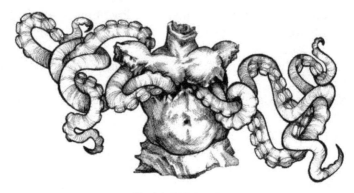

CHAPTER 15

THE GREEN

NEDDA DE AQVANCIS'S FACE IS A MOSAIC. Her conch-pink scars meet the brown skin of her forehead and cheeks in fine barbs, but the borders around her newborn eyes are bold, perfect circles. When her eyes are wide open, her eyelids make dark rings between pale scars and pale eyes like her irises used to make between whites and cataracts.

"How is your imagining going?" I call, scraping a flat edge across my sculpture's lower eyelid.

Nedda turns around, holding a lump of grey clay in one hand. It's a lump I left out overnight by accident, dried as hard as a stone.

"Really great," she says.

"Yes?"

"Yes. I have my eyes open nearly all the time. Even when it's bright or busy."

"And do you like having them open?"

"Sometimes. In here. Watching you make statues."

Nedda blinked out her cataracts last year, half a year after her healing. When her crying made Ersilio sprint into her bedroom in the middle of the night and light her lamp, her scream woke the whole village. I arrived in my nightclothes to find her grizzling in his arms, with her eyes ground shut and soft white tissue glistening in the tear tracks on her cheeks. When I touched it, she screamed again and threw her arms over her face.

For months, coaxing her to open her eyes was like coaxing her to walk on a broken ankle. She made herself a blindfold out of one of her stockings, and Ersilio found himself burdened with guiding and carrying her in a way he hadn't when she was blind.

The first therapy we devised was for the terrible shock she got upon opening her eyes. We would take turns sitting in front of her and, whilst her eyes were closed, describing ourselves to her.

"I am sitting with my legs crossed, my feet tucked under my knees. My skin is dark brown and my hair black and curly, just like yours. I have a big beard which makes my chin longer. My arms are big and strong, but they won't hurt you. I made them like that so I could carry you. I love you so much, pulcino.*"*

"I have short brown hair, and green hose underneath green trousers, and gaps between my front teeth and my canines."

"My nose is big, like a knot in a tree. I am wearing black tunics with tall collars. There are scars on both of my hands, like white gloves made of barnacles, from trying to kill God. There is another scar on my forehead from a rock."

Nedda was to imagine each speaker before her, draw a picture of them under her eyelids. We wanted to lessen the shock of opening her eyes and seeing us there, but the only one she never jumps or whimpers at the sight of is me. Perhaps, because I was the first thing she ever saw, there's a ritual, a comfort, to opening her eyes and seeing me. She and Lagia spend plenty of time in my sculpting workshop, now a canopied structure tacked to the skeleton of the church, but when her sister leaves to find her father, she stays.

The nave's wall beams are up, a base for a first attempt at a ceiling and second attempt at flooring. The first floor was too heavy for the supports, and Ersilio ordered it torn up, so crossbeams could be added in the crypt. When he suggested that I forget about building and return to my list of gravestone commissions instead, I was frightened that the builders would think me spoilt. However, they either love my statues or know that they're the only thing I'm good at. Between Ciecherella's death and Nene's, I made five gravestones. This is my tenth.

"Papa wouldn't like me asking you," I say, "but would it help if you spoke to me about why you're afraid? Why it feels different to see clearly without your cataracts?"

Nedda shrugs.

"I dunno," she says. "It doesn't feel like I'm seeing clearly. It doesn't feel like seeing. Not the same as seeing before."

"Like it's... a different sense entirely?"

She gives one large nod. "When I was seeing blurry, it just felt like being a baby. It didn't feel new."

I stare. "You think you remember being able to see when you were a baby?"

"I guess. I dunno. Seeing, like, blobs of colours and people moving around in front of lights."

"And you felt like that when your eyes first came back?"

"Uh-huh."

Hoping to soothe her by averting my eyes, I focus on my sculpture. Watching my scalpel dig a crisp line between eyelid and eyeball makes my stomach feel hollow, so I move to work on the teeth instead.

"And now, now it's like..." Nedda says.

"You don't have to tell me if you don't want."

I know what she's trying to describe. The advent of a new sense. Something too bright and too loud, which plunges endlessly backward, which tilts none off-kilter in the aspect and all off-kilter in the belly.

"Well, I heard you and Papa talking about cataracts and

about blurry, but I didn't even realise what you meant. I didn't even realise I wasn't seeing properly. And then suddenly there were edges on things, and... and... different blurriness for close things and far things and... people *looking* at me. When the stars twinkle in the sky and the sea twinkles in the sun, I get dizzy. And when Uncle Malacresta licks his teeth and Signora Vpezzinghi makes her eyes dart around. And when there are flies in the air. When I see flies in the air, I feel them crawling on my face."

I grind my teeth. I pray that she's speaking because she wants to speak, not because she wants to please me.

"I can't help it feel smaller," I say. "There are a lot of things I'm not big enough to understand. Noise that gets in your head without going through your ears and animals that crawl on you without touching you at all. But sometimes, you don't need to understand things to trust them. If you believe that the huge, terrifying, confusing thing isn't going to hurt you, being near to it can be... fun. It can feel nice."

Nedda walks to stand beside me. As she gazes up at my statue, her hands twitch upward.

"You can touch if you like," I say.

"Can I close my eyes?"

"Yes."

Nedda closes her eyes and reaches up to touch the statue's face.

As I watch her, a shaft of guilt cores my throat. I oscillate always between feeling like the healing gave her more than she could handle and like it stole from her.

"Do you remember when we brought you to meet Nene?" I say.

She nods.

"You were four, weren't you?"

"I dunno."

"What do you remember about him?"

"Um, that it was really cold and smelled old. And his voice

sounded like when Papa climbs the cliff and gets tired, even though he was sitting still."

"He was very sick. Talking took a lot of effort."

"And then I remember you said, 'Nene, stop,' and Papa picked me up and ran out of the place with me."

"Did Papa tell you what happened?"

Nedda sucks her teeth. "Said same as you, that he was sick."

There's a rush of footsteps from the direction of the square, and the draped sheet which serves as a wall flutters up. As daylight floods the workshop, Nedda jerks her head in discomfort.

Malacresta and Prasede have come in. In one hand clad in a grey plush glove, he's holding her hand, seems to be dragging her. He isn't smiling, but there's a familiar giddy flush in his cheeks.

"Come see what I did," he says.

I fold my arms. "Did you make a sheet finally?"

"No. Just come see."

As Malacresta leads us uphill to the furnace, Nedda dashes ahead to walk with him and Prasede, tired of being dragged by the hand, falls back to walk with me. "What'd he do?" I ask her.

Prasede rolls her eyes. "Don't know. Won't bloody tell me. Must *show* me."

"As if we plebs can see the difference between a clear batch and an extra extra clear batch."

She snickers.

As the months have passed, Malacresta's devotion to collecting sand, burning plants and fussing with fire has made me feel increasingly like I'm giving a child a toy to keep him out from under my feet. Knowing what I knew about his rocks, that he likes the act of polishing more than he likes the finished jewels, I gave him the idea of the glass knowing there was a chance he'd decide he couldn't be bothered with colours and pictures. I didn't realise that that wouldn't mean he'd stop. He brews huge bubbling vats of clear glass and then leaves them in the crucibles to harden. Prasede and I watch him get giddy day after day not at progress in the craft but at the lava and fire, the noise, the pole-spinning.

"This was a stupid idea you had, Sole," Prasede says. *"Stained glass?* Rich gentlemen in cities go to school for years to learn how to colour and draw and set. You really expect *him* of all people to work it all out on his own? By what—chucking things in and seeing what happens?"

"No," I say. "I just think he's having fun."

It's a half-truth. I don't expect it now, but I did when I asked him. I didn't realise colouring glass isn't like dyeing clothes. It's chemical, not physical.

"And you'll stop him when? When he's devoured the whole beach? Burned down the forest?"

"I don't know. When he stops having fun."

"Oh, good, it's still hot," Malacresta says to his niece from inside the green dome of the furnace.

We walk in to the sight of him buttressing a crucible of white-hot glass with his leg. There's a blowpipe in his gloved hands, connected to the crucible by a thick red frond.

"Mal, we talked about leaving the furnace on when you leave," Prasede says. "It's not safe."

Malacresta ignores her. "Ersilio told me metal oxide means the rust on his boat."

There's a declaration like this once a week. A farce of interest in a lead.

"But when I mixed that into the glass, it just made a gritty soup. Caro said maybe I needed to burn it off, that that'd make it do something."

"Burn it off?" Prasede says.

"Tried it. Just went to ashes." The blob of glass on the end of the pole has turned black. "Tried a bunch of different temperatures and then got annoyed and dumped it in seawater instead."

"Seawater," I say. "That's possibly what Caro meant by *burning off* in what language?"

Malacresta gazes at the doorway behind us. "Exactly. I was smacking my forehead and saying stupid, stupid, stupid the whole time."

In the backlight of the crucible, the blob of glass has turned green. Deep jewel-green, like his trousers.

Nedda hangs forward off his arm, her mouth agape, immune to the smouldering light.

"Ta-da," he says.

Prasede and I exchange glances. My eyes are glittering, and hers are guilty. "Mal, that's amazing," she says.

"It's the colour of you!" Nedda shouts.

"It's the colour of you. We should have an early lunch to celebrate. Fetch Ersilio and Lagia."

Malacresta moves to put the pole down in the crucible.

"You're just going to let it harden?" I say.

He stops.

"Before lunch, you should blow it and sheet it. Like you saw Caro do."

"I haven't done it before," Malacresta says. "I need to practice with clear first."

"I want you to do it with the green."

"I'll ruin it."

"Like you ruin it by letting it harden?"

He rolls his eyes at me, and slings the pole out of the crucible in a wide arc. When he feints the molten end at me, I flinch. "Caro had Papa hold it while he blew. I can't hold it by the end by myself."

"You should come to the beach and exercise with me and Ersilio, then," I say, taking my end as he fastens his mouth around his.

As I watch him blow the lump into a bubble with jolts of breath, swing the pole up out of my hands, and slice the bubble open like a peach with one of the long blades from the floor, I can't stop smiling. Though he knows exactly what he's doing, he carries on his chant. "It's going to stick. It's going to melt. I'm going to break it. I'm so stupid." After a minute outside the crucible, the glass resists his cutting like leather hard clay, and by the time he lays it open on the table with his gloved hands, it's cool enough for me to touch.

"There," I say, grinning at him. "A green sheet. Come to my workshop this afternoon and show me what you're going to make with it."

After lunch, I clear the scalpels, buckets and crusts of dried clay from the table in my workshop. When Malacresta comes, he stands in the doorway with the sheet of green glass like he's worried he's intruding. He waits for my instruction to sit at the table, select a sheet, pick up the pencil.

"I just thought you might like to draw with me," I say. "You don't have to."

"I want to."

After an hour of scrubbing hard with the nub of charcoal, rubbing his hands on his trousers, and covering the page with his arm whenever I try to look, he finally shows me. It's a face in profile. There's a thick, drizzling border around the profile and the rhombus of cascading hair and the features—long, shallow nose, lipless mouth, an eye drawn as though from the front—are wispy and nervous.

When I see the mane of hair and the big nose, I think it's me. Then, I remember that my hair is short now, and my nose is a hook, not a thorn.

"I thought you were staring at her at lunch more than usual."

Malacresta huffs and puts the sketch down. "She thinks it's stupid, the glass, so I thought I'd make her first. No way it looks like her, though. You should draw her for me."

"No." I spin the sketch to face me. "You're wonderful. Because you're learning to draw as you learn glass, you're drawing things that will work in glass."

As he snatches the sketch back, I think about asking him whether Prasede really said that to him. That the glass was stupid.

Instead, I say, "Does your name tire her mouth?"

He frowns. "Huh?"

"She calls you Mal. Does your name tire her mouth?"

"My name tires everyone's mouths."

I don't reply. I watch him carefully stroke an eyelash out from the portrait's eye.

"She…" he finally adds, "assumes I'm embarrassed by stuff. You know what I'm like. You had to tell me to sit down. It's an initiative she took, I guess."

I open my mouth to ask him whether it was the right initiative, then change my mind. Therefore, instead of a shrug, I get,

"It's green. Like this green."

He picks up the sheet of glass.

"Malachite, I mean. It's a jewel. Mamma jokes that's why I'm so weird. Because I'm double-malachite."

A solid fractal of jade rolls across the tabletop and darts up the wall. When I turn back from watching it, Malacresta is looking at me with narrowed eyes.

"Why aren't you talking?" he says. "You're being creepy."

"Because you talk more when you feel like you're talking to a wall."

He rolls his eyes. "Whatever you do, don't start calling me Mal too. She likes having a name only she gets to call me."

I get up and walk to the corner. "I'm not in the habit of calling people names they haven't claimed."

He is probably about to say *Can't imagine why* when I drop the burlap sack onto the table, making him jump.

"I have something for you," I say. "I kept meaning to ask you what colour your clear glass really is, when it's just the gabbro sand and the plant ash, but you've never taken it out of the furnace, so you wouldn't see if it was a little bit purple."

224

I unsheathe a plum-coloured icicle from the sack.

Malacresta's head jerks like I elbowed him in the chin. "Where'd you get *that?*"

"God made it. Last year. In the sand and seaweed. Most of it got crushed or washed away. But I grabbed these in case you wanted them."

Malacresta thrusts his hand into the sack and pulls out another purple crystal. This one is violet and milky, but just as bright.

"I'm sorry I didn't show you before," I say. "I knew you'd love them. I was just worried about giving you false hope. I knew you wouldn't be able to find the part of the gabbro that made the purple this bright as easily as God did. But I see now that you don't need it to be easy. You just need it to be possible."

Malacresta's mouth stretches into a grin beneath a visor of purple glass held between his palms. Even though his clothes are green like the first glass and his name is green like the first glass, something about the grin makes those words come back: *It's the colour of you.*

Unlike Malacresta in the furnace, me in my workshop, or Ersilio, who spends most of his days in the same scrunch-faced stance against a beam, Prasede is a lover of odd jobs. It doesn't matter that she's our nimblest climber, shimmying up behind people on ceiling beams to check their harnesses, or that her knife skills make her a prodigy with hammers and saws; if she hasn't finished a job before nightfall, she abandons it for someone else to finish. Something about it must be the key to why she won't marry Malacresta. Because she'll wake up the next morning bored of him.

A week after the green, with Malacresta busy crushing, burning and soaking handfuls of gabbro to make purple, Prasede comes into my workshop. As she explains that two joists have become jammed at the wrong angle, and she needs to borrow a slim chisel to hammer into the join, she wanders to the table, thumbs through the pile of sketches, and flicks at the sheet of green glass, which Malacresta hasn't touched yet.

I give her the chisel. She thanks me, walks to the door with it, pauses, then says,

"Oh, I don't like that you did that."

I freeze, my arms slung over my statue's shoulders.

"What?" I say. "Gave him the purple?"

"Crowned his victory with another task."

My stomach tightens. Prasede says what she thinks. All my friends say what they think, but it's caustic in her because what she thinks is that I'm an asshole.

"It isn't a task to him," I say. "It's fun."

"It's *obsession*. He hasn't left the furnace in a week! His parents keep fetching me to make him come down to bed. You've seen him sneezing black everywhere. He's got burns all around his wrists. Every time he comes to me, I pray he's coming to tell me he's given up, but it's always, 'Come see what I did! Come see what I did!'"

"If you think he's starting to love you less, you're wrong," I say. "He must look at you all the time, to draw you so well."

"To *draw* me," she scoffs.

"People can show you they love you that way. Don't you think? What must you think of me if you don't?"

Prasede grins at me. "You know exactly what I think of you."

We stare at each other from opposite sides of the workshop.

Then, she says, "Where *did* that purple glass come from?"

I narrow my eyes. "From God. On the beach. Don't you

226

remember all the seaweed, multiplied, like the wood?"

"Yes, I do. What did God want, though? What was He coming to do? Did He speak to you? Did He call you there?"

"I don't understand," I say. "Do you not believe me?"

"Of course I believe you. I saw the house."

She walks towards me. I freeze, my clay-grained hands against my chest.

She lifts her hand and, when I don't recoil, tucks a curl of my hair behind my ear.

"You look different," she says. "I've been trying to figure out why. And I think it's your face."

Terror roars in my ears, slings my eyes out of focus.

I freed myself from the corpse of the seaweed monster with an aching neck, a sinus headache, and hands which weighed down my arms. The changes are threefold. My wrists and knuckles are thicker, the veins breaching between the tendons in coils. My collarbones have been pried upward in the middle, turning their V into a line and giving a pinched peak to each shoulder. My jaw is only a little longer, my chin sharp enough to balance with my widow's peak on the pivot of my nose. I fawn over my hands more than my face, running them up my neck and across my mouth and gazing at them covered in clay.

I had expected the first physical changes to render me hysterical with ecstasy. I had expected to tear through the streets declaring the miracle to every neighbour who would listen, builder or heretic. But when I first looked at my reflection, with the monster dead and the flesh hard, I felt nothing but calm. For the first time in my life, a trough of despair did not invert into its equal and opposite. There is a hole inside me where self-loathing isn't. I am no more blessed by that than I am blessed to breathe.

I meant, at least, to tell my friends, the way I'd told my mother. Then, I didn't.

I rip my head from Prasede's grasp. "It's my haircut," I say. "Go away. I have to finish this before dark."

227

I stay in the workshop to sculpt long after dark. The last builders go home, and all around and above, the blue bones of the church creak and heave as they cool.

My workshop is not quite a tent and not quite a room. The timbers are joined with quick tacks, and the skin of white sheets is only nailed down on the ceiling. I think about asking Ersilio to add it to the plans, like a little chapel. I am going to make gravestones for the rest of my life, and keeping the dead people out of my bedroom would be good for me.

As I wash my hands in my water bucket, I spend a minute rubbing at a grey welt on my palm before I realise it's not clay. It's skin. I first noticed the dryness of the new skin a week ago, as I ate lunch in the square. My jaw, neck and hands are tight and cold.

Just as I've settled into the peace of solitude in the church, footsteps approach the wall. I sigh. If it's Malacresta coming to drag me up the hill, I'll tell him I'm too tired. If it's Prasede coming to interrogate me, I'll tell her everything.

Ersilio slides the sheet of the wall up around his shoulders. "Shit," he says. "Your mamma said you hadn't come home."

"What time is it?"

"Past midnight, Sole. What's so important?"

We gaze up at the statue together. It's another solid pillar of an elderly father, triangular beard and smiling eyes, and it's been finished for a week. I've been sculpting sloppily on purpose, leaving fingerprints and grafting details on dry, so I have excuses to keep working on it. I hate the process of starting a new statue, hacking the rough shape free from the block.

"Nothing." I run my thumbs over the prints on the statue's neck. "Prasede came in earlier. I was just annoyed."

From his belt, Ersilio produces the chisel Prasede borrowed. He grins at me as he sets it on the table. "So was she."

In his other hand, he's holding a bottle of wine. He tips it to me and raises an eyebrow.

I narrow my eyes at him. "Sure."

I don't know what I'm expecting. A pair of crystal glasses produced from his belt. He hands me the bottle.

I take a slug and nearly choke. It's strong, pure wine, with aniseed which crawls into my nose and honey which coats my throat when I swallow. "What'd you trade for *that?*" I crow.

Ersilio skips back to sit on the table. "I told them I was sharing it with you."

The winemakers in Magmate are the Totollo family, two brothers and their wives. Their mother was the final victim of the earthquake I sculpted. I spent months savouring garlands of plaits and the fine lace of her wedding gown. And thank Heaven for it, because months after I finished her, Nene was dead, and I needed wine like water.

The bottle is passed back and forth between the table and the statue, and is soon nearly empty. When Ersilio cranes his head back for a long slug without closing his eyes, I realise that he's watching me. Watching me prevaricate, press fingerprints in and out of the statue's neck.

He gets up and comes over to me. I put my hand out for the bottle and get his hand instead. He puts his palm flat against mine, and spreads our fingers wide. I frown at him as he reaches for my other hand. Both of my hands are caked in clay, from the fingernails to the square knobs of the wrists.

He wasn't watching me work. He was looking at my hands.

"You made a deal with God to change you into a man, didn't you?" he says.

I stiffen. It's typical of Ersilio to notice my hands before my face. As my heart softens with fondness for him, I realise my unfairness. To be worked out by Prasede was to be nagged, mistrusted. To be worked out by Ersilio is to be loved, known.

"Yeah, I did."

"That's why you're doing it. All of it."

"Yeah."

"Have you changed anywhere else?"

229

My knees tighten. He can see that I still have breasts; the hardest squeeze I can achieve with my stays makes my chest like a third roll of belly. There's only one change he might not be able to see.

"No."

"What are you going to do once you can't hide it anymore?"

"What? I'm not trying to hide it. Mamma knows. I would have told Prasede if she was nicer, if it didn't feel like she…"

"Like she'd be furious? Like she'd mount your head on her wall?"

"Yeah, because she thinks I'm making Malacresta sick and she doesn't want to be happy for me."

Ersilio sighs. "Are you stupid, Sole?"

"What?"

"Because I don't want to believe you're lying. Did God ever threaten to destroy Magmate?"

It takes me a moment to understand. Then, my heart plunges into my bladder.

"I think so," I say quietly.

"Does that mean no?"

"I… think so."

"Oh, Sole."

"It was never going to happen! We're building the church! We've answered."

Ersilio takes another slug of wine and gurgles: "Oh, *Sole.*"

My voice comes damp as well. "Would they *ever* have come to build if they'd known why I was doing it? I could never have made them understand. They think I want to look like a man because I think it's beauty, or… or… power. You know that I need this like a resurrection. It's not good, but it's… animal."

Ersilio hums into his hands, three syllables.

"But you could have told *me,*" he says. "When we were sitting in the street. When I told you I wasn't going to help you. I didn't come back because of Nedda's eyes. I came back because I thought it was what you wanted. You wanting a man's body makes more sense than you wanting a goddamn church, but whatever it is, I don't care! If it stops my best friend from killing himself, it's holy."

We finish the wine. Ersilio hasn't been drunk since he buried Ciecherella. As comical as the memory seems now— him setting aside six hours to drink three bottles, then rising up like a revenant at dawn to return to his duties—his utter abstinence since then makes me think he was scared he wouldn't be that strong twice. I wish I'd been that strong even once. I drowned the memory of Nene in wine. I boiled the sea with him in it. I was drunk on the arrival of God. I was drunk when I healed Ersilio's daughter.

Tonight makes me think that drinking doesn't have to be drowning. Or that drowning is okay if you're drowning in a person, not a memory. I abandon the statue with a sweep of my knuckles against its neck and curl up with my head on Ersilio's shoulder. He puppets my hands through the air and sings, "Too big, ridiculous, too big for your face." I command him to look at my face, and grin when realisation breaks through his squint. "Oh, that's wonderful, that's sunshine," he says. "No wonder that's your name."

Once we're nearly asleep on the table, with the lamp burned out and cold wind making the curtains breathe against the ceiling, he says,

"Is it good? Seeing Nene?"

I turn to look at him.

"Would you see Ciecherella again if you could?"

"Of course I would. I still talk to her every day."

"What if coming back wasn't good for her? Only good for you?"

"Isn't that the whole point?" Ersilio says. "How selfless can it be, wanting someone back from the dead? Of course I feel like it wasn't fair on her to die, but she's not still hurting, is she? Neither are the girls. They never knew her, and to hell with the people who say they're broken because they grew up without a mother. It's me who's hurting. I think about it every day, the life I could have had if she was here. Not just loving me and loving the girls but… absolving me of the need to ache. I've spent so much life aching. I'll never get it back. I'll never know what kind of person I could've been if my wife hadn't horribly died."

I rest my chin on his chest. "Mm-hm, well, the monster aches. Being inside it and having a headful of its voice makes me feel like I'm going to die."

"Because it's not Nene? It's the thing that killed him?"

"I don't know. I told it the first time that I knew it wasn't Nene. That I knew it ate him. But if I really thought that, it wouldn't make me feel like that, would it? So much pain and yet so much pleasure. I think what it makes me think is that it was Nene who ate Nene. Maybe I watched him eat himself and crawl out of himself every day he was alive and every time that thing comes back, I have to watch him do it again. I don't like that that's the part of him that survived, Ersilio. The part that eats itself."

There's silence. I grow frightened that he's not as drunk as I thought he was. Sentient enough to be harrowed.

Then, he snickers, "So much *pleasure?*"

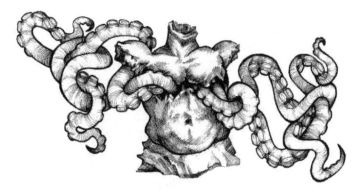

CHAPTER 16
THE PURPLE

N OW SHEETED, the purple glass from the beach glows on the furnace's windowsill, a maddening contrast to the sallow lilac Malacresta is blowing. He hasn't told me the intricacies of his experiments with the gabbro, but around us in the domed chamber roost jugs, boxes and papers spread with grey powder. He kicks the pole upright with the toe of his boot and picks the still-hot fruit. Draws his sword. Pierce, cleave, splay. It's absurd to see a craft so brutal and heavy, bubbling lava and parrying poles and blades as long as our thighs, result in a product so delicate.

"Ersilio's going to have measurements of the windows for you soon," I say.

Malacresta, smoothing the glass with his gloved hands, jerks his head up in a nod. His quiet isn't panic-induced today. I know Prasede has told him about her fight with me, so he must, in revolt against the idea we are fighting about him without him, have refused to choose a side.

The job of the moment is the erection of pillars and joists to support the second floor. With the walls hung with fabric and the window frames not yet reinforced, the church's skeleton will be completely sketched before a thought is given to texture and detail. I told Ersilio to fetch measurements for the metal frames of the eight arched windows, but not to start making them. Malacresta still hasn't touched the green glass on the table in my workshop, and I'm not sure his devotion to sheeting and colouring will lead to devotion to designing.

"Do you want to make them yourself? Or should I ask Ersilio to make them for you?"

"Don't make frames," Malacresta says.

There's a pang of pain in my heart. "Why not?"

"Didn't mean it like that. I meant *they* don't make frames. Stained glass window makers. They stack the pictures out piece by piece." He doesn't look up as he worries his hands together in an act of stacking bricks.

Just as I say, "Okay," two people darken the doorway. It's Ersilio and Prasede. Both are wearing leather tool belts.

"We've been sent by the people to fetch you," Prasede says with a sunny smile. "We're to have a meeting."

I frown. "A meeting?"

"We were waiting until the floor was finished. We're going to commune on it."

"What about?"

Prasede stares past me at Malacresta. "About, uh, whether it's strong enough to hold us all."

Later that hour, Malacresta and I traipse down the hillside to the church. Forlorn at his listlessness, I scour my mind for something that might excite him.

"I've been thinking," I say. "Perhaps the purple wasn't so bright because of one tiny part of the gabbro. Perhaps it was something to do with the speed. Sand became glass in flashes. With big clangs."

"Well, I can't make it in flashes," Malacresta says.

I look sadly at the floor.

"But," he mumbles, almost to himself, "it might be

something to do with the temperature. On the beach, without ash, the reaction would have been much hotter."

I grin at him. He stares beyond me.

"What's wrong?" I say. The expression on his face is almost frightened. Like he's frightened by his own knowledge, or perhaps his own passion.

"Me and Prasede, um," he says. Then, he violently shakes his head. "Doesn't matter. Tell you later."

We enter the church through the side wall and walk across what will be the chancel. I feel like the Curato, walking out to give a service.

Fifty people are waiting for us in the rectangular clearing between the wall beams. It's a bright yellow day, and the ceiling lies down on them in bands of blue shadow. Nedda, Lagia and Prasede are sitting in a line on one of the ceiling beams, tied in place with ropes around their waists. Ersilio leans on the beam underneath them, like he's waiting to catch them.

The first thing I say is shouted up at Prasede. "I thought this was a meeting about whether the floor could hold us."

She leans down, her copper hair flashing with wind and sun. "And?"

"You're not on it."

Prasede stands up on the beam, untying her harness. We all watch anxiously as she swings to the supporting beam and shimmies down it, kicking away Ersilio's hands when he reaches to help her. When she springs onto the floor with a thump, I flinch, expecting it to give way beneath her. It doesn't bend.

"Seems sturdy to me!" she chirps.

Malacresta leaves my shadow and slinks into hers. He sits down beside her, but she stays on her feet, so I do too.

The crowd are looking at me with a kind of expectation.

"So?" I say. "What should we meet about?"

It's Prasede who answers. "Well, I thought we ought to talk

about what's going to happen after the church is finished."

I narrow my eyes. "What do you mean?"

"Well, surely you know that when God said 'Rebuild the church,' He didn't mean *put the building back*. He meant *rebuild the congregation*. What's the nature of the religion we're bringing back to Magmate?"

I curl my lip, annoyed that she lied. Brought me in front of the crowd to gripe.

"For instance," she continues, "and this is an obvious question: Who's going to be the Curato?"

It is an obvious question. For the last nine years, Magmate has felt the absences of church and Curato in three places only. Mass and confession hold no appeal where God holds no appeal, but christenings, funerals and weddings had mites of ceremony which could be salvaged. Babies were anointed with saltwater on the beach, dead bodies anointed with earth in the forest, couples married around bonfires at the top of the cliff. Our ancient prayer, *"Ex magmate exoriebamus, et ad magma revertemur,"* changed. Now, it was, *"Ex Magmate exoriebamus, et ad Magmate revertemur."* The literal meaning remained, but the implicit meaning was different. We were no longer children of God's earth, but of the village we'd built from it. The Creator we worshipped was us.

I must pick a Curato who allows the worship of our creations to exist in harmony with the worship of God's creations. A Curato whose blessings are embellishments, not imperatives.

Benghi Cvradi is the first person I think of. He's sitting at the front of the crowd with his daughter and wife, squinting up at me like he's trying to look at the sun. Since his healing, he has greeted me in the street with heavy hugs and exaltations of God and asked me, like my mother, if he can help. Unlike my mother, I let him.

I imagine Benghi giving sermons, gilding each one with the anecdote of his unconditional, Heaven-sent healing until we're all sick to the bowels of it. I imagine sitting in his audience, guilty to have put him there and angry to be misrepresented. For as the only one who didn't see the moaning, drooling machinations of his healing, his view of God is gilded.

"I am," I say.

The gathered crowd nod, smile and shrug at each other. To them, it's a relief that I want to be the Curato. That I'm committing to the church for life.

To Prasede, it's enough to pale her face.

"Oh," she says. "Well, then. As our sculptor and our Curato, I assume you will want to reinstate the sculpting ceremonies every ten years?"

My throat shrivels with horror at the thought. Stuffing my church, Ersilio's church, Malacresta's church, with flimsy, ugly, amateur sculptures.

"Absolutely not," I say. "Those ceremonies were designed to belittle people."

"But you of all people should know how to make them good! Make them lessons in glorifying God with beauty!"

"Prasede, don't you remember that horrible horde of wraiths? You were so frightened of it."

"I was a *child.*" Prasede's teasing laugh is tinged with irritation.

"Don't you remember how it broke us to be forced to make ourselves?"

There's a syllable of silence. As Prasede narrows her eyes at me, shame climbs up my spine. *No*, she might say. *It only broke you.*

She doesn't avert her eyes from me as I walk to stand with Ersilio.

"I must ask," she says. "Why, *how,* does one who claims to loathe the way he looks sleep in a bedroom full of self-portraits?"

Anger throbs in my chest. Ersilio interjects before I can shout at her.

"I hated it too," he says. "The stupid sculpting thing. It was fun, of course, but I thought the sculptures should've been melted back at the end. It was the hoarding I couldn't stand. That bit of clay Sole took from my hideous childhood heap and mixed into his statue of my Ciecherella was much better used by him than by me."

I resist the urge to throw my arms around his neck.

"It seems," Prasede scoffs, "everything's better used by Sole than by us."

"Look!" I say. "Why don't we do it, then? On the night the church is finished, we can have a big sculpting ceremony in the square. I can see to the clay and the tables. Everyone makes a likeness of themselves, and, at the end of the night, comes up and squashes it back into the vat. It will be a moving tribute to everything that has happened to us. Destroying and rebuilding anew."

Prasede glowers at me.

Someone in the crowd calls, "Will it just be for us? The ceremony? For the builders?"

I consider the question. There's a stab of inspiration in my belly as I imagine announcing as much to our neighbours. That they're only invited to take part in the lovely new ceremony if they join the church.

But the second stab of inspiration is stronger.

"No, it should be for everyone. Like good Christians, we will rejoice in the name of God, but for the benefit and joy of our neighbours."

Prasede gives a quick laugh. "Oh, splendid," she says. "What a fine farce of goodness. That will do a grand job of endearing the sceptical."

"I'm a Curato, Prasede. Endearing the sceptical is my job."

"You offered to be the Curato five minutes ago. We haven't accepted you yet."

"YOU ACCEPTED ME WITH THE FIRST NAIL YOU HAMMERED INTO A BEAM IN MY NAME!"

I don't realise until the moment after my shout, when silence falls in a rush, that our bickering had put a buzz into the crowd. It is like I dragged a knife through empty air and ripped a hole.

The people in the crowd swap frightened glances. Ersilio rubs his mouth with his palms, and Malacresta reaches up to hold Prasede's hand.

"Tesoro," she says. As I watch, she kneels and kisses his fingers. "I told you, didn't I?"

"Mm-hm," says Malacresta.

"Loud as bells, was he not?"

"Mm-hm."

Terror squashes my lungs. The escaping air almost tugs out a whimper.

I remember Malacresta trying to tell me something on the way here. That him and Prasede had been talking.

It's like when Ersilio found out about my deal. I don't care if Prasede reviles me. If anything, it's a relief.

But if she makes Malacresta revile me, she'll stab me through the mouth.

"In *your* name, Sole?" Prasede says. "Not God's name? You failed to think about how we would worship God in this church because to you, it is not God's church. It's your church. We are all slaves enlisted for the restoral to glory from disgrace and embarrassment of *you.*"

"Of us all," I manage.

"You think you can convince me you see us as equals? You just told us you don't want our art in the church."

"I want Malacresta's. Why do you think I asked him? He's not a great artist yet."

"No, but he is your friend. You think you can control him."

"Well, which is it? Am I favouring him or am I using him?"

"All under your favour are used, Sole. Your favour is a force which uses. Chews up and spits out." She jerks her chin at Ersilio, as if to add, *you too.* "And you were chosen by God for

no better reason than that God was chewed by you too."
There's a ripple of cries in the crowd, and Ersilio gasps low in
his throat. "He was just a child once, and you chewed Him
until He haunted us with those wings and those tentacles, until
He could only speak to us from *your* mouth, until He was a
creature which cut its teeth on pain, on power, on making
deals—I will not hammer one more nail, Sole De Gasinis, to
hold your tongue down in the Devil's mouth."

Ersilio puts his hand on my chest as if to stop me from
attacking her.

There's a chink in the storm of Prasede's resolve, as if she
was expecting me to attack her too. As if she's scared I'm going
to start crying instead.

All of this happens before I fully grasp her meaning. I'm
staring at the side of Malacresta's face, beseeching him not to
leave me with unrequited eye contact, when I realise she's
talking about Nene.

"You really think he's the Devil, you... child?" I say.

Ersilio presses his nose into my cheek, pleading.

"The fucking Devil? This thing, which claims it is God, is
conniving, is grotesque, is uncontrolled, and therefore, *it must
be the Devil instead*. What a tidy invention the Devil was, a
perfect evil to oppose a perfect good as if the very idea of a
being which calls itself perfectly good isn't perfectly evil! Did
we not tear the old church down on that conviction? Did you
ever think that the God which was born from Nene
Karafantoni came back as a monster because his neighbours let
him die believing he was a monster?"

Prasede bares her teeth and growls low in her throat. *"You,"*
she says. *"You* let him die believing he was a monster."

Tears swell in my eyes, hot and sharp.

When Prasede storms away towards the square, Malacresta
jerks to his feet and follows her.

"LET GO OF HIS HAND!" I yell. "If he agrees with you,
he'll follow you without being dragged!"

They stop. Malacresta lets go of Prasede's hand and turns to face me with his hand aloft.

"I'm just quiet, Sole," he mumbles.

"You've had enough of me? You don't want to do the windows anymore?"

He shakes his head.

"Why? Because it was making you sick?"

He nods.

I bare my teeth and wipe my eyes with both hands. "Do you think that about Nene too, then?" I say. "Since she told you to?"

"She didn't—"

"DO YOU THINK THAT TOO?"

He flinches, like I slapped him.

"That he... loved you because he was turning into a monster... or he turned into a monster because he loved you?"

Malacresta doesn't answer his own question, but he's careful about the way he orders things.

I hiccup. More tears fall down my face.

"I'm just scared," he says to the floor. "She made me feel like I was gonna end up..."

His splayed hand turns downward, points at the crypt, for just a second before he turns away.

And then, followed by all of my hopes and none of my builders, Malacresta and Prasede are gone.

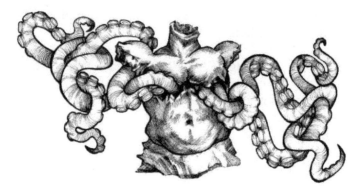

CHAPTER 17

THE RED

TO BE TOLD that your tongue is nailed down in the Devil's mouth is a sweet and rotten pang, but to be told so in front of fifty people and watch them take your side is a sweeter, rottener one. When the white curtains of sunlight in the square swallow Malacresta, I bury my face in my hands, quell my tears in two hard sniffs and tell Ersilio to help his daughters down from the rafter. Then, I tell the crowd to take the afternoon off.

"Are we allowed to stay, Signore?" Abriana Cvradi answers. "We haven't finished measuring the windows."

Warmth spreads down my neck like a bruise. "Of course you are."

It was obvious to the builders that I was favouring Malacresta. Whilst they sanded and hauled timber, splintered in beige and brown, he cavorted with lava and rainbows, and whilst Ersilio's leadership drew them along at a clip, he wasted months. Before sunset, I hear a hundred accusations. How dare he suggest such a pleasant job was making him sick, such an easy job, such a *pointless* job? How dare he spurn such

242

generosity and patience? But perhaps he's too stupid to be blamed. Prasede seduced his simple mind away from God. She wielded against his softness the old, enormous horror we do not speak of.

For the first days without Malacresta, I only grieve the loss of his respect. Then, Caro Tegliacci, Sitha's father, visits me in my workshop. Though a farmer by trade, Caro used the furnace to remake windows after the earthquake. He also nurses a hobby of making jewellery, twine hung with pendants of seashell and wood.

When he asks me if I'd like him to take Malacresta's place in the furnace, I blink at him. *Oh, yes,* I think. *It's the windows I should be grieving.*

Like me, Sitha prevents her elderly parents from helping with the building. That means I cannot reject him by pretending I need his labour elsewhere. I cannot claim Malacresta was more qualified, either.

"Signore Malacheti's betrayal," I say at last, in a heavy-tongued twang like I'm drunk, "has made me loathe the idea of stained glass. I'm going to put clear glass in the windows instead. A heretic entering a house of God should feel from whence he is missing."

Caro shrugs. "It was you leaving his things out that made me wonder if you wanted someone else."

I haven't been back to the furnace since the morning of the meeting, but three little sheets of glass—a green, a violet and a clear—sit on the table in the corner of my workshop. Alongside them is a nub of charcoal and one of the glassmaking blades, rusty broadsword glistening with dewy white blood. I forget why Malacresta brought it here. Probably absent-mindedly, slung over his shoulder or sheathed in his trouser leg.

"I didn't leave them, Signore Tegliacci. He left them."

Caro leaves, and I go back to my statue.

I didn't ask Malacresta to make me stained glass because I liked stained glass. I asked him to make me stained glass because he liked stained glass. Whenever he dragged me up the hill to show me a mite of progress, as dull as a new cutting method or as magnificent as a new colour, I absorbed it in a couple of blinks and then turned like a worshipper to his face. His face was the stained glass I liked, aglow in its fissures with pride.

And I want to see it turn to stone when he looks at the boring windows I make without him.

Days turn into weeks with the glass sheets on my table, searing my eyes at the corners as I sculpt. I fantasise about Malacresta coming into the workshop by happenstance and being moved by the fact I kept them. One day, I prop the green and violet up against the wall, where the setting sun slices through the gap between two sheets. When I glance over my statue's shoulder and see the fractals seeping like blood across the floor, beginning to climb up the leg of the table, I lose my temper in a flash and run to kick them over.

The green glass skitters through the sheet and comes to rest in the street. I burst out after it and stamp down on it with my heel. It shatters into a spiderweb over the dome of a cobblestone. When I do the same to the purple one, it snaps cleanly into two, then four. With stragglers in the square watching, I limp back into my workshop like it was my ankle I snapped.

The church comes along steady, steady. Lintels for the windows, the timber ribs of the second floor. The moment Ersilio declares the roof structurally sound, I climb up there to sit and gaze across the valley. When I try to do the same the following day, I get a sunburn which rubs off my lips, cheeks and neck in black gnats like clay, so I relegate my climbs to nighttime. I tell the builders I'm climbing up to check they're safely tied in place, as Prasede used to, but I'm just occupying the best vantage point from which to watch people obey me. It's all I have. Ersilio, my voice, and people obeying me. As I sit cross-legged on the roof, I imagine the fifty of them detaching the church from its foundations and lifting it up onto their shoulders to add a new ground floor, then another, then another, lifting me higher and higher.

I decide to treat the church as my largest, finest sculpture. Though the windows must radiate Malacresta's betrayal, the rest will be mine. I can send people to the city to find me some hard stone, marble if they love me, limestone if they don't, and carve friezes to mask those hideous joists. I can paint the walls. And I can make as many statues as swarmed the old church. Statues which are ghoulish on purpose.

My workshop becomes a forest of sculptures of God.

Nene writhes on the table, and bones jut in haloes around my workbench. One day, I try to sculpt God's shape in the dead whale, but find in the streaks and crags of its tentacles no pleasing form. As I begin a sculpture of the ruined house with the ceiling-beam wings, I twist the shape of it as much as I can, barnacle the walls with moss and rot off the ends of the planks. Nothing sucks the life from a sculpture like a straight line.

I have just grafted on a wing which unbalances the sculpture, and frantically scooped the whole thing into my arms, when a group of visitors wanders into the workshop.

Visitors come in to chatter every day. Some treat me like a poor lamb, and assure me that two less friends in this life is worth the love of God in the next. Some treat me like a sculptor, asking questions about my half-conceived horrors, and some treat me like a Curato. I find it no enormous task to give advice to people with dilemmas. The first person who presented a struggle was a woman who wanted to give confession. I chastised her for allowing me to see her face, and told her to go outside and speak to me through the sheets. As I worked on my statue, she shouted from the bustling square that she'd let her husband punish her four-year-old son for breaking a bowl that she'd been the one to break. When I nervously asked about the nature of the punishment, she said, "He, um, bounced him on his knee and called him a little hurricane."

With my jaws pressed against my statue's shoulder to muffle my laugh, I told her I'd make her a new bowl. I wish I'd told her to break it in front of her husband and son.

This is a group of older women. Amena De Aqvancis, Ersilio's mother, Papena Tegliacci, Sitha's mother, and Fotena Del Meda, my second ever gravestone client. I welcome their sunny greetings with grunts as I search for a safe place to lay the floundering sculpture.

"Oh, what a splendid one," says Fotena, stroking one of the wings flopping over my shoulder. "What is it?"

I peel the wings away and lay them flat on the table. "Do you remember the apparition on the hillside?"

"Of course. Well, I heard the birds, and saw it dead the next day."

"It's all around us still," Papena says. "That's the wood they're building the church with."

Fotena sucks her teeth. "Mm. I heard Signores Barostaldo and Di Chremasco saying it's cursed—Can you believe that?" She nudges me. "And you call those boys your friends."

She's talking about Ario and Lalo. "I've called worse my friends."

There's a syllable of silence.

Ario and Lalo saying that I'm cursed behind my back, Malacresta and Prasede saying that I'm in the Devil's mouth to my face. Even Ersilio's loyalty can't soften the stream of betrayals. As the best of us, he should never have come back to me, and as the best of us, he will never leave me again.

"Do you believe in curses, Amena?" Fotena calls.

"*I* believe," Papena interrupts, "Poor Signora De Gasinis deserved a softer apparition. It didn't help her find favour at first, did it?"

Two mosquito bites. The first in a few days. The first not immediately corrected in a few months.

My friends are the only ones who make mistakes and then correct them. The people who don't see me as a man structure their sentences to avoid using any name, title or pronoun at all, and when they use the wrong one, they stay quiet, as if they're hoping I won't notice. Really, they're hoping I'll pretend not to notice.

"*Signore* De Gasinis," I say, exaggerating the last vowel with a drawl as I drag my finger across a wing, "deserved a truthful apparition. Worthless are the followers of God who believe He is not monstrous."

"Why did you take the wings off? Would they not fix on?"

"There's a balance problem. Too much weight on the top."

"Why, couldn't you make the base bigger by sculpting the hill?"

"No, Signora Tegliacci. That would be ugly."

She blinks at me, offended.

"I think I'll have to make the roof wider and flatter. Graft the wings to a stronger spine."

"Oh, I wish *I* could have a stronger spine," Papena says.

Shit, I think. *Shit shit shit. I've done it again.*

Moral pains aren't the only pains my visitors complain about. I first noticed the pattern on the day Ersilio carried Lagia into the workshop and pointedly said that she'd twisted her ankle on the cliff path. When I asked him if he wanted permission to take wood for a splint, his *yes* was disappointed. Now, every other visitor happens to mention a headache, a backache, a cough. It's a miserable existence. To be capable of healing pain is to learn that everyone you love is in pain. I picture them all, driven mad by my rejections, gouging at their arms and throwing themselves from the roof. Desperate to be worthy of my luting hand, to be hurt enough.

I started calling the power *luting* after Benghi. After I closed his wound with a hand smeared in gore, like I was luting a clay seam with slip.

Papena's complaint is a substantial one, to her credit: Scoliosis. Sitha told me that the curve of her spine is blatant on her naked back, and she has a crease in the right side of her waist not mirrored on the left. She has agonising days and easy days, but going to sleep every night wondering whether tomorrow will be painful is a pain that never wavers.

When I ignore her quip, she continues. "Oh, how it hurts. I was telling your mamma the other day how lucky she is not to have an affliction her daughter is doomed to share."

This bite makes me bristle. "Indeed, because she does not have a daughter. She has a son."

"Oh! Of course." Papena laughs and hits her face against my shoulder twice. "Sole, Sole. I've been calling you Solavita all afternoon."

"You have."

"Oh, I'm just a silly old woman. Don't esteem my opinion of you too highly."

"I don't."

"Anyway, yes. Her *child* is not doomed to the disease which manifests in, ah, how do I say it? The female bodies in the family."

"A woman's body?"

"Yeah, give it back."

I start to pull pieces of clay from the roof of the house and blend them into a new beam. The remembrance of what silence feels like, an oasis where *female* and *Solavita* aren't, bloats the small of my back with luting power.

"Do forgive me the mistake," Papena says from behind me.

"I'd rather you forgave yourself and saved me the effort."

"I beg your pardon?"

I turn, seize her by the throat, and slam her backwards into the table. Amena and Fotena scream. We crash into the sculpture and buckle it. I yell, "Shit!" and crush the mess of beams into the back of her bodice.

An immense lustrous CRACK crystallises the air. In a wire, it shoots up Papena's spine and into my hands. At first, all I feel is a shockwave. Then, a burgeoning freeze between the bones of my knuckles, as if my fingers are bending back slowly.

Papena's back arches and her eyes bulge, like I've impaled her on the sharp wings of the sculpture. All I think as the luting floods out, pops my fingers back in and pours my bones down like pewter into my bladder, is that I miss Malacresta. He watched me heal Benghi the right way. Horror and love squashed like bugs against his mouth.

I let Papena go. She looks taller. Too tall to hit her face against my shoulder.

"Wasn't expecting it," I say, fat-lipped. "Thought it only worked when it served God. I suppose it serves God for you to leave me alone."

But of course I'm not left alone.

I finish the house statue, abandoning the spine and balancing it with a new pair of wings which drag their knuckles on the ground. The night it's finished, Ersilio comes in with Lagia, whose ankle is nearly healed, and before he's finished greeting, "Now, don't feel obligated—" I'm on my knees with my jaws around the splint. The bones in my hands break again, heal again. I sculpt an inaccurately whale-shaped version of the whale and lute a nine-year-old's rickets, bending my fingers like molten glass. I sculpt the starfish covered in crabs and lute a fluttering heart, making my tendons bubble in their trenches. I sculpt a slavering tower of intestines and bulging eyes and lute a cracked thumbnail.

My echoes, the mutations which occur in whichever part of my body God last changed, always vanish in time with their sources, but luting Papena brews in the base of my spine an ache which doesn't fade until the following noon. I am entranced by the idea that I absorbed her affliction, that I'm a pain-eater, the way Jesus was a sin-eater. But luting Lagia puts the ache back in my spine, not my ankle. It's a food-poisoning squeeze, a brown and red weight which bends viscera down to my groin. It slithers for a week, shrunk by eating in the morning and enlarged by eating at night, then settles clawed into my back. One night, Ersilio notices me bending to hold myself on the roof and grabs my thigh, thinking I'm falling.

"Is it just the luting?" he says. "It's just tiring you?"

"Or what?"

"Or is God using the luting to… deliver something to you? A change?"

"Or an eviscerating death."

He doesn't dignify my joke. "Please don't say that."

I sit up, try to stretch my back. There's a cloud of gulls overhead, black against the blue dusk.

A wet film of nausea envelops me. I dig my hands into the bare timber of the roof beam.

A knife stabbing me in the belly I know. The buried knife turning like a winch, drawing my guts in until they pull taut in their fastenings, turns me blind in a flash.

When Ersilio flings himself on top of me, my head jolts like he punched me in the face. I was falling. The floor of the church unfurls above me, abandoned hammers the new cloud of gulls.

As I hang upside-down, the winch turns again. On the back wall of my ribcage, something twangs loose. My scream is an "Mmf," a gurgle of vomit.

"Are you awake? HELP US DOWN!" Ersilio is close to tears. "Is it something moving? Is it God? Is it going to rip out?"

I struggle upright in his arms. "You… that scared of a period?" I slur. "I'm going to sleep in the workshop."

I'd rather exhibit my pain to all fifty of my builders than to my mother. The builders don't see me dragging hay and blankets into the workshop that night, but they see Ersilio bringing me a bed warmer the next day. When I insist at noon that I'm being dramatic, that this is an ordinary kind of pain, and probably an ordinary intensity of pain for many of my builders, I'm swarmed in the side aisle by a crowd of them asking if I'm well. When I inhale to reply, a serrated sword of a cramp bump-bump-bumps through a gap between ribs, makes my answer judder.

By the evening, my legs are unreliable. The fronts of my

thighs are numb and there's a yellow swamp of ache on the muscular side of each calf. I tell Ersilio to fuck off home to his babies, but when he comes back minutes later to drop off my refilled bed warmer, I ask him through whistling gasps not to leave me. My stomach muscles slide over one another all night, a cat's cradle trying to pull back into a circle.

The next morning, a young woman comes into the workshop with her baby boy. He's been coughing, she says, abysmally, for a week. The sound coming out of him is like a pepper mill. The fear of twisting his tiny head off is washed away by the frenzy of power. The mother finishes saying thanks to God and leaves the workshop just before I vomit into my water bucket.

The next day, another. Someone else smashed her thumb with a hammer. She refuses to give me her hand until I tell her I'm well enough, and I surge up and put her in a death roll. I wonder why they're all happy to be licked and clawed to heal such petty injuries.

"I'm going to tell them to stop coming," Ersilio says, twisting my hair into a knot as I lie face-down.

"No," I say. "When the people who haven't joined the church hear I'm doing it freely, they'll join. It won't be forever before Malacresta polishes through his fucking hand."

"Sole." His voice comes in a shiver.

I have to look at his face before I can follow his eyes. It's as grey as my statues.

There's blood on my blankets. A scarlet sprawl, crowning the peak of my thighs like the snow on a mountain. It's still growing.

The pain becomes a sharp-toothed mouth made of ribs. It gnashes on my innards and slavers them out. It grinds its jaw in its sleep and awakes with its whole head burning. Ersilio, Lagia and Nedda change my bedding every morning for three days, but when the blood is still coming ripe and fast on the fourth, I tell them to stop before the village runs out of bedding.

Finally, when my legs are numb and my whole body white from blood loss, Ersilio storms out into the nave and shouts that the lutings are making me sick and I'll do no more. It's so I won't be seen. We're both praying it isn't the lutings. I've felt before the same pain with earthly strength and he's seen before the same mess with earthly cause and if I can survive the crescendo without screaming myself inside out, we may never have to suffer it again.

The noises coming from inside me are hollow, wet thumps. Pieces of me sloughing and falling. I am barren with promise, the dark before thunder, the receding of the sea before a flood. The crescendo, whether it's the rotting or the struggling to life of my womb, is close.

"How-are-they-taking-my-absence?" I ask through jittering teeth.

"You're not absent, Sole. They hear you screaming. They see me washing the bloody things in the fountain. People keep asking me if you're miscarrying."

I curl my lip in disgust. I wonder whether that rumour names God as the father, or him.

"You tell them," I say, "that no matter what they hear tonight, they are not to come in. Tell them God told me He would kill them for it. He would fry-them-alive-in-my-aura."

It's a night for thinking of Nene. Spasming like there's a panicking dog trapped in my trunk and tossing my head like I'm going to spit heartsblood down Ersilio's back. He can't let go of me because he loves me and I can't let go of him because my arms locked in place when the first tremor came and he happened to be between them. He puts me on my back, staggers on top of me with a winded *oof.* When I press my hands into my belly, he seems lost without the embrace and joins his hands to mine. He pushes down so hard I think he'll crush me, but that's the way to keep the fist of God down. *The wing. The wing wreathed in guts.* Pain, short and red, grows out of itself into agony, long and black, and agony grows out of itself into pouring white light which makes me daydream and sing. Just to see how it tastes, I shout, "I don't want to die like him!" and then, like I'm trying to finish a song to get the tune out of my head, I say it again and again: "I don't want to die like him! I don't want to die like him! I don't want to die like him, Ersilio!"

The blood on my blankets and thighs bristles with tissue, black clots and purple fronds and long yellow flounces. Like the blood, it stinks of rot, sweet gas and sweaty iron and mouldy paper. Ersilio sobs that he wants to get Teglia and I, with memories of women giving birth on their backs, tell him I'll fucking kill him if he does, fucking kill you, Ersilio, excoriate and cremate you in my aura, feed your ashes to a whale. At dawn, the bulk of it comes out. It looks like a dead jellyfish. We stare down at it on the bed like we're about to argue over who gets to kick it first.

"That's for making me bleed every month," I say. "Now y...urgh...*you* get to bleed!"

I collapse on my face, cackling. Ersilio collapses on top of me, weeping.

"That's... that's... *pointless,*" Ersilio says in the morning, as I hammock the bed into a stinking bundle. "What, do you look more like a man now? Is my mamma less likely to call you Signora at breakfast?"

Covered in blood and corpse-pale, I grin at him. "I will *feel* more like a man next month, when I do not have a single heart attack in my asshole."

I spend the day scrubbing the blood from my hair, legs and workshop floor. As night falls, I gather the gore-blighted sheets and walk to the cliff to burn them. For the first time since I started bleeding, I am wearing my beautiful trousers. Ersilio's best trousers, black with braided cords. He said I was his best.

He wanted to come with me, in case it wasn't over, but I told him I needed to be alone. Annoyance is all I feel when I reach the back of the forest and see movement.

There's a light in the furnace. As I walk closer, I hear a quiet roar which pulses in time with the fire. Then, the hollow rumble-clang of a door closing.

Only when Malacresta turns around and drops his blowpipe, shocked not only by the presence of me but the white-faced, bloody-sheet-enrobed state of me, does the possibility occur to me. I had thought it was Caro, or someone else making glass for the houses. In the new world of blood, luting, Ersilio and more blood, Malacresta was not a figure. He was gone over the mountain, under the sea.

"Should I have checked the trees for Prasede?" I say at last.

"She knows I'm here," is his reply.

In my mind's eye, my innards run down my legs again, run out of my mouth and eyes. I know he heard I was sick. Builders whispering or me wailing. The sheets in my arms reek of dead dog and cow, and the colour of my face makes it clear it's my reek.

On the end of the pole in Malacresta's hands is a crimson pomegranate. It oozes syrup in the backlight.

The wooden sideboard next to the furnace is a murder scene. Something copper mutilated around a glassmaking blade, which is impaled upright in the table.

He turns his hand, as if to say *ta-da*. Two quick stutters might be the first syllables of better explanations. "It's... red."

"You said it was making you sick," I say.

"Making it for you was."

"So what are you making it for?"

He shrugs. "Dunno. For me."

I snort.

Replacing me with himself. It reminds me of the way we replaced God with the village. To the worshipper, it's more grounded, more introverted. But if God made the earth, God made the village.

And I made him.

"Just making colours and stacking them up?"

255

"Just until I feel better. Prasede calls it weaning me." He jerks his chin at the sheets. "What's that about?"

"None of your business. Ersilio held me through it. It's over now."

Ersilio's name softens Malacresta's eyes.

"You're thinking poor him, aren't you?"

He looks at the floor, saws the lip of the crucible with his pole. "Prasede reckons he'd go too if he wasn't desperate, yeah."

"Desperate for what?"

"For, uh, for all the time he invested in you to be worth it."

It's obviously a recitation of something Prasede said, but only because of the phrasing. He might believe the same.

"And what do you think?"

He shrugs.

"I miss God," he says, to my surprise. "I didn't want to think of my sister dashed to smithereens by some brute. I wanted to think of her loved and healed in Heaven. You took that from me."

"You know God is both."

"Yeah, I know. I got obsessed with the glass after I watched you heal that old man."

I blink at him. Rot spreads through my chest, the stink of anger and the sweetness of pride.

"What do you mean? You were going to make a window of me luting Benghi?"

"Doesn't matter if I was."

I say nothing.

"I'm weaning," he continues. "Prasede says I'm done for good after red."

I say nothing again.

"Copper red's a pleb's gold red. It's all dark and barely see-through. I thought I'd try burning the copper into oxide, like the rust. It didn't make it brighter, though."

He turns and reaches toward the windowsill. The sheet of

glass he selects looks green until he holds it up to the white-hot crucible, when it lights up, seems to smelt, into oceanic blue.

A croon of praise tries to thrash out of me like a cough. *Beautiful.*

Don't do that!" he exclaims. "Stop it!"

I feign surprise. "Do what?"

"Make me... talk to a wall. Stay quiet so I'll tell you more. Prasede says that's what you're doing."

I smile.

"She thinks you're rebuilding the church because God said He'd give you a man's body."

I almost tell him. Secret for secret. Red jewel for red jewel.

Then, I picture him running through the street on cycling legs, poles and blades overflowing from his arms, yelling, "Prasede! Prasede!" Another meeting. An exodus of builders. No church, no body.

Apocalypse.

"You torment me by suggesting such a thing," I say. "Making me daydream about it."

I leave, and trek up the cliff with my sheets.

When I feel a tug in my bladder, attaching me to the quarry, I curse God under my breath. All I wanted was one lonely, painless night.

I assemble my bonfire, waddling on legs turgid with pleasure, lolling my tongue and biting at the flames. Once the fire is large and hot, I throw the first sheet on, watch it mushroom into a dripping black dome and float down to its doom. Black spreads across the whole. Gore and cotton burn to powder.

Please, please, keens the hand upon my belly. *We parted last on a note of pain. Let me make it up to you.*

As I kick the ashes off the cliff, walk to the quarry, and follow the tug down the basin to the caves, the bonfire stays burned into my aspect in a blue triangle. When I stop in front of a cave, a black wound in the gabbro thrice as tall as it is wide, the blue triangle takes root between the teeth.

To nail your tongue down in the Devil's mouth. The cave has fangs, long gabbro stalactites which dripped and climbed into existence in symmetry. In the moonless night, the teeth are rotten with shadow at their roots, and spire together silver-blue as though suspended in the air. If the cave walls were bark, the light could have been peeled, stripped out of it. Though the teeth are God's spell, I have no idea whether the cave itself has always been here or whether it opened as I climbed the cliff. Opened just to cry for me. Nene opened his throat before his mouth, gazed at me with his neck bulging and his tongue floating, when he wanted me.

I walk into the cave. Squeeze myself between its teeth. They throng not in rows but in rings, and as I squeeze deeper, the rings grow tighter. I lie down on my front, my hands trapped under my belly. The possession has imbued a heat, a dampness, a stink like dog's breath. I'm in a warm, wet maw, and everything from the roots of the teeth to the crown of the head far above jitters with the desire to chew.

"Hello, *dolcezza*," I yawn against the ground.

The cave slams shut and chews.

The teeth don't touch me, but noise and pressure effervesce me in an instant. I am chewed into gristle and bone, into liquid. My hands claw into my mouth and scrape the screams from my palate and tongue. An ocean of pain and cliff face of pleasure petrified in the space between my thighs is a shock which ratchets me up onto my elbows.

I am chewed small. I am chewed until my ankle swells up in my shoe. I am chewed until Sole De Gasinis with a fresh cut on his face turns to me in the street and shoves me over. He's the pressure on my broken ankle, the terror in my air. He is everywhere except the gaping hole inside me. I taught God to heal as I tried to make Him bleed, and now He has made me bleed, He will crown the wound He made with something new. He will show me what it is to thrust a full unbending spire into the hands that twist me.

The two peaks of the break strain towards one another until the pressure gives. They crash together and climb over and through one another in a burgeoning molten pile. It is born, leather hard. I could use it to dig a hole in the gabbro floor inside which I might snap it off.

I rock onto one elbow. Claw my trousers open. Palm the length, weight of it. I can't believe how much the pleasure hurts. A membrane once sequestered inside me turned outward and inflated until the pores stretch. The sensation makes me moan, and the moan makes me shriek.

I dig my teeth into the quarry floor, wrap my hand around my girth, and sculpt. I sculpt like a jailed genius who will be beheaded the moment he finishes. Squash and stretch, cosset and wrench, dent and lute and dent again. I can't thrust long and deep enough into the earth, so I roll onto my back and thrust upward instead. My free hand stops groping in the dark. I should be yearning for my Nene, but I pleasured my Nene with only my hands. This is mine. It's all mine.

The cave and I finish together. We throw back our heads and cleave our mouths open with our tongues. There are tears running down my neck. I'm still yelling as the spell wanes: "Holy God! Holy God! Holy God!" The wetness webbing my fingers is *my own,* and could be my blood, the last gritty black clot of my blood, for all the tremors it took to get out.

I hear they carve small ones on the marbles in Rome, to symbolise intelligence. Yet again, and vindicated by the fact I am lying in a filthy quarry cave with my cock in my hand, my good God has declared me as dumb as a rock.

CHAPTER 18

THE FEVER

NENE'S EYES WERE HALF-LIDDED MOONS at the moment he penetrated me, and mine were wide and mad. With him on his back and me sitting tall on top of him, we were the earth and the church. Even though I'd pushed him under my skirt and snarled "Yes," whenever he'd faltered against new flesh, I was thinking about a dirk searching for chinks in armour. My fantasy that every thrust scoured open the wound between my legs, made him spire higher out of some ragged exit wound on my back, ignored the fact that it was me doing the thrusting. This was revenge. I was breaking my jaw to swallow him, gutting myself to imprison him. I thought Nene was beaming because he loved the pain of our rhythm skinning his back against the rock. Only when I collapsed onto my elbows, and he turned his head to keep gazing at me, did I realise he loved me too much to feel it.

"*Sei il mio fuoco,*" he said. "You are the one who taught me how to feel."

I flinched. I was so dense from thighs to shoulders with visions of violence that his tenderness went through me with painful friction. He didn't know I was thinking about eating him. He didn't want to be eaten.

And he wasn't hurting me. I was turgid and torpid and I liked it.

"Are you alright?" he said when he felt me shaking. "We can stop. Sit up. Stop."

I clawed into his shoulders and sobbed, "*Sei il mia dolcezza*, please shut up the thing in my head which is making this look like us killing each other. I'm so tired of it."

Nene laughed. "How could this look like us killing each other?"

"I don't know. You could be a sword. Coring me of my spine. I could be a fanged mouth. I could bite it off and spit it out."

He kissed my cheek. "Oh, but we can put it all back when we're finished."

I held his head against my chest and sat up. Every pang of fear I galvanised into a push of my hips, which eased from him a moan, which blossomed a new pang in my chest. I was hoping that my pleasure would soon grow great enough to drown my panic, but I was a monster for seducing gentle Nene and then a monster for betraying my village in his favour and then a monster for liking the way it felt and then a monster for not liking it enough. I was a female temptress and a male brute, a conniver and a blight without a brain. I gave up on my pleasure. I would drown in Nene's instead.

He was too busy moaning to wonder why I wasn't moaning too. When his mouth opened wide and round above the neckline of my dress, my mouth stretched into a grin against the curls at his temple. I stroked his cheeks in circles with my thumbs. Turned the key, tight and frictious, of his music. Louder than the tide and surer in rhythm. This was angelsong.

When his moaning crested white, I nuzzled his face away from my chest and covered it with kisses. My mind made the kisses into nails, made me nail down his tongue and nail open

261

his eyes and nail shut the jaws of an iron trap around his head, but I kept kissing him anyway.

He slid his cold hands between our thighs, cupping mine. "Do you need my hands?"

I tilted his head and kissed the corner of his mouth. "I am finished," I said. "You were too loud to hear me."

We lay clinging to each other on the slimy yellow rocks, as soaking wet and manic as if we'd washed up from a shipwreck, until dawn carried back the smell of dead fish.

I awoke in bed the next day feeling like I'd been thrown down a mountain. The aching was worst where I was softest: Behind my knees, inside my elbows, behind my collarbones. I was reluctant to plant my feet on the path into the valley, untie the tent door, and touch the sculpture of Ciecherella. Every contact between my flesh and solid matter seemed to spread my bruises into it, dye it dark with pictures of bitten mouths and glistening thighs.

Reaching up to Ciecherella's hair strained my shoulders, so I worked on the filigree on her bodice instead. Thankfully, I wasn't brought any children to watch. Ersilio brought Lagia and Nedda in, found them a brick of clay to paddle at, and sat down behind them to guide Nedda's hands. With him giggling over his games with the baby's arms, answering the toddler's questions in coos, and gazing up at the statue, my focus was already impeded when Nene came in.

When I saw him, I reflexively retreated behind the statue. His slinking straight up to me, and putting his hand against the opposite side of the bodice, seemed just as reflexive.

"Oh, wonderful," he said, beaming over at Ersilio as if he was talking to him. "The patterns are just how I remember them."

Ersilio pulled the baby up into his lap. "Haven't seen you in days," he said. "Has the great sculptor driven you mad yet?"

"I daresay I'll drive the sculptor mad much faster," Nene said. "You should let me come back and build before she starts throwing things at me."

"You're not building, Pipsqueak. You're hunched in the back just standing there."

"Am I?"

"And white in the face."

"I have grazes on my back."

"*Cazzate.* Show me."

Nene turned his back to Ersilio, pulled his tunics over his head, and showed him the grazes like pink shiny petals on his shoulders.

Calling him name after name in my head, I fixed my scalpel back into its line, but my eyes soon wandered back. There were six grazes. With each I focused on in turn, I hallucinated a moan.

When Nene lowered his tunics from his face, he looked at me. His smile and my glower diluted one another into the same stupid gaze.

Ersilio left the tent in the evening, taking Lagia and Nedda with him. He was always wary of the balancing act between being a good father and being a hard worker, but after accepting the offer of the stone house, he'd started choosing his daughters more. He walked with Nedda on his hip and Lagia holding his hand until he grew tired of walking bent double and scooped her up as well.

"I'm sorry," Nene said straight away. "I talked myself into a corner. I couldn't avoid it."

"Oh?" I said. "You couldn't have given him a reason, even? Said you slipped down the cliff?"

"How would slipping down the cliff make me forget you were a man?"

I turned. We blinked at each other.

"I was talking about the grazes," I said.

"I was talking about calling you *she.*"

I rolled my eyes and turned my back. I should have known he'd feel no shame about the grazes.

"If Ersilio finds out about us," I said, "it's me he'll think less of. He'll think I manipulated you."

"What a disservice his assumptions do us both." Nene flopped to the floor with a thud. In fright, thinking he'd fainted, I dropped my scalpel and spun around. He was lying on his back, playing with his fingers in the air. I gazed at the profile of his face, slightly turned away from me, with open lips, gauzy eyelash, and nostril flared in the tiny nose like a wing.

"Don't ask me if it hurts my back," he said.

"I wasn't going to."

"Then what were you going to say?"

"That I've never wanted to sculpt someone so badly."

Nene turned and beamed at me. I knelt down, putting my clay-slick hands into the grass without wiping them. His distracted face was a sculpture, but his beaming face was a painting. His red mouth opened in dark fissures at the corners and his cheeks were petals, a gradient from green to gold-freckled pink.

Whilst I'd spent the day brooding, wringing my hands of sin, he was nothing but delighted to see me. This sweetest of all beings should have been loved by someone as sweet as him, and I would have killed every sweet being in the world to make sure he stayed mine.

"If they won't let me build," Nene said, "and they never want the church back, I'll worry about not having a trade. I hoped you'd let me stay and be your assistant."

I danced my fingers, gloved in wet clay, through the air above his waist. "You don't know what a sculptor's assistant does."

"Fetch buckets of water, and keep the children's hands off the masterpieces?"

I scurried across the tent, grabbed the plank and slab of clay the babies were playing with, and brought it to him. In quick, subconscious pushes, I worked a sphere the size of my shoe, added a prism of jaw and slots of eye socket.

"A sculptor's assistant," I said, "does all the sculpting whilst the sculptor fucks around with details. What the great sculptors are truly great at is teaching their boys how to sculpt, and convincing them they're still no better than assistants."

Nene sat up and crossed his legs. "Are you making me?"

In answer, I made a show of smearing on a nose, squinting long and hard at his face, and then pushing my thumb into the tip of the nose to make it snub. When he beamed in delight, there was a twinge in my chest which made my blood feel thicker and warmer. I held the sculpture up next to his face and pretended to frown in vexation before reaching out and pushing my thumb into the tip of his nose. It left a firm black oval of clay, like a puppy's nose. Instead of laughing, he half-closed his eyes and tilted his head to one side.

The thumbprint dried silver on his nose as I formed the likeness, smearing layers onto the cheeks and off again, peeling at the nostrils. I textured the lips the way I always did, with a drizzling of slip poked into ridges with a scalpel. With Nene gazing at me, my dents were lopsided and my guidelines needed luting and rescoring. He opened his mouth for me when I put the sculpture down, leaned over, and smeared the slip from one corner of his upper lip to the other. Hunger at the sight of his open mouth made me sick of the game, so I closed the gap and kissed him, bringing a black slippery hand first to one cheek and then the other. The clay's taste was disappointingly dusty and chemical, and the breath and gore of his tongue beneath it was delicious.

"How should I best sculpt you?" I said, as he continued to bite and lick at my mouth. "Finish that little lump, or cover you in clay?"

"So that's how you're so good," he murmured.

I seized his thigh in my filthy hand and crawled, pushing him onto his back. "That's why," I said through his yell, "I can't have assistants."

When I looked down and saw the mess I'd made of his

trousers, I felt a pang of regret. I tried to decide whether to apologise, tease, or ask what we'd tell our neighbours.

"Again," Nene said. "Quick. Before they get us for dinner."

I smiled in amazement. "They'll smell me on you."

"It doesn't matter."

"Let me tie the door shut."

"It doesn't matter."

I left black handprints in his hair when I enveloped him, on his waist when I pulled his tunics off, and on his thighs when I unlaced his hose from their belt. With his arms thrown out in the grass, his torso was leather hard, taut between the four canid fangs of his ribcage and hips. I used both of my hands to arc a black outline from corner to corner.

"My guidelines," I muttered.

"For what?" he said.

I plunged my head down into his belly, mouth open.

Nene was soft everywhere, but his belly and thighs were where his softness was ripest. As I kissed, the skin's tautness and film of curly hair made him feel like a peach, made depriving myself of a penetrating bite pure torture. Every sound from the hillside made me turn towards the tent door with his fists tight in my hair, and at the third pause, he arched his belly up against my cheek and whined, "Don't stop." The whine warmed my blood. I moved my kissing to his thighs, waited until his sighs bubbled with voice, and then turned to the door again.

"Please, please, I'm going to die." Nene pressed me with all the flesh which could reach me. His hard sex digging into my throat was not a dagger, but I gasped like it was. There was a thud inside my head, fossil brain falling against fossil bone.

I would make him forget every word except *please.* I would make *please* his curse, his prayer, his hello.

I pushed his hose to his knees and unwound his undershorts as carefully as though the fabric might pull lumps of him out. Naked, his beauty would have boiled off in paint and shivered into powder in clay. It was only fit to be looked at, and then only in flinches. As I grasped his ache, settled us into a strongarmed, burrowing rhythm with my head down on his chest, I made some joke about adjusting the tilt of the head by moving the neck only, some joke about wetting the mouth before you ratchet it wider open, some joke about being aware of the centre of gravity when you change your mind about the bend of the legs, how high they lift into the air. And being careful that the details are grafted on strongly before you start to push, pull, push, pull at them in neurotic dissatisfaction, or they'll slide straight off in your hands.

"But... above all... you must... know when to *stop,*" I gasped into his neck as he convulsed and yelled his last. "You must *order* yourself to stop. I do it by signing my name."

I dashed my wet thumb against my lips, brushed his hair aside, and kissed the curve of his neck.

In the afterglow of a rough, foolish joke, a joke which had robed and crowned us in damning handprints, we fell still in a heavy embrace, his naked body cocooned in my skirts. I wanted to be naked too, not so that he could pleasure me but so that I could squash our bodies into one.

When I stood up and went to wash my hands in my water bucket, Nene held his arms out to me.

"Your turn now," he slurred.

"I just wanted to do you," I said, picking up my scalpel.

His voice turned sad. "Because it makes you feel like a girl."

I tilted my head at the scalpel. "Because I like seeing you greedy."

After two more weeks of fussing, I declared Ciecherella's sculpture finished. As we watched Ersilio and Malacresta carry it down the hill to the crypt to be fired, I muttered to Nene that I was going to make myself stronger, so I wouldn't have to trust others to carry my creations. My belly and back were broad beneath their fat, my calves solid from a lifetime of cliff-climbing, but I wanted arms like Ersilio's.

The graveyard was clear of rubble, imprinted in the centre by the wooden church floor. The first statue in the flat plane of graves, Ciecherella was like the church spire in the razed village.

I had offered Fotena Del Meda a sculpture of her father first. Della Del Meda was not only my first promise to Magmate but my entire promise, and I had made Ciecherella first because I loved her family. She was indulgent, vain, unprofessional.

The Malachetis were animated with ecstasy. Malacresta took to driving his head into the statue's shoulder and turning to grin at it whenever we laughed, as if he was checking she was laughing too. Their parents spent more time hugging and kissing me than they did looking at the statue.

Only Ersilio looked at the statue intently enough to make me fear he'd decide it didn't look like her. He stood as close as he could without standing on the grave, hanging forward on his toes, gazing up through the net of carved hair into the carved eyes which looked over him. I knew Ersilio well enough to know that this was happiness. Since Ciecherella's death, he had expressed happiness in these trances, these rare moments of inattentiveness to the babies' wriggling in his arms. I felt not only that he was on the verge of climbing up onto the pedestal and kissing her but that if he had, she would have come to life and kissed him back.

I had convinced myself that Ciecherella was the reason I couldn't tell Ersilio that Nene and I were lovers. I had convinced myself it would be cruel to burden him with happiness for my love whilst he grieved his.

I had tried not to ponder the possibility that he wouldn't be happy for me. There was an image in the back of my mind of him shouting that he'd told me, *told* me not to take advantage of the victim of my bullying. Another scene, more tangible and somehow more noxious, where he called me Nene's victim instead.

In another scene, we were all Nene's victims—me, Ersilio,

Malacresta, Ciecherella—and in another, those victims of the earthquake were my victims too. No matter how massive or purposeful the crime, I could more easily bear the role of perpetrator than the role of victim.

I knew that a statue for a family I loved less would take less time, but it was with dread that I hauled in Della Del Meda's clay. I scored my measurements, settled on a simple pose with arms grafted to its sides in long sleeves, and then saw Nene slung across the tent doorway, bent at the hip with his arms spread. I decided to sculpt him as a warmup, and hacked Della's head off.

That night, I sat on the table in the tent with Nene's head in my lap and stared at the two sculptures of him. The head I'd made during the jest of the lesson was now a bust, lying on its back with its hair sprawled out in spider-legs. I had spent all day on the new one. Peeled folds into the sleeves in jagged streaks, refined the face and hands until my eyes were cold.

"One's an exercise but two's an interest," I said, stroking Nene's hair.

He staggered up onto his elbows to look, grunted, and toppled back into my lap face-first. "It makes sense you'd sculpt me a lot," he said, muffled. "I'm in here with you all the time."

I chuckled. Nene didn't see the difference between a loving study and a practical one. He didn't see the difference between Ciecherella's hair, sculpted strand by strand as I shivered soaking wet, and Della Del Meda's randomly gouged curls. He didn't see the difference between a pose with delicate arms out in front and delicate skirt flared behind to counteract the weight and a pose hacked in one pillar. He didn't see that my obsession with his beautiful face oozed from every scalpel-cut in a lip, every smiling crease around an eye, every parting between curls forged by a big, protruding ear.

Perhaps nobody else would have noticed either. Perhaps, if nobody looked at Nene closely enough to notice the minuscule jewels of his beauty, nobody would look at my sculptures closely enough to notice that I had.

"I'll get in trouble for wasting clay," I said.

I hacked the two sculptures hollow, waited for them to dry, and then hid them under a white sheet posed as a tablecloth. I used the scooped innards to sculpt him a third time: A full body, swimming with its hair in its eyes and its naked legs drawn up to its chest. Vindicated, I sculpted him a fourth time and then a fifth and then a sixth. I secretly loved the idea of Ersilio or Fotena wondering where the first two had gone, tearing up the sheet, and discovering a tangled dozen.

There came a sunny Saturday, a month into Della's sculpture, when I found myself in charge of a dozen children. They were all older than five, old enough to take care of each other on the beach or in the forest, but they came to the tent to play with Nene, and were crestfallen when they saw he wasn't there. I had sent him to the quarry to ask for more clay.

At last, I looked up from placating the crowd of children and saw him coming up the hill, shining in the sun like a white and gold seashell. When he saw us, he beamed, dropped the burlap bag he was carrying, and ran out of sight, around to the back of the tent.

The first the children saw of him was his hand pushing through the canvas, making a long spire with five points. One by one, they shrieked in glee and ran to grab it. As they leapt up against the wall like cats, the hand arced down and away. It was a game he'd invented to play with them whenever I wanted them kept away from my work. I bear-hugged my statue to hold it steady as they barrelled past in pursuit.

"Nene," I called, "can you come and help me turn, please?"

He didn't hear me. He was shaking the canvas at the side of the tent, the children leaping to grab and shake back. Their laughter was already so hysterical I was worrying about them throwing up.

"Nene," I called again.

Nene stuck his face through the tent canvas, to the

270

children's screaming delight. When he ran back the way he'd come instead of answering me, I muttered, "*Merda,*" and joined the children. That none of them were kicked aside was a lucky coincidence as I lunged at Nene's protruding hands, chased him along the back of the tent. The children's laughter couldn't have grown any more hysterical, so he had no idea I'd joined in until my enormous arms reared out around his shoulders, grabbed him, and yanked him in.

There was a syllable of quiet in the children's laughter as they looked at us. I drew Nene closer. The canvas at my shoulder bulged with the shape of his head.

"I said I need help turning," I said to it. "You can play later."

After that, we grew bolder. I decided that although there was something noxious about announcing we were in love, there was nothing so noxious about being discovered. In front of the children, I let him rest his head on my shoulder as I sculpted, and reach into my pockets for tools. Our beds on the clifftop were separated only by a small stretch of grass—I had made mine on the outskirts and he had made his on the outside—and one night, when he caught my eye and realised I was awake, he sat up and looked over at the Malacheti family.

I knew what he was thinking. Prasede often slept in Malacresta's bed with him. Though they fell asleep demurely side-by-side, they were both restless enough sleepers to wake up entangled, and nobody gave their excuse, that she was soothing him away from nightmares about his sister, any scrutiny.

If I had still cared, I would have told Nene that they were different. Magmate wasn't looking for reasons to shun the brother of the impaled young mother or the butcher who'd ended the animals' suffering. But I didn't care, so I opened my arms, and kissed Nene on the nose as he slid into them. Immediately, I noticed that his chest and face were hotter than usual. His eyes were pale pink, his forehead shiny.

"You've got a fever," I half-mouthed, half-whispered.

I knew he'd assent. What I wasn't expecting was a smile and a croon of, "My lungs are full of embers."

Dread soaked down my spine, pooled around my tailbone.

"Do you feel sick?"

He gazed at me torpidly.

"Faint? What about your heart? Is it going fast?" I fumbled my hand under his tunic and pressed at his bare chest. He threw his head back in pleasure. He didn't want to talk about it. He just wanted me to know.

With his quartz eyes and red staining his nose, he continued as usual in the tent. He ran for clay and water without being asked, chattered and played with the children, and dragged me to his mouth whenever we were alone. Sickness made him kiss in hungry bites and gulps and smear heat onto my skin like it was liquid. One day, as Fotena indicated the shape of her father's beard under the statue's ears, Nene flounced in with a bucket of water. I watched over Fotena's shoulder as he set it on the table, stared at it for a moment and then, like a fairy's victim entranced to drown himself, plunged his whole head down into it. My stomach clenched when I thought he was only cooling his face, but when I saw his throat bobbing and realised he was drinking, I nearly fainted.

Nene tossed his head free, splattering water across the ceiling and down the wall. Fotena gave a grunt of disgust. As he beamed at us, swept the empty bucket off the table, and flounced out of the tent to refill it, she leaned close to my ear and said,

"I don't think I realised just how completely demented he is. I understand why you mind the children, but putting that cumberground in your way was a step too far."

I ground my teeth. I wanted to lambast her, punch her, but Nene would have hated it. There were ways to defend him more gently, tell her he was useful or harmless or pitiful, but they would have clashed with the way I was gazing at

272

his wet face.

By the next week, everyone had noticed that Nene was sick. Pink and manic looked healthier than green and wan, but a change was an excuse to gossip about him. His refusal to lie in from work was neither admirable nor pitiable and was instead irresponsible, the callous exposure of *their* statues and *their* children and *their* sculptor to *his* disease. Fotena stopped visiting the tent, and parents stopped bringing their children. A rift had been chiselled between Magmate and Nene, and I had no desire to teeter on the bridge. I held him, wiped away his sweat, and told him he was going to get better. I was the only one on either side of the rift who would.

We lay in silence one night, surrounded by sleeping neighbours. Nene's belly was pouring heat into mine and I fancied the air around his eyes was shimmering. When I brought my hand to his face to wipe a tear away, he brought both of his hands to mine.

"Tell me if it burns," he said.

How it burned. After the white shock passed, there was a long, red pain which dripped down my neck.

"It burns," I said.

He giggled with his tongue between his teeth and pulled me closer.

A shadow fell over the bed, and Nene looked up past me. "Here," said a voice.

I rolled over. Next to the bed, now kneeling, was Prasede. Her face was blue in the moonlight, and her hair was plaited for bed. She'd been asleep with Malacresta when I'd checked the coast was clear for Nene to lie with me.

She reached over me and laid her hand on Nene's forehead. When I instinctively shuffled out of her way, I saw Malacresta standing behind her, looking at us with his arms crossed. Panic tore through me with friction.

"Madonna santa," Prasede said when she felt the fever. She turned her hand over and offered Nene a wet rag. He let her lay

it on his face, then dragged it down to his neck. From the other hand, she offered a little pile of tan-coloured seeds. "It's coriander. It'll calm your fever. Eat half and put half in Solavita's pocket for later."

"Thank you." Nene tipped the seeds into his mouth. I gave him an uneasy smile as he tried to crunch them up.

"Look at this," Prasede said, nudging me. "Never ask but never say no. What will we do with these quiet boys, hm? At least mine throws a fit when he needs something. Yours? Nothing."

I stared at her, hugging my knees, as she stood to leave. Malacresta followed her to bed without giving us a backwards glance.

I'd fantasised about being discovered. This wasn't being discovered. This was realising we'd been discovered long ago.

Prasede was right. I had to roll over in Nene's arms after he'd fallen asleep, and uncoil the rag from his tightly clenched fist, to see that it was blotched pink. The pink hadn't come from his mouth or nose. It had been sweated and cried. I used the hours I lay awake to convince myself that meant it wasn't blood.

When his fever broke, Nene took me to the beach. Since we'd made love for the first time on the outcrop, we'd learned that the tent was more comfortable, but he was hungry for a cold, slimy rock against his back. He threw his belt and tunics into a rock pool, sank down with a sigh, and wriggled his shoulders like a dog.

It was a clear black night which blended sea and sky, and the ribbons of reflected moonlight on the water looked suspended in the air. As I listened to the waves lapping against the outcrop, I wondered how people who didn't live by the sea dealt with the silence. I didn't imagine that different places made different sounds. Heaving cities, windswept deserts and squalling forests were silent in my head.

Behind me, there was a noise. A noise which scratched a

smarting line down the inside of my cheek. Nene heard it too, and fell still.

"Come down," he said.

He was naked to the waist, where the white pleats of his undershorts swelled from the tan sash of his trousers. His chest and shoulders still wore the red welts of his fever, so bright I thought I could lick them off. Although Ersilio's body was the one I wanted, Nene's body was the one which made me sure being male was what I wanted. I looked more like Ersilio than Nene did, but if I could have sold my soul for Nene's flat chest and spiked throat, I would have. Our love was poisoned by it. Marriage was poisoned by *bride,* sex by *let me wear your skin.*

"Let me wear your trousers," I said.

Nene beamed.

"I've been expecting you to ask for such a long time," he said. "I wouldn't know how to bide my days in a dress."

He unfastened the drawstrings on his belt. I leapt on him, kissed his hands, and pulled his trousers down. I realised as I kissed my way down his legs, which were like wattle-twigs wrapped in red hose, that the trousers weren't going to fit me. Already embarrassed to have asked, I closed my eyes as I put them on.

It wasn't fair. As I pawed with my eyes closed, what I felt were gouts of *woman* overflowing from a membrane of *man.* Ersilio could have put Nene's trousers on for a joke, and the fly gaping open a hand's length and the way they cut his fat thighs and buttocks into four would have made him feel no less masculine.

Bigger trousers would have held me. I was not embarrassed that I didn't fit. I was embarrassed that Nene had seen me want to.

When I opened my eyes and saw him gazing at me—at my blatant desire, at my undone belt—I began to change my mind. As I stepped out of my dress and stuffed the hem of my white chemise into the waistband, I saw that this could be the outfit of a man half-undressed. He'd cast his tunic onto the rocks beside his lover, and undone his trousers to relieve the aching appendage that was his sex.

"How do I look?" I said.

Nene gave me a gibbous smile. "Vain."

"Vain?"

"Vanity becomes you."

When he opened his legs, hunger pulsed between mine. I knew he'd done it subconsciously. He wasn't deducing which poses might make me feel masculine. Nene didn't think in deductions.

I grinned like a mad thing and fell on him. He cried out and threw back his head. When I hoisted his legs around my waist, he locked his ankles together and wrenched, pushing my hips down against his.

Nestled between his thighs with his hands in my hair, I fell still for a moment. I wanted to sleep like this, I thought, instead of stomach-to-back, keeping watch for witnesses.

Nene keened, and his ribcage kicked me hard in the face. There would be ten thousand nights for sleeping. We would have our own bed soon. Our own curtains to draw around it. Our own house.

"I have no idea what I'm doing," I said, and thrust up against him with my hips. He dug his nails into my scalp, scratched me down to my neck.

As I ground against him in a rhythm, my mouth open in the curve of his shoulder, his hands went down between our bellies and started scratching. I pushed down against his knuckles, put pressure on the bone between my breasts. Our toothy frenzy slowed into sucks, gasps and drags. As hunger swelled my brain out of shape, I tossed his legs around in indecision. My legs around him were the solution to the burn of arousal below my belly, but his legs around me were the cause. With his head thrown back to moan, I was the only one who saw the flutter in his chest.

I planted my hands, stilled my hips. It was like something under his skin had pinched it up by one corner, braced its elbow against the sternum bone, and given a twitch. I remembered the kick against my face, the way he'd been scratching himself.

"Nene, Nene."

"It's just fever," he said, seizing my head in his hands. The blight reared up again above his nipple, and with wide eyes and open mouth, I followed it.

It wasn't in his skin. It had free reign to duck away from the plane and retreat into his belly. When it breached again, Nene said, "Oh, yes, yes," and ground me down harder. I bit at it as it burrowed away, fastened my teeth around his rib. "I missed your mouth so much, *fuoco mio;* I'm so glad I'm better," he said. I opened my mouth to tell him he wasn't better and dragged it down his belly to his sex. Took a mouthful of his undershorts, stopped to think. And the thing inside him pressed its full flank against the swell of fat around his navel, allowed me, for a moment, to see its shape.

Pitching the white canvas of his skin, five perfect finger-points.

Nene's legs bent up around my head.

I pressed my hand against the skin. I thought about Ersilio slapping the surface of the water to make the fish jump up.

"Don't make me beg," Nene said. "I will."

I looked up at him from between his thighs, my mouth open. I could have asked him. Did he know? Could he feel? And since he did and he could, what kind of monster would deny his request for relief?

I bared my teeth between his legs. "If you tell me you will beg, I will make you," I said.

"Please."

"Please what?"

"Fuck me like a man. With your hand. Until I can't think. Until I'm knocked out."

I moaned, low and starved, his plea nefarious in vague

shape through a red fog of pleasure. I pushed his shorts aside with the flat of my hand, penetrated him with one finger, then two.

"Oh, sweet *fire!*" Nene laughed. "You could burn the blight from every mite of me."

"Could I?" I said. "And would that make you better?"

He moaned for three pushes, the sound high and skittering. Then he said, "It would make me... bigger."

There was another movement on the surface of his belly. His hands moved to trap it.

"That is your hand!" he snickered. "All the way inside me! It's not deep enough yet."

"What?" I said, stilling my arm.

He stared at me. There was a pink ring around each of his eyes, like a soreness which shimmered.

"I like it," he said quietly.

"You like what?"

He blinked, confused. One of his eyes turned red.

"I like it," he said again.

I rolled my eyes and resumed. My arm ached, but it was my favourite kind of ache: the ache from giving. Nene thought I didn't care about my own pleasure because I had the wrong kind of sex, but if I could have fucked him with my sex, I would have done it to watch him be fucked. He lifted his hips on the ratchet of my hand, stretched his arms out around his head. One of his legs rested on its calf on my shoulder and the other kicked at my back, making me feel like I was sparring underwater with a huge red starfish. His head rolled on the rocks, spilling his hair to one side. When he spoke again, it was in a gurgling trance. "*Fuoco mio,* towering Devil, heat in my blood, hands which hollow me in my sleep..."

"Nene..."

"Faster, faster! Hollow me! Split me in two! In twenty! Unspool me to my blackest fibres!"

"Nene!"

He climaxed. His wail was glottal and unary, a waterfall in a cave. His thighs slammed shut around my head, and if they hadn't, the arch of his back might have broken his neck. Still working, I opened my jaws against his knee and bit hard. He rolled his head and gaped at me with a pink tear running across his nose.

Up in his belly crested a twitch. Two peaks, like the pectoral and dorsal fins of a rolling shark.

"I thought you were asking me to make it stop," I said. "To make you forget about it."

He smiled at me like a drunk.

"You... what... you want me to make it worse? You think I'm making it worse?"

I dragged myself from him, went to dash my hands clean in the sea. When I turned to face him again, he was still lying there on his back. He hadn't moved since we'd arrived. Only his head had followed me. Glazed eyes and terrible smile.

"You're frightening me," I said.

Nene opened his arms. "Hold me."

I crawled over, lay on top of him with my whole weight. I went face-first into the crook of his neck, and he nestled kisses into my hair.

"It just frightens me," I said. "You only say what you want when I want it too. What if you're frightened? If you're in pain? If you don't really see me as a man? If you're miserable about the way those prats in the village talk about you..." I extracted my head from his neck.

"I would never lie to you," Nene said.

"Then maybe I just... can't bear that you don't care. I care so much, Nene." I brought my hand to his face, to wipe the pink tears away. "I *broke your ankle,* Nene. I tried to *slit your throat.*"

Grinning, Nene seized my hand, which was still on his cheek, and brought it to his lips. He looked straight into my eyes as he kissed my palm, but it took me a moment to understand. He was kissing the burn scar he'd given me. When he pressed his mouth to the scar on the ditch of my elbow, I discovered a new favourite place to be kissed.

I pulled back and crawled down his legs. Closing my eyes, I pictured the night I'd knocked him down in the street. Left ankle. Left.

I lifted his socked leg into the air before I kissed it. He beamed.

"We ought to tell the builders," I said, kissing my way up his calf, "that we only need one house."

His eyes widened. He understood immediately that I was asking him to marry me.

"There's no church," he said.

"I know!" I bounded back to lie on him. "We could be the first Godless wedding."

"Who would witness us?"

"Prasede and Malacresta and Ersilio."

Nene's bafflement only deepened. "But you'll have to be a *bride*."

"Why? What if you put flowers in your hair and walk down the aisle to me?"

"But if they make you…"

"Then I will." Nene continued to stare at me. "There's nothing I wouldn't do to share a hearth and a warm, dry bed with you."

Realising, perhaps fearing, that I was serious, he cracked an uneasy smile.

"I like this game," he said. "What else will we do at our wedding?"

"Oh, you think it's a game?" I leapt to my feet. "I'm going to climb up the cliff and wake the whole village up shouting that I'm going to marry you." I held out my hands. "Come on. I'm tired. I want an official blessing to sleep in your bed before sunset."

Nene looked at my hands, and didn't take them.

"I can't," he said quietly.

"You can't? Why not?"

"Because I'm stuck."

Dread filled my throat. At his tone, not his words.

"What do you mean, you're stuck?"

Nene twitched his shoulders as if to sit up. Something seemed to grab him, maybe around the neck, and hold him there.

"Che cazzo?" I threw myself down and crushed my face into the seaweed, trying to see the fissure he was lying on. I saw a narrow shadow which attached his shoulder to the rock. When I thrust my hand underneath him to feel it, he squirmed and gasped.

"Does it hurt?" I said.

"Does it bleed?" he said.

My hand was slick and hot.

I climbed on top of him on my knees, wrapped my arms around his waist, and pulled. His eyes bulged, and he clawed at his throat. His shoulder didn't budge.

I wanted to slam his head to and fro and scream at him. Why hadn't he told me? How long had he been stuck? But I knew. I remembered the sound of something scraping against the rock, the way he'd frozen when he felt it. The moment he lay down.

I dropped him, got up, and ran from him towards the jetty. As I sprinted past the cliff path, I realised I hadn't told him where I was going. I turned back, hunched and panting, and yelled, "I'm getting a knife!"

I reached the jetty with the waistband of Nene's trousers cutting into me like wire. I leapt down into Ersilio's coracle, threw aside the nets which carpeted the floor, and snatched up the first knife I saw. It looked newly hewn, with a driftwood handle and serrated obsidian blade.

As I jogged back to Nene, I said, in one heaving breath, "Please-don't-melt-this-it's-another-of-Ersilio's."

Then, I saw him properly. There were tears pouring down his face. Tears as red as cherries, two from each eye.

"I thought you left me," he said. "I didn't hear what you said when you ran off."

"I said I was getting a *knife,*" I snapped, nauseous at the thought. "I just asked you to marry me! How could you think I'd *leave?*"

I straddled him again, and dug the knife into the gap between the protrusion and the rock.

I pulled him upward again and again. I wrapped my spare hand around the protrusion, trying to pull him up away from it. Then, I heard the scraping noise again, and the protrusion came free with him. He flopped over my shoulder face-first, caped with seaweed.

At first, as I blinked down at his shoulder, I still thought the thing sticking out of it had come up through the fissure and stabbed into him. There were plenty of bones on this beach, gull bones, splintered and rotted sharp. Malacresta had once cut his foot on one.

Out of Nene's shoulder stuck two sheaves of bone, as thick as forearm bones. Like maggots they coiled, yellow-white and newborn, in a wound like a round red rock pool. They seemed to arc from beneath the shelf of his shoulder blade, and I imagined the agony of them rutting against it, trying to find a way around it.

"Do you feel better?" I said weakly.

Nene threw his head back and laughed.

The laughter was red, thumping, cavernous. The moment he started, I wanted to pin him down and shove my fist into his mouth to make him stop. I didn't realise he was laughing because it wasn't over until his belly kicked me hard in the ribs. He gurgled, jerked like a corpse with something jerking inside it, and threw himself down onto his back. Even as I saw that his whole torso had swollen into an oblong, the skin stretched transparent over something blue and purple which swirled beneath it, I wondered miserably whether lying on his back was hurting his shoulder. His hand slithered over his thighs, holding Ersilio's knife. I didn't know whether he'd taken it from the floor or straight from my hands. Thick, dark blood swelled between his smiling teeth and ran up his cheeks, bisecting the tear tracks.

Nene gutted himself in a quick slash and out of him exploded a wing.

I tried to scream and tried to gasp at once, and my throat knotted shut and was silent. Wanting to spring forward to help him and backward to escape him left me sitting up on my heels, unmoving. The wing was as tall as a wall beam, with feathers as long as our arms, and it was saturated with blood which in the silver-grey night glistened black. It stood bolt upright in the sky, twisted backward on a broken spine, strange fractures which jammed the feathers into lattices like bonfire twigs. Garlanded around the wing and pooling on the rocks around us were black eels too smooth to be feathers. They were Nene's intestines.

I knew that the death of a loved one was something which took time to dawn. I didn't have the thought that such a thing would kill a person until I heard him laughing.

When I crawled under the arch of feathers and flesh, over the edge of the outcrop hung his head, upside-down and with the smile of blood still on its cheeks. He answered to his name with a moan, an open-mouthed, "Ha...ah!" and if he had wanted to soothe me, he would have answered my, "Does it *hurt?*" with a promise that yes, it did.

CHAPTER 19

THE MONSTER

AND I DIDN'T FEEL THE TIME PASS as I stood in the water under the outcrop, cradling Nene's upside-down head, staring at the thing which slithered in the sky. I didn't feel the difference between pleasure, stupor and horror in Nene's moaning, even when he put his hand against the wet black spine of the wing and followed it into the geode of his belly. *Stop, stop it,* I thought without emotion as he shoved his arm inside himself to the elbow. He shoved up, as if reaching into the opposite armpit, and when the marshy sliding and popping sounds of parting membranes paused, the pierced shoulder and wing juddered as one.

"Yes," he said in his blood-bubbling voice. "It's the same wing."

Like a baby in breech. It had forced out a joint bent back on itself and had to be cut out.

I didn't feel surprised that Nene had lived with his innards in a flower above him and I didn't feel sick as I put my elbows on the rock shelf and said, "Do you want me to fetch your guts down, *dolcezza?*"

He smiled. "Yes please."

I kissed his cheek and climbed out of the water.

I stalked around the wing—thrawn like a rag, taller than me, fruiting with gore—and shivered only when I looked down and saw Nene's red-hosed legs fidgeting their heels together. When I reached up and shook loose the first loop of gut, he jerked, making the wing jerk with him. I could only imagine it felt like being constipated. There was nothing to signal to his head that the cramping belly was in the sky.

The guts slunk down into my arms like molluscs. The smell of bovine gas and blood was white at the edges with sweetness. As I piled them up, I noticed the perforations of rot in the flesh. Small, precise nicks. I tried to remember the last time he'd eaten.

Nene tried to stretch his belly open for me, but the flesh blistered aside by the wing was blue and hard, already calcified in its crumpled rings. I pushed his guts in coil by coil. He rolled his head and scratched his neck with his blood-mired arm and I didn't feel like I was hurting him.

All I felt was that we hadn't been discovered. We were immune to discovery, Nene and I, wiped from existence by tent walls and thin blankets. Whether for our sake or for theirs, if a neighbour had come onto the beach or peered down from the cliff, the sea would have moved to conceal us.

When sunrise turned the sea bronze, and I realised he wasn't going to die, I said, "Let's go to the tent."

He nodded vigorously.

I leaned down and nuzzled his scrunched nose with mine. Laughter burst from both of us at once.

Nene rolled onto his side and let the weight of the wing drag him into the sea. We held him down in the water until the blood blossomed out, then dragged him up the cliff. We tried to wrap the wing around him, but it was so badly broken that it only bent far enough to drag on the ground behind him. Nene couldn't move it like a limb. It was a dead weight.

As I helped him down through the forest, I thought about how I'd promised to shout my love for him to the whole camp. Now that it was help I needed instead, not even a prybar could have opened my mouth.

The moment we reached the tent, I fell to the floor and started clearing sculptures out from under the table. I didn't tell Nene why I was doing it. I turned at last, and saw him panting against the wall. I had fenced him with sculptures of himself. Heads with open mouths and stupid eyes and scrunched noses, busts propped on their hands, bodies floating and lying.

When the blood had washed out of the wing, I had thought the feathers were white feathers dark with water or stains, but now they were drying in the light of dawn, I could see that they were the same golden colour as his hair.

"I wanted to see," I said, offering him a shaking hand, "if you'd fit. Under the table. To hide."

Nene stood, flopped first forward onto the wing's gnarled back and then sideways into my arms. The enormous weight, yellow tufts and wet stink put me in mind of carrying a sheep. We bent the wing to his back, I pulling to alleviate the weight on his shoulder, he shoving without care, and rolled him under the table. It was a tight fit. When I fell in on top of him, I was crushed up against the tabletop.

As we lay there, I registered my own mania. Mania had made hiding him from the village seem like a next step, rather than a choice.

"Prasede... knows..." I said in a drunken drag.

Nene understood that I was proposing telling her. He widened his eyes.

"About us," I added. "Not about you."

He smiled.

"I know. I'm sorry. Just thinking. They see you're... even *of* God and you're dead."

Nene threw his head back. "No," he said lucidly. "They are."

286

I tossed my shoulders, making tools and buckets topple above us. Nene giggled.

"This is stupid," I said. "I'm making you a bed."

"A bed?"

I lifted the table clean off him. "What, you'd live under the table when you've got a whole tent? Does it hurt?"

I asked him again and again that day. As he lolloped determinedly back and forth in the tent. *"Does it hurt?"* As he tried to decide between cradling the wing at his belly or dragging it behind him, pulling it shut like a lid over the crater. *"Does it hurt either way?"* As I hauled hay and blankets off the cliff to make him a bed, begged him to tell me how to arrange them to support him. *"Does it hurt if you lie on your back? Your side? Your front?"* I eventually made an L-shaped bed, one arm for him, a nest in the middle for the wing, and another arm for me to lie perpendicular. That was the only thing he seemed worried about. How I was going to hold him.

Before I lay down to sleep, I pulled the table over the wing to cover it. Then, I stretched my legs out and pulled it into my lap. As I gave it long, slow strokes, Nene sighed dreamily.

"You can feel it?"

"Like having my hair petted."

"But you can't move it?"

He closed his eyes, focused for a moment, then shook his head.

I gently scratched the golden feathers along the wing's spine. The arrangement of bone beneath them felt like a forearm. Two joists with a well in the middle.

"There's something not right about it, don't you think?" I said.

Nene yawned. "Beyond the fact I can't feel it and it's coming out of my stomach?"

"That it... I don't know. It feels incomplete. Just bones and feathers. And it's heavier than you."

"Like the bones aren't hollow."

"What?"

"You remember Malacresta told us bird bones are hollow so they can fly."

I looked down at the wing.

"Yeah," I murmured. "It's like when scars feel like they're made of fingernail. Just your bones, and your hair. Maybe it wasn't made to fly. Maybe it was just... made."

As I lay on my arm of the bed, scratching Nene's hair from behind, I saw that the bones protruding from his shoulder were now surrounded by a purple keloid.

His other shoulder was purple too, with a swelling that looked like the same wound in a later stage of healing. I knew it was really the opposite.

I knew he'd felt it, and decided not to say anything. Before the dread of sleeping in the path of a second explosion, of double the volume under the table, double the weight in my arms, I felt a rush of fondness.

The second wing grew tentative and correct. It was a violet tumour at first, smooth and hot against my face when I held Nene from behind. It grew on his shoulder with such rapidity that the pores stretched into slits and the first barbs of feather dropped out onto the pillow. Then, it was a shivering golden animal. Curled into a ball and slowly sitting up on its haunches, craning its head. After a month, Nene looked, on his side on the bed, like a golden whirlpool. One upside-down wing arcing down from his belly and one arcing up from his back.

All month, I worked in a dogged trance on Della Del Meda's statue. Nene's fever had chased away most visitors before the wing burst out, rendered the tent hostile enough that keeping the door shut kept out the last. Ersilio asked me if I was fleeing my mother as I hauled my bed down the cliff and Prasede asked me the next week if Nene had told me where he was going, but I was allowed to make a recluse of myself. Knowing that a wordless ban wouldn't last, I devised a lie.

It was sunset when I went to Fotena Del Meda and told her

that the statue of her father was finished and waiting on the hillside. Unfortunately, I said, as I was sure she'd noticed, I had closed my tent to visitors, because Nedda De Aqvancis had pulled down a tablecloth with knives on it and nearly skewered herself, and I didn't want her to feel excluded because she was blind, so now everybody was excluded. Fotena didn't care. She just wanted to see her father.

It was dusk when I went to the Del Vaccas, the mother and father who'd lost their little boy Pippo in the earthquake, and told them I'd like to see to their gravestone next. I had chosen the child strategically, to create the largest, most sensitive crowd to give my warning. It would be monstrous to ask a sculptor what he's hiding in his out-of-bounds tent whilst there's a wailing parent on each of his shoulders.

It was nightfall when I found Ersilio, sitting in his coracle with his babies, and asked him to help me carry Della's statue into the crypt to be fired. As we walked up the cliff, I whispered that I'd told the village a huge fat lie about Nedda to keep the ankle-biters and old hags from annoying me while I worked. He snickered, and told me he'd keep my secret. But of course he couldn't come in either, I said. I'd already raised eyebrows by sculpting Ciecherella first. I couldn't be caught favouring him again.

The truth came up like bile with every silence as I walked with Ersilio and with every exhale as I stood in the crypt, gazing from the kilns to the mossy floor above.

There's an angel in my tent.

The force that shook down Magmate stuck on his back.

Come do unto him as he did unto you.

It was midnight when I untied the door of the tent, looking to and fro along the cliff to check I wasn't being watched, and was greeted by the sight of Nene beaming at me from the bed. He was propped up on his side, with each wing extended flat along the floor.

"You shouldn't lean on your elbow like that," I said as I

double-knotted the door. "It's pulling on you, isn't it?"

Nene tilted his head to one side.

I narrowed my eyes. "What's funny? Why are you smiling?"

Still balancing on his elbow, Nene held his hands up, and then crossed them over each other like a choir conductor. Both golden wings—first the shoulder, then the belly—lifted at their ends, braced on their elbows.

They fanned slightly aloft for a few seconds, then lay back down on the grass.

My mouth fell open. Nene giggled.

"My back can't carry them, but they can carry themselves. Wave back."

I shook my head slowly.

"Wave *back.*"

I sighed and lifted my hands in a wave.

I was terrified that my friends would bypass my new boundary on the assumption that they were exceptions, but, as my friends, they treated it with even more delicacy. Whenever one of them shouted for me from outside the tent, I emerged to find them standing in place at the bottom of the hill, as though that was my doorstep. The closest call came from a group of men crashing past on their way to the forest. When two of them raised their voices in a jovial argument, Nene and I froze and looked at each other, and when one of them fell hard into the side of the tent, ripping up the peg in one corner, Nene's wings flinched from the ground in fright.

"Sorry, Signora De Gasinis!" someone shouted.

A pair of hands appeared between the flapping canvas and the ground, groping close to Nene's wing. I stormed over and kicked at them until they receded.

"If your fucking around squashes a statue of a murdered little boy, you'll be the one apologising to his parents!" I yelled.

"Geez, I'm sorry."

"With more emotion than that!"

My rage stilled when I saw Nene's smile. What broke my

heart infinitely more than the knowledge he missed our neighbours was the knowledge they didn't miss him. I had designed all my lies to explain my own absence, not his, and I had been right.

One morning, I went up onto the cliff to make an appearance and saw Ersilio acting strangely on the beach. He was alone, with Lagia and Nedda playing in the sand a few paces away from him. There was a boulder in his arms, not a gabbro boulder from the beach but one of the white bricks from the old church. As I walked down the cliff, he carried the boulder ten paces one way, set it down, sat on it for a spell, then carried it back to where he'd started.

When I was close enough, I saw that his beard and thick forearm hair were beaded with sweat, and his tunic was soaked under both armpits.

"What the hell are you doing?" I said.

Ersilio put the white boulder down with a wheeze. "I've got to exercise somehow. Those clowns banned me from helping build my house. My own house."

"That's because it's meant to be a gift for you."

"Well, what do they want me to do instead? Sit on my arse playing pat-a-cake? I'm getting fat and feeble already, look."

It wasn't a delusion. In the months since I'd finished Ciecherella's statue, Ersilio had gained fat and lost muscle. His belly hung over his trousers and the cheeks above his beard were rounder and gentler.

"Fate wants you cuddly," I said. "It saw that you were now a sofa for babies and resolved to make you look like one."

"I'm not a fucking *sofa*. I'm Ersilio De Aqvancis. I'm manly and mean. I'll punch you for looking at me." To punctuate his disgust, he got up and heaved the boulder back into his arms.

"Go back to fishing, then," I said as he staggered away with the boulder. "It kept you strong for ten years."

He ignored me. Everyone in the village, including the other fishers, knew why Ersilio had stopped going fishing. Because he couldn't plop his daughters down, close at hand, on the floor of his boat.

"How long have you been lifting?" I said.

"I'm going to do it every day."

"When did you start? Today?"

Ersilio glowered at me.

"I'm not bullying you. I'm asking if you need a partner. I want to get strong too. We can make each other do it."

"I don't need you to make me do it. I'm motivated by purpose. *Noble* purpose."

"Then I will best you, also, in the nobility of my purpose."

It took us an hour to realise that carrying boulders back and forth was not good exercise. I came out of it with only my hands and feet hurting. Over the weeks, we devised repetitions of squats, lifts and passes that made us burn along our arms and backs, burn like we were dying. The ever-present toddlers were kept in hysterics, Lagia by our prancing and Nedda by our wheezing.

For the first month, I lay with Nene in the evenings in agony. My hands shook when I sculpted and helped him move his wings. But the intensity of exercise required to induce the agony increased. Neither Ersilio nor I grew thinner. We grew muscles on our arms and bellies which made our fat solid and dented like hammered copper. If anything, we looked fatter, and we didn't care, because we were stronger.

The sculpture of Pippo Del Vacca crawled towards completion. I ran out of clay before I added the hands to his flung-out arms, and fiddled away at his doublet as I wondered what to do. I hollowed him out to an inch of thickness, scraped shreds from the curls of his hair, and then turned, as Nene watched from the floor, towards the table which contained all my sculptures of him.

"What's the matter?" he said.

"I need more clay," I said quietly. "I promised the parents I'd finish tonight. I'm scared they'll come in if I don't."

"So go and get more!"

"I'm scared they'll *come in,* Nene."

As I looked at him, I noted again how quickly his wings were growing. Each was three times his length, and the healthy one lay flat on the grass all the way to the wall. The broken one often spasmed and struck the walls and ceiling. I lay awake at night worrying that they'd slide under the walls and be seen.

He still couldn't carry them. The wings bent and straightened on their elbows at his will, but only their spines were designed for their weight. His spine was not. He couldn't lie down fully, choosing every night between lying on his back with the belly-wing twisting in its keloid and on his side with it pulling against his back. For the delirium caused by his sleeplessness I was grateful, as I was sure it was dulling his despair. We had made love three times in four months: on our sides, with three hands yanking back on his belly, to stop the wings from rearing up into the tent roof when he climaxed, and in the dark, to stop our neighbours from seeing a shadow-puppet play of an eagle being strangled by a snake. Nene's pleasure had always served us both, but it now served us chiefly with mutual exhaustion.

He didn't eat. Whenever I tried to ply him with food, he gestured sleepily to his middle, where the organs lay blanketed only by shadow in the chasm between the wing and the keloid, and said something which started with, "Nowhere."

"I'll keep this one," I said, lining the sculptures up next to my water bucket. I was cradling the first one I'd ever made, the bust with the perfect profile. "And this one." A lounging full body with tentacular legs.

Nene struggled to his feet, dragged his wings with hissing breaths, and threw himself upon a third. It was the one of him swimming with his hair floating. "*This* one."

"Three's good." I turned to the rest. "Let's do it quick."

"Why can't you spoil them one at a time? Take the clay out in little pieces?"

I tilted his miserable face and kissed his nose. "*Dolcezza,* you know that would look much more frightening."

Together, we hydrated the dozen sculptures until they melted. Nene was soon laughing as he pounced to flatten stubborn faces and protruding limbs. Only when all traces of him were gone from the vat of clay did his misery crawl back.

Soon afterwards, as Ersilio and I exercised, I realised what his 'noble purpose' really was. Malacresta brought Lagia and Nedda onto the beach, set them down, and told them to "Run to Papa." Ersilio picked up Nedda first, now two years old and learning to walk, and, as was the nature with siblings, Lagia crashed into his leg and yelled to be picked up too. He often preached to me the vitality of treating the girls equally, no matter that Nedda's need was greater.

I watched Lagia warily as we finished our exercises. I didn't know whether four was old enough to sense secrecy in such innocuous words as,

"Are you free to help me with something tonight?"

Ersilio looked at me with both toddlers holding handfuls of his hair. "What kind of something?"

"I need to take something heavy into the water. I want you to dock your sailboat by the path at high tide and help me carry it down."

"A statue?" he said with a frown.

"Sort of."

The night was a teal, buzzing one. Nene could tell that I was scheming something, ducking out of the tent door every time I heard a noise, but I couldn't bear to tell him I'd betrayed him even a minute early. I fought the urge to turn and ask how bad his pain and delirium were, to confirm the betrayal was justified. But Nene was as allergic to *It hurts* as I was to *I love you.* I could only pray it hurt as much as I loved him.

When Ersilio appeared at the bottom of the hill, I gasped and slammed the tent flap shut.

"What's wrong?" Nene sat up. "Is someone coming?"

"It's Ersilio," I said, with tears welling in my eyes.

"Is he coming this way?"

"I hope. I asked him to."

"You what?"

I ran out of the tent and crashed into Ersilio. The door fell shut behind me.

"*Merda!*" Ersilio sloughed off his shock. "The boat's on the rocks. I moored it on a plank, so we'll have to be quick."

"Ersilio." I was crying now, terror bubbling green in my throat. "I need to tell you what we're carrying, before you see."

Ersilio's face fell. He seemed to instantly marry my words to the banning of visitors from the tent. Perhaps even to the disappearance of Nene.

"What have you done?" he said quietly. "Have you killed someone?"

From between my sobs burst a cough: "HA!" Ersilio jumped, and I hissed, "If I'd killed someone, why would I need your arms and your big boat?"

"I don't know," Ersilio said soberly. "Because you were scared?"

I realised then that if I had killed someone, he would have helped me.

I slammed my face into his shoulder and wailed, "Oh, I am! I am!"

"Just show me. Don't tell me. I'm prepared."

"I need to prepare him too," I said, and ran back into the tent.

Nene was standing up now. "Is he gone?"

I squatted and wrapped my arms around his belly-wing. "Can I lift this?"

Nene, in his confusion, managed to curl the wing into my arms a little. "Support the bottom, where it bends."

I slid my arms down around the wing's golden elbow. I formed a shadow of a plan: If I could manage the bulk of the wing, from the elbow to the end, Nene could manage the rest.

But as I lifted, grunting and sobbing with the effort, Nene only stared at me. "What's happening?" he said.

I spasmed and put the wing down.

"I called... Ersilio... to help me carry you. You know we've been lifting weights together."

Nene liked my new muscles. He hated that I was trapped with him and was pleased I had a hobby, and he liked the way they made me look, broad and firm and of the outside. I had never told him I had wanted them so I could carry him.

"You did what?" Nene said. "Carry me where? I don't want to go outside."

"Yes you *do,* Nene," I said, trying again to lift the wing. "You ache for it. Day and night for half a year you have ached for it. And you can't sleep in here with the weight of them, the pain. We're going to take you out in Ersilio's boat and float you in the sea, and you're going to sleep there."

Nene pushed the wing out of my arms.

"You lifted rocks on the beach for half a year so I could have one night of sleep?"

He was staring at me with crumpled eyes and a kidney-bean mouth, a breath away from sobbing. It wasn't quite love. It was horror at the size of my love. It was self-loathing.

"It doesn't have to be one night," I said. "I'll hold you there for as long as you want."

Nene cried out and collapsed on his side. When I knelt and tried to hold him, he thrust out his arm and hit me away. It was this scene that Ersilio, tired of pacing outside at my disposal, walked into the tent and saw.

Nene saw him first. He seemed to feel him even before that, stiffening in my arms and lowering his arms from his face. As we looked at him, Nene gazing up, I glowering over my shoulder, from inside the golden nest of wings, none of us were afraid. I was angry, and I thought that Ersilio and Nene were dreaming of the first time they'd seen each other. Standing on the pew, sticking his face out from the blankets.

296

Or perhaps Ersilio was wondering whether one of his daughters could have gone missing for six months without him noticing.

"He's been in here all along," said Ersilio dully.

I got up. "It wasn't safe to tell anyone."

"Because these are…" Ersilio stalked, upright and unsteady, down the side of the tent, and nudged at the back-wing with his foot. "…attached to him."

"They're attached to him like tumours," I said, "meaning his back can't support them. It's like his body decided to make wings for some reason, but all it had was heavy bones and hair, so they just lie there… and he can't sleep… I wanted him to sleep in the ocean."

"Are they getting bigger?" Ersilio said.

"Yes—When the first one grew, it was only about—"

"Look at me when you ask questions about me," Nene said from the floor. "And when you answer them for me."

Finally, with a lockjawed, burning effort, Ersilio and I managed to lift Nene's wings between us. We waddled sideways through the tent flap one at a time. Nene walked with the strain of shame in his throat and cheeks. Ersilio and I had the greater weight to handle, but it was Nene who tired first, swooning into our arms at the top of the cliff. It took an hour to get him to the boat. I told Ersilio to take us out past the cove, somewhere Nene could spread his wings and I could stand in the water and hold him. Nene lay in my arms as Ersilio sailed, stared up into my grinning kisses with stunned eyes.

As Nene submerged himself, Ersilio clung to one wing from the prow and I the other from the stern, slowing his descent just enough to prevent a capsize. The boat gave a thrash when we let the wings go, and I threw myself into the water after him. As I put my arms around him, relief creased his entire face. He lay curled on his side in his red hose, with the wings around him in a green cyclone.

"Do you still feel the weight?" I said, a disguised *Does it hurt*.

"No. Just the pull. I have never... I can't believe..."

He was already falling asleep.

"*Dolcezza mia,* I will hold you," I said. "I will hold you here if you sleep for a decade. If you die here, I will hold you until you are seafoam. I will never let you go."

I kissed him again and again until his eyes listed shut.

Ersilio watched from the boat with his arms folded, slowly shaking his head. It appeared that he found the kissing a greater abomination than the wings.

"*Dolcezza mia,*" he scoffed.

I wiped a tear off my face. "Sweetness is better than Bread Roll and Chicken." Those were his nicknames for his daughters.

"*Dente di lione.*"

"What?"

He coiled the anchor rope around his arm. "I called Ciecherella Dandelion."

My feet turned blue and my hands shrivelled into plastercloth for the ten hours Nene slept, but his fever kept my belly warm. I thought all the while about how little I knew about God. Maybe Nene was designed to die on his first night of peaceful sleep. Maybe I'd washed out of him the last shred of fight. Through me went the terror that I might not know whether he'd died, that I might hold his corpse and force Ersilio to wait for days, weeks, years, never sure enough to let him sink.

But he woke up, reached his green arms around me out of the water like a siren.

As I hauled him back into the boat, a horse's weight in sodden feathers trussed around my upper body, something moved against the crook of my elbow. Only once Nene was lying in the boat could I flatten the wing against my lap, splay apart the feathers, and uncover new tissue. It wasn't more wing. It was a cream-coloured, slimy snake, a strange hybrid of the feathers and the guts that had come out with them.

299

With relief too thick in my head for terror to pierce, I clawed along the length of the wing. I found another coil on its elbow, a third pressed against his belly. Poking down, I found that the tentacles had ends, notched white points like earthworms' heads.

Nene watched me placidly.

"There are more inside me," he said. "I can move them."

I slammed my head down into the wing. "Oh, what have we done?"

"They didn't grow because of the sea. I don't think. It's just because of the sea that they look like that."

"Because the wing felt the seawater? Because it went into the wound?" I groped, trying to feel the tentacles' roots. "Are they growing out of the wing?"

Nene threw his head back and said with pleasure, "Maybe they'll push the wings out of me."

I ran down the side of the boat. We were almost at the shore, and I wanted the sails to hide our conversation from Nene. "We can't take him back to the tent," I said.

"I know," Ersilio said. "He's going to knock it down."

"He's going to *swallow* it."

I thought. Somewhere large, solid, and sealed. Somewhere nobody would go, somewhere their sensibilities forbid. Somewhere over which I had jurisdiction, like I'd had over the tent. I made a show of thinking because I'd known the answer since I'd fired my last statue, and I dreaded it.

In the middle of the graveyard, the church floor, shielded along its front edge by the steps, lay under rugs of gabbro dust and runners of dandelions. The stone stairs which led down into the crypt were narrow and low-ceilinged, and it was with unanswered apologies that we crammed Nene down them with his wings crushed against his body.

The crypt, cut into the gabbro hillside and armoured with grey bricks, was three houses long, three houses wide and three houses deep. My first breath of the underground air brought me

300

my favourite rain-and-stone smell, but the following breaths were drier and sweeter. Nene closed his eyes as I laid him on the stone floor, and I wasn't sure whether he was relieved by his long sleep or the total cold.

I left him there and went up to Ersilio. He was at the top of the stairs, swinging the open trapdoor back and forth by its brown iron ring.

He had looked at me all night, and he looked at me now, like he was one blink away from slamming me into a wall and crushing my throat in his hands.

"So what is he?" he said calmly.

I could have lied. I could have told him Nene had a disease, was a witch, was a fairy. But Ersilio knew when I was lying, and I would rather have watched him sob at the truth than cling to a lie.

"Of God," I said. "He might be God."

"Did he kill my wife?"

With almost imperceptible smallness but almost frantic speed, I nodded.

"Is that why you hid him? To keep him safe from... me?"

I had pictured it. Ersilio murdering Nene. My mind couldn't make him meaner than he was when he played with his daughters, shouting *"Rar-rar-rar,"* and pretending to gnaw on their legs.

Malacresta incensed but ineffectual. Prasede lethal but passionless. The imagined mob strong enough to paint the tent walls with blood, mine and then their own, didn't have familiar faces.

"No. He's got a power which prevents him from being hurt. He wouldn't mean to, just like he didn't mean to send the earthquake, but he'd... kill anyone who tried to kill him."

"Like his mother?"

"Ersilio, please." I seized his hand. "He doesn't want to do harm. He just wants to lie here."

"For how *long,* Solavita? You can't hide him forever! What

301

will you do when they build on top of this floor, or tear it up for the wood? What end do you imagine that *isn't* the one you're scared of?"

I sniffed. A tear coursed down my cheek. Ersilio's face withered.

"It wasn't about being fat," I said. "Lifting the boulders. Was it?"

He managed a weak smile.

"She's tiny now," he said, "but she won't always be tiny. She's not scared that she can't see now, but she might be one day. I thought I'd better start training now. Just in case she still wants my arms when I'm eighty."

Nene beamed at me when I came down through the trapdoor that night. His smile dropped when he took in the dullness of my manner. The burlap sack which bumped against my leg with silvery clangs as I walked.

I was a living temper. My love was primal. *Tell me what you want and I will find it. Tell me what you fear and I will kill it.* Being married to a creature who told me nothing did not absolve me of my duty. It gave me the additional duty to want and fear on his behalf.

I knelt beside Nene. The sack spilled its contents as it deflated against the floor. I kissed his hot forehead and slid my hand up the slippery back of the belly-wing until it reached the keloid. The white tentacles converged into a peak around my elbow as I pushed my hand inside him. Invisible slugs of tissue swelled to push my walking fingers away from the wing, but I pressed back. Nene gave a closed-mouthed, wide-throated, "Mm."

I hadn't expected the inside of a person to be so hot, so tangled. I'd been thwarted in my hope to know the difference between lungs, heart and bone by position and texture, but I couldn't say that I didn't know what I was feeling. What I was feeling was a shell crammed to every wall with tentacles. If his innards were still there, the blight had shoved them down or burrowed through them. I felt less the horror of reaching inside a body and more the horror of groping in a warren for the hackles of a creature which might bite me. Nene was rolling his head and moaning like my hand was making love to him, but it didn't feel discordant, a noise of pleasure born from pain. I was caressing membranes too tender to be exposed, searing them, saturating them.

The wing ended in a hot tumour of stone and gristle in his centre. It was large enough that my hand splayed flat against it. My hope of finding a root thwarted, I took a hard hold of the wing's spine and groped in the sack for a knife. Nene had seen the knives filling the sack, encircling it on the floor.

"Please," he moaned. "Please, please."

I didn't know what he was begging for. For me to cut the wing out, for me to stop, for me to keep touching him no matter the reason. I slid the knife inside him down the path of my arm and fixed it into a ridge of bone.

"Will you die if I do this?" I said.

Nene panted, "God does not die."

I flew up on the ratchet of the wing and sawed.

The wing kicked up behind me like it was mine. The white light could have been born from the friction between bone and knife for how quickly it came. It shot out of Nene's body in a wire, knocked my head back and scratched a painless line from my chin to my eye. That was the end of the first knife. I reached my hand, dripping a slag of black rot and molten metal, back into the sack and found another. I stabbed down with this one. Watched as it split lengthwise and the two halves spiralled in opposite directions. It was as the third knife bent into a bracelet and impaled me through the wrist that Nene started telling me to stop. "Please, I don't like it, don't make me watch it again!" A fourth knife melted and a fifth unwound into a spidersilk of wire and wood. When I reached towards the sack, Nene grabbed my hand. I thrashed in his arms, terrified to leave a gap in my mania for pain to seep into. "You had to try, had to try, I know. But you've seen it won't work and now you must stop! You won't get closer each time, and deeper burns won't hurt less once they catch up to you, not unless you burn yourself down to the bone."

I dropped the sixth knife without using it. I pressed myself into his lap, slid my legs beneath the wing. I could tell from the way he was panting that the defence mechanism had drained him, and as the pain of my wounds began to dawn, we rocked together in a heavy-headed rhythm. I whimpered when it bubbled in my cheek, moaned when it wormed in the bone of my elbow. When it burgeoned down my arm, burrowed through my impaled wrist and split my palm along the lines of my old scar, I wailed and bit down on Nene's scalp.

"I said that to my mother," Nene said. "'Mamma, you know God does not die, and you have to stop trying.' When she poisoned me, I cried the poison out. She thought I was crying because it hurt and held me on her lap, waiting for me to die, until she smelled the tears. It was hard to tell what happened when she held me down in the fireplace, but I think the fire and I swapped places. I was lying on cold embers, and the fire was above me, clinging to her arms like I had. The sickle turned on itself and stuck in the wall. By the end, I really think she only kept trying because she was fascinated. To watch God work. And..."

I thrust my hand out towards the crypt wall. It wore a gauntlet of pulverised knives, wire coils fountaining from the impaling bracelet. Through the lattice, I could see wet red pits in the burn-whitened skin. I pressed it against the brick, hoping to cool it, but all I felt was powder.

"I said, 'Here, Mamma. You want me to be dead? I will be dead.' I took the sickle blade out of her hands and tried to cut my own neck."

"That didn't work," I said.

Nene picked up the knife I'd dropped. He put it against his own neck.

And a flinch dug a tiny cut into his skin.

We stared at each other. His face was as shocked as mine.

"No," he said. "No... the sickle... it snapped in half."

Against his flesh then.

Against the wing now.

Not against his flesh now.

I had thought it from the moment I realised the wings paralysed him.

Nene, my sweetness, I fear that God inhabits you as He inhabits the earth. That you are God no more than the mountain is God. That you will never feel holier than you do now, as He splits you and crawls out of you.

If collecting the knives had been the chisel-crack, this was the breach. After six months of quiet, of barely caring, of trying to keep him comfortable, I howled, "What's *happening,* Nene?"

"You know you told me about your first sculpture?" Nene said. "You laid air into clay as God lays spirit into flesh, as God laid Himself into Jesus?

"But the clay wasn't vented, and the air was trapped, and when they heated it up in the kiln, it expanded.

"Kerblam."

Nene was right. The tentacles did push the wings out.

Just as the convulsions had exploded into being with two earthquakes and then settled into flutters, the metamorphosis after the disembowelling birth of the first wing was one slow, continuous growth. The tentacles stretched longer on the floor of the crypt at the same rate as the wings on the floor of the tent. A man's length a month, new growths sticking out in cowlicks until they grew heavy enough to lie down in the golden vaults. As I watched the wings creep up to the walls of the crypt and breathe crushed against them, their newborn roots bright and seething with tentacles, I thought they were growing larger underneath. Then, one day, I wrapped my arms around Nene to sit him up and felt a sliding THUD.

Nene rocked his head back in my arms and gasped.

"Has it come off?" I said.

Nene reeled forward and lay down on his front, bending the belly-wing into his face. In the mountain of tentacles which forested and quarried his insides, he rolled and laughed in relief.

The tentacles bore the expelled wings up the walls of the crypt. They spidered the feathers outward and bore through the gaps between bricks with the bones in their coils, darning long golden lines through the gabbro. Nene still waved his arms to conduct them. He lay in the middle of the floor and beamed as golden feathers and ivory tentacles strained down towards him, showering us with brick dust.

I first learned that the stale smell in the crypt was mould when he told me he was growing something new, bid the tentacles at his belly lay back, and pulled forth three walnut-coloured flounces of fungus. The fungus which grew from his shoulder lay on his arm like a caped sleeve. As it dominated his body and burgeoned up through the tentacles, it put me in mind of a flood, white ocean chased back by rocky black beach. I lay down at his side and sculpted him, dipping raw-edged discs of clay into my water bucket until they were wet enough to fluff with my fingers.

I had not lifted the ban on visitors to the tent. In the year the horror had been gone, sculptures of him had swarmed to replace him.

In the autumn, Prasede told me she was glad Nene was gone. Not because she didn't miss him, but because she believed, without a mite of doubt, that he was somewhere better.

"With his father," she said, when I asked her idea of a better place.

"The Marchese Di Mantua?" I scoffed. Living in a crypt blanketed with mould had given me a rotten cold, chewed through my cheekbones and spat the cud into my throat.

"No. Someone soft and humble, like him," Prasede said.

"Someone with a cottage. A garden full of primroses."

"Keeps your heart hardy, does it? To think that?"

She smiled at me. "Yes. I *shudder* to imagine what you think."

I went down to the crypt that night with a bushel of yellow primroses I'd picked from the woods. I sat Nene up in my lap and told him I thought he'd look sweet at the heart of the black biped with his hair full of yellow flowers. His golden hair had grown out into a cloud around his face and then down past his shoulders, and the longest curls rustled in a hairnet of mould. I pared them clean and then wove them into a pair of plaits encased in flowers. Nene plucked every fifth flower out of my hand and crushed it into his mouth, and the next week, his belly and back were domed with primrose. The yellow blossoms were as large as mixing bowls, and mutant. One was a tube of petals encircled by their black middle like stalks bound with string. One was a sphere of spindles like a dandelion clock. One was hackled down its stem like a lionfish.

I remembered what he was like as a child, blinking under duress at flowers and sheer cliffs alike. With God in his mouth, he licked up droplets of life and gave birth to glaciers.

In two years, there were sienna tree roots, purple glass, great barrels of moss, and my least favourite layer: volcanic rings of gabbro. Born from a taste of the dust in the walls, the stone choked the breathing carpets of colour in crusts, fossilised them into friezes. Its weight dragged feathers and tentacles down from the ceiling, peeled fauna from the walls and crushed glass and moss against the floor. For an eternal month, Nene lay petrified inside the floor, the stone at his belly and shoulder convulsing with growth after growth. Then, blissfully, a new layer began. A layer which lengthened quietly beneath the stone, breathed against it in gentle rhythm, and burst to supremacy on the walls, floor and ceiling in a single afternoon.

It was viscera, red lacework and purple bladders, which slid against itself with pops and squelches like mud. Suffocated in

His bed by the stone, God had been starved of material to eat, and had eaten a piece of Nene.

Unencumbered by the wings, Nene was comfortable. He gained control over the growths—the growths which his body could not lift, but which could lift themselves—and used them to lift his body. The days on which I found him lying on the floor were the days on which he was pious, confused, listless. He asked me if I'd come to kill him, and why I'd done this to him, and why he was so cold. On those days, I thought that nobody was God. I thought that God was just a voice which filled any shell of a person something else had hollowed out. It was on the days I found him in the sky, hanging from the walls on arms of tree root or upright in gowns of red flesh, commanding huge cyclones of gore with his arms, that he was most lucidly himself.

And how did I know he was lucidly himself? Because he moaned. Moaned like a sybarite at the slithering of his guts. Swayed his head with *Mm-hm-ah-hahs* as he pulled long red slugs out of his stomach. The hard thudding movements inside his chest and head that made blood pour out of his mouth and eyes were the same movements that made him trap his tongue between his teeth and roll back his eyes, making wells for the blood to run into. I promised I would keep kissing him for as long as he had a mouth, and one kiss sent ecstatic shudders through the crypt from floor to ceiling. When I touched his keloid, the blight sat upright on the walls and buried us in avalanches. He nodded and pleaded and made the crypt nod and plead with every brush of his eyes against movement, of his tongue against air, of my flesh against his, of his flesh against blight, of blight against more blight. Even when he wasn't moaning for me, I lay down on him when he moaned, felt the spires of viscera and bone on his belly kick me up and down. I felt more like the leviathan anchored by our bodies was mine, was under my control, the more Nene and the leviathan swallowed each other.

308

It wasn't that he could only feel love. It never had been.

It was that he took pleasure in everything.

"Fuoco mio," Nene said one night, as I came down the stairs. "I cannot see you."

The way his tongue cleaved at his palate gave magnificence to the idea that he'd sensed me without sight. He could have heard my footsteps above him or the creaking of the trapdoor, but as I staggered across the breathing floor, red tentacles and feelers slithering up my legs, I decided that he had tasted me.

He was lying on his back in the sky, suspended between two red poplars. One cascaded down from his shoulder and the other fountained high from his belly. He hadn't had legs for a year, though I hadn't noticed whether they'd been eaten by his belly or his back. Gut and marrow hung in garlands around his waist. His hair, longer than mine and tarnished bronze, hung in a curtain which his red bone arms pillared. The newborn red of his mouth was a vicious slash in his green face, but his eyes had disappeared. His eye sockets were streaming red tissue.

I ran my hand down the tentacle coming from his left eye. It joined like a root to the base of the poplar on his shoulder, and the one coming from his right eye joined likewise to his belly. The texture of the flesh was a web of round boils, like seaweed.

"Were your eyes pushed out, *dolcezza,* or eaten?"

Nene grinned and moaned through the open corners of his mouth. Beneath the moan, beneath his mouth, somewhere inside his chest, I heard my answer. With the shortness of a POP and the texture of a CRUNCH, it was the sound of a turgid boil bursting.

"Oh, *fuoco mio!*"

There was a second POP-CRUNCH, the mastication of the second eyeball. Nene spasmed and threw his head back.

"Yes, *dolcezza?*"

"I can't see myself! I see inside myself! God is everywhere and I am nowhere! Not a piece of me left that is turned outward!"

His reverie slammed through the room. Swaths of tentacle peeled up from the walls and tore bricks out with them. When I threw my arms around him to kiss his bloody forehead, the ceiling began to rain. The crypt beat like a panicking heart, and every THUD shook my head white.

"It's alright," I soothed him. "Blindness is human, Nene! I can bring you someone who will make it stop, help you turn yourself outward again! Would you like that? I will bring her."

Nedda De Aqvancis was four years old. As her father looked at me darkly from the doorway of my tent, she would tug on my skirts until I lifted her up to touch the faces of my statues. She was my only cause to regret the consumption of my portrait work by savage, stretched things without features.

Ersilio hadn't seen Nene since he'd put him in the earth. The friendship which persevered through building and exercising was a deaf, unconscious one. I had concussed myself into forgetting that Ersilio knew, and Ersilio had concussed himself into forgetting that Ersilio knew. The best part of him, I thought, believed that Nene had died. That he'd died from his wounds not long after he'd slept in the sea, that my grief had come and gone, and that I didn't want to talk about it.

But when I asked if I could borrow Nedda for an adventure, the worst part of him said, "Only if I come too."

I was smiling when I said he could. He'd already come into the tent, and seen the wings, had he not? *Not a man, but an angel* was a larger more difficult shock than *Not an angel, but God Himself,* was it not?

As I led them down the stairs, I began to feel the crypt as they might. First, the smell. Lush greenery split by the axe-wound of copper and sweet rot. Then, the fear of being underground, the way the air above you feels heavy, alive. Perhaps awe at the size of the room our ancestors cut into the valley, the waste of material used to armour it, first the bricks and then—

When his foot hit the last stair, sheer horror made Ersilio fall over. He walked into horror like it was a door slammed in his face, jammed his foot in the crack beneath it, flailed downward on that pivot. Nedda sat up on his stomach, giggling. I giggled with her, and bent to scoop her up.

"Silly Papa fell on the stairs," I said.

Ersilio stared at me, huffing air through a square mouth, like I was the one with fourteen wings made of intestines. Maybe, now that Nene was made of intestines too, I was.

Horror held him down, by the shoulders, by the legs. He couldn't move to stop me from carrying Nedda away from him, into the crypt. He only watched.

And watched as the buttressed spire of intestines broke apart and Nene Karafantoni poured out of it. He was hanging from the ceiling upside-down, with red maypole ribbons streaming from his hair and eye sockets and black marrow prongs like chandelier chains for legs. As he threw his head back and spread his arms, every facet of the room bent towards him.

Isn't he beautiful? God, isn't he beautiful?

"I have brought you little Nedda," I said.

"I am not *little,*" Nedda said.

"Ah, no? I am sorry. How old are you? Tell Nene how old you are."

"Four!"

"Nedda..." said Nene in a slow heave. "The last time I saw you you... were a little baby... up on the cliff. Do you remember when I looked after you and Lagia?"

"Yes," Nedda said. I knew she was just being polite.

"I am so happy... that you came to talk to me about being blind. How brave you must be. Does Papa still hold your hand to help you walk?"

"No," Nedda said.

"Ah, do you hold Papa's hand to help *him* walk?"

Nedda beamed back at the staircase where she knew Ersilio was. "We hold hands just because we like to."

311

"Ah, that's what he tells you," said Nene, "but I know he would be lost without your hand to hold. Don't ever stop letting him hold your hand, Nedda. Promise me."

"I promise!"

"I won't ever let Solavita stop holding my hand. Solavita is the only thing that keeps me here on the earth. Without my eyes, I worry I will be like a balloon, cut strings and flying away… full of nothing but myself."

Nene wasn't stammering in pain but in suppression of his pleasure. Blindness had saturated him with taste, sound and touch. Full of himself he already was.

"Well, I don't miss my eyes," Nedda said. "I was too little when I lost them. You must miss yours a lot if you only lost them today, and you are twenty or thirty or whatever."

"I am twenty-two," said Nene, the pile of nothing and everything.

"That's so big. That's ginormous. And ancient."

"And they used to call me Pipsqueak," Nene said, with a gaping smile which swallowed his eyeless face. "Do you really not covet the eyes of others, Nedda?"

Nedda shook her head. "My hands."

"Ah, your hands are your eyes?" She nodded vigorously. "May I touch your face? I'd like to see you."

Ersilio gave a moan of terror.

"Yeah!" Nedda said. "And can I see you?"

From inside the red pillars of Nene's arms, white-skinned hands emerged. I believed not that he'd unearthed his old hands from the cocoon but that he'd germinated new ones for the purpose.

Two ribbons of gut detached from him with twangs and fell at our feet. I looked up, and saw that his face was now the right way up in the sky, upside-down on his body. It hung there unsullied, black-eyed and red-lipped.

Nedda ran her fat, clumsy fingers down Nene's nose with a distracted grin. Nene cradled Nedda's neck, and put his thumbs on the shells of scar tissue over her eyes.

As he touched her, something fluttered through his purpose-grown face. A whisper of brown through his white cheeks, a whisper of pink through his red tentacles, a whisper of black through his bronze hairline.

He let her go.

"It's a..." he said—in a babyish chirp of a voice— "*relief...* to talk to another person who is blind, not only because you can teach me how to be blind, but because you are my equal."

The toddler gazed happily up at the monster whose face was busy turning back upside-down.

"You are not committing the rudeness of looking at me when I can't look back, so as I... learn to look back... I will avert... my eyes... from you."

In the aerated flesh which poured out of Nene, from his belly to the ceiling and his back to the earth, eyes opened.

They were round and black, and the thin crescents of their whites rolled like suckers in the dark. They did not blink.

At the revelation that he was seeing again, and seeing so enormously, Nene shrieked with laughter and threw his arms out. His buttresses clawed at the walls, and all around and above us, there was a throaty ripping sound, like the earth beyond the crypt was shifting. Another tremor. Stirred by his limbs, rather than his spirit.

Nene surged down, seized me, and jounced me from my feet. Nedda jerked in shock as the wet bone of his arm touched her cheek. "Nene, stop!" I laughed.

His trance vapourised, Ersilio cleared the roiling floor between himself and his daughter in a second, ripped her from our arms, and fled. We moved only to close the gap. Nene's delight breached in stalagmites. Arms grew from his shoulders and the crypt walls. Ribs grew like fins from the marrow of his waist. As he commanded the ceiling to spit him out and grew again with back-breaking weight in my arms, crouched on his crab-legs with his head thrust forward in an endless inhale, all eyes in the room gazed at me. Gibbous whites in the corners and pure beetle-black on his face.

"I am God," he said. "I am!"

"You are, you are, beautiful sweet thing!" I spread my arms, and he lashed me with tentacles and pulled me up into the air. And it was this scene, this scene of *I ams* and *You ares* and me hanging by my legs from the crypt's quivering uvula, that Ersilio walked back down the stairs, without Nedda, and saw. My wild eyes flickered with apology as Nene reared up and swallowed my head.

"They're frightened," Nene breathed against my throat. "Nobody can look at me but you."

The trapdoor slammed shut. Ersilio was gone.

"Block it, bring it down!" I yelled. "Make the staircase collapse! Keep them out! Keep them all out!"

In the stairwell, there was a rush of dark which choked the last rays of daylight, chatter-chatter-BANG-CRASH. I cackled, pushing my body up against Nene's with all my might.

"They'll never look at us again!" I said.

Nene slid a wreath of bone into my skirt, baring my thighs.

"I can see the world," he said, "known and unknown, dark and light, inside and outside, but I only want to look at you."

I whimpered, half hunger, half terror.

"Let me look at you. I will make you God as well. I will make you so lucid the world razors the ichor from your eyes, and so naked the world's eyes go through you." I moaned and threw my head back as he slithered further up, making my stiff bodice roll and crest. "Only one who has watched me change too slowly to feel that I have changed could fear I might look upon the things which grow uninvited out of a man, and say they make him less of one."

I tore open the laces of my bodice. Made him swell out like my heart was erupting. The tentacle, finned and club-footed, reared back as if to regard me and then lunged to rub itself against my cheek. I nuzzled back with an open mouth.

"I'm the one who taught you how to feel," I said, "and *you* are the one who taught me this wasn't us killing each other!"

"How could this look like us killing each other?" said the red skull skinning its jaws between my breasts.

A cathedral grew out of the beam inside my dress, and tore it off me. A too-long tongue slurred his whimper of my name, and I forgot it. His arms seized and hoisted my naked body a hundred times, because he grew for me two hundred arms. As the red body I gripped between my thighs broke apart and the first tendrils found their homes inside me, Nene encased my ear in marrow and said, "Look what I can do."

Two perfect legs, cold as marble and soft as moss, grew around my waist and into my hands.

"Hold them as tight as you want. I'll keep them whole for you. I promise."

They were the only thing he kept whole. Upside-down on the ceiling, clasping those beautiful legs like they were an original fragment of his body unearthed for me, I saw in rhythm with our thrusts his skull cracking in half as its jaw unhinged, his jawbones growing until they lay along the floor and the ceiling, the massive mouth's tongue curling up and growing a new skull. He grew heads to spread my legs, bent arms to arch my back, bucked hips beneath my hips to pour me over the precipice of one body into the pit of the next. Those bodies may as well have been mine, as my back joints burned when the tentacles strained and the thousand eyes rolled on my face, as the red blight disintegrating in my mouth and sex wove all of my innards anew. Gnashing and gurgling, soft-bodied and spineless, he pulled me tongue-over teeth down his throat into a belly which could not dissolve me. I came in a long rip, with his jaws around my head, my jaws around his tongue, his legs around me and my legs around him. He came. Shuddered, bent, lunged like a collapsing tower, erupting mountain, drove me down into his flank neck-first. Saturation burnt a white hole through my carol of his name, and I forgot it.

"Are you…" I said. He ground his teeth at my temples, at the back of my neck. All I could see was flesh. Soft red dark like the insides of my eyelids. "Are you…" He opened around me like a flower, slithering down my legs and splaying me out.

Who am I? Who are you? Have you eaten me?

"Are you going to turn into me now?"

This, this body, this melting and reforming tower of legs which broke in one step and eyes which opened as punchlines and tentacles which draped without strangling, this creature which only felt its limbs for as long as they kicked in its womb, this tremor which shook down buildings and made little girls cry, this rot with its roots through a man and his room and its street and its village and its valley but not a spore in his beautiful mouth, this angel, this monster, this lover, this mountain of flesh, was Nene. It was God, love and madness and blood and filth and massiveness, but it was Nene. It was the death of the tenderest thing I'd ever known, his whole being multiplied and, in its multiplication, rendered useless, but it was Nene. How could I mourn the death of two black eyes when it'd born me a thousand, mourn a moan against my neck whilst I lived in a cavernous red tunnel of moans, mourn filmy-haired skin in my mouth whilst I was blanketed in pure naked muscle? How heartless would I have to be? How eyeless?

Nene, Nene, Nene, Nene, Nene. The light on my world and the world beneath it. He grew from a thing I loathed into a thing I loved not by turning from headache into heartache but by surging from the back of my head to the front and then bursting out. I staggered with the hilt of him stuck between my eyes, dragged him behind me, fell, flowered, *haemorrhaged*. It was so slow. It was so fast. I forgot his name every time a climax wrenched my mind tight, but as I lay in the red dark unspooling, it came back, through the blood: Nene, Nene, Nene, Nene, Nene.

When he melted into the mortar of the crypt, the crypt became him. When he touched Nedda and became her mimic, wearing her brown skin over his jaws and her pink scars over his eyes and chirping two syllables in her voice, I forgot Nedda for him. When he said he was God, God ceased to exist, and when he was me, I was nobody. As we lay on the ceiling, I leant over and burrowed, naked arms first, into the cavern of his chest. The red arch of his body grew Solavita like coral. Solavita's chin creased triple, Solavita's blue eyes rolled back, Solavita's breasts tracked with blood, Solavita's cunt streaming tentacles and vertebrae.

When the mimic tilted her head at me, I tilted my head at her. We were still connected by my arm, which was buried to the elbow in her chest.

I twisted. The mimic's head juddered forward, down. From her mouth fell a cry I knew well in a voice I did not:

"Please."

My own voice. Perhaps a glottal wheeze, perhaps a perfect copy. It bent out of shape in my head.

I raised my free hand to cover her mouth, leapt on top of her... *him, him...* slammed his hips into the ceiling with my own. He opened around me with greedy laughter. Solavita's lips split by my tongue, Solavita's legs split by my fist.

I will copy you until you look like me. Echo you until you sound like me. I will fuse with you and make you disappear, an extra finger or a voice in my head. I will press my hand down through your head and shatter your brain against the floor, make you surge out into the world and rip it in two. I will make the earth beat in time with us, Nene, Nene.

In my sex, down my throat, red light over my eyes, a burn of cold behind my nose. He was always attached to me, but I noticed it rarely. I never wandered far enough for the thread to pull taut. If he was keeping me alive, as God kept him alive, he was doing it in the way he used to feel for me with his legs as he slept. The way he used to follow me through the street. Knowing he needed to touch me, but not why.

You are keeping me alive. I don't know why.

I lay on my back naked and blight-webbed. The crypt hadn't made the shape of Nene for days, weeks... The red tissue had darkened into marrow, cruel spindles which pointed at me.

"How are you feeling today?" I said.

"I am so happy," Nene breathed from the ceiling. "I love you."

I smiled. "What do you love about me?"

"You are the one who taught me how to feel."

"And you are the one who taught me this was not us killing each other."

He laughed his beautiful laugh. Flushing his cheeks on the tent floor or rolling its tongue on a fossilised ceiling, it would always be his laugh.

"How could this look like us killing each other?"

I slurred the line as always. "You could be a sword coring me of my spine I could be a fanged mouth I could bite it *spit* it out."

Ever patient he was. "But we will put it all back when we're finished."

"We will never be finished."

The stairwell had collapsed. I lived in the dark now.

"I am so happy. I don't want to go outside."

"You're the one who taught me this wasn't us killing each other."

"How could this look like us killing each other?"

"You could be... The one who taught me this wasn't us killing each other."

"How could this look like us killing each other?"

"How are you feeling today?"
"I am so happy. I love you."

"You're frightening me, Nene."
"Hold me."
"I can't."
"Hold me."
"I can't hold you. You're too big."
"Hold me."

"Where's Nene? Who are you, who only regurgitates his words?"

Who are you, who only stimulates regurgitations?

"How do *you* feel today?"

Like I could rip the world in two.

"Do you want me to hold you?"

You cannot. I am too big.

"And… what about loving me? Do you love me?"

I like that you love me. Is that the same thing?

"No! Please, no! Stop it! Make him come back!"

"Please don't cry, Solavita. There's a horror about you crying I just can't bear."

"Does it hurt, Nene?"

"Tell me it doesn't hurt! Just tell me it doesn't!"

From my mother's marrow to my coffin's hackles it hurts. From the first death of dark to the last death of light it hurts! Why does it still hurt?

Why does it still hurt?

It *hurts*!

THE PICA
AND
THE BLOODTHIRST

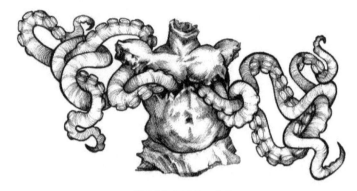

CHAPTER 20

THE YELLOW

I
T IS ARIO BAROSTALDO who reaches me first, spat into my workshop by a commotion in the nave of the church.

"Uh," he says. A small crowd of builders, identically wide-eyed, arrives behind him. "Malacresta's just walked in."

Sitting at the table with my head buried in my outstretched arms, I groan. "Oh. What does he want?"

"To speak to you. S'all he said, to speak to you."

"Who's got him?"

"Oh, we're not touching him." Ario glances nervously over his shoulder. "Just ran faster than him is all."

He dashes out as quickly as he dashed in.

I stand up, wave my hand to dismiss the other builders, and set about arranging myself to look annoyed. I lean against the table with my arms braced behind me.

Malacresta Malacheti walks into the side aisle looking like death. Having cropped his hair identically all his life, he can't hide even the slightest neglect of it, which makes tufts stick out around his ears and down his neck. His eyebrows are full of red scabs, pimples crushed and torn open. He has gained muscle and lost fat, making dents on his throat like long grey bruises.

He crashes into my anger like it's a wall, and blinks at me as I glare at him through my hair.

Then, he holds up a disc of yellow glass and says, "Yellow."

Magmate is too small a village and my builders too diverse a cross-section for my enemies to be strangers to me. Prasede is teaching Malacresta as her apprentice in the butcher shop, but keeps him in the garden, lest her patrons be cowed by the sight of him with a knife. When a rumour spread through the church that he'd smashed his bedroom window, we assumed he'd done it in a temper. Perhaps tossed a rock or blowpipe through it. Then, someone snuck around the back of the white stone house and saw that it wasn't the glass which was gone, but the lead grate. Caro, who made the clear glass for the church windows, spent hours every day cleaning crusts of black glass out of the crucibles and collecting poles and blades from where the nocturnal glassmaker had left them: Impaled in the table, kicked down the hill, hanging from trees. Nedda and Lagia are now constantly at Ersilio's side, because the last time their grandparents took care of them, Malacresta went into a stupor in his bedroom and started sandpapering empty air between his knees. This isn't the first time we've seen each other even in days, but it's the first time we've spoken. He's been flashing the forest to smithereens in my periphery and I've been clawing my life back from blood loss in his.

And his greeting was *Yellow.*

"Just thought you'd like to see," he says, fat-lipped. "So you knew, uh, what I was up to with all the lead. It was really difficult. It goes yellow in the lowest temperatures, but I've been having blackouts, see, where I zone out after adding the ashes and come to with it overcooked to treacle. Ochre, brown, black. Ha, blackouts."

Is he drunk? The way he's slurring his words isn't quite mechanical. It's less like his tongue is too heavy for his mouth and more like his words are too heavy for his head. It's not that he's anxious either. He's always anxious.

This, I think as I stand and stare at him, is what it was like to talk to me whilst Nene was in the crypt. He's pulling words free like scabs, in shapes decided long ago, dry on one side and oozing on the other. He's letting a fleeting idea possess and steer him like a mission. A fleeting idea to visit a friend and play at being present.

His brain is still in the furnace. He thinks that because the things spidering in his head in its place are things we don't understand, we won't see them at all.

"But don't worry," he says. "I didn't use all the lead up. I had enough left to figure out the setting."

He reaches into his belt pouch and pulls out a little knot of lead and green glass. Four black-outlined petals, like the interlocked wings we drew together.

I curl my lip and sneer.

His face falls.

"Don't be like that," he says. "I'm proud of it, and everyone just treats it like a symptom of disease. I am sick, but I want to feel like it meant something. I thought you'd understand that."

Rage knots my groin to my stomach. He *thought I'd understand.* He *thought I'd like to see.* Whether he's asking to come back without apologising for his disloyalty or asking for praise despite continuing his disloyalty, he's asking me to swallow the pain he caused me. Swallow my pride.

If his brain was in his head, he'd have remembered who he was talking to.

"Let me show you." Malacresta walks to the wall. When he hunkers down with his back to me, I leave the table and go to the corner.

Propped up with my rulers and saws is the long glassmaking blade Malacresta abandoned on my table a year ago. I pick it up without looking at it, and am amazed by the amount of time which passes before the tip slides loose.

I walk over and stand behind him. He has propped the yellow glass up in a sunbeam between two sheets, saturating my grey floor with a primrose of fractals. As I watch him gently nudge it back and forth, like a father tying the laces on his baby's shoes, I decide to kill him.

"I could make Nedda now." He turns to me. "Like you said."

I drive my elbow into his throat and swing the massive blade at his head. He ducks, and it embeds in the beam with such ferocity the whole structure of the workshop shakes. Daylight surges over us as a sheet slides off the wall and the yellow glass falls over with a thunk.

"I don't," I say, my forearms framing his head as I hang from the stuck blade, "give a single fuck about your god-damned fucking glass. I never gave a fuck about your glass, Malacresta. I wanted to help you make something of your hobby instead of hanging it raw around your beams, and now that you are dead to me, *traditore,* I don't care if it hangs you!"

Horror rends Malacresta's face open. His eyes are like tiger's-eye in the way they turn yellow with a light behind them, and I suppose the light must be coming from his brain.

He thrusts up his arms and seizes the handle of the weapon. A downward flail and stumble forward dislodge it from the beam and an upward swing rips it out of my hands. In the moment it takes me to feel that he's cut me, he swings it down from above his head like an axe, gets it stuck in the table, frees it with a TWANG.

Is trained with blades and blowpipes, I think as I scramble backwards onto the table. Is now trained as a butcher, I think as he comes down on top of me and my head crashes into the flat of the blade, suddenly stuck upright in the tabletop. Sweet flowers of glass belie the armouries which make them. If it comes down to slashing, he'll kill me.

As I grab his hips, I know I'm stronger than him, but as a single shove lifts him off me, I realise he's even thinner than I

335

thought. He frees the blade from the table. Over his head like a dagger, down into my shoulder. The impact is painless and rotten and deep, like he's prying my collarbone out. I roll and pin him underneath me. He rips the blade out of my shoulder and slashes my face. As I rock forward to choke him with my forearms, something slams into my stomach. Thinking I'm impaled, I thrash and fall off the table. It was his knee. He gasps for air on his back with his leg still bent.

He pounces off the table, holding the blade above his head.

"All this for your fucking glass!" I say, with blood cold like grease on my neck. "Are you *crying?*"

"You're just like Prasede!" Malacresta yells. "Do you know what she used to say to me when I was making the green and purple? 'Look at me, Mal, look at me.' I've never looked at people when I talk to them! I'd read my own wedding vows to the floor! You made me feel like you gave a shit about the windows, like you'd picked me because I was best for it, like for the first time in my life I could be *useful,* and all you were doing was... *babysitting* me like everyone else! There's no Malacresta in Malacresta's eyes—" I get up to run, and he chases me, rebounds the blade off the table so hard it completes the reverse of its arc. "You want to see me, you look at the things I make for you!"

I sweep the tools from my worktop. All I find is a cheese knife covered in clay. I'm expecting Malacresta to laugh at the size of it, and when he only bares his teeth, tugs at his fringe and swings, I laugh instead. I duck, and the huge blade attaches me to the table by the ear. On the floor, pulsing with pain from left ear to left thigh, I pull him down on top of me. TWANG. He brings the blade with him. Staring at the cupboard door above my shoulder, he pushes it slowly and steadily against my neck.

With a thud, he slams his forehead into the cupboard. I recognise it as a defence mechanism against being looked at, but I feel it as the impact of his brain, left behind in the furnace, surging down the hill and back into place.

I stab him in the back with my cheese knife. To escape it, he shunts his hips forward in my lap. Blood seeps up under my skin, making all of my wounds burn as one.

I've just realised that my knife is stabbing at the leather of his belt, not his backbone, when the sheets fly back and Ersilio and Ario run to drag him off. Sitting alone against the cupboard, my body registers a pang of cold, like I've pulled away from a hug.

"Holy God, holy God!" As Ario and Sitha pin Malacresta against the table, Ersilio throws himself down in front of me. I don't realise how badly I am hurt until I slither to the floor, unable to move my arms. "What happened?"

I convulse on my back as the pain settles. Deep, shimmering, total. Severed ear. Cored shoulder. Cut throat. Slashed up the arm, leg and cheek. I feel like I'm being sawn in half.

Sitha wrests the glassmaking blade from Malacresta and hurls it across the floor. It leaves a bracelet of blood droplets on the wood with every bounce. As Ario yanks his arms behind his back, I see the deep cuts on his hands. Black seams in crimson gloves. That's how hard he was pulling the blade out of the wall. Out of me.

"What HAPPENED?" Ario yells. The sound Malacresta makes is scarcely human. A wiry shriek of laughter which fractures into chitters. When I lean on Ersilio's shoulder and stand up, I see that he's biting the table.

"What's wrong with him?" Sitha says. "Is he drunk?"

"He's been eating lead," says Ersilio.

Drooling blood, I slur, "Can't a man go mad on his own?"

They all look at me. For a moment, I think they've discovered me. In my guilt for starting the fight, or in my skinless, bestial arousal from being beaten.

Then, Ario says, "What should we do with him?"

I greet another throb in my shoulder with a moan.

"Mm. *My* God demands we… pull the teeth from his mouth with his own pliers. But he told me last year that his God is a gentle one. I am nothing if not curious to learn. Take him home, and fetch Signora Vpezzinghi to bandage his hands."

"No!" Malacresta yells. "Don't tell her!"

Ario crushes his wrists together, making him curse. "How dare you argue with mercy?"

"Being denied a luting is punishment enough," I say. "Do as he says. You're to take bandages from our supply and do it yourselves."

There's a flash of black pleasure in my head as I imagine luting Malacresta. Then, I imagine what the echo would be, *where* it would be, and shudder.

The crowd don't take Malacresta to the door. They take him to the wall. I run to rescue the sheet of yellow glass from their boots.

When I stand up, Ersilio is watching me, bewildered.

I tilt the glass and flick fractals onto his face. He breaks his stare when one hits him in the eye.

"We… should've built you walls and a door months ago," he says. "I'm sorry."

"If we'd been shut away, he would've killed me." A grin burgeons on my face. "Oh, to be a cow. I bet he gets them minced before they've finished mooing."

"I'm worried about you. Someone's going to notice."

For the six months since the blessing between my legs, every brush of emotion against a membrane has inflated it into a weal. Irritation swells my brain against my eyes, pity stretches my sinuses until they split and leak and lust makes me want to crush my cock until it rots off in my hands. It was a breath from getting hard under Malacresta, with his throat against my cheek and my throat against his blade, but it's gotten hard for less. Sights, noises, thoughts. It's my tender thing in the dark now. Unlike my breasts when they were new, it is evil, and it is driving me mad through my stomach, mouth and skin, and

338

it is *wanted*. It is the most male thing I can imagine: A mite of
maleness stretched for and clawed forth, just to be hidden, for
no eyes and no hands but my own. In a land where maleness
is money, Ersilio and Malacresta are coddled princes and I am
a magnate.

My thirst is constant, slip-throated. I drink a bucketful of
water a day and sweat it out again. I'm so thirsty I cannot get
hungry; the closest thing I feel to hunger is a grey ache which
is like the ache for a strong smell. My skin rolls black off my
neck and palms when I spend too long in the sun.

It's all delicious. If the weals inside me split and slough my
fragile skin, I will die moaning. If my builders discover my
attack of rage against Malacresta and connect it to a bodily
burn, the same burn which leaves the coddled men at eighteen,
I will take off my trousers and show them.

I rub the yellow glass against my face, beading it with black
blood clots. He did this to me; I did this to him.

Weeks later, after violet scars have closed my wounds and the
builders have blessed my workshop with walls and a bolted
door, Ersilio knocks with Nedda. She is eleven now. Her eyes
have grown darker and sharper in their round pens of clear
skin, and she is fat like her papa, rather than like a baby. She
still holds his hand, for his sake, not hers.

Nene and Nedda's meeting, when I lured her down into his
red coils on the chance it made him happy for a moment, was
seven years ago. At once, I feel like I've lived a thousand
lifetimes since and like I fell asleep in the crypt yesterday. Like
I'm still asleep, and everything from the whale to my near-

murder by Malacresta is a dream agitated by the blight.

With practiced apologetic stammers, Ersilio tells me that Nedda needs luting.

I tilt my head at her, straining the stab wound on my shoulder. Her chest is jouncing like she's panting.

"What's wrong?" I say. "Her eyes?"

"No, just very thirsty, aren't you, *pulcino?*" When Ersilio strokes his daughter's cheek, she sways a little, delirious. "And her skin feels like sand. I'm worried it's porphyria. Or diabetes. Or, I suppose, I was, until I remembered her uncle's magic luting hands."

With unease hollowing a fissure at the base of my spine, I kneel and place my hands on Nedda's face.

"Ready?" I say.

She grins and nods.

I push out my belly, push down my shoulders, and shake a shudder up my back. The bloat rises, gets stuck in my elbows.

To my mind, luting is devouring. It's holding my breath for so long I grow delirious, only in a quick flash. It's embracing someone hard enough to push them through me and out of the back of me. That's why I can't lute myself. When, after Malacresta was dragged away, I focused my power on the slashes and gouges he'd given me, it felt as impossible as trying to turn myself inside out.

When I stretch it out to Nedda, her flesh seems to press against mine but refuse to pass through. The plane of it seems fragmented, half-reacted, liquid glass mixed with sand, clay slip mixed with gabbro dust.

My wrists cramp when I let her go.

"Better?" I say.

Nedda nods.

"Did it feel strange?"

She shakes her head.

"All better?" Ersilio says lovingly, lifting her down from the table. They leave the workshop with their arms linked.

My dizziness recedes. It consumed me enough to put a gap between touching her and letting her go, so I have forgotten why I was uneasy before I tried to lute her. But I'm uneasy now that I can't lute the same person twice.

Days later, Nedda is back without Ersilio.

"Uncle Sole?" she calls from the side aisle.

"The door is open."

I turn from my statue as the door opens.

She emerges with the shadow of something around her mouth.

"It's bad again," she says.

I drop my ruler. With terror pounding in my head, I jostle her inside and slam the door. Now that I'm close, I can see that the darkness around her mouth isn't a stain. I'd been thinking about her father in the forest with wine around his mouth, and Nene moaning out his own blood.

It's a sunburn like mine.

Black flecks, like eraser shavings or dead gnats, stuck to the shiny raw skin they were rubbed from. Crowds at the corners of her mouth, and two snagged in the baby hairs above it.

With a thumb caked in dried clay, I stroke her brow. The skin there rubs off too, in the same shavings. It must have rubbed off around her mouth because she put her fingers there. It's a common place for sculptures to buckle, the corners of the mouth, if the mouth is too hollow or the hair too heavy.

"Does it hurt?" I say.

"Not now," Nedda says. "But it stings when I eat."

"Do you eat? Are you hungry for something which isn't food?"

She frowns at me.

"Sorry. That was a stupid question. Just Papa said you were thirsty."

"I put pebbles in my mouth on the beach," she says placidly. "Without Papa knowing. The taste makes me feel much better. I like the smooth flat ones best, squashing my whole tongue."

I stare at her.

"Uncle Malacresta saw me doing it once. He puts rocks in his mouth too, pointy ones on his teeth, so he didn't snitch on me. He snaps his glass in his teeth too. Papa says he's going crazy because he's eating glass and rocks, but it must just be the glass, because eating rocks makes me feel good."

I barely hear her. I'm sick of Malacresta this, Malacresta that. I'm stuck on the taste of rocks.

"Are your eyes okay?" I say.

"Yes, there's nothing wrong with my eyes. I promise. It's just, um, my face and my arms, and my mouth and my tummy."

"So, um, everything else."

"Yeah."

What unites Nedda and me? God-grown things, of course. My voice, and then, a perfect few weeks later, her eyes.

I straighten my back and clutch a handful of my tunic, rubbing peas of clay from my hands onto the floor. Horror swallows my stomach without chewing it.

There's a blight in us both. We're decaying. We're going to split for it like Nene did. We're going to birth wings and hang from the church ceiling. I joked about turning him into a statue, and now he is doing it to me.

Grey ache. Licking rocks. Cracked at the corners of the mouth. Rubbing off in black gnats. Thirsty.

I let go of my tunic and stare at my hands. Then, I put my thumb into my mouth, scrape a small amount of clay onto my bottom teeth, and hold it on my tongue.

Is this hunger new? I know that I have always loved the smell of cobblestones after rain, the silver-green miasma I want to lick out of the air. The clay's taste is that miasma liquefied. It clangs green through my head like the taste of Benghi Cvradi's blood, but I was struggling out of a stupor then, and I am lucid now.

I have spent my life with holes inside me, holes I didn't

know were there until something suddenly filled them. Feeling like girlhood was torture, because I wanted to be a man. Swimming with Nene until I nearly drowned, because I wanted to be his lover. Burning with the agony of existing after he was gone, feeling like the slightest sounds cored my ears and the softest light flayed my eyes, because I wanted to drink a lot of wine. For as long as I have had my voice, for as long as I have lived in this workshop surrounded by the smell of clay, I have echoed and yawned with hunger. Is this hunger new? The hunger to fasten my jaws around a fresh, sharp-cornered, marshy block of gabbroic clay and take an enormous bite?

Nedda watches me anxiously as I gnaw at my hand. She doesn't notice that I'm eating the clay off my fingers. She must think that this is what I do when I'm panicking, and that I'm panicking because I don't know how to help her.

I turn my back on her and go to the table. Scattered between the bloodstains and stab wounds in the wood are a bucket of water, a cube of clay, and the jar I use to mix slip. I dip the jar into the water bucket and add to the wet rim a finger-sized dollop of clay. The slip I mix is weak, but it's darker than water and thicker than ale.

I hand the jar to Nedda.

"Drink this," I say, "and tell me if you feel better. If it tastes bad, stop."

She does.

There is a certain way that toddler children drink. I saw it every day in my sculpting tent after the earthquake. Holding the cup with both hands, jamming it into their eyes as they finish, gurgling for air like plugholes. *Sip-sip-sip-gasp.* That is how eleven-year-old Nedda De Aqvancis drinks the slip. The tight-eyed, tight-fisted ferocity of her drinking tells me that she can taste the clay, and she more than doesn't care. It's as delicious to her as it was to me.

As I watch, my mouth falls open and my hands fumble to grip the edge of the table. I feel my best friend's gigantic hands closing around my throat and twisting until my head comes off. I see him turning around to kill me as I climb onto the pew to see Emerenzia, as I slope up to him in the quarry, as I ask him to pull the church down, as I tell him my womb is moving, as he pulls Malacresta out of my lap. In every memory we've made together.

Nedda lowers the cup from her mouth. A grey tongue darts to safety behind her teeth. The slip glistens around her lips where the shadows were.

I reach out a shaking hand. "May I?"

She nods.

When I rub the corners of her mouth, the shavings of skin melt back into place.

"Is it going?" she says happily.

"Oh, fuck," I say, rubbing at the welts of sunburn on my own neck. "Sorry, darling; that's a bad word you should never say. Oh, fuck!"

I turn back to the table, pick up the wet block of clay with a squashing fist, and bite off the piece which oozes over my thumb. Nedda charges up behind me. She says, "Does it help? Can I have some?" and in the manic relief of plugging a haemorrhaging hole in my soul, I break the block in half and oblige her. And Ersilio, as is his great talent during my wickedest, least dignified moments, opens the door and sees.

"Hello," I say with my mouth full.

Ersilio doesn't realise what's happening for a long time. Porphyria or diabetes, he said. All better after the luting, he said. You're like my brother, and I'd trust you with my children before any other, he said. Disgust and confusion come over his face in quick flashes, then recede.

"Papa, Papa!" Nedda rushes up to him and seizes his arm. "I'm better, look!"

She smears at the corner of her mouth, and shows him that the skin is strong again.

He stares down at her.

"We," I say, wiping my mouth with the back of my hand, "have discovered that the luting causes a sickness. That sickness. Thirst, the flesh drying in the sun and rolling off on the fingers. Luting doesn't fix it. Eating clay and hydrating ourselves fixes it. Like we're sculptures."

"Sole gave me clay slip to drink, and I feel so much better!" Nedda says. "I'm not hungry anymore, not even a bit!"

"I'm going to tell Benghi Cvradi and the... couple of others I luted after him. Papena Tegliacci and the baby. Oh, the baby..."

And Ersilio says, with his daughter hanging from his neck,

"Do you have *any idea* how many people you luted while you were sick?"

And do I have any idea how bad the sickness can get? And do I have any idea how long satisfaction lasts before we need to eat again? And do I have any idea whether that tiny baby whose cough I luted can drink slip before he's weaned? And do I have any idea how to break it to my builders, my churchgoers, my *followers,* that I've infected them with a disease I know nothing about?

No.

Every apology I could offer must begin with a preliminary apology: That I don't remember whom I've luted. My touch is so important to them as to cleave their lives in two, into the time before and the time after, and I don't remember touching them. The sickness will come over Benghi Cvradi soon, and quickly, because he is elderly and weak. The others will have to dread it for two more years, believing that every crackle of hair on their faces is their skin beginning to peel off.

Nedda and Ersilio don't want me to go, but I have to remove myself before they notice my terror. Ersilio kept his tender faith in me through all possible displays of bad leadership, bad prophethood, bad personhood, but he will demand wisdom and decorum now that Nedda is at stake.

In a jolt, I remember putting my jaws around the splint on

Lagia De Aqvancis's ankle. An ankle which was almost healed. Because she couldn't wait a week to walk, she is blighted too. People became blighted for *cracked thumbnails.*

I blighted both of Ersilio's daughters. His entire family.

I blighted my congregation. With a sickness which requires them to eat and bathe in clay. They will expect wisdom and decorum from me as well—

—because I am both their Curato and their sculptor.

They need me twofold.

In the mire of terror in my belly, power breaches, with bristling back and wolfish eyes.

On a lilac evening, fuzzed with rain, I find myself standing in the graveyard.

When we peeled the old church from the hill, the graveyard lay powdered with clay. The people who salvaged chunks of their dead loved ones' statues laid them in the grass as placeholder gravestones, scratched with names, dates and pet names. As I started to work on my gravestones, I promised that they wouldn't need the placeholders for long.

I was wrong. Before Nene dragged me down into his belly, I made Ciecherella, Della Del Meda and the three other victims of the earthquake. So far, in my new workshop, I have made twelve, rewarding myself for every three half-remembered grandparents with one sorely grieved young beauty. I grew efficient and confident, sloughed the fear of being accused of sculpting passionlessly by a client blind to the intricacies of sculpting and tried, as the years went on, more diaphanous garments, more precarious poses, more likeness-unseating expressions.

And all of them are hideous next to Ciecherella.

I nearly always prefer my rough work. Twists and gapes scream *This is art* more loudly than refined realism. Ciecherella, however, maintains those twists and gapes in spite of her refinement. The intricate embroidery on her bodice is creased by the turn of her waist, and the petticoats froth from the hem of her skirt as if they were smeared on raw and squashed out. I remember the week I spent stripping my dress off to drench my long, heavy hair, stuffing my wet body back into my dress and running back into the tent to sculpt, over and over and over again. How I shivered as I worked, my hands around my tools and my whole body on its feet. How I coughed at night. How, as I stared at the tangles of hair I had carved, swinging in a net over those divine eyes, I was numb to my own suffering. When I saw the way Ersilio gazed at her, numb to his daughters wriggling in his arms, I felt that it would have been worth it if I had caught a chill. It would have been worth it if I had died.

I know exactly how to give to Malacresta. He wears his wants in colour on his teeth. He wailed for his sister for a week, then filled the hole she left with polished rocks. It was me who made him want more.

The hole she left inside Ersilio is so intricate, so perfect, that it has always seemed that only she could fill it.

I throw myself to my knees on Ciecherella's wet grave and shove my hands against the grass. The force with which I rock my power into my shoulders and down into the earth is the force with which, if I had no power and no pride, I would scream *DON'T LEAVE ME!* It is tidal. It makes me chew off slugs of my cheek and grind my teeth until a headache comes with a snap and cross my arms flat on the floor. It makes me jerk and keen like Nene before the first wing tore through his stomach. It makes me cry.

And Ciecherella has no flesh left, so nothing happens.

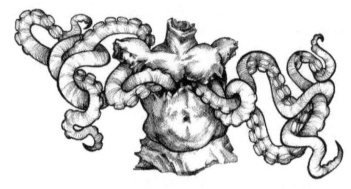

CHAPTER 21

THE OPAL

I STOP TO SLAM MY HEAD INTO TREES three times on my way to the furnace. I'm not embarrassed to stoop. I'll grovel to Malacresta, tell him I was wrong to attack him and my church is ugly without him and oh, God, Ersilio's too good and he's going to leave me. I need the friend who, at least for the eternal minute after I swung a blade at his head, might have been as mad as me.

As long as it makes him come back. If he rejects me, I'll put another blade in him.

I notice the darkness and silence of the furnace before I'm halfway up the hill, but seeing it empty when I arrive at the door still makes me groan. Though Malacresta isn't here, he was the last one here. The two crucibles look like someone was disembowelled inside them, drooling a dark ichor of glass down their bellies, and the eye of the furnace is stuffed with dirty blades and blowpipes. In the mess of it all, the sideboard is bizarrely clear. There's no lead grating, no yellow glass. The only sheeted glass in sight is a black arrangement, much bigger than the green one Malacresta showed me.

I pick it up. It's shaped like a ram's head, a big rectangular base with two prongs bent upward and outward. It wears lead in the joins between the five pieces. Each sliver of lead has been carefully hewn not only into the right snake or arc, but with a long slit for the glass piece on each side.

I've walked out of the forest, down the hill and into the square before I realise I'm still holding the black arrangement. Though the hunger to beg Malacresta is waning, I keep walking past the church, towards his house. I expected to find the furnace cluttered with colours, and I need to check he's only taken them somewhere else.

Malacresta's bedroom window faces the cliff. As I stand in the street outside the white stone house, I see that he's also taken the lead grates from the two front windows, leaving rust-bruised nail marks in the limestone.

I knock at the door. When, after a long period with no answer, I hear a THUMP from the back of the house, I try the handle and let myself in. The kitchen, with its ashy hearth and low wooden cupboards, is as gloomy and tidy as the furnace.

I let myself into Malacresta's bedroom without knocking. He is sitting at his desk in the corner of a cavern drenched in smoky pools of yellow and bronze light. As I stare at the thing propped to cover the window, he turns and sprawls out in his chair, nothing more than a fleck in the corner of my eye unfurling.

It's an enormous shard, a serrated archway, of a stained glass window. True to his explanation the day he left me, he has built it out in portions from a central piece, and that piece, an umber oval with a clear gash like an ink splash across its middle, is Nedda De Aqvancis's face. She has two jagged loops of plaited hair and, in familiar yellow, a bolt-straight bodice with long sleeves. Beneath the bodice is a porthole of empty space which stretches down to the windowsill.

Malacresta gets up from his desk and walks to block my view. I only see that he's holding two more yellow pieces when he reaches up to lean them in place. The tiered tulip of blowing skirt sits in two halves, and doesn't fill the entire gap.

Reptilian in his skin of yellow fractals, he turns to me and reaches out. When I don't react, he storms up and wrests the black arrangement from my hands. When he places it between the halves of Nedda's skirt, with the ram-horns reaching up around her bodice and towards her face, I realise what it is. Albeit headless, its head thrown down beneath its shoulders, it's me.

He turns his palm, scalloped with purple scars, towards the ceiling. *Ta-da.*

I stagger. Miss the bed, and sit down on the floor.

"How did you do her face?" I say, shock weighing down my tongue. "Paint? Or did you mix the brown and clear in the crucible?"

Already grinning from the sight of me on the floor, he quirks his eyebrows at the second.

Then, he gathers the three loose pieces, lifts the window down, and slinks to his desk. There's another picture standing there. One with a flower of skirts at its centre I suppose he was copying Nedda's from.

When he places it in front of the light and paints the room turquoise, I think it's a picture of Ciecherella on her wedding day. Then, I see the black splashes on every other vertical band of skirt, the cherrywood hair, and the oval of clear glass on the bodice.

"You were only… five when she got here," I say. "How did you remember?"

He scowls at me.

"I suppose I was only six."

He sneers.

"Is that Nene in his blanket? He's so round. I love that I can see outside through him."

Malacresta's sneer turns into a big, pleased grin. He pulls the picture down and replaces it with another. Another with a

350

clear body floating in its centre. Another body which wears my black arms as a belt.

Malacresta has used the first colour he ever discovered, horizontal waves of deep jade and organic ruffles of a grassier, milkier formula, to make a picture of Nene and his wings basking in the ocean. There are four wings in the picture instead of the correct two, and they spire around him in sharp, interlocked geometry, like the drawing we did together in my bedroom. The little green knot he brought to show me in my workshop was a test.

He hasn't had time since the fight in the workshop to half-finish three windows. He had some of them waiting. Perhaps all of them apart from Nedda.

As I stare and stare at Nene in the waves, I draw my knees up to my chest like a child. I'm not sure which of them my heart is aching for. I am stunned that he worked it all out on his own, without a supporter in the world. I am furious that I didn't see his face when he learned how to set, how to design, how to mix two colours in one sheet. That's what he wanted when he visited me. Not for me to see his yellow. For me to follow him and see the rest.

Malacresta leaves the window and stalks past me. When the sound of scraping metal alerts me to the fact there's a fourth picture, I say, "Please don't change it yet."

He assents. He leans to look at Nene with me, resting his bent knee on my shoulder. His clothes smell so strongly of smoke that my nose twitches when his arms fall around my head.

I reach up to hold his hand, then remember the wounds on his palms and hold his leg instead. It's a different contact. Perhaps because it presses his knee harder into the scar on my shoulder and perhaps because one tug would bring his whole body down into my lap.

"You picked just the right moment for him," I sob. "He was in so much pain, nearly all the time, but you didn't trap him in his pain. You let him sleep. And the sun shines through him harder than it shines through anything else. Harder than it shines through the wings. Do you see that? Do you see how beautiful that is?"

There's a tiny click as a smile separates his lips.

He gets up off me, making me pang with cold, and drags up to the window the fourth picture.

"Please don't, Malacresta. Please don't change it yet."

He thrashes his head in disdain and changes it.

There's something mythic, something classical, about the flash from green to scarlet. The way Malacresta slams the picture into place and strides back says *This is it. My favourite.* For the first time, I find myself following him with my eyes as he sits down on his bed, spreads his legs about my shoulder, and glares up into the bloody light with his tongue oozing out. When he sees that I'm looking at him instead of at the window, he leans down, takes my head in his hands, and redirects it with a violent twist.

It is the best one. It's divine. Benghi Cvradi lies on his back on a cobblestone floor, his naked torso a chessboard of bronze and red, the closest forearm sprouting up like a rose from the bottommost border and the farthest lifted flush against the rightmost. The oblong of fountain wall behind him is clear marbled with sunny, translucent red, but the haemorrhage which frames him in an arc, jagged and outlined like a great broken beam, is iridescent opaque mahogany—the untreated copper glass he disparaged in the furnace. There is such immense variation in the shades, mixtures and opacities of red that the picture looks like it's moving.

"You made the fountain marbled the same way as Nedda's face, mixing it with the clear?" Malacresta's head nods against my cheek. "And that's how you got it bright and see-through, too?" He nods again. Given the proximity of his mouth to mine, there's a chance he's disappointed I'm not asking about the way he's drawn me: Straddling Benghi in a black dress as harshly outlined as the haemorrhage, my bronze head rocked back behind my arms. None of the faces have features yet, but this is the only picture of me which has a face at all. Seeing it floating in the mass of black clothes and black hair puts me in mind of a night sky with a low, yellow sun in it.

"I'm in a lot of them," I say. "It's... I was going to say it's strange to see a picture of me made by someone who doesn't hate me, but of course you hate me. And of course that monstrous thing looks like you hate me."

I turn to face him. I find my mouth full of his tunic, warmed by his stomach. The smoke in his clothes has put a heaviness in my head, and opening my mouth against him snaps it into an ache.

"It's so *ugly,* Malacresta," I say. "The church. It's exactly what we said it'd be when Ersilio gave us the plan. Without you, I'm the only one who cares that it's ugly. I told myself I could stuff this boring thing with crazy things and make it symbolic of something, of Nene before he split, of the way we think of God, that it might be funny to entice people in and shock them with how monstrous it is. I was going to cover the walls with mushrooms and tentacles, hang Nene from the ceiling with the chandelier hanging out of his eyes, but I just... think it'd be better in glass."

When he winds both his fists into my hair, hunger spreads from my nape down my back.

"I was lying," I say. "About not caring about the glass. I stopped caring about it when you left because I didn't want to share it."

I extract my head and look up at him. He's glaring through me with narrowed eyes.

"I know you know what I'm asking you. I'm begging, actually. On my knees. I'm the right hand of God. I don't beg. You know how lucky you are. You're just letting me keep going because you enjoy it, aren't you?"

He grins, a dark ribbon of space between his teeth, and nods.

My redness burns white. With a snarl, I surge up and tackle him onto the bed. Headbutting down into his stomach draws his limbs in, elbows into my face and knees into my thighs. My only weapons are my fists and my mouth, and with two catches and a bite, he takes them from me.

He tastes like soot and iron. I am surprised he doesn't belch smoke when he opens his mouth.

It's a good thing we are fighting, because we don't know how to kiss. I bite his lower lip and lunge on top of him to pull it in a death roll. He digs his nails into my cheeks to unhinge my jaw and yawns around me with his tongue back. We gape and snap at each other like dogs, thwart bites to the throat with headbutts and turn them into bites to the face. When I bite his neck, he curls up and kicks. One knee slams into my sex and the other my lung. My groan is unary.

I rock my hips down between his thighs. He stretches his legs up again, not beneath me but around me. When he feels the hard spike of my arousal, he makes a rattling, hissing noise in his throat and brings his heels down like hammers on my spine. When I bury my face in the laces of his tunic, he drags me out by my hair, but when I hook my hands into his trousers, he drags me back and takes them off. Clad only in his hose, dyed green in the same bath as his trousers but kept dark as jewels in their shelter from the sun, his legs knot shut around me harder. The last thought I have before the molten weight of my sex pulls my brain out of its socket is of him sheeting a green glass bubble with his blade. Pierce, cleave, splay.

Once my brain has slid away and I'm fucking him in back-scratching, head-hanging shoves, hard enough shoves to shake his shoulders and trunk off the bed, Malacresta throws his arms out, and hangs upside-down by his legs. To keep him from falling, I grind my head into his neck, impale him on the pike of the mattress. He parts my hair from his face with a two-handed scratch. We're one beast now, one black beast which fucks itself with two green legs sticking out of its back. We yell

KYLE WAKEFIELD

in single and pant in double until my concussing orgasm, when Malacresta's panting turns into a lurid mockery of my moaning and his moaning turns into the kind of cackling I only hear when a racket frightens every seagull in the valley at once.

I shriek in shock, crash down into him, claw about in the blankets around him. My shriek seems to finish him; his stomach bucks and he screams with laughter with his head thrown back over the bluff. Once he's laughed so hard he's on the verge of slithering to the floor, he clenches his thighs around my waist, opens his mouth against my scalp, and says,

"You talk more when you feel like you're talking to a wall."

I stagger up, dripping from my hair and drooling from my mouth, and stare. Horror at his action, a horror which is half awe, is beaten to my stomach by horror at its consequence. He can speak. He stayed quiet to agitate me.

He wanted me to tell him about my lie, and I showed him.

He grins at me, crinkled and toothy and proud. His throat is still trembling with laughter. His lower lip is huge and purple from being bitten, his sweat soaked down the front of his tunic, the dark comma of my release on the inner rim of his hose. Kept safe from the eyes of the world by three little strings.

"You're blackmailing me," I say. I plead.

He rolls his eyes. "Yeah."

"So what do you want?"

He swings one green leg to and fro on its heel. His thighs make the same wet click sound as his lips when he smiled.

"Uh, I want out of this room. I want… to talk to myself and not eat and not sleep somewhere my mamma can't see. Don't you have walls now?" I nod. "I'm putting my sketches up on them. You still have the table I butchered you on?" I nod again. "It's my table now. You're not to let your people treat me like a traitor. You're to point to my windows and say they make me better than them, as good as God, as good as you." He stops swinging his leg. "But you came to offer me all that anyway. Beg me, actually."

355

"So you're not blackmailing me."

He frowns. "I guess not."

Despair spreads through me in a burn.

"Then why did you stay quiet until I came?"

The answer seems strung between his teeth. That he's going to show everyone. Burn my kingdom to the ground. That there's not a thing I can do to stop him.

"Funny," he says instead.

The commotion Malacresta flowers in the church is distinctive. My builders shout, their tools clatter, their shoes squeak on the floor, and he is silent. When I walk out of my workshop into the side aisle, he's standing in the centre aisle with Benghi, Benghi's brother, Ario and Sitha holding his arms out.

"There he is," Sitha says. She calls to me: "He insisted you'd want to see him again. We grabbed him in time."

"Thank you," I say. "Your dedication to my neck honours me. In this especial case, though, the vow I made to be gentle to his hands outstrips it. Please let him go."

The four exchange bewildered glances as they release Malacresta. He keeps his arms spread wide.

"Right hand of God," he says, "I've, um, come to beg you to take me back. If your noble hands can heal the unhealable, then your noble heart can forgive the unforgivable."

"Practiced that speech, did you?" I say.

"In the mirror."

The swelling I bit on his lip has ripened into a red sore he might have bitten himself. He might have burned the bite marks on his neck, jabbed the black rings into his belly and thighs with a blowpipe. The latter, in their ripened state, will never be seen by anyone but him.

"Have you told the Devil's bitch yet?" I say.

Malacresta shakes his head.

"What will she do when she finds out you've come back?"

"Follow." Malacresta rolls his eyes back. "Or be dead to me."

"Is our fight dead to you too?"

"I'll impale myself to make penance."

"And when you remember it was me who started it?"

"I'll… beg you to impale me again."

Confusion, lust and relief knot inside me, pull tight.

"Very well," I say. "Bring me, uh, whatever bits of stained glass you've ferreted together in your absence, and I'll make up my mind whether you can be of use to us."

"Merciful angel!" Benghi cries.

Ario mutters something which ends with "—killed," and kicks a hammer across the floor.

The interior of my church is barren and grey. A floor tracked with chalky footprints, a nave bordered by wooden joists, a chancel backed by framed rectangles of cliff face. It is, to the neighbours who have visited for the first time as of late, exactly what they expected of me.

Everything changes that night, when Malacresta carries the turquoise and green windows into the side aisle.

By the time he returns with the red and yellow, the clattering and shouting has grown loud enough to draw Ersilio, Nedda, Lagia and me out of the workshop. Builders entranced away from their work and visitors entranced away from their sneering alike are jostling each other and dragging beams and ladders to stand on. Parents are holding up their children, holding their hands out to catch the marine sparkles.

I sigh in delight when Malacresta reaches out to Benghi, who is gazing at the picture of Emerenzia with his hands clasped at his chin, and solicits his help with lifting his own portrait. The consumption of a rectangle of daylight by the tight twist of red viscera sends a thump of a gasp through the crowd. When Benghi seizes Malacresta's hands and draws him close, I know exactly what he is muttering to him. Something about being lost and found again, about the Curato's golden heart.

Ever unsmiling, Malacresta looks across the nave and beckons to Nedda. She gasps, Lagia squeals, and the two of them race each other to see the picture.

"Guess he finally polished through his hand," Ersilio says.

I say nothing. I am beaming at the side of Malacresta's face like it was me he beckoned to.

I shouldn't have expected Malacresta's return, but I did. Later that night, there's a return I should have expected, but didn't. As I lounge in the rafters, with a bird's-eye view of the side aisle which makes the four windows' capes of fractals look like coloured beams laid along the floor, Prasede, with long black shadow and spectral step, walks down the centre aisle.

Malacresta notices her, gives her a two-handed wave, and goes back to talking to his nieces. Prasede marches up to him and pulls him to face her. There's a conversation of jerking hands and shaking heads and words that I can't hear, but that the crowd turn to listen to.

Ersilio, Nedda and Lagia never saw the windows. When Malacresta takes Prasede's hand and leads her to look, it's impossible to tell whether this is his first attempt to convince her they're beautiful or his hundredth. Between red light and yellow, she looks up into the rafters and sees me, and a prey animal's murderous terror comes over her face.

For four days, she stays. She sits slung down on the benches or up in the rafters with a scowl on her face, like a child dragged to a boring tea party by its mother. When we start fitting Malacresta's windows, measuring the lead frames and removing the clear glass, she shows a glimmer of willingness. She untangles knots in ropes, but doesn't run to fetch. She holds things steady as we lift them, but doesn't take any weight.

She and I don't exchange a word, but we are connected by the question squashed narrow between our foreheads: *What did you do to him?*

Malacresta and I haul the drafting and assemblage tools from his bedroom into my workshop, lay upon the table covered in bloodstains and stab wounds the huge sketches, the cement, the clay dish of paintbrushes. He sits there in a tangle from midday to midnight, drawing the construction lines for his eighth and final sketch. The fifth, sixth and seventh are pinned to the wall around the chair like wings.

The fifth will be orange, and depict Ersilio and me on the steps of the old church. The sixth will be deep blue, and depict Lagia lying in her blanket on the ruins of her house. The seventh is the long-expected tribute to his sister. The least disconcerting reason he is depicting her statue in the graveyard instead of her living body is that he wants to make her purple. The slow sketching, constant erasing and vicious disparaging of the eighth is painful to watch over my shoulder as I sculpt. It's a self-portrait.

On the fifth day, Prasede comes in to sit beside him. Sick of the pain which pulses between my eyes whenever her head moves to a new part of the drawing, I go outside to sit on the chancel. I haven't been sitting there long when the spire of lanternlight which reaches into the side aisle from the workshop slides away, and the bang of the door shakes the rafters.

Ersilio comes to sit with me. "Have they kicked you out?"

"No," I say, my eyes glazed.

There's a buzz of chatter from inside the workshop. A syllable of silence, then the same sound again. Malacresta's reply must have been pressed down into the silence.

"Didn't he say he came back without telling her?"

"Yeah, he did."

"What changed his mind? Do you think it was her?"

Thump, thump, thump, sweep goes my head. I jounce him

off the edge of the bed and pull him back. His socked feet dig into my bare hips. The bruises pang under my pockets.

"It was me," I say.

Like it's the first time I've opened my mouth since he bit me, pain lances my cheek and shoulder.

"What?"

"The morning before he came back, I went to his house. And—"

"Oh, you saw the windows there?"

"Yeah."

Prasede's voice rises. She isn't shouting, but the final note of each sentence mewls, like she's begging.

Then, suddenly, she's shouting. He says something which ends with her name. She spits two repetitions of the nickname she calls him: Mal. The door of the workshop slams open. Light stabs the floor of the aisle, withdraws. Nobody comes out.

Ersilio gets up to investigate. I follow, bent around my stomach in terror of throwing up.

We enter the workshop to the sight of Prasede pinning Malacresta to the table, but the moment she sees us, she shoots towards us, copper launched from a sawblade. Ersilio steps to shield me, but the shouting which pours over his shoulders is for him.

"Did you know? You knew! You were out there washing his sheets! You knew he was lying! This isn't shame or privacy! He let people think they'd *die* if they didn't obey him! That their houses would be crushed and their children would burn alive! All to gild the identity we already accepted with *pure gluttony!* Do you think that's holy, or are you just stupefied by how much you love him?"

"I think it's holy," says Malacresta, who sits on the table with his eyes rolled back.

Prasede unleashes a stuck nettle of a scream. Then, she runs from the workshop, crashing into a joist and using it to throw herself sideways.

"She knows?" Ersilio murmurs. "*He* knows?"

When he looks at me, he sees me glowering at the side of Malacresta's face, drafting a hundred pictures of his murder.

And he realises what I did.

"You didn't," he says.

I charge and seize Malacresta around the neck. My knees never impact the tabletop, because Ersilio seizes me around the waist and hauls me back. He doesn't stop once I'm upright. He backs me up against the statue next to the table and says,

"Tell me he went to bed with you."

"What?" I spit my hair out of my mouth. "How else would he know?"

"I didn't ask if *you* went to bed with *him!* He's a fragile person, Sole—"

There's a THUMP-THUMP-CRASH as Malacresta leaps up onto the table, strides across to the worktop, and hooks his boot under Ersilio's chin.

"Call me fragile again," he says, looming above us. "We'll see how fragile your neck is."

"Oh, God! Fine! Fine!" Ersilio pushes his leg away, making him half-leap, half-fall to the floor. "I'm going to fetch Prasede back, and we're going to sit and have a conversation about it. Like adults!"

He staggers out of the room, rubbing his neck with one hand.

"Need a best friend like that," Malacresta says. "Mine didn't guess."

I stare at him for a moment.

Then, I yell, "Prasede doesn't KNOW how you found out?"

He shrugs. "She won't believe I tricked you. She'll believe it if you tell her."

"Why in God's name would I tell her?"

"Because she's going to tell your whole congregation, and you need something to shout back at her." Malacresta backs me against the statue like Ersilio did. "How did you think this was going to work? Would you have shaved if God gave you a beard? Stuffed socks into your stays if God took your tits off? Were you going to lie for the rest of your life that the voice you demanded because it made you feel like a man was a coincidence, an accident? Course you were. You hid Nene. Even though none of us would've died killing him." When I open my mouth, he raises his voice and shouts, "You put a knife to him *twice!* A hundred knives the second time! You *told* us! And what happened to you? You got hurt, and you stopped. You were *lying,* Sole. You lie, lie, lie. You hid Nene because you knew he was unravelling and you wanted to fuck him until he was a cobweb the size of a mountain."

I roar, seize Malacresta's throat again, and hurl him forward against the table. As the pain withers his eyes, he juts his chin and opens his mouth in a smile.

"I know you better than Ersilio," he says. "I know you live these half-lives out of laziness. I know you don't feel bad and you never have. Watching you pretend to feel bad is like watching Ersilio pretend to be big and tough. It's like… it's like… watching me try to look at you! It's embarrassing. You don't have to pretend anymore! Those people *love* you! Why do you think people love God, even though He does terrible things? Because He does terrible things and lies that they're good? No! Because He does terrible things, tells you that they're good, and *so makes them good!"*

Nene fills my head. Not pleasure masking pain or pleasure in pain, but pain made pleasure by a declaration it is pleasure.

My belly is so tight with anger I'm bent around it. In my mind, I bludgeon him wide open, hang him with his own guts. In my mind, I march out into the side aisle and smash his windows one by one. *Blackmail involves keeping your mouth shut!* I yell as I do it.

But it wasn't blackmail. I won't break his windows. They're still gaining me followers. And oh, how I love them. For all his obsession—begging for compliments, fantasising that I'm on top of him with a hammer, mixing and cutting and soldering my black shoulders and hair into every glass rainbow—I am entirely at his mercy.

"This is a trick," I say feebly. "You pretended to come back and fight with Prasede, just like you pretended in your room. Telling everyone the truth wasn't enough for you? You wanted to trick me into doing it?"

"Sole, she called me sick in the head." Malacresta pulls at his fringe. "She looked at the red one and called me sick in the head. She's dead to me."

"PROVE IT!"

Malacresta blinks.

"I can do that," he says.

When he pries my hands from his throat and stands up, I think he's going to kiss me. He goes past me to the table.

I watch with narrowed eyes as he picks up his dish of paintbrushes and shakes it upside-down. Two pieces of stone which look like teeth fall into his hand. Their pink is clotted with gentle green and gold. Opal.

"I made these. They're tooth caps. See." He slots one onto his canine. What looked like the root of the tooth is the long prong of a fang.

"Nedda already told me you wore them. *That's* you proving your loyalty?"

"Hang*ong,*" he says with his fingers in his mouth. The tooth cap falls out, and he catches it with a palm-heel against his chest. "They fall off. Hold."

He dumps the tooth caps into my hand, shaking at the long string of spit.

As he darts to the table and picks up his glassmaking pliers, I say, "Malacresta, that was me telling you to kiss me."

"No, this is better." He puts the pliers into his mouth, fastens them around his canine tooth. "I'v'in finking about it all week."

364

Like the deft first slice of the blade through the bubble, a quarter-turn, stopped when his knuckles meet his cheek. He stares at the wall above my head as he does it, and the first crunch sends a thin fracture of light through his eyes. Blood swells up onto the shelf of his upper lip, then emboldens the side of his mouth as it runs down.

Cold pleasure spreads between my shoulders. When I tilt my head to follow the pliers, it brims down my back.

Malacresta rips his tooth from his mouth with a violent thrash of his head. Slams the pliers onto the table and staggers back, like they're a glass of something bitter.

And the act is answered by a rising roar from outside, as if the whole congregation saw it through the wall.

From the chorus of yells rises Ersilio's—a livid bellow I haven't heard in fifteen years: "DON'T DO THIS, PRASEDE!"

Prasede's shout comes from the ceiling.

"Listen to me! Builders, neighbours! Sole De Gasinis is a parasite and a LIAR! He told you God would destroy Magmate if you didn't build this church for him, but he really forced you to do it to PAY the DEVIL to TURN HIM INTO A MAN!"

Malacresta walks to me, wiping his mouth, and gouges the tooth caps from my palm. Pain pulses from his whole head, pumps apart the hinges of his jaw and the halves of his crown. He tries to jerk his eyes at me in command, makes them roll like marbles instead.

"You're right," I say. "That was better."

I emerge into the organic gloom of the nave to the sight of Prasede standing in the rafters, panting so hard she rocks. She hangs by one arm with her feet together, ill at balance, well at ease.

"LOOK AT HIM!" she screams, straining forward on her arm. "LOOK AT HOW HIS FACE HAS CHANGED! His hands, his shoulders! Don't you see that it started with the breaking of his voice? Didn't you see the gore of a miscarriage on his bed last winter and think for a moment that it wasn't a child he was giving birth to?"

The crowd's heads turn in a ripple. The closest people are a man's length from me on the chancel and the farthest have stopped in the square on their way past the door. Eyes crawling over me, eyes in pits on the walls and floor and ceiling. As I comprehend the size of the beast, I force my mind to reverse the direction of its body. Convince myself that I am its head, and Prasede, suspended in her orange dress, is its bait.

I open my mouth with a hard tongue click and say,

"Did Malacresta tell you willingly, or did you wrestle it from him?"

Prasede snarls, "Don't play that game."

"Did he tell you to convince you he was capable? It was a brilliant deception he worked on me. You didn't even believe he could *recognise* deception, did you?"

"Don't play that game, *porca puttana,* or I will gut you."

"You know—" I raise my voice to shout over the crowd. "I abhor the view you have of him, but the view you have of me is intensely funny. Three years into a well-hidden pact, but recently blessed with my Devil's-flesh cock, I am so unravelled by pomposity that at the first challenge from my enemy, I fall into his lap, open my mouth—and *tell* him all about it." The prevalent sounds in the crowd are gasps of disgust and parents jostling their children outside, but as people understand my confession, there are laughs. Muffled giggles and a shriek. "Oh, Malacresta, let me describe to you the size of it, shape of it. Oh, Malacresta, the primal ache of... secrecy lamented!" Prasede lets go of the rafter to cover her mouth with her hands, and I almost yell at her to watch her balance.

"And you would tell the whole village just to embarrass him?" Prasede says. "Discard him now you've taken his windows?"

"Prasede, he's only finished *four* windows. If I don't get to see the others, I will die incomplete. I'm going to cram this church with him until it bursts at the seams. I'm going to put him in that one too." I point to the enormous clear window behind the chancel. "After that, we're going to collaborate on a sculpture of Nene Karafantoni and his blight. For the ceiling."

"I don't believe you." Prasede gazes down at the workshop. "Where is he? I want him to tell me himself."

"I can get him to come out," I say, "but I don't think I can get him to talk."

Malacresta slinks down the side aisle and up onto the chancel, his mouth and neck ivied with blood.

Ario, who is standing next to Ersilio, squawks. Ersilio locks his jaw inside his mouth and opens his eyes until they're round. Both are remembering the threat I made after he gutted me. They think I ripped his teeth out myself, to punish him for his espionage. It's almost true.

But as Malacresta reaches me, puts his palms out to say *ta-da,* and gives me a grin thorned by a single pale fang, I feel that it isn't true enough. His is the art I wish I had made first.

The hole in his gum, left by a canine displaced so far up, faces out rather than down. That means that the opal tooth cap, which he has pushed deep into it, protrudes forward like the fang of a snake. The bleeding has stopped, but the stone is as orange as his teeth. The keloid is dark and thick, like the swelling I bit on his lip.

The people at the front of the crowd see it too, and curse and laugh when they realise it's impaled in his mouth. Prasede, sequestered up on the ceiling, says in a thin voice,

"What? What have you done? Mal, what did he do?"

Malacresta wrinkles his nose in disgust.

Prasede crouches, twists until she's hanging from the rafter, and lets go.

There's a fountain of screams and a thump. The crowd collapses in the middle, then rolls back. Prasede surges out,

square-mouthed and wild-eyed. I think she's running to
Malacresta, and I am wrong. Her thumbnail pierces my throat
before we're horizontal and she lands on top of me with such
force that her whole body seems to go through my neck and
stake it to the floor. Knee in my belly, knee behind her
shoulder, hair cracked across my face like a whip. "YOU
MONSTER!" It's not a noise from her mouth but an exorcism
from her chest. "YOU FESTERING SORE IN THE HEELS
OF THE GENTLE! I WILL PESTLE YOUR HEAD IN A
BUCKET AND EAT YOUR HEART!"

She punches me in the face over and over again. The first
blow is a rockfall, the next blow fleshier, all subsequent blows
superseded by the shock of her whole body slamming against
mine with the effort. When she flies up away from me entirely,
gurgling on her screams, it feels natural. I wait for her to crash
back down, put her fist through my skull, through the chancel
and into the crypt.

Instead, I open my eyes and see her lifted in the arms of the
crowd. Benghi Cvradi has his arms around her waist, and a
dozen others are pulling at her clothes and hair.

I stand up, heavy-tongued with concussion. My eyes burn
and my nose feels crushed against my face. Like I'm a shark
and they a shoal of fish, I walk into the embrace of Prasede's
attacks and watch the crowd bend around me to remove her.
She punches me until they yank out her arms, kicks me until
they haul her off her feet. Only then is the storm of rage in her
eyes broken by fear.

"He LIED to you!" She starts to cry. "He lie-hi-*hied* to you
all! Look what he does to the people who love him! You're just
his… arms! He'll… disintegrate you when your purpose is
served!"

She stretches her hand out to Malacresta, not like a parent
but like a child. Malacresta looks through her.

"Nene… For the years he was missing, we thought it was
you." The corners of her mouth open, make wells for her tears.

"We talked about you and Ersilio dumping his body somewhere. When I found out what really happened... whatever in sweet Hell really happened... It was like you'd dumped his body every day for all those years, and never wavered... Oh, Mal! Oh God, Mal!"

"Don't call them a *monster's arms,*" I say. "They're people. We're scared people."

"You *slink between your victims again,* Devil's whore?" When she bends double over the crowd's arms, her hair comes down over her face. "What are you scared of in this world?"

I wipe my mouth. "I'm scared that you're so beautiful when you're angry that you'll take him with you after all."

She gives a snarl made staccato by a snap of her jaws.

"I'm scared that they love me enough to tear you to flinders."

Behind the crowd, someone wearing blue is walking in the light of the square.

"I am scared," I say, "that God loves me enough to gild every sin with a more absurd miracle."

"Hello?" Ciecherella De Aqvancis calls from the doorway. "Is this Magmate? It looks different."

Still facing the chancel, Ersilio stiffens, like her voice was a dagger jabbed into the small of his back.

She walks into the gloom of the church at a creep. The path she forges through the crowd is blocked by people kneeling on the floor. People trip over their kneeling neighbours, panic, and kneel behind them, forging pews perpendicular to the aisle.

Ciecherella and Prasede lock eyes. Relief clears Ciecherella's fear like sunshine.

"Oh! Thank the Lord! Why is everyone staring at me? Why... have all the houses..."

Prasede's mouth is square, her chest heaving. Just as I think she's going to faint from panting so hard, her stone shell shatters and she turns and runs from the church as if for her life.

Ciecherella whimpers.

It is not her presence, but her fear, which draws Ersilio out into the aisle behind her.

He stumbles up to her. She turns. He stops.

Then, he lunges and seizes her like he wants to eat her. He claws up and down and up again to gather her into a smaller and smaller bundle and then falls, first to his knees and then his face, with her underneath him.

She laughs. "Fi-*ore!*"

She stops laughing when, with his face buried in her chest, he screams. High and violent, the sound is all relief and no horror, like finding Lagia alive in the wreckage.

There is a dead woman on the floor, my best friend is wailing on top of her, my nieces are crying because their papa is crying and they're frightened, and the whole crowd in the nave is kneeling to me. Malacresta, sitting back on his heels and gazing over its heads at the doorway, must wait. Now is not the time to ignore my followers for my friends. Now is not the time to scour my face against the floor or cackle at my power. Wisdom and decorum are not traits I lack. They are tools, and they fit in any hand.

"Every day," I say, "I hear God speaking to me not from the earth but from the sinew of my throat. Though He speaks in a language I do not understand, in tremors, He has built my body to withstand Him, and so I withstand. Today, we have witnessed two miracles in which my hand's only role was to hurt thereafter. Perhaps Malacresta's sister's return was a reward for his return, and perhaps it was only an echo, but it is clear I am not the one you should be worshipping. I would ask you to get up, turn towards God's strongest warrior, and kneel to him instead, were he not only a stride from me."

I turn to Malacresta, take his face in my hands, and unhinge his jaw with my thumbs.

"Prodigal son," I say, "It is harder to claw your way home from the wilderness than to never leave it. Harder to cultivate a scar than nurse the open wound. *Arcobaleno mio,* as much as I love the taste of your blood, you will be no fun if I drain it from you. One wound is enough to earn your healing."

"Good," he says. "S'why I made it."

I kneel to murmur into his ear.

"There is a sickness, which overtakes the luted. Their faces crack and they need to eat clay."

I feel him smile.

You lie, lie, lie.

"Is there enough?" he says.

I make a seal around his ear with my mouth. "For you, there is."

With the luting in my mouth like an apple, I lunge and splay him out on his back. He spreads his arms and lashes me with his legs as our tangled heads hit the chancel. He bites. The heat pours out of his teeth onto the floor.

And when the echo splits me from hip to hip, making me growl, "Huck! *Huck!*" with my lip trapped between his teeth, he laughs.

He laughs as his mouth fills with blood again, as his opal fang digs true, as the keloid pales and shrinks around it. Benghi Cvradi's hammer was ripped out, but this is a wanted intruder. Into my hair and mouth and hand, into the ears of the kneeling crowd, into the air which fills my boring church, he laughs.

The effort of unsoldering our jaws is tragic, but it isn't final. As he sits up, pushing me upright with his legs, he pulls the pliers from his pocket and shoves them back into his mouth. Like the man of pact that I am, drained by giving and hungry to be paid, I press my cheekbone against his, so I can better feel the crunch.

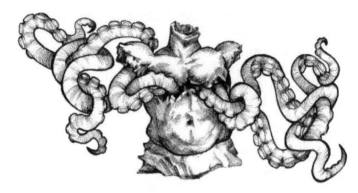

CHAPTER 22

THE PICA

CIECHERELLA DE AQVANCIS isn't acting like she just crawled out of her grave. From the moment she walked into view, the amnesia of her questions clashed with the lucidity of her voice. *"Is this Magmate? It looks different."*

She is wearing the blue wedding dress she was buried in. Unlike the woman who gave it to her, she bore it into the church spotlessly clean, and although it isn't raining, she bore it into the church soaking wet. The blue linen is uniformly dark and moisture flashes in the embroidered lines of the bodice.

"Who are you?" Ciecherella says as I kneel before her. When I bite my lip in awe and reach out, she flinches.

I run a wet, glittering rope of her hair across my palm. A rope of hair which was once mine. Drenched and referenced.

Staring into each other's eyes, we tilt our heads in tandem. Recognition.

"Solavita…" she says.

"It's Sole now," I say. "Don't fear my hands. They're the hands that made you."

A gallop to the churchyard confirms what I already knew.

372

Ciecherella's grave is undisturbed. The pedestal set into it is bare, branded by a long splatter of water.

"I was sitting at the kitchen table, watching the rain," she explains, stroking Ersilio's head in her lap. "I was thinking about how badly I wanted to go outside and feel it on my face. I heard rumbling out at sea, and suddenly I *was* outside. Wet, but the rain had stopped. I got down and saw that the pedestal—had—my—name on it…"

There is a point at which terror becomes so total that the smallest comfort wipes it clean. If Ciecherella had woken up already in Ersilio's arms—if he had kissed her back to life, as I used to imagine—the horror of her own death which burgeoned to core her would have cored her of his comfort as well. Because she crashed into him after the coring was done, he found a foothold inside her. He held her together, instead of holding her as she broke apart.

I expect Malacresta to lunge on her, but he, like me, is set in place by awe. His expression is cresting with disgust at her story long before anyone else has realised, in uncanny shudders, that it is a much more frightful story than the one about six feet of grave-earth and a hole in the chest stuffed with rags.

Minute by minute, Ciecherella becomes a sunbeam. When Sitha flinches away from her greeting kiss, her eyes crumple and she runs across the nave to cry on Ersilio's shoulder. When Ario does the same, she stretches her hand out like she's beckoning a traumatised pony, and when she suffers it a third time from her own father, she laughs with her mouth open and says, "Oh, Papa, are you scared I am cold as iron and wet as well-stone? Do you think I'll melt and stain your doublet?" To her and only her, guessing whether each new person will welcome her with delight or terror is a hilarious game. She is welded always to Ersilio, soldier-marching between the church and their limestone house with her feet pressed to his insoles and his fat arms around her middle, but it is he who is afraid to let go.

In the world before, she was terrified of the blue dress. She wore it like it would disintegrate at the slightest strain. Now, because she was born in it, she strides, grasps her skirts and lifts her arms as confidently as if it's her own skin. At last, twenty-five years after Emerenzia gave it to her at the fountain, it is her turn to say, *"It won't break! You must touch! It was made to be touched!"*

She says it to her father first, but to her husband most.

On the table in the workshop, Malacresta assembles the central geode of the fifth window. The orange he discovered is the ripe shade of molten glass just raised from the crucible, and its home is a tongue of flame which haloes Ersilio's umber body as the haemorrhage haloes Benghi. Ersilio is sequestered in the workshop for the week, helping me draw the plans for our chandelier. Though he ignores the portrait of him seeping outward on the table, Ciecherella is enthralled. Perhaps because it unifies her husband and brother, who so hated each other before she died.

"Have they told you yet what happened to the old church?" I ask her.

Ciecherella's fingers tap-tap-tap along the arch of fire, finish between her brother's hands.

"You ripped it down before dawn," she breathes, "because it dared to stand as I fell."

Yesterday, I found her alone in the side aisle, staring up at the picture of Nedda. To her, it is not Nedda's eyes which are the strange miracle, but her scars. I feared Ciecherella as an outsider to my church thrust suddenly into the epicentre, but with every new shock she accepts, I find it a little harder to believe her smiles are a stupor. Her husband ten years fatter and jowlier, her babies young women she doesn't know, me holy-handed and baritone-voiced, her mousy brother a lunatic with opal fangs, and Nene Karafantoni's death spelt in charcoal spires and spores on a fresh sketch page: This is too much horror for any mechanism to compress.

That night, when I think I'm alone in the church, footsteps shuffle down the side aisle and stop outside the workshop. After a pause, Malacresta calls,

"Signore Cvradi said you were doing confession now?"

"Yeah." I expect him to open the door. "They stand in the aisle and shout."

"Oh, um, bless me, Father, for I have sinned. It's been… twelve years since my last confession."

I grin down at my sketch. "May God, who has enlightened every heart, help you to know your sins and trust in His mercy."

"So, like, for orange, nice orange that isn't just muddier yellow, you need silver."

I look across the workshop at the window.

"Two days before Ciecherella came back, I boiled off all her jewellery."

That's how he greets me whenever the door is closed. *Bless me, Father, for I have sinned.* I suppose he feels he's too bold to knock but too shy to come in without knocking. The next time he says it, he has abandoned the orange window nearly finished for the cobalt blue one. I expect him to tell me he stole the cobalt from a baby or a defenceless old woman.

"Bless me, Father, for I have sinned. It's been three weeks since my last confession."

"May God, who has enlightened every heart, help you to know your sins and trust in His mercy."

"I hated you and Ersilio for burning down the church. You know I did. But I hated that you'd left me out of it too. That, and rebuilding it with you, and denouncing it with Prasede… it's all the same want. I just want to be part of carnage."

375

The chandelier swarms us. First, I sculpt the wings, which I designed to cradle the pulpit. They will twist around me when I give sermons the way they twisted around Nene: One spread long and straight down the wooden stairs and one splayed aloft like a great fountain. I keep the slag-heap of clay wet for weeks so I can shove the wings harder against the floor, trying to convey their dead weight. Every night, I fall asleep in the corner of my workshop with ease, then wake up an hour later with a fresh vision juddering in my head. Every time I assent to the vision and get up to sculpt judders me sicker, judders me awake more ferociously the next night, but I would choose a lifetime of sickness over a morning of waking up with last night's vision forgotten.

The sicker an idea makes me, the better it looks. When I wake up with a vision of fauna, the big mushrooms wearing little mushrooms on their heads like hats, I sit up in bed to make shapeless, stained sketches; when I wake up seeing nothing but intestines, the purple and orange slugs Nene uncoiled from his stomach like rope from the ocean until they pulled taut in fastenings between his bones, I go to the nave and sculpt gorgeous pillars of braid and bladder until I fall asleep face-down on the floor. I wake up in a puddle of drool which ululates **It hurts, it hurts, it huuurts** as I haul myself up to start hollowing. I'm wet and green with nausea, but I never throw up. I can't drag myself from one side of the church to the other without needing to sit down on the floor with my head between my knees, but I never faint. God wants me to finish my masterpiece. Only then will He cut my strings.

The closest thing to rest is watching Malacresta make tentacles. Instead of devoting a day each to forging a batch of glass, cutting a batch of lead, and assembling a clutch, he brings a single tentacle from conception to completion a day—long, glittering pastel things like pleated ribbons—and hangs it from the rafters of the workshop like a conquest. The greater my exhaustion, the purer and brighter the lava he leaves in his

wake. Like an angel with a flaming sword he is, as tired as me
and in infinitely more danger if he falls asleep at work.

I wait in vain for someone to mention the fucking. For
Ersilio to tell me his brother is a low blow, or it's my job to
explain to his thirteen-and-eleven-year olds what a Devil's-
flesh cock is. For someone's mother to say it's abominable I
don't want to fuck women now I pass for a man, stupid that I
decided to pass for a man when it makes it harder for me to
fuck men. For someone to voice the natural assumption that
we, labouring side-by-side in the workshop every night, are
sleeping together again and again. The speed of our progress—
the tentacles multiplying on the ceiling, the wet wings twisting
back and forth, the sandcastle heaps of lead filings and clay
shavings—should make it clear that we aren't. Our intimacy is
making art together. It's a deeper intimacy than sex. A
finer one.

Then, on the dusk of a day which he has only broken at the
edges, dragging his feet like his skin is a gown which doesn't fit
him, he thumps against the workshop door.

"Bless me, Father, for I have sinned. It's been…" He makes
a fart noise with his mouth. "… since my last confession."

I don't want to play. I put my face down on the table and
slur, "May God, who has enlightened every heart, help you
know your sins."

"I let a crooked Curato ride below my crupper."

There's a snap inside me, a frictious meeting of tiredness
and incredulity, and I burst out laughing. Why am I surprised
that the congregation have forgotten the act beneath its
consequence? So have I.

I fucked him. I gave him my cock as I once gave Nene my
hand, but my hands are practiced and strong. I was a beached
fish on top of him, a hungry dog. Malacresta's greatest feat
wasn't choking back pain or fright. It was choking back
laughter.

"That's an—especially egregious one!" I manage between

laughs. "You'd better come in and apologise to me personally!"

I'm only trying to keep up the joke. When Malacresta walks in with soot on his face and his fringe sticking out like a chimney brush, I throw my head back and guffaw. Unsmiling, he crawls up onto the table, grabs my collar in his gloved fists, and kisses me with his teeth out. Amazement makes me fall off my chair, and the shock of hitting the floor is echoed by the shock of him pouncing down on top of me. With fatigue-drunk arms, we drag his tools off the table and my tools off the workbench only to set ourselves back on the floor, scarcely on the bed. Nuzzling the warm inside of his thigh, I mumble, "What do you want to do?" and he crosses his arms over his face and hisses, "Go to *sleep.*"

We squabble over who gets to lie down, finish soft-mouthed and chest-to-chest, and fall asleep without moving.

I'm awake an hour later, with him face-down in the crook of my arm. As I roll him onto his back to free myself, I lose all sense of what woke me up and what I'm going to work on in the space between our throats. Inside me rises the sickening need to be violent—pin his wrists to the pillow, cover his mouth with my hand, bite him hard on the neck—but I'm scared he's sleeping too deeply to wake up and fight back. In another hour, he's awake too, filing lead.

"Bless me, Father, for I have sinned. It's been two days since my last confession."

"May God help you know your sins."

"You're only in all my windows because my yellows kept turning black."

The nave is walled in rainbows, with all eight stained glass windows in place in the side aisles, when Benghi Cvradi's skin starts peeling off.

He has just turned sixty, and the black gnats are trapped in the wrinkles between his eyes. As he rests on a pew, I place my hand on his back and sweep into a crouch. "My dearest friend," I say, "you wear the marks of God's love on your forehead. Allow me to vitrify them for you."

I give him a mug of slip, and smooth down the blisters on his face as he drinks it. As I explain the sickness and entreat him not to tell anyone, so as not to prematurely panic Papena, Lagia and the smashed thumbnails, he smiles at me stupidly. He doesn't need an excuse. He's just happy to share a secret with me.

The sickness of art, cobwebbed eyes, thoughts as loud and repetitive as carol-choruses and feeling my heartbeat in my bones, drowns out my own decay for a while. The skin rolls from my palms when I push too hard against my tools and an iron-coloured sunburn spreads across the apples of my cheeks when I venture outside. When I scratch my neck one evening and tear off a black piece of skin thick enough to hurt me, I stare at my hand for a while in shock. The graze it opens on my neck is silver and sticky, and I spend the week pulling my hair out of it. My pica is unbearable. I want to lie flat upon the chandelier until my ribs have chewed it up, regurgitate it mutilated and redoubled, and eat it again.

It isn't long before Malacresta, cutting glass cross-legged on the table as I sculpt, asks me when clay will start tasting good to him. When I tell him I don't know, he jumps down, picks up the block of clay I'm sculpting with, sinks his teeth into it and twists, like he's biting the head off a frog.

As I watch him swallow and take another bite, I think I'm discovering that the cravings begin at the luting, long before the skin peels. But I'm not sure.

"When d'you think you'll tell them?" he says, as I wrestle

back what's left of the clay. "All the others?"

"I don't know."

"And how?"

"Well, I'm running out of clay soon. I'll do it all at once. Prepare them clay to eat and have it ready when I tell them. So they don't have to pass a moment in fear."

"So they'll be too busy eating to be angry, you mean."

"I do."

"Where will you do it? In the square? Show the whole village?"

"Not yet. And the sun might burn us."

"Well, they'll smash up the chandelier if we do it in the church."

Malacresta has moved to making primroses, deep green crystal shard leaves and yellow petals stained pink in the middle, and I to gore. Pieces of the chandelier have overflowed from the workshop and lie at wading depth between the pews. Malacresta might be right about the congregation's hunger. Even though Nedda didn't know what she wanted to eat until she tasted it, her relief undammed a frenzy.

"They won't be that hungry," I say.

"I mean they'll panic. I mean, what does it mean for us, really? If we're made of clay, will we shatter like clay? Or go hard and still over time?"

I look down at my hand. The pads of my fingers are smooth and pink from sculpting, the rest of the skin sallow and gnat-speckled.

"I'm going to find out," I say. "It's why I'm not eating. I'm going to find out how bad it can get."

Malacresta sinks his opal canines into his wet black bottom lip.

"Oh, they'll love that," he says. "You clever devil."

I reach out and rub my thumb against his lips. Because his fangs protrude forward from his teeth instead of downward, they don't affect his eating or his speech, but they affect his visage, giving him bigger catfish whiskers and making him rest his mouth in a dimpled smirk.

"I'll bite yoffingers off," he says.

"Better my fingers than my statues' fingers."

I am sculpting an arrangement of viscera, round bladders with disembodied hands protruding between them. Malacresta pushes past me, breaks off three leather hard fingers, and shoves them into his mouth.

"Just don't eat that one." I point. "Spent all day on it."

He thrusts his head against the carved hand I'm pointing to and bites it off. Warmth spreads through me.

"What're you smiling at?"

"You eating."

He rolls his eyes. "It's not that bad."

It is. In his years outside the church, starvation caved in his cheeks and scraped the fat from his muscles. His limbs and neck are pure gristle, beams without crossbeams. Since the people who told him to eat were also the people who hated his glassmaking, he found a triumph in refusing. Maybe, now that he can offend their morals by eating, he'll get his appetite back.

"Am I an experiment too?" he says. "You're fasting, and I'm the glutton? Double-luted? You going to triple and quadruple-lute me?"

"No," I say. "Unless you want more fangs."

There's a pause. Then, he says, "I cut some aventurine ones."

Tonight, there is no dogfight. The way Malacresta kisses my mouth, feinting and slashing with his jaws, is part passion for violence and part hatred of eye contact, but he carves his teeth into my neck and shoulder like he's carving slots into lead settings. I roll up his tunic, roll down his hose, and stamp a repeating pattern into his belly and thighs, giving wine-dark centres to the old yellow flowers. He's so thin that sucking his flesh makes my jaw ache.

"You want to be on your back?" I say.

He rattles his throat. "You want me to choke on my blood?"

He kicks me upright, rocks up onto my lap, spreads his legs to straddle me. I dig my thumbnail into a tooth mark on his hip as I penetrate him. While he's slack-jawed from the shock, we shove our tools into his mouth. My sculpting tongs clink against his glassmaking pliers. When we wrench his lower canines out, his tongue rears up like a centipede. Blood pools in the dark well of his jaw, then froths out vivid.

As he uses his hips to jounce the pain out of his head, I reach for the new teeth. Aventurine is green, with an even white glaze like frost. They're as sharp as the opal ones, but their curve is shallower. I push them into place with my free hand grasping his face, his hisses vibrating from his jawbone to my elbow.

I lute him, and the echo cleaves a sickle crescent between our navels.

I growl low in my throat, so hard I nearly retch. The pain of the echo is fleshly and turgid, small wounds prevented from gushing by thorns of obstruction. A sense of being filled with blood which can't escape, it chases the tail of my arousal. Malacresta laughed at the echo on the chancel, understanding at last what they meant and where they settled, and, when I told him I'd grow teeth on my cock every time I gave him new ones, he told me he wanted to see it.

He meant he wanted to feel it.

Malacresta arches his back, throws his head back and cackles. Like a stag with an arrow through its head, he ruts against the impaling not to push it out but to scratch its delicious raw itch. I wrap my arms around his waist, try to slow him, as if he might fuck me hard enough to snap it off inside himself. If he does, we'll be swollen too flush against each other to get it out. My embrace makes him push down harder and headbutt me backwards, and I then become rapt in his expression. Pain stamps yellow cracks through one of his eyes and pleasure melts the other down his cheek violet. When he opens his mouth wider, the green fangs dam his blood-reddened tongue like the leaves around a rose. My fantasy that every thrust chisels off another facet of his face, bares another spire of crystal or mucous rainbow, ignores the fact that it is him doing the thrusting.

He is held up entirely by me, leaning back in his hose belt with his head slung back in my hand, when the echo recedes. The moment he feels that he's healed, he lunges down and bites me on the shoulder. His climax levers his four fangs down to the bone.

Weeks later, he skips up to me with a blowpipe slung over his shoulders, gouges an apple-sized chunk from the mushroom I'm carving, and shoves it into his mouth.

"Goxum amethyst," he says with his mouth full. "S'prolly whadidis anyway."

"What?"

"Ansome serpentine."

"What?"

He points to his fangs in turn. "Ping, green." Then to the teeth behind them. "Pupple, yellow."

He already has more fat for me to suck. Bared in shards between the hose, shorts and undershirt he never takes off, the flesh smoothing and softening his muscular parts glows red like agate. I have never seen a man so ripened by madness. I feel so weak when I look at him that I start believing he's sapping the ripeness out of me. That he's a vampire in more than mouth.

Weeks after that, he uncoils an entire wet grey intestine from the pillar into his mouth.

"Pig!" I yell, swiping at him. "There's a whole block right there!"

"D'you ever wonder where it's going?"

I narrow my eyes at him. "Where what's going?"

He scrapes his palms with his bottom teeth, striping them with silver grazes. He pulls a face with a vast underbite to eat the skin off his lips.

"If we must eat clay, because we're made of clay."

383

I think about gabbro. One vein on this coast of Italy, another on the southern tip of England.

Looking intently at Benghi Cvradi, who is resting on a pew by the chancel, Malacresta traps his pewter tongue between his teeth. "When the quarry's empty," he says, "I'm eating the old man first."

"Bless me, Father, for I have sinned. It's been three days since my last confession."

"May God help you know your sins."

"I feel nothing for her. My sister."

This morning, when Ersilio and Ciecherella came into the church together, Malacresta and I agreed that he'd told her how she died. Her blue dress was unlaced, and he had both of his hands pressed in a coffin-cross against the hard part of her chest, where the beam had impaled her.

Before me stands the clay which will become my statue of Nene. He is nothing yet but a block with a hole in its middle, from which our clay and glass blight will germinate. I carved the hole with my fist dug hard into my belly, holding my organs in place.

"I'm sorry for the waste of your gift."

"I didn't bring her back for you. I brought her back to stop Ersilio from leaving me."

Malacresta's forehead thuds against the workshop door.

"Thank God."

Nene's face consumes me first. I cover every surface of the workshop with my sculptures of him. The pretty faces I made from life in the tent, the sublime blighted bodies I made from life in the crypt, the disgusting half-formed demons I made in grief and drunkenness. Even though I know the faces are perfect, copying them feels a second degree removed, like tracing someone else's work. The upper half of his face, with the huge pensive eyes, heavy brow and pointed nostrils, soon stares out at me, its mouth submerged in the clay as though underwater. Every night, I have a dream which seems to make me remember what he looks like. No, his nostrils only flared when his brow was furrowed; no, his hair was redder than blond, and who cares that you're sculpting in monochrome; no, he shimmered always with slime and film, walked among us like a jellyfish only half-cursed human. The sensation of an epiphany fading into an embarrassing delusion as I stand at the statue with my scalpel aloft becomes part of my morning routine.

I score a horizontal guideline for his mouth, then carve vertically. He ends the day with finely honed tentacles hanging in a beard from his cheekbones, crowned by the negative space of his cupid's bow.

I think about luting him as I luted Ciecherella. Tentacles pitching my trousers.

I think about luting him as I luted Ciecherella.

I cut the tentacles out and carve his lips.

Malacresta walks in on me kissing them, peeling them off from corner to corner with my teeth and then swallowing them, first the bottom and then the top. He stalks to the table and pushes a tentacle down his throat, whole.

I carve his lips again. Lute the gaping hole in his face.

I remember Nene's torso because I thought about it so much as I looked at the ruin of it, but this statue is of the ruin of it. He must make do with generic raw-boned legs and generic raw-boned arms.

I realise, not as I stand on the tips of my toes to kiss the new lips but weeks later, as I recall it, that I made him too tall. He was such a tiny thing.

As the builders hoist the sculpted blight into place, Malacresta and I lie down in the centre aisle to watch.

In shape, the chandelier is a dead octopus suctioned to an upturned bucket; in texture, it is a crystal cave skinned by a blow to the ceiling. In glass, yellow primroses strain on their roots, indigo geodes and pearly tentacles jut in geysers. In clay, guts drip slip down the pillars, fungus gouts the angles between beams and wings snarl the pulpit. Last week, I decided to rip the carefully sculpted broken wing from its place and start it again, this time by sculpting a replica of the intact wing and pulverising it myself. I punched it, kicked it, bent its spine up into my arms, beat it against the chancel floor like a sandy towel, then luted the cracks and blended it into place around its sibling. It's ugly, but it pierced a nerve in my stomach which hadn't been pierced since it burst out of Nene, and that means it's good.

"Beautiful, beautiful church," Malacresta says.

"You know what's more beautiful?" I say.

"That we made it."

I turn my head to look at him. "Do you know what's more beautiful than that?"

"You're not gonna say it's me, are you?"

"No, Malacresta. The most beautiful thing is that everyone will say we made it, but really, we fucked around with the beautiful bits whilst the peasants made it for us."

His grin bares all the colours on the ceiling.

Nene stands in my workshop like a corpse chained underwater. Fastened to the floor on the pedestal which will fasten him to the ceiling, he has a kelp pillar of hair and arms crossed at the wrist above his head with a strain which scoops out his collarbones. When the time comes to hollow the sculpture, I tighten my stays and belt until my breasts ooze out, until I can't twitch without feeling how hard I am held together.

As I gaze at him with my mouth open to declare him

finished, I worry that his face is too peaceful. His body is posed in tension and agony and his eyes are torpid, his smile gently puckered to show three top teeth. But there might be something right about that. As the centrepiece of the chandelier, he will hang inside a cocoon of candles and emerge as they melt. The people who climb up to light the candles might get used to the fountains of blight and clawing limbs, disdain them as the product of two broken minds, but their disdain will never find a place for that face.

"We'd better hang him up quick," Malacresta says. "Before you eat him or put your cock in him."

"I thought I'd have a service to hang him up."

He slaps his thigh. "Oh, *good.*"

We've been squabbling for weeks over when to start giving services. I wanted the sculpting ceremony in the square to be the first. How, I said, could an unbaptised church perform baptisms?

But my beautiful Nene fills my head with carols.

"Bless me, Father, for I have sinned.
    "I'm so hungry."

I climb up into the pulpit. I think about how lucky I am that it isn't attached to my backbone.

"Good evening, my patient, treasured friends," I say to the congregation of seventy. "Welcome to your creation."

They are all standing up. Though we ripped religion from our minds eleven years ago, we couldn't rip its instincts from our bodies. Stand when the Curato enters. Wait for him to seat you.

"I'm sorry there wasn't a hymn. Or a door, or a roof. We'll get our façade in order before the first real service, but I wanted your attention for a matter of blessing. You all see him standing there. I hope you like him."

Nene is standing on the chancel where the tabernacle will be, a grey ghost trapped in eternal gust.

"Please don't fear my manner. I am still learning the art of decorum. You had every right to disparage me as a poor choice of prophet and Curato, and I am grateful for your faith, not only for my own sake, but because I will not stand for the disparagement of the creature who chose me.

"Please feel free to sit."

Rainstorm in forest, large flat leaves patter-pattering. The shoulders of the crowd sink into the pews.

"When He was a child, our God felt nothing. The God before Him didn't seem to remember what meek and mild meant. Or perhaps He felt that He felt much too much the first time, and sought a simpler experience. As He grew, those close to Him went mad with frustration. For His lack of feeling, He was despised by you all, but would not despise you in return.

"And at the same time, one of your own was nursing an equal monster. You told him he was a girl, but he did not agree. He did not think he lacked beauty, power, opportunity or acquaintance as a girl. Indeed, he did not think at all. He only felt his body stretching out of shape the fabric of his soul. As he putrefied, making girls fear that they were meant to hate being girls and brutalising boys who had what he wanted, he despised you all, but you did not despise him in return.

"Now, you might bristle with fear that God chose me as His prophet to force you to love Nene. But there was not a dreg of Nene which felt it deserved to be loved, no dreg even for God to mutate enormous. I unite us in prayer today not to make you forgive Nene, but to make you forgive yourselves.

"Unless your legs or backs forbid you, please kneel."

The crowd sinks further. Melts into the cracks.

"I had planned to do this in repetitions, but it would rather hurt all of our heads, so what I will do is this: For every line I give, please answer 'It was holy'.

"Nene Karafantoni, your birth in the arms of a washerwoman?"

"It was holy."

"Oh, you honour me. Your smallness?"

"It was holy."

"Your apathy?"

"It was holy."

"Your bellyful of earthquakes?"

"It was holy."

"Your lunatic lust!"

This puts smiles in the crowd and laughs in the chant. "It was holy."

"And your *evisceration* when the God before tried to claw His coward way away from it?"

"It was holy."

"Wasn't it? Wasn't it beautiful too? That's why it's on our ceiling. The mountain of your flesh?"

"It was holy."

"It is holy. Its roots are still stuck in the ground all around us. I believe that they are the reason God came back, and that God is nowhere but Magmate. The church of the mountain of your flesh?"

"It *is* holy."

"The no-good parasite prophet of the church of the mountain of your flesh? Hang on! We changed the tense, and now we must change the pronoun."

"He is holy."

"For God needs not purpose to be power, needs not gentleness to be beautiful! Desire needs neither goodness nor cause to be *holy!* Thank you for indulging me, my darlings. Please sit yourselves down."

As the crowd settles back in the pews, I settle forward against the broken wing's spine.

"Nene Karafantoni cared not for a moment about himself," I say. "Not until he was so unravelled that his very voice was spread through the mountain could he tell me that it hah... *hurt.*" I always retch on the word. "And though none can say whether he concealed a desire to be whole again, the desire he displayed was the desire for *us* to be whole again." I hang my hands down from the pulpit for the crowd to see. "On that note, might I ask all those I have luted to come to the front? Signore Malacheti marks the spot."

Malacresta bounds up from the front pew and slings himself across the pulpit staircase.

For the first time, I am frightened rather than pleasured by the size of the upheaval. Five, ten, twenty people join Malacresta between the transepts. In the front pew, Ciecherella and Ersilio exchange frightened glances as Nedda and Lagia get up.

"Ciecherella, dearest, you are included also. Please bring Ersilio if it soothes you."

The couple get up and join their daughters.

"I know that *the luting* is the name we've given it," I say, "but I have come to understand, with the help of my first and fondest, Nedda, that the sealing of seams is not the whole of it. God's holy touch blossoms in its wake a sickness which, over a period of years, changes the flesh and the appetite. Nedda and I discovered that our skin was rolling off in the sun, and we were hungry for something which wasn't food, something which tasted like earth."

391

The fifty people in the pews look at each other and whisper. The twenty luted gaze up at me placidly.

"We discovered that the thing which melted away our blisters, our thirst and our hunger was... gabbroic clay."

The commotion in the pews increases and the silence between the transepts does not tremble.

"I am sorry," I say, "that I didn't tell you the moment I found out. I was desirous to find and stockpile your medicine before I frightened you. And I understand that you must still be very frightened. That is why, with Signore Malacheti's help, I have been fasting."

Now, the luted begin to look at each other.

I rub three fingers across my jaw, and show the congregation the black rot which comes off.

"I have starved myself of clay since the baptising bite. I have come to believe that the disease's progression is very slow, but until I am completely sure I know how to care for you, until I reach the very end of my endurance, I will not eat. The creature who could not heal himself gave me the power to lute you. The creature whose body disintegrated on contact gave me the power to *vitrify* you. And now, that burden, the power to hand out relief I cannot experience, is mine."

There's kneeling. All of the luted and half of the ordinary. Malacresta mock-bows against Ersilio's back and grins up at me. I wonder which instance of me eating clay he's thinking about. I'm thinking about the time my mouth was too full to reply to his confession.

"Don't kneel," I say, to make more of them kneel. "Stand tall, and let me guide you to relief."

"Where do you guide us?" Ciecherella calls.

I point back from the pulpit. In the corner of the chancel, a gabbro-skinned hole has been torn in the wooden floor.

"Away from the sun's bite, and into the earth."

As I stand at the crypt stairs, encouraging people downward with smiles and hand-squeezes, I notice that the entire congregation has risen from the pews. Instead of protesting that there's not enough space for seventy, or asking why they should want to watch their loved ones eat clay in the place God melted, I say, "Please bring as much as you need for comfort."

Ersilio and his girls slog down the stairs as one body. Sitha and her sister accompany their mother. Lalo and Ario shove their way down with the awe of spectacle on their faces. My mother holds out her arm for me to help her down the stairs, and I tell her to wait until everyone is safely beneath.

Though the deep roots of his mountain are broken off in the earth all around it, the crypt is not Nene's anymore. A new floor means a new ceiling, and for the week that the far wall has been cluttered with troughs of clay, insulated by heavy white sheets, it has smelled like me. I am thinking about giving Malacresta the room upstairs and making it my workshop.

I am accosted on my way to the troughs by Ciecherella, who seizes my face and gives me a hard kiss. Nedda and Lagia copy her, and I squeeze Ersilio's hand as I give him my mother's. Then, everyone is touching me. I walk through a grass of cold, fragile hands.

I drag the first sheet from the line of troughs. "I know," I say, "you have no choice but to fear a trick—"

Malacresta and Nedda sneak after me with stooped heads, she giggling as he mutters, "Quick, quick!" The moment the sheet is removed, they throw themselves at the vat of clay and wrap their jaws around enormous bites, like two cats eating from bowls. Nedda is giggling so much that most of her bite falls out of her mouth. Malacresta pumps the air with his fists and yells, "I win!"

I glare at him. As Nedda bends to pick up her mess with her mouth, he scoops up a second helping.

"What?" he says. "They're hungry."

Lagia and Ciecherella come up to eat. So does Papena, whose daughters pull faces at each other over her empty place. I sigh and remove the final sheet. "Signore Cvradi," I call towards the stairs, "don't subject yourself to the crush. I am bringing you a cup."

One more performance of selflessness is the last I need. Before I can walk out of the back of the crowd, the crowd, whose placidness upstairs betrayed that they have panted with pica for months, surges forward and spits me out.

I am always wrong about how much my village will doubt me. When they unearthed me from Nene's belly in this room, I thought they would call me a murderer. When I begged them for wine for my grief, I thought they would throw me home. I thought that when they saw the horror of the luting, they would call me a witch, and that when I told them I was a man, they would call me a deviant. I expected rebuke at the revelations that I lied about the end of the world, that I filled my paramour's mouth with gemstones, that I blighted their bodies with clay.

But after they pulled Nene from the ground in colossus spires, they lost their appetite for making the eldritch their enemy.

"D'you ever wonder where it's going?" Ciecherella closes her jaws around her own hand. Nedda sucks a gout of clay out of her plait. The lady with the luted baby kisses his wet grey brow and coos, "Is it good? Is it yum-yum-yummy?" The crowd depresses in portions as people duck into troughs or sit down in relief.

"D'you ever wonder where it's going?" Malacresta slings one green leg onto the lip of the trough and foists himself into a crouch, then a stand. As he hangs there swayback as if on the crowd's shoulders, he rolls his head toward the stairs, where Ersilio, my mother and the untainted stand, and grins, giving jewels to the black bracelet of his mouth. Then, he loses his balance and falls. When my blood turns into pewter and I realise that God is coming to change me, I am terrified. Without me, who will stop him from force-feeding them clay or biting their throats out? He doesn't wonder where it's going.

As I slink down the wall, I see a gabbro brick bursting out of the ceiling and never landing. It seems to vanish in a puff of dust, leaving only the black groping root which expelled it. Then, I realise that the groping root *is* the brick, stretched, like a canvas hit from behind, into the shape of an arm.

The arms born thereafter reach for each other. Grow long. Grow elbows.

They are born across the ceiling in a great spiral, a conch with spines and a central point which sags in three quick quakes. They grow down the walls in cockle-shell rays, deep, straight trenches, like buried ropes are being pulled out. A trench opens around my head, and I slouch backward into a grinding jaw of gabbro hands.

Through me goes the terror that my congregation will be splayed out too, that their arms will fountain into tentacles as the bricks fountained into arms, that they will elaborate on themselves until they are one black mass of fine filament. It isn't just hunger causing the frenzy. It's not that they were hungry for clay, and I offered, so they ate. It's that they are so bewildered to be hungry for clay that reality has melted out of them. By bringing them out of the square and into the church, I blindfolded them to the daylight, and by bringing them beneath the church and into the crypt, I reached into the dark head sequestering each of their brains and whispered, *Don't you want to rest a while?*

And as God struggles to life on the crypt floor, an ever-extruding ouroboros of stalagmite and arm, and gives a toss of His back which sloughs them like parasites, they scream like playing children.

I stand up, spread my arms, rub my back against the wall. Gabbro arms kick my belly, pull my hair, make belts around my thighs. As all below my waist tessellates, the crowd's heads begin to turn. Recognition takes many forms. Ersilio falls to his knees, pulling down on his eyes, and Lalo and Ario laugh at him. Ciecherella and Nedda's open smiles are mirrored by all those I love less, and Malacresta is surging upward again, rocked one-legged by a ripple in the floor. As a tug from the wall lifts me off my feet, he crashes into me with his teeth out, already knowing I am a shard of pure light to be tasted.

"Is this holy too?" he says.

Two quakes. I am sideways with hands in my hair, then upside-down with hands on my face. Malacresta gapes and my mother screams as they part the skin from my neck. Clean sweep, like it's already liquid.

"It'll be holy tomorrow," I moan as blood runs up into my eyes.

God drags me up the wall and I drag Malacresta with me.

"Shit! Holy shit!" he cackles through my screams as he coils down into my gown of arms. A spire of gabbro pushes our heads apart, and drags the skin off my face. When my pain stretches from red to white and I start laughing, Malacresta ducks and drives his head into my neck. *Poor wisp doesn't like gore,* says delirium, *is probably trying not to faint.* And then he rears up with my neck skin hanging out of his mouth like a dead rabbit.

He thrashes his head to dislodge it. It tears up to my cheek. I whimper. There's a syllable of open-aired calm, all havoc rolling back in a crater. The instant the first churchgoers summit God around us, Malacresta opens his jaws against my face and licks the whole wound down his throat.

God's body tock-tock-tocks beneath us, sinking, erupting and turning. I'm on my back, Malacresta splayed out on the ceiling above me. Ciecherella is pulling my bloody hair out of my eyes, Lalo pulling my hand up against his face. Others are arriving and pressing themselves against any mite of me they can reach. As I heave with the agony of being skinned alive and they marry their movements to mine, the pile of us inflates and flattens like a lung. I'm wattle and daub, the fine weave of my flesh widened by holes which whistle with cold air. As Malacresta eats my face, his teeth get stuck in chewy knots of chin and nose, in bare cheekbone, in *my* teeth. He unfastens my tunic, peels up my undershirt, and sloughs my stays down with a horse's head-nod. He unlaces with his teeth the red gouts of me stretched into strings by the friction. I am stuck in the fast dark thudding aspect which comes before an orgasm, which persuades me without proof that I must be fucking, because my cock is hard against his ever-indifferent thigh and he is licking a long ribbon of my stomach from my arm. There's a baby crying somewhere, crushed between bodies. As I throw my head back to see the ground, I see Ciecherella pulling her bodice down to bare her white and red breasts and rubbing clay against her front with scratching shoves, as if it can lute the memory of a wound too. I realise what God has done to me when Malacresta bites down on my face and a thick, sharp stubble crackles against his teeth.

I wonder, as the frenzy of stone abates into a frenzy of flesh, who will be the first to wake up. To see my blood on their hands, to hear their baby crying, to bristle along a naked breast or thigh, to feel their scratches start to burn. To notice that the embrace between me and the glassmaker has halted with my forearm shoved between his jaws and gore shimmering everywhere but his eyes.

At last, I see Ersilio.

He is sitting on the crypt stairs with his wife's clay-covered breasts against his neck.

And he, as is his bothersome habit, is staring with horrified eyes not at the horror, but at me.

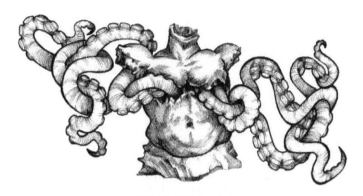

CHAPTER 23

THE CHANDELIER

BEFORE WE BEGAN, Malacresta said something about Nedda which made me picture the ugliest possible church. A gabbro anthill with boils oozing rainbows. Before I knew the misery of boring and the pleasure of viscid and mad, it was with dread that I imagined another blind sweep killing us all, leaving no monument to our existence but an *ugly thing*.

God doesn't seek to be loved. God seeks to be known for the monster He is. It is not His fault that some of us love Him for it.

There's a new stained glass window above the chancel. Four thin slices of God. A coracle between clear green sky and milky green ocean, buffeted by white whale tentacles, a violet moon stabbed by the narrow wings of a wooden house, a golden beach winged by red seaweed, and a blue eel-mouthed cave. There is no need for a picture of the arms in the crypt. They're still there, tangled together on the floor and walls, a fossilised coral reef.

We walked out of the crypt in a body of seventy,

Malacresta's bloody face hidden in my tunic, my neighbours' hands inside my sleeves stroking the stubble. In a fortnight, the stubble grew into thick hair all over my body. It covers my limbs down to the backs of my hands and feet, christening my hard-earned muscles like the chandelier christens the rafters. It runs in a feathering line from my throat to my sex and blossoms into a carpet on my chest. My breasts persist perhaps because God knew I despised them first, despised the way He had formed my body to match them, and wanted me to see them not belong. They hang deflated and covered in chest hair between my hard shoulders and pot belly like a pair of dead rats.

My beard is much redder than my chest and head hair, and flecked with silver at my ears. It's a bulbous-moustached, square-chinned, elderly beard, and inside it, my mouth is as gnarled as my eyes inside my eyebrows. My congregation don't comment on it, finding it inevitable or frightened I'll murder them for reminding me my face was once naked. Malacresta finds me setting up sculptures in the side aisle, stares at the profile of my face, and says, "It's scary, you know, to not know what your mouth's doing."

I soften my eyes at him. "I'm smiling," I say. "Always."

"That's what I was scared of."

We set up the tables and clay for the sculpting ceremony during the day, delirious with pica and wiping the skin from our brows. Neighbours who aren't part of the congregation stand spectral in the streets, then sidle up to ask what we're doing. None of them ask why we're holding the ceremony at night.

And just like the voyeurs who turned into builders, they all show up at sundown because they're curious.

We set the square ablaze with bonfires and candles and fill the tables around the troughs of clay with wine and fruit. For the first time, the church is aglow from within. The side aisle windows paint a uniform rainbow on the neighbouring houses and the chandelier rolls a great tongue of fractals and tentacular shadows down the front steps and into the square. It's an accidental consequence of the design. That an ugly thing stuffed with mad things keeps them inside itself during the day, but vomits them out at night. I am so enchanted by the dark little gemstone-warted monster that I spend the first hour of the ceremony gazing at it cross-legged on the doorstep of the bakehouse, not speaking to anyone. I am doomed to squander my sculpting ceremonies. Stamping my foot through my baby-brick earned me my life, making my six-year-old sculpture explode earned me my best friend, and flattening my sixteen-year-old sculpture earned me my trade. I remember thinking that letting people see that I'd sculpted myself with Ersilio's stubble and jawline would end the world.

My luted ones are eating as they work. Ersilio watches with a tight mouth as Nedda wipes a sticky blob of slip onto her sculpture's head, plunges her hand into her mouth to clean it, and then bends to bite the blob off the sculpture as well. Malacresta drops a chunk of clay into his water jug and takes a slug from it. The lady with the luted baby is feeding him clay on a spoon from the tool table. I thank God we made so much clay. We anticipated gluttony after what happened in the crypt.

There are as many outsiders as insiders. People who smiled at me in the square, cooed at the stained glass windows, and now sit paddling our clay, but never helped build. I roll my eyes between those people and my people, seeing the clay-eating as they might. Perhaps they'll see Papena Tegliacci scraping the clay from her fingers with her bottom teeth and think, *What a disgusting way to clean your hands.* Perhaps they'll see Benghi Cvradi mixing slip in a mug and think, *In a minute the old codger will mistake it for his ale mug.* Perhaps they'll see stained faces next. The little ones, or Malacresta, who likes to strut around with it on his mouth. Perhaps, the way I noticed injured people after the earthquake, they will move in a maddening sweep from noticing one clay-eater to realising they are surrounded by clay-eaters. And what will they do then?

They will allow me to convince them, with kindness, rainbows, and a person masticated mad in every second seat, that they are the mad ones.

I get up to stroll between the tables. The appearance of each sculpture betrays which God the sculptor loves. Some are passionately dense, as heavy as lumps of lead from the number of layers on every facet, and some are passionately sinuous, stretched and coiled by stylisation. Some are passionately untouched, raw everywhere except for a single feature which has been cut out and remade a hundred times, and some are just untouched.

I stop at the Cvradi family's table. Benghi's wife is making something abstract and pastry-long and Benghi is making a pastiche of Malacresta's red window, a sausage of a haemorrhage with a spitball of a hammer perched on top, but their daughter is finished. She sits with her cheek in her hand, wheedling a pencil against the scratched mouth.

"Not enjoying yourself?" I say to her.

When she doesn't reply, Benghi's face flames. "Abriana, you answer Signore De Gasinis when your laziness offends him!"

"I'm not offended," I say. "I just want you to enjoy yourself."

"Just not very good at it," Abriana mumbles.

"You don't have to be. Being good at it isn't the point."

"Then what is the point?"

The clench in my stomach is bitter and tragic.

"I suppose I don't know," I say. "What right do I have to tell you that, when I am good at it?"

I move to the De Aqvancis family. Nedda has rendered a beautiful pair of eyes and is tattooing the pattern of her scars with a serrated knife. She has thrust her face so close to the table's shared mirror that her parents and sister don't stand a chance of a turn. Lagia's sculpture is a sweet doughball of a girl with a cross-shaped mouth which looks nothing like her now, but very like her as a baby. Ciecherella's has a bell-shaped skirt and hair blowing up from its face. As I smile down at it, Lagia exclaims, "No, *no,* it didn't blow up. It blew down, like a fishing net."

Ciecherella seizes my hand. "I am making you a commiseration for your loss. I hear I was the most beautiful statue in Italy."

I smile. Ciecherella has skipped through the world which grew out of her blink like she's skipping through a dream. It's like she thinks she will wake up soon, with the bellyache and the babies crying through the night, and she might as well have fun whilst she's here. She doesn't mind that I miss my statue. That its wet hair has dried, its divine expression cooled. That it doesn't belong to me anymore.

"You were," I say, "but I will make you again one day. Perhaps tonight, after I've made your brother."

Ersilio stiffens when I throw my arms around him. I am horrified to see that his sculpture looks like Abriana Cvradi's.

"You know what would make it sing?" I say. "A big ugly nose."

"Would need to steal Ciecherella's clay for that," he says without turning around.

"Do *not,*" Ciecherella says, swiping playfully at his arm. His body locks up when she hits him.

I unwind my arms from his shoulders.

I find my way to Malacresta, who is sitting alone on a table with his leg behind his shoulder. I pull up a chair and tell him to sculpt me in return for a sculpture of himself. He gouts on my beard without looking at it and scores it into a rhombus. I grow angrier and angrier as I try to keep his fangs inside his mouth, and eventually resort to adding a tongue and carving them out of that.

"Prasede's here," I say.

Malacresta grins down at his sculpture. "I know."

"With her cleaver."

Prasede and Sitha arrived in the square an hour ago, wearing aprons and tool belts. Prasede is holding an enormous meat cleaver and Sitha a scythe.

"Yes, they're very busy at work and can't stay long."

"They might be here to kill me."

"Might be."

I nervously titter. "I think she's proud. Because she's the one who suggested the ceremony."

"Got to see if she makes a sculpture or just stands there."

When I look over at Prasede, I feel a ripping pang of anger. This *isn't* her ceremony. Godly and godless alike are enjoying themselves together, and she is poisoning it with her glower. All who don't want to be here poison it. Abriana. Even Ersilio.

I heave myself to my feet. "I'm going to make her make a sculpture."

I think I'm going to the doorway Prasede is standing in. Instead, I stop on the church steps.

"If I may say something," I call across the square.

Everyone turns to look at me. The sceptical turn immediately and the congregation nudge and giggle.

"I was just asked," I say, "by Abriana Cvradi, what the point of it all is. When I was a child, these ceremonies oppressed my spirit, and I told Signora Cvradi what my mother told me then. That being good at it isn't the point. I still believe that. That it's a joy to make things even if you're bad at it. But I also believe that a person must not be *told* not to try to be good at it. There's pleasure and hilarity in trying to be good. A bad sculpture can be interesting, but a boring sculpture can never be good.

"You might say that I'm a sculptor and I can't expect everyone to have fun sculpting. Of course I can't. All I can say is that the day I decided to become a sculptor was a day I made something so frightful that I threw it down on the table so nobody else could see it. I was disappointed that I'd failed, and

404

I tried again. I needed to prove to myself not that I was already good, but that I could be. Even if I found no fun in it, I could be. Even if I gave up for good, I always could be.

"Our founders believed that in order to be humble under God, we had to make bad things on purpose. Had to cobble them together and abandon them quickly, lest our hands grow vain and gluttonous. And that's a performance of inferiority, not a demonstration. If God is so brilliant a sculptor, His efforts should stand tall above our most earnest, passionate efforts, and He should have nothing to fear!

"If you hate sculpting, I thank you all the more for coming tonight. If you hate *me,* might I suggest that you come up and waste a heap of my clay? Make the ugliest thing you possibly can, hold it up to God, and say, "Look! Look what I've done with the earth You made! Look what I've done with earth which could have been beautiful in the hands of Sole De fucking Gasinis!"

Prasede steps down from the doorway. Sitha looks up at her anxiously.

"And to those I see already trying to surpass me, I challenge you, implore you, to do so. A true leader welcomes His people's creations as elaborations on His own. Why else would God make gabbro and not clay, clay and not statues? The child and not the adult? Nene Karafantoni and not the monster? *My* body is the church in which God Himself made worship, and when I told Him I hated the shape of it, He helped me rip it down and build it anew.

"I want to be honest with you. I was wrong to lead you all to hate God. I was not *born wrong.* I did not only mould my body to match my soul but also, before that, my soul in spite of my body. I'm a mess of my own making, and that is all a sculpture ought to be. A waste of God's earth with your soul pacing inside it. That is all I will ever ask you to make for me."

I pace back to the church door, trying to mimic the finality of descending from the pulpit.

"And eat *slowly!*" I call.

The smattered clapping swells with laughter from the churchgoers.

Abriana digs her thumbs into her sculpture's eyes and grins at her father's as if she's mocking it. Prasede quirks an eyebrow at Sitha, slings her cleaver down into her belt, and gouges a lump of clay from the troughs. I look hopefully at Ersilio, and see him staring over my shoulder and into the church.

He's the first one I see. There are more. Ciecherella has grasped his shoulders to stare past him, and at the table next to them, a group of teenagers are hitting each other in the chest, pronouncing, *"Look! Look!"* Malacresta puts his sculpture down, stands up on my chair, then steps onto the table, his mouth open in awe.

I stand frozen on the steps. At the revelation that my speech has had a punchline at my expense, my belly plunges. It keeps plunging. It pours onto the floor through the hole the thing behind me is boring in the small of my back.

When I turn, and the door blinds me with rainbows, something in my head snaps. A nerve, a nerve which came out of my ear and connected to a rivet in the floor, was stretched beyond its limit by the turn.

And what I see, to explain the plunge and snap, is Nene Karafantoni standing in the pulpit, gazing at me with his cheek against his crossed arms.

He is smooth and beautiful. Green neck and strawberry cheeks, wet black bites of eye. He is wearing red and white tunics turned purple and grey by age and his golden hair is long, as long as mine was before I cut it. Short broken curls froth around his throat and the rest pours down in heavy curtains. It's like he went away after his fever crystallised, before his wing burst out, and came back when he was better. Like he didn't want me to watch.

A thrill judders my shoulders. What has happened? Is he luted? I never luted him. I want to run into the church to see

406

him better, but the rainbow air between us crackles and creaks, bubbles and drips. Everything is undulating, and my brain has hallucinated a pinhole.

When Nene comes down from the pulpit, drumming his hand along the banister, there's a flash of terrified noise in the crowd. He shouldn't be able to do that, I think, to climb down out of the nest of his wings and leave them behind. He shouldn't be able to walk through that air, that air which is attached to him. Tock, tock, thud. The world claws at his back as he walks, but still he walks.

He stops inside the foyer of the church, safe from the monster which settles its elbows above the door, and beams at me.

I'm sad you stopped, he says. **I love to hear you speak.**

There are screams behind me. A lone scream followed by a multitude, the way screams so often start.

His voice pours into me, stretches my skull away from my brain. I sway. "What would you have me say next?"

We both know what you're saying doesn't matter.

There's a squashing shudder in the flesh of my chest.

Smiling back at Nene, I unfasten my belt, throw my tunic off over my head.

He does the same. One purple sleeve at a time, he picks his way out of his tunic like he's scared to dislocate his shoulders. Something massive slides up the wall of the church in creaking coils as he bares his chest.

He drops his tunic onto the stairs on top of mine, and holds his arms out. When I throw myself into them, he snags in the doorway, unable to be pulled outside.

He turns me to face the crowd and presses his body against my back. His chest is cold and gritty and leather hard, just like mine. As he forces my hands against my breasts, I realise I'm not sure whether he made them malleable when he arrived, or whether they were already malleable.

At first, they hold strong. The flesh is elastic, and troughs beneath my fingers. Nene lets go and presses his hands against my heart, smelting my blood white and thick. I moan in a gurgle as my index fingers, together, pierce the sinew at the tops of my breasts.

Harder, Nene says.

I grit my teeth and toss my head. The effort makes me dizzy. Rich flash of rainbow limbs on the church. Dark phantom of gabbro hands on my chest. Thumb meets finger in the middle of my left breast. Sinew snaps and sticks to my wrist. Handful of beach worms. The pain is wide and deep and tense, like the breast is a stake driven all the way through me. The crowd doesn't matter. It wouldn't matter if they were trying to run and it doesn't matter that they are instead standing in silent terror, gazing up at the thing I won't look at.

Harder, Sole. Harder.

Thumb meets two fingers in the middle of my right breast. Nene pushes his cold, stuck-open mouth against my ear and laughs as I moan and hiss. When, eliciting a brown, ripping growl, both of my breasts slide off into my armpits, he pushes his weight down onto my shoulders, too high and upside-down. It doesn't matter. It doesn't matter.

With my breast flesh still dripping from my armpits, I thrust my hands against my chest. I'm not sculpting. I'm just clawing. I want to drag this hard plane across every surface in Magmate, across floors and windows and trees and sand, across faces and bellies, across fire and knives. Anything which jars the bone without its cushion, which reminds me *it is flat.*

There, says God, as my ichor joins his on the steps. Fractals split my aspect as their source rolls outward and upward. **My church rebuilt.**

I look down at my black tunic, and see that there is no red tunic beside it.

"Please don't go," I say.

I will always be with you. I am in everything and everyone.

408

"I don't want to share you."

I turn around in his arms.

A Charybdis of stained glass and clay clings to the outside of the church, pouring out of the open doors. Its crab-legs drag themselves barb-over-elbow up the walls, snapping at every joint with jolts of dust and lashing back together. The tentacles which sway in the sky slump drunkenly at the troughs of their cycles and drag themselves up with the same creaking efforts. Two tentacles as thick as my waist corkscrew down the steps on either side of me, creaking, belching dust and reforming in perfect symmetry. Every mite of material is mutant, clay extruded into hackled gouts and colours of glass melted together in waves and blossoms and gashes. The pointed barb of one tentacle on the floor is creamy yellow and pink, the flank of a limb sliding over the roof is a fruiting orchard, and the monster's massive belly, which heaves against the door with Nene's statue stretched upside-down over it like a black thorn, is the orange, plum and indigo of dark clouds over a sunset.

So that's why Malacresta was smiling.

"Oh!" I wail. "That took us months!"

God laughs, thud, thud, tocking against the door like His tentacles against the roof.

And I did all this in a moment.

It's not the statue that speaks. The crowd were watching me embrace and address a puppet hanging dead from cits innards. The gabbro figure moves on its own axis, spasming its shoulders and the lips of its gaping, tongueless mouth, but its hair and limbs are splintered and lashed to the glass blight around it. It is an oasis in the vicious chandelier the way its face once was in its vicious body.

"Can you put it back on the ceiling when you're done with it?"

Could I put you back in the pulpit with your breasts and high voice, now that you have tasted life?

I fall to my knees on the church steps. My head sinks into

the river of fractals between the front tentacles. My horror at the sight of the statue jouncing limp with the tremors of the voice beneath it is primal, primeval. There's an oceanic seethe behind me as the crowd kneel as well. Sense pulls out of me in viscid strings.

I stagger back to my feet. The statue stretches out its arms, gapes wider with its upside-down head. *Hold me.*

I think about—

I throw myself on top of it. Foetal scrunch.

I lute.

I think I've broken the statue. There's a sense like the reverse of the tackle from Prasede, like my whole compacted body going through it in a disc. As God split my chest with molten white, I split His chest with stony black. My belly bloats and my thighs lock. My body passes through the strain of an hour of work in a second. My hair crawls up to cling wet to my neck and there's a CRUNCH of a headache behind my eyes and the hands which direct the power numb and blister under its heat. The glass cyclone tenses in shock, headbutts the doorframe. As God tosses like a bull, I straddle Nene and open my jaws against his face and give a tongue to his mouth. The fibrous shell of the clay body shivers, lashing dust into my eyes.

My chest explodes with echoes. An impaling pain joins left shoulder to right rib and a tentacle slithers from under my collarbone into my face. Another cradles my breast from sternum to armpit. A fissure opens in the hard bone and hard bone fingers lever the halves of it apart from the inside. Nene's murder swarms my flat chest. It says his pain is worse than mine. It says my body never mattered. It asks why I didn't scream like this at the sight of his carcass when I had the body of a woman.

One of the statue's eyes bubbles like seafoam, as if there's something moving beneath it. Still luting, my hand spasms up to brush away the clay. There's pearly skin there. A wide black eye with pink for a white.

It's working.

When my shock sends out a massive jolt of power, the chandelier bucks and the eye rolls back in agony.

I'm killing. Killing God. Clawing Nene out.

There's another bubble in the belly. Instead of flesh, what pours out into my hands is red glass. A mudslide of snakes of it. There's a bubble in the mouth, but when I reach up to it, the mouth burgeons into tentacles which coil around my arm and crush hard. I scream.

Would you like to feel what you are doing to me?

A glass tentacle loses its grip on the church and topples to the ground, dead weight. The statue convulses in pain as it shatters against the floor.

I nudge forth the tentacles which lattice my chest. "I feel it, *dolcezza*. I feel it."

You don't.

Clay hands with new white fingers shoot up and seize my face, and my chest swells fat.

My breasts are back.

"No," I say.

The black eye in the mire narrows. The white fingers on my cheeks contract. Cold wind gushes against every hairless pore from my face to my belly. "No," I say in a silvery voice crack. "No!" I shriek as my hands splinter like frozen puddles and my shoulders dislocate and sink, stabbing the flesh in the base of my throat. "NO! NO! NO! NO! NO! NO!"

Soft and shivering I lie. Naked and yet caged I lie. Raped and crucified I lie, eaten down to my tongue-hollowed bones and yet splayed out into a mountain. This body is everywhere and nowhere. Was my costume at birth and will choke me to death. I only parted from the last piece of it five minutes ago, but because I tasted perfection in those five minutes, it is nightmarish and ancient as a long-forgotten god. With Nene's murderous hands sloughing clay down my naked face, I see a hundred faces staring, Malacresta pulling his hair with his

411

elbows up like wings, Ersilio and Nedda with their hands over their mouths, Prasede laughing with a gibbous mouth and flaming eyes.

I throw my arms around the statue's neck, numb to the tentacles bruising me to the elbows. "You *can't!*" My old voice floods my mouth like vomit. "You can't do this to me! I understand! I understand! How do I put you back? Just tell me how to put you back!"

I put myself back.

God lifts Himself up, tossing the statue onto His back. I try to stand up with Him, but He leaves me on the floor.

Colour splits the dark as a new tentacle grows down the stairs, flush to the corpse of the tentacle I shattered.

The statue strains its head back. It still wears Nene's eye in a pink and white fissure.

I flower and die a thousand times a minute. I'm a cauldron of voices and a sediment of thoughts. Can you tell me, truthfully, if my reason for rebuilding the church was always the same, or if the desire was implanted just now, by your blasphemous hands?

By Nene.

"What desire," I say. Dead men can't make questions tick up at their ends, and I have been dead for a hundred years.

The desire to kiss it with immunity and scorch the earth around it.

I should feel something when the meaning dawns. I don't.

"You never told me why."

Would God want to do that?

"I don't know."

Would your *dolcezza* want to do that?

The last piece of the sentence is luscious and red. He must have stolen my anger when He stole my body. My soul.

"I don't know."

What about you? Would you want to do that?

"I want my body back."

Would you give up your people?

"For my body back."

Your home?

"For my body back."

Would you watch the one crushed by the other?

"I would."

Lead-veined snakes swarm me on the steps. A hard push on my chest, and flesh mudslides into the crooks of my arms. **Would you watch your *dolcezza* flower every morning and die every night?**

"I WOULD!" I scream, shuddering on my back on the steps. "I WAS GOD ON MY OWN! I WOULD LIQUEFY YOU ALL TO LUTE MYSELF!"

I claw my breasts off, wipe them down God's arms. The moans He rocks from me roll down into a baritone as He breaks my bones, forests me with hair, dislodges my womb in three quick bright-white thrusts. I stream gore and sweat down the steps, and no pain. Having tasted perfection, I am empty until I reach perfection again.

That's why I chose you, says God. **I think.**

He braces His elbows and lifts. I stand up with him, take six drunken steps towards my tunic. Here ends my speech. My mind is exhausted, my crowd entertained. I scratch and rub my flat chest, hum a scale in my restored voice.

I am furious that Malacresta hasn't come down from the table to hold me. He isn't even looking at me. He's looking at the monster made from his glass.

And the monster, crouched on its buttresses on the church roof, is only getting bigger.

Tentacles burgeon in every direction, caging the church in a helix, winging the roof in a flare. They grow longer and thicker with such speed that the sound of glass breaking and reforming is like a hailstorm. All around and inside me. Tentacles knuckle into the earth, tense, and lift. Nene's white-eyed, white-fingered mimic hangs its head as it kicks into the air, but cannot hang its hair.

"We made that," I say.

Malacresta looks down at me.

And behind him, God tilts Nene's head and lights the world on fire.

White light pulls tight through every tentacle, stamping a spiderweb crack in the sky. Noise pours forth from leaking Heaven in a convulsing CRACK-BOOM. Malacresta is thrown from the table and I from my feet. The boom recedes into something silvery and spectral which could be the whole ocean singing, but is truly the whole village screaming. Smouldering fragments of sky crash down on the houses and start crushing them in slow, bitter clenches. Windows shatter as their frames constrict and roofs slough thatch in oozing scabs. Nene thrashes back and forth in his bonds above the valley, and my animal impression is of a child playing dumb. God isn't looking as His clay squashes the bakehouse in a whipcrack or as His glass knuckles trenches through the street or as His candles hang curtains of waxy white fire along every wall of the square to trap us inside, but He is conscious enough to cling tightly to the church, guard it with His legs as His arms cycle in tantrum.

Running and screaming perpetuate one another. The screaming of adults who sound like they are already burning alive and of babies who would sound the same if they wanted milk in the night. This isn't like the earthquake, which came in one white seethe. Staccato thuds shake silent the air, shake black our aspects, shake upward the buildings, recede, then come again. When Malacresta falls onto my back, I think he's a building.

"We have to get in the church," he says.

Someone hears him. "INTO THE CHURCH!"

"You can't," I say.

God's legs may be holding the church steady, but they are kicking. The tentacles tear up cobblestones as they knuckle and

414

claw, a destruction of the ground which mimics the destruction of the church. Magmate spirals around the entwined pair like a pyroclastic flow around a volcano. Anyone who tries to enter will be crushed.

People bolder than Malacresta swarm me and haul me to my feet. Lalo, Prasede, Sitha.

"What do we do?" Lalo shouts.

I stare at them blankly.

"HOW DO WE GET INTO THE CHURCH?" Prasede is now holding the scythe and the cleaver. She thrusts the butt of the scythe into the ground with a stamp of her foot.

I dig my fist into my flat chest and shrug.

"Then I do what I came to do," Prasede says. Sitha slinks from her side.

Her swing of the cleaver requires no backswing. She cracks it like a whip into my head. Yawns around her bottom teeth as the hilt of the blade stops between my eyes. I jolt, but I'm stuck fast to her arm until she lets the cleaver go.

The scythe rears up like another shining limb of God and crashes down on me. The blade is so long that when the blow knocks me down, the tip lodges in the street before my knees bend.

I land on my face. If I hadn't rolled, she would have beheaded me.

I landed on Sitha. When she kicks me out of her lap into the path of Prasede's next swing, I realise what's happening. I cross my arms, take a cut which bites down on the blade. Prasede is the heaviest fighter I know. Hers is a hunger which stares past the killing blow to the peace of the dissection. She kicks my arms open and drives her boot into my head, grinds me cheek-down into the floor. I close my hand around her ankle as she roars with percussive gasps, "PIG WHORES LIVE LIKE WHORES AND DIE LIKE PIGS!" and strikes true through my heart.

Bright-white, ice-cold BANG. She impales me so hard she

falls over backwards, leaving the scythe driven through me and the street.

The first sputters of noise are funny. Lalo says, "Hoh," and Ario says, "Aw," as if they're watching a cow take a shit in the street. Sitha says, "Jesus, he's heavy," and Prasede slurs, "Toh—hoh—*old* you he would be."

The noises after that, the ripple of shock, the annealed sheet of a scream from my mother, tell me how dead I look. How dead I ought to be.

I sit up. Try to kneel, but am stopped by the blade, which is stuck deep as a fence post in the street. On some blind instinct, Malacresta walks over, puts his boot on my chest, and wrenches the scythe free. Only when I am on my feet can he pull it out of my heart. I yell in pain, and he pats me twice on the shoulder.

Together, we put our fingers against the wound. Cleavage in my flat chest.

We smear it shut.

Smiling open-mouthed, Malacresta seizes my cheek with one hand and the cleaver with the other. When he wrenches it up and out, eliciting another yell from me and not a drop of blood, he screams with laughter.

Frustration undoes Prasede's fear. With Sitha staring over her shoulder with wide, horrified eyes, she reaches into her leather pocket and pulls out a wicked sickle. It's this which undams the crowd's realisation; in the middle of the end of the world, she laid a killing blow on me, the one who can heal any wound—

A mob of churchgoers surges up behind Prasede and drags her off her feet.

—and my leather hard body took the wound like a fingerprint.

"THE LUTED DON'T DIE!" Lalo screams.

God laughs in the sky like a thunderclap.

Two frenzies begin at once. The frenzy of the congregation

416

attacking Prasede is the tightly twisted core to the wide, unravelling frenzy of people cutting themselves. They cut themselves with sculpting tools, scalpels and knives and needles. There's a gonging sound as someone knocks a metal mirror onto the floor and dives to saw their arm with it. Sure that they will be healed in moments, they are making cuts where it is convenient, not safe or painless. They cut their faces and necks, their palms, and the insides of their wrists, where the blood spurts out hard and black. Ario tosses himself into a stampede to snatch up a dropped scalpel and Lalo dives after him and snatches it first. There's an exchange like *Oh, sorry, were you going for that one? After you,* and Lalo stabs Ario in the neck.

The first person to reach me with a wound is a mother, carrying a little girl of five or six. She's holding a knife against the child's face, which already wears a small cut under the eye, and says, "Is that enough? Do I need to cut deeper?" In answer, I seize the child's face and lute her. God could have taken the power from me when He finished my body, but how could He resist this feast of the terrified? "Thank God! Praise God!" the mother cries. Only when her daughter is safe does she raise the knife to her own cheek.

There's a father with his son next. He also has me lute the child first. The four lutings leave me with a fist squashing my windpipe and an impression of sunburn across my chest.

"Mamma!" I cry, and see her already running towards me. There's a moment of peace as we meet each other, identically dark in the red and white screaming mire. I feel like I'm ten, running to meet her on the jetty after she's been out at sea for weeks. Like I've forgotten what she looks like.

She looks more like Ersilio now. Cold, trusting eyes with something screaming behind them.

When I dig my nail into her cheek and drag, she squeezes her eyes shut and nods. I kiss the graze as I lute it, then pull her up the steps of the church.

"I can't go through," she says, staring at the wall of tentacles.

"You can. You won't die now. Close your eyes."

People claw at my back until I turn around.

The crowd of the luted is a blossom squashed down in the middle, like the crowd which carried Benghi to me. Benghi is in the middle again. He and his brother are holding Prasede down on the floor. Too afraid to rip her belly and take her guts, they settle for ripping her belt and taking her weapons. As they shake the leather pockets upside-down, out rain more knives than I can believe fit inside. Boning and paring and carving and peeling. There's a pair of snips and a shower of T-hooks. She was going to butcher me to the gizzards on my own sculpting table. Someone seizes her legs, two people spread her arms, and someone rears up under her and lifts her into the air. Malacresta, who until now was watching in a daze with the scythe balanced on his foot, kicks it upright in his hands and uses the handle to force a path through the crowd. She watches him approach upside-down with her eyes bulging, jerks an elbow in an attacker's grasp like she wants to reach for him. At the moment that her body pulses, seems to break, loose to stretch in every direction, Malacresta grips her neck between the blade and his boot and beheads her. He catches her head upside-down between thigh and elbow, belts himself with her orange hair.

It's a mercy. A quick, efficient death to preserve her from the clumsy one.

But Malacresta keeps hacking.

The luted drop the corpse and retreat, glanced by the backswing of every massive, spiralling blow. The first brings the weapon down from his chest, the next brings it high enough for the blood to flash like ruby glass above the shadow cast by the crowd, the next makes him feint and spin in and the next makes him leap in the air. He embeds the blade as deep into the cobblestones as Prasede did, every clang of steel against stone sending shockwaves of laughter through his shoulders, and kicks it free with enough force to lash blood onto the faces of the cheering crowd. He hacks and hacks and hacks until he's hacking at cobblestones, and when they're sure he's either sated or jilted, the luted swarm up to spread his arms and kiss his hands. Someone holds aloft what they expected to be Prasede's head. It's a gob of her hair hung with red ribbons of scalp. Malacresta lunges, throws back his head, and takes a long step which coils the ribbons of scalp up into his mouth. When he sees me watching him, he shrugs and grins, his teeth glowing in a black mask of blood.

Some people are standing in torpor. People who don't understand what is happening, are frozen in fear, or are watching God. The people who don't want to be luted aren't standing still. Near a curtain of fire to the left, Benghi Cvradi's wife is holding Abriana by the waist and screaming for her husband. Abriana retches, claws and strains towards the fire as her mother brandishes a scalpel and cuts her arm—a nick turned into a long slash by her writhing. Abriana wriggles free and sprints towards death, only to crash into her father, who is covered in blood from kissing Malacresta. They drag her to me, stroking and kissing her hair.

It's a sputtering burst of a luting, thick gouts through a tiny opening. Abriana grizzles like a baby as her parents carry her up the steps.

As I turn to the next person, Malacresta falls against me and knocks me sideways. There's gore hanging out of his hair and he's holding the scythe on his shoulders the way he holds his blowpipes. He jerks it over his shoulder to point it at the woman in my arms. "Present your wound," he says, "or go and make one."

"Wh… what?" the woman says. "Is that why everyone's bleeding?"

Malacresta says, "Ugh," and swings the scythe, severing the tips of her fingers.

419

As I put my hand over her screaming mouth and lute her, the people in the line say, "Shit," and "Oh God," and start fumbling with the knives in their hands, preferring to choose from whence to bleed.

Pain cores my chest, slow and deep. "Remember their wounds become mine," I say.

He laughs at me. He's pleasure-drunk.

The next in line are Lalo, Ario and three of their parents. Ario is cupping the gushing hole on his neck with a wet red hand.

"What are you so glum about?" Malacresta asks him.

Ario sneers. "We don't all clamour for the Devil's tongue inside us, *frocio.*"

Malacresta impales him. He touches the point of the scythe to his chest with a tired blink, but as he forces it upward and through a hand's length at a time, jouncing Ario's head forward, his hand from his neck, and his feet from the floor, a smile burns a hole through his face.

"There are sharper things than tongues, Baby Barostaldo," he says into Ario's hanging leg.

I look for Ersilio, and what I see is Lagia, Nedda and Ciecherella on their knees under the table, tearing into him like lions. He's got his knees up to his chest and his arms crossed over his face, and he's crying so hard he sounds like a saw against wood, he-ha-he-ha-he. Even though there are three of them, and his daughters aren't babies anymore, he could slough them with a breath. He could slough them so easily it wouldn't hurt them. Just make them sit down hard on the street with little oofs.

But he doesn't even want to do that.

Above the church, God blossoms larger, ripping His roots from the ground. The thrashing of the earth intensifies, and the dozen people left in the square scream at the CRASH-CRASH-CRASH of boulders rolling down the cliffs. When I see the girls carrying Ersilio to the back of the crowd, I raise my fist and scream, "PART! BRING ME ERSILIO! OR I WILL KILL YOU ALL!"

The girls beam at me. Ersilio hangs from their shoulders, Ciecherella under one arm and his daughters under the other. In their agitation, they have scratched and grazed and cut him all over his face, neck and arms. There's blood under their fingernails and a dark print on Nedda's cheek, as if she wiped her finger there. I notice the way they're holding him, with their hands under his arms and on his chest. They aren't carrying him. He's carrying himself, so his weight doesn't hurt them.

Nedda and Lagia are wild-eyed, and not in panic. They look on the verge of giggling through their teeth. The wide, vacant shock on Ersilio's face tells me that he thinks so too.

I thrust my hands against Ersilio's head. He tosses them off.

"Ersilio." I lift his chin to make him look at me. Knowing I can lute by touching anywhere, he tosses again. "Ersilio!" I seize him hard, and he moans and thrashes, making us all fall to the floor.

"They cut me," he says, mournful and confused.

"I can make it stop hurting!"

He shakes his head. "No. They cut me."

I hurl myself into his lap. He headbutts me in the face with a vicious grunt. Stupor creaks behind my eyes.

"I won't *live,*" he wails, "in a world where they're this! Where *he* is this! Where it was *you* who did it! I love you… You've got my blood on your face! Look at you! Look at you! You've got Papa's blood on your face!"

Nedda whimpers and grabs her mother's arm.

"This is mercy," Malacresta says above me. In the darkness between me and Ersilio, the gleam of his blade snakes, all red and no silver. "Don't make me extend it to you."

I yell and tackle Ersilio sideways. Ersilio fights me with all his might. I can't cough the luting up in the time between his blows. He punches my throat and makes me choke it back, kicks me in the stomach and deflates it, slams my head into the ground and shatters it in my mouth. As we roll in the effort to knock each other out, Lagia, Nedda and Ciecherella throw themselves at Ersilio's back and the crowd, unsettled by the delay, throw themselves at mine. Malacresta whirls above us, keeping them back with his boots and his blade. There's a thin, hammering impact from the forest to the square which flattens the last buildings and bares us to the cliffs bordered only by fire. Ersilio crashes down on top of me, choking me hard with both hands. Nedda is on his back like a monkey with her hands on his face, shouting, "Papa, Papa, please, please stop!" His eyes are utterly blank. It's worse than bloodlust, worse than hatred. It's a sadness so total that it has maddened a man incapable of either. Malacresta wraps his arms around Nedda, lifts her off and throws her, then forces Ciecherella back with the blunt edge of the scythe. Just as I think my luting-squashed skull is about to cave in, the red gleam crescents around Ersilio's throat and jerks up.

His blood tumbles down in a velvet curtain.

I scream. Nedda, Lagia and Ciecherella scream. The only one who doesn't scream is Malacresta, the practical one, who knew that I could more easily resurrect a dead man than heal a fighting man. But even Ciecherella, dropped into the world not a year ago, understands that Ersilio is dead. Being cat-scratched by his daughters made him say he didn't want to live, so what about being killed by his brother? His body will come back without his soul. His eyes hollow and haunted, his mouth maundering misery into air which treats it like silence. He will be nothing.

As he bleeds in a steady gush, Malacresta and I haul him onto his back. Before the wet blood on my face can go cold, I crawl on top of him and nuzzle it back home.

I could sleep. The amount of pain which has gone through me since I last lay down, the amount of noise, the amount of power, has squashed me flat. And so quickly. God crawled up the church, dug His tentacles down, and twisted. The last time my village fell in a flash, I was on my back with Nene holding me.

When the crowd notice that I'm not luting, they push forward. Someone grabs my collar, and Malacresta shouts a curse and kicks him away.

I can't live in a world where my best friend tells me every day that he wishes he was dead.

I'm not as strong as him.

I stagger to my feet with his blood in my mouth and up my nose, half-swoon, then run.

"Sole!" Malacresta shouts.

"NO!" Nedda screams.

I slam into the wall of God's tentacles. They stamp me flat against the floor, coil around me to throw me, sweep me down the steps. After a battering to the head and trunk which would knock a human man out, one blind sweep tosses me inside. I land on my back in the centre aisle, staring up at the bare, riveted ceiling where the chandelier was. The church groans under the weight of its protector, shudders with impacts against the walls and sways with undulations hinged on the roof. The stained glass windows flash like coloured fire as tentacles pass behind them in long sweeps, and since there is nothing but stained glass, the nave wheels slowly through phases of colour. Green, turquoise and yellow illuminate the faces of the people I luted. Crouched, with their children curled staring in their arms or their parents crying on their shoulders. Crowds look bigger when they're on the floor.

"Don't be scared," I say, bearded and bibbed in blood. "It's almost over."

I run to the stairs which lead to the second floor. The attic is a little square room more useful to the church's outside than its inside. The behemoth crouches close and invisible, burdening and charging the air like a thunderstorm.

I crawl onto the windowsill and stare up. The rainbow cyclones above me, tock-tock-thudding against roof and sky.

Tentacles carpet the carcasses of the houses, the wattle and thatch and limestone and iron, like ivy over buildings which fell a decade ago.

The monster's epicentre is no longer a mountain of blight with the statue stuck to it. The two have grown together into something tall, black and spindle-armed with glass wrought in hackles down its back. The hair is a mat of jagged rays. The face is as peaceful as the statue's and as mutant as the blight. Eyes all over it. A neat arch of red, pink and golden eyes from cheek to cheek, marred by the pearly slash of Nene I luted. That eye is rolled back, as if frightened to see.

I haul myself onto the roof with the tingling numbness of death in my arms. I want to beg the monster to lift me.

There's still screaming in the square, but it isn't pain or panic anymore. It's just grief, keening, splintering howls. Everything beyond the square is silent. The people who didn't come to the ceremony are as dead as the ones who came to mock it or tried to escape it. As dead as the ones who were in the way of the wrong building, the wrong tentacle, the wrong surge of fire. Dead, dead, dead.

Malacresta puts his head out of the window. When he sees me sitting against the iron cross on the roof with my knees up, a canary on a perch in a stained glass cage, he grins.

As he scrambles up to join me, using the scythe as a pick between the tiles, he points up into the sky, where a red-barbed tentacle swings. "Tha..." he pants as he seizes the cross. "Tha... Gold red."

I squint at the colour. It looks the same as his copper glass mixed with clear to me.

"See how it's pinker?"

He is redder. Before, he wore a second skin of blood, but now it's clotted and fibrous on him like he's skinless. There's a ring of white around his mouth, and that's it.

"People who wanted luting..." he says. "You can do it in your own time. When you're ready."

424

I gaze back up at God. "I'll start with Prasede. It seems only fair."

His silence is harrowing, hilarious.

"Not really. Just wanted to see your face."

"Have to look at me to see my face."

Another tentacle arcs past him, low enough to scrape against the edge of the roof. It's patterned with feathery ovals, in yellow, red and blue. He bends down to stroke it like it's a cat.

"Careful," I say.

"Can't die."

"The only people who say they can't die are people about to find out how they can die."

God strains down towards him. At first, I think it's a random sway, but He tilts beyond His point of return, rearranges His tentacles for balance. Impossible glass spirals around Malacresta and the scythe.

"Pipsqueak," Malacresta says.

The gabbro insect turns its face upside-down for him.

Rabbitfish.

"I made you, you know."

Did you?

Malacresta puts out a hand thick with gore. A tentacle arches its belly into his palm. When he raises the other, a tentacle slides down his back.

He brings up the scythe, cradles a moss-and-daisy tentacle with the blade.

"Will you let me take a piece of you?" he says. "Before you break?"

More tentacles roll forth and cradle him. Gabbro limbs knock their knees at his throat, lifting his chin.

When the blade bites up, Malacresta says, "Mm," and thrashes his head. I recognise the reaction, but it takes me a moment to notice the cause. The tentacle has grown pink, yellow and orange hackles and impaled him through the wrist.

He and I stare at his hand with the same awe. The glass mutates under his skin, dappling the blue of his veins and making their branches blossom.

When the tentacle forces its nettle-back against his arm, he gasps and throws his head back. The rainbow on his arm is double, opal flecks inside and saturated icicles which hang and spire out.

He drops the scythe and offers his other arm. God cripples it likewise, grows in through his hand and ivies up to his shoulder. He arches forward. God penetrates and twists, jerks him up swayback. Colour peaks in his cheeks and jaw, stretches wide his collar, pitches his tunic and hair. Steeples out of his belly like gabbro out of the sea, pauldrons on his shoulders, a tick-ticking shudder down his back which spines him like a lionfish. Both of his eyes flash as shards stab out of his cheekbones at such angles as to stab back down into his eyebrows. One yellow, one milky pink.

God stabs Himself in the belly with the glass which comes from Malacresta's. Three barbs between their mouths stop Malacresta's head from rolling back. There's less human shape in the elaboration of his flesh than in the elaboration of God's clay. He's abstract. He's a staircase, a conch, a great hanging jawbone.

His smile is dopey, the great fibrous spirals of his arms stuck open. He must be dead. The glass must have crystallised his brain, his blood, his marrow, killed and possessed him in the same thrust.

Will you let me take a piece of you?

With the same broken-elbow creaks as the tentacles climbing the church, Malacresta raises his arms. Opened to the neck like an eel, he gurgles,

"Yeah."

God doesn't swallow him tongue-over-teeth, but by opening glass mouths and rearranging him into them. His arms splay into such fine filament that I don't hear the bones breaking or the flesh squelching. His spined backbone and belly braid and coil into God's stomach. I am so busy watching their thighs knot together in an iridescent cat's-cradle that I don't see what happens to his head.

"Told him," I say.

No, God says, skinned in glass. **He told you.**

I stand up. My stomach tightens and my aching eyes crease. When I stagger down the roof and crash into God, the mask of glass on His face draws back for me. I press my forehead into the diadem of eyes.

When red gore crawls out of God's stomach and over His shoulder, I wonder whether He is copying Malacresta's body or the fabric of his soul.

His body, of course. His soul isn't dead.

"Oh," I say.

From the square comes a noise like a little girl is being eviscerated. "SOLE HEAL MY PAP-AAH-AAH!" screams Nedda. Lagia's scream elaborates in a higher key.

"Oh," I say again.

Is this the ecstasy you wanted?

With hot tears pouring down my face, I nod. It is. The ecstasy I wanted was the room in my heart to feel agony for others.

"Where is he, then?" I say.

Glass crawls over the gore again, helmets it.

Dreaming lovely dreams.

"Could you give me a lovely dream too?"

If you don't mind your *dolcezza* armoured in yet more *dolcezza*.

I laugh.

The rainbow sky dies down to cold black night, and Nene shimmers out of thin air in front of me. He stands in the clothes from the pulpit, the red tunic and brown trousers, but his hair is wriggling and thrashing in the air above him like fire.

He beams and opens his mouth for a kiss. I reel my head

428

back and examine the expression, the way it creases him.

"Hm, not quite," I say. "Something wrong about the eyes."

I slide back down to the window, haul myself inside.

As I walk down the stairs, there's a silvery seethe in the air outside the church, followed by stillness. I go outside, squeezing myself between two tentacles which have frozen bow-legged around the doorway.

I walk backwards into the square. Gore sucks at my shoes, pulls taut and trips me. God has died standing up, with His statue shattered over the roof and His legs in a spider-crouch.

There is Ersilio. Dead on his back with my face-print in his slit throat. The sight of me doesn't invigorate his wife and daughters. They know a monster is not to be begged.

I sit down at his side, throw my arms around his head. Nedda gives a wet, delirious, "Mmf," and Ciecherella shushes her.

I look up at them.

"You couldn't have carried him on your own," I say. "He helped you with his legs. Remember that. Cling to it."

They give shivers of nods.

I lute. My chest chasms again. Through me goes the terror that the power will melt us together, melt us into one man who claws and spits at himself, begs himself for death without requital.

Ersilio wakes up screaming.

CHAPTER 24
THE NOTHING

Y OU WOKE UP IN A SCULPTING TENT *banded with sunlight. There was a mirror on the wall where it couldn't have been, and in it, you saw yourself, with long hair, white breasts and a round, naked face.* This won't do, *you thought.* I'm getting married today.

So you changed yourself into a man with a hard glare.

You were sure you were dreaming as you pawed through the dawn-dusted air, changed each breast into a plane with a deft squash, wrung your hands between your legs until your sex lengthened into them. You used the flesh of your breasts to broaden your shoulders and scooped a dollop from each hip to wash your hands with. The stubble that grew under your glare wouldn't grow into a beard no matter how hard you glared, but that was okay. It grew down your throat. It gave a hard twist when you tried to speak. You still didn't have a name, but that was okay.

Nene waited for you at the end of the aisle on the cliff. Prasede had filled his hair with yellow primroses, and when you reached him, you plucked one out to place in your collar. "You look different," said the golden-haired boy without a mite of intestine slithering out of his eyes

430

as he kissed you in the sun.

After the wedding, you pulled aside Ersilio, the Curato, and apologised for turning up as a man without proper warning. He clapped you on the shoulder and told you all a wedding needed was two people and a kiss.

So you kissed and kissed. With your rings scraping together in the nest of your entwined hands, you stole down to the jetty, where you'd kissed for the first time, and he'd tasted like salt, and lay down. People whooped at you from the top of the cliff. They saw everything which happened on the beach. They only pretended not to see for their sake, their sake, their sake. *Nene grew down your throat and twisted. Nene pushed his hand between your legs, and beamed against your neck when you swelled. "That is better," he said.*

And then Prasede ripped the root out of my throat and Ersilio tore me out of the wall of the crypt.

I came out in a gust of dead things. They floated and pattered down around me as Ersilio laid me on my back. A carpet of them was snarled around my legs, and beneath that, I was naked. One of them was scratching my eyeball, and I couldn't raise my arm to brush it out.

"It's okay," Ersilio said, as shivers shocked me through the neck like a seizure. "You're here with us. Do you hear me? Do you know where you are?"

On the cliff getting married.

In the crypt forested with blight. The first wings, rotted to fluffy bone, one extended and one contorted in a bow, hung from the ceiling like a chandelier, having grown away from each other on the floor and then back together. Mushrooms as big as barrels, tentacles turning on threads like loose teeth, fauna and eye sockets and sublime shapeless viscera were fossilised in a grey, stinking crust. The monster had died.

But before that, it had swallowed me, put a root down my throat, and jostled me up inside the wall.

And before that, I had curled up on the floor and told it to. I needed nothing, not air or water or food, as badly as I needed the slithering to stop. The peeling up of arms that weren't arms, the fat hard pops, the keening of *"Hold me, hold me, hold me"*— all around and inside me, like the crypt had crawled into my brain, my brain out into the crypt—

We weren't alone. Malacresta was panicking by the wall, spinning to look at the whole corpse. Ario, Lalo and Sitha were there, and so were their parents. As more people poured down the crypt stairs, lunging with their torches and shrieking when the dead behemoth lunged back, I realised that the ones closest to me were just those who'd run the fastest.

"H… how…" I said.

"Don't speak."

"H… how long?"

"Months," Ersilio said.

I thrashed. He crawled on top of me to hold me. "What have you DONE?" I wailed.

Ersilio shook his head. "He was dead when we came down, I promise, I promise!"

"Why did you come down?"

Ersilio sobbed into my chest, "I-thought-he'd-killed-you!"

"What is this shit?" Ario kicked a protruding part of the carcass. "Ersilio! What is it?"

"It's Pih-ih-ipsqueak," Ersilio sobbed. "It's Nene."

I thought they were going to put their torches against him right then. Disintegrate him in a flash, scatter him to the air. But I wouldn't watch him burn. And they couldn't imagine the smell.

So they tore up the floor and took him with it. They sloughed great scabs of him off the walls. They pulled enormous roots from between the bricks, weeds and tentacles and bones like cruck blades, but they all came free with SNAPS. They couldn't get him out of the earth without tearing up the street they'd just paved, so they left him there. They left snapped pieces of him under the street.

They piled him into fishing nets on the jetty, where we'd

432

kissed for the first time, and he'd tasted like salt. Oh, how much of him there was. Three sailboats dragged a pile of him on it and a pile of him behind it.

I was an obsessive exerciser, an obsessive lover, an obsessive sculptor. I had never devoted so much of myself to a task as I devoted to trying to throw myself into the sea after Nene. Ersilio spent the whole ride bear-hugging me from behind, pinning my wrists to my tailbone, because he knew I was going to try, and he was right. We were perfectly matched in the fight. I thrashed against him and screamed until I vomited and kicked him in the stomach and tried to claw his eyes out. I threw us both so hard against the side of the boat I nearly capsized it. I would have killed us all, sunk us all into the behemoth's grave, if Prasede hadn't pinned me to the floor and knocked me out with two hard punches to the chin. I slept in my bed for two days and woke up begging for wine.

Neither air nor water nor food as badly as wine. Examine my emaciation if you must, but only to measure how long the monster has been dead. It's just for one night, and it's not about Nene, only me. Neither friend nor passion nor sunshine as badly as to stop the slithering.

Ersilio stayed with me. Swallowed my maundering without tasting it. I told him that he should have never pulled me out of that wall, that he was the total cause of my agony, that I'd rather be stuck in a corpse's belly, dreaming happy dreams, than out here in abyssal nothing. It was a realisation he couldn't save me which made him leave at last, but as he got up, he told me he was going to wait in his sailboat, to save me when I tried to drown myself.

"I'll kill us both the moment we're on land," I slurred back.

Through his heartbroken eyes and his tear tracks, Ersilio smiled. "Then I'll just tell you you washed up."

THE END

ACKNOWLEDGEMENTS

This novel is the behemoth mutation of my undergraduate dissertation. Thank you to Phil Langeskov, my dissertation tutor, for putting up with a barrage of gripes to the tune of, "Not in six thousand words…" and "When this is a novel…" and for praising the scene where eight-year-old Sole contemplates pushing five-year-old Nene off a cliff. My plan for the novel consisted of putting a pin in that scene and twisting everything else around it.

Thank you to WKD-X, an evil potion which turns silly side characters with bowl cuts into glassmaking tooth-ripping priest-fucking mass-murdering maniacs and would also probably turn a cartoon flower with a smiley face into a cloud of ash shaped like a skull.

Thank you to my wonderful beta readers: Achilles Sinclair, Atlas, Bethany Lane, H.S. Wolfe, Lemony Wakefield, Lillian Frasier, Lucy Davies, Luke Eavers, Marat Earendel, Mars Adler, Molly Looby, Tegan Anderson and Zachary Goodliff-Cook. The novel needed every last one of you. Have you read it? Fucking size of the thing.

Thank you to walking alone: to a roadside warehouse for nighttime sculpture classes, to a hospital in Livingston for a double mastectomy, to a thousand bridges to watch the water.

Thank you to the mountain of my flesh, for shambling on. I'm sure I'm still alive in there somewhere.

K.W.
June 2024

www.ingramcontent.com/pod-product-compliance
Lightning Source LLC
LaVergne TN
LVHW091053260225
804621LV00006B/177